THE HIDDEN CIPHER

A Knights Templar Conspiracy Thriller

The Hidden Cipher. A Knights Templar Conspiracy Thriller
Copyright © 2025 by Rich Petrelli

For information, contact:
Color & Quill Publishing Co.
Cover design by Saba - @art_gallery49 (Fiverr)
First Edition : November 2025

ISBN: 979-8-218-94278-4

First Edition
10 9 8 7 6 5 4 3 2 1

THE HIDDEN CIPHER

A Knights Templar Conspiracy Thriller

Book One of the Templars Legacy Trilogy

RICH PETRELLI

Dedication

For those who search for truth in history,
And for those who dare to imagine
what lies between the lines.

Acknowledgments

Writing a novel is never a solitary journey, and this book would not exist without the support, guidance, and encouragement of many incredible people.

To my early readers and ARC group — thank you!

Special thanks to Mrs. Hope Cusick and Mr. McIntyre of Seaford High School on Long Island, NY, for instilling in me the love of literature.

To my family, friends, and fellow alums. Thank you for your support.

To Zona, thank you for your love, strength, and belief in me — you are my world.

Mom and Dad, I miss you both.

To Peter, my brother, who helped me jump over the cracks in the sidewalk of life.

This book includes a special tribute to my stepfather, Tony Bongiorno, the inspiration for the character who shares his name.

And finally, to you, the reader. Thank you for joining me on this journey with Elena. I hope you enjoy the adventure.

Between History and Imagination

The Hidden Cipher is a work of fiction. All characters, organizations, and events portrayed are products of the author's imagination, except where historical references are publicly known.

Real Elements

- The Knights Templar was a real medieval order, founded in the 12th century. Their influence and mysterious dissolution in the 14th century remain subjects of fascination and speculation.
- Lisbon, Tomar, and the Aqueduto das Águas Livres are real places in Portugal, rich with history and architectural marvels that still stand today.
- The martial arts techniques described in the fight scenes of this novel are genuine movements from Wing Chun Kung Fu, a close-quarter Chinese martial art. Additional techniques draw from disciplines including Jiu-Jitsu, Krav Maga, Taekwondo, and Arnis.

Fictional Elements

- The Guardians, the Cipher, Prefect Valerius, Isabella Guiomar, Dr. Elena Voss, Antoine Rousseau, Liam Hayes — and all other characters and organizations depicted herein — are products of the author's imagination. Any resemblance to actual persons, living or dead, is purely coincidental.
- The vellum fragments, cipher, inscriptions, and encoded riddles are fictional constructs used to drive the plot.

- While historical cities and landmarks provide a setting, the events, dialogues, and character actions within them are imagined.

This blending of fact and fiction is intended to convey a sense of realism while keeping the heart of the story firmly rooted in narrative imagination.

Other Books By Rich Petrelli

- ISOMETONICS™ – A Guide to Fasting Fitness
- Wiggle & Giggle – a children's rhyming picture book
- The Adventures of Pman & Pookie – a children's book
- The Ultimate Guide to Boondocking in the U.S.
- Classic Cars Coloring Book
- Adorable Animals Coloring Book

Sign Up For My

Author Newsletter

Be the first to learn about Rich Petrelli's new releases and receive exclusive content.

www.TheHiddenChalice.com

CONTENTS

Prologue

Seven hundred years ago, as the last Templar fortress burned, a knight lay dying amid the ruin. Flames danced against the night sky, the air thick with screams. An arrow pierced his shoulder, blood soaking the white of his surcoat.

His apprentice—barely more than a boy—knelt beside him, tears cutting through soot on his face.

The knight pressed a vellum scroll into the boy's trembling hands, his voice raw with urgency.

"Tear it, cut it into nine fragments," the knight rasped. "Hide them across Christendom—where no pope, no king, no person will ever unite them again." He coughed, blood flecking his lips. "It contains a secret unworthy of this generation—or any generation."

"Master—"

"Go!" The knight's grip tightened, blood dripping from his gauntlet.

"They come."

The boy looked past him—and saw them. Dozens of figures advanced through the smoke, blades drawn, armor gleaming red in the firelight. Their formation never broke. Their eyes fixed only on the parchment.

The Guardians.

The apprentice ran.

Behind him, his master's last cry drowned beneath the clash of steel.

That boy was Brother Martin of Troyes. He fled to the sea caves, waves crashing loud enough to mask his footsteps. There, with shaking hands, he cut the scroll into nine pieces under his knife and swore an oath. Each fragment would sleep in a different corner of Christendom, hidden where even kings couldn't reach.

He scattered them. And for seven centuries, they slept. Until tonight.

✠ ✠ ✠

Lisbon. Midnight.

Rain slashed across the cobbled streets, turning stones into black mirrors. A monk in a dark cassock ran hunched, clutching a leather satchel bound with iron clasps. His breath came in ragged gasps, each exhale echoing against the alley walls.

Inside the satchel, pressed between the pages of Psalms, hid something far older—a fragment of the Cipher.

Behind him, shadows moved with precision. The Guardians. Silent, relentless. Protectors of a secret that had slept for seven centuries.

He darted through the alley, cassock flaring, rope sandals slipping on rain-soaked stones. His whispered prayer was almost inaudible above the storm:

Novem nexus tenebrarum. Novem unum faciunt.

"Nine bonds of darkness. Nine makes one."

A flash of steel cut across his chest. Crimson bloomed through dark fabric. He staggered, slammed into the wall, and slid down. The satchel fell from his grip, spilling across the cobblestones. Rain and blood mingled in the gutter.

A figure stepped from the shadows—smaller than the Guardians, moving with a different kind of grace. Hooded, silent. She knelt beside him without pity, her gloved hand resting on his shoulder. Not to comfort. To confirm.

His eyes dimmed as she reached for the satchel.

She worked quickly. From her cloak, she drew a fine needle and dark thread. Her fingers moved with ritualistic precision, opening a seam in the satchel's lining, tucking something inside, stitching it closed with practiced care.

Not taking. Planting.

When finished, she set the satchel down beside the body and disappeared into the rain. From a doorway across the alley, another figure emerged. Older, broader, wearing the dark cloak of the Order. A Guardian. He'd been tracking the monk all night, trying to reach him before the Guild of Shadows could strike.

Two minutes too late.

The Guardian knelt and pressed two fingers to the monk's neck. Nothing. He bowed his head—not in prayer, but in acknowledgment of failure. He scanned the alley. The killer had vanished. He knew the signature. Guild of Shadows. If they were moving this openly, their leader had sanctioned it.

Guiomar.

His eyes fell on the satchel lying in pooled rainwater. He lifted it, searched through soaked papers and prayer books, looking for what the monk had died protecting. Nothing. The fragment was gone. Stolen. He pulled out his phone and dialed.

"Prefect," he said. "Lisbon cache compromised. Brother Paulo is dead. They have the fragment."

Valerius, at the other end, spoke coldly. "Guiomar?"

"Yes. Her signature." A pause. "If she has one fragment, she'll want the others. She'll need a scholar to decode the locations. Doctor Elena Voss arrives in Tomar tomorrow. She's researching Templar ciphers."

Then watch her," Valerius said. "No interference. If she locates what eluded us for seven centuries... we secure every fragment.

The Guardian ended the call, looking down at the monk's body, then at the wet cobblestones. From his pocket, he drew a piece of white chalk and knelt. But he didn't write words. Instead, he drew a single symbol—simple, geometric.

A broken wheel with nine spokes. Ancient. Unmistakable. Any Guardian who passed would recognize it instantly: *Fragment compromised. Hunt active. Protocol engaged.*

To civilians, it was nothing—a child's scrawl in the rain. He stood, took one last look at Brother Paulo, and disappeared.

Dr. Elena Voss arrives tomorrow. She and the Guardians are unaware that the thing they seek is close, hidden in a satchel she will soon have.

Seven centuries of sleep. Tonight, the Cipher had awakened.

1 – The Chase

The morning sun broke through the clouds as Dr. Elena Voss's rental car crested the hill overlooking Tomar. The town sprawled below—terracotta roofs clustered around the Nabão River, and above it all, perched on its limestone hill, the Convent of Christ rose like a crown of stone.

Seven months of grant applications, academic committees, and bureaucratic red tape had led to this moment.

Elena pulled into the cobbled square near her hotel, the Pensão dos Templários, a converted merchant's house with ivy climbing its whitewashed walls. She'd chosen it for location, not its luxury—two blocks from the Convent, walking distance to the municipal archives.

As she stepped from the car, the proprietor emerged—a woman in her sixties, gray hair pinned back, wiping flour from her hands on an apron.

"Doctor Voss?"

"Yes, Senhora Carvalho?"

"Welcome, welcome! Your room is ready. You are here for the Templar research, yes?"

"That's right. Ciphers. Encoded manuscripts."

Senhora Carvalho's expression shifted—something flickered across her face, too quick to read. "Ah. You'll want the archives. They open at nine."

She gestured toward the entrance. "Come. I'll show you to your room. But first—" She turned back toward the small reception desk just inside the doorway. "Something arrived for you this morning. Very early. Before dawn."

Elena frowned. "For me? I haven't told anyone I'm staying here, except—"

"The University, yes. Perhaps they sent materials ahead?" Senhora Carvalho produced a leather satchel from beneath the desk, its surface darkened with age and water damage. Iron clasps held it shut. "A courier left it, stating that I must give it to you immediately upon your arrival."

Elena took the satchel, surprised by its weight. The leather is soft, worn smooth by hands and time. Old. Ancient.

"Did the courier leave a name?"

"No, he was..." Senhora Carvalho hesitated. "He wore the robes of a brother. From the monastery, I assumed. Very serious. He said that you would understand."

A monk.

Elena's pulse quickened. Her research proposal mentioned reaching out to local religious communities to gain access to their collections. Perhaps one of them had responded.

"Thank you."

She followed Senhora Carvalho up narrow stairs to a corner room with windows overlooking the square. Simple and clean—a bed with white linens, a wooden desk, a crucifix on the wall.

"Breakfast is at seven. If you need anything, call down."

The moment the door closed, Elena set the satchel on the desk and unfastened the iron clasps. They clicked open with surprising ease, as if recently oiled.

Inside: a worn prayer book, pages of Psalms in Latin, its edges yellowed and brittle. She lifted it— and froze.

Beneath it, tucked into the satchel's lining, something crinkled. Elena reached in, carefully opened the seam with her penknife, and found it—her fingers closed around the paper. Old paper. Vellum. She drew it out.

The fragment was no larger than her palm, its edges cut. The vellum had darkened to amber with age; the ink faded to rust brown. But the symbols were still visible. She did not recognize any alphabet at first glance. Geometric shapes interlocked with abbreviated words. Numbers scattered throughout—some Roman numerals, others in a notation she'd only seen in one context before.

Templar ciphers.

Her breath caught. She'd spent five years studying Templar encryption methods. She'd written her dissertation on the fragmentary nature of their encoded communications—how they deliberately separated information to prevent capture.

She pulled out her field notebook—the same system she'd used since graduate school.

Right margin for symbol frequency counts.

Left margin for pattern observations.

Bottom corner for her mnemonic anchors. The mental hooks she'd learned in fourth grade from Mrs. Cusick, her elementary school teacher, who'd taught her that memory was about mental pictures, not repetition.

The fragment on her desk was authentic, and someone had delivered it directly to her before dawn. Elena sat down, fragment in hand, and tried to think through the implications. It's not official. No university or monastery would send a priceless artifact via an anonymous courier. No provenance, no paperwork, no authentication. Illegal. Or dangerous. Or both. She should report it. Call the local authorities, the university, someone.

Even as the thought formed, her eyes traced the symbols, her mind beginning to decode the patterns. Frequency analysis. Substitution markers. Not random—it's deliberate, systematic. Part of something larger. Every symbol she translated felt like opening a door that should have stayed sealed. The world wanted truth—but some truths should stay buried.

Her phone chirped. A text from her department head back in Boston: *Settled in Tomar? Remember, this is preliminary research only. Don't go chasing treasure legends. We need publishable scholarship.*

Elena stared at the fragment in her hand, then at the text message. Too late.

She pulled out her laptop, opened her cipher analysis software, and photographed the fragment. When she uploaded the image, she noticed something she'd missed—faint marks along the torn edge. Intentional.

Numbers. A sequence, *1 of 9*. This fragment was part of a set, and someone had sent it to her.

✠ ✠ ✠

She checked her watch. 8:45. The archives will open soon. Elena tucked the fragment back into the satchel's hidden pocket, gathered her research materials, and headed out.

The Arquivo Municipal de Tomar occupied a renovated building near the river, its stone facade weathered by centuries. Inside, the air smelled of old paper and preservation chemicals—a scent Elena had come to love during her years of research.

A young man sat at the reference desk, bent over a laptop, his fingers flying across the keyboard. Early twenties, dark straight hair that looked like it hadn't seen a comb in days, wearing a faded university sweatshirt. Stacks of manuscripts and photocopies surrounded him like fortress walls.

Elena approached. "Excuse me, I'm Doctor Elena Voss. I have an appointment to access your Templar collection?"

The young man looked up, eyes widening.

"Doctor Voss? *The* Doctor Voss?" He stood, almost tripping over his chair. "I—I'm Liam Hayes. I've read all your papers. Your dissertation on fragmentary encryption was brilliant. The way you proved the Templars used deliberate document separation as a security protocol—" He caught himself, face reddening. "Sorry. I'm sorry. I just—you're kind of a legend in cryptographic history circles."

Elena couldn't help but smile. "Thank you, Liam. That's very kind."

"No, seriously." He was already pulling out reference materials. "Your work on the Chinon Parchment decryption? I used your methodology in my thesis. I'm getting my Master's in Medieval Studies—well, trying to. I'm working part-time as a photographer to help pay for school. When Senhora Mendes told me you were coming, I may have *requested* to handle your research access personally."

Liam smiled, remembering his first day in the archives.

"Senhora Mendes runs this place like a fortress," he said. "But she's been kind to me. Last week, we stayed after hours talking about an illuminated manuscript she restored in the nineties—she said it was her favorite piece in the entire collection. She loves these books as if they're her children." His voice softened. "She's one of the good ones."

"I appreciate the enthusiasm." Elena set her bag down. "I need to see any documents related to Templar cipher systems, particularly anything from the early fourteenth century. Encoded manuscripts, fragments, anything with geometric notation."

Liam's fingers were already dancing across his keyboard. "We have twelve primary sources from that period. Most are account ledgers, but three contain encrypted sections. Nobody's been able to crack them." He paused, looking up at her. "Maybe you can."

Perhaps. Elena took out her laptop. "Can you start with these three?"

"Sure. Give me ten minutes." He hesitated. "Doctor Voss? If you don't mind my asking, why Tomar specifically? There are larger collections in Paris, London..."

"Tomar was a Templar stronghold. The Convent of Christ was their headquarters in Portugal. If they were hiding something, encrypting something important, they'd do it here."

"Hiding what?"

Elena thought of the fragment upstairs in her room— 1 of 9.

"That's what I'm here to find out."

Liam grinned and disappeared into the archives.

For the next two hours, Elena worked through the manuscripts he brought her. Liam hovered nearby, offering insights, fetching additional references, thrilled to be helping. He has a sharp eye for detail. More than once, he spotted connections she'd missed.

"You should be teaching," she said after he'd found a pattern linking two separate documents.

"I'd rather be learning." He pushed another manuscript toward her. "Look at this one. Same geometric markers as the others, but the frequency distribution is different. Like it's using a secondary encryption layer."

Elena studied it. He was right. "Liam, this is excellent work." He beamed.

A new text message arrived on her phone.

Stop looking. Leave Tomar. You have no idea of the danger ahead.

Elena's hand tightened on the phone.

"Doctor Voss?"

"Everything okay?"

She looked up, aware of how quiet the archives had become. They were alone in this section. The windows looked out onto a narrow alley.

"Liam, do you know anyone named Brother Paulo?"

He frowned. "Paulo? There was a Brother Paulo at the monastery. But—" His expression darkened. "Wait. He died last night. I heard Senhora Mendes talking about it this morning. They found him in an alley near the docks. The police are calling it a robbery."

Ice crept up Elena's spine.

The courier. The monk who'd delivered the satchel, Brother Paulo.

"Doctor Voss?" Liam was staring at her now. "What's wrong?"

Before she could answer, the archive's main door opened. Footsteps echoed on stone floors—measured, purposeful—multiple people. Liam glanced toward the sound, then back at Elena.

"We're not expecting anyone else today."

Elena's instincts screamed. She grabbed her laptop and the manuscripts. "Is there another way out?"

"What? Why—"

"Liam. Now. Please."

Something in her voice must have convinced him. He snatched up his bag and moved toward the back corridor. "Storage exit. Leads to the loading dock."

Behind them, voices drifted through the stacks. Speaking Portuguese. Searching.

Liam led her through narrow passages between shelving units, past preservation rooms, toward a metal door marked Saída. He pushed it open—

And a man stepped into their path.

Tall, broad-shouldered, with close-cropped dark hair. He wore dark tactical clothing. His stance was relaxed but ready—former military.

Liam stumbled back. "Who are—"

The man raised a hand. "My name is Antoine Rousseau. I'm here to get you guys out."

"How do you know—"

"No time." Antoine's eyes flicked past them, back toward the archives. "The people looking for you aren't here to talk. There's a car two blocks north. Let's move."

"We're not going anywhere with—"

The sound of shattering glass cut through the air. Footsteps, running. Antoine's expression didn't change. "Your choice. But make it fast."

Elena looked at Liam, whose eyes were wide with confusion and fear. She thought of Brother Paulo, dead in an alley. Of the fragment marked 1 of 9 and of the warning text.

"How do I know we can trust you?"

Antoine met her eyes. "You don't. But I'm not the one who killed Brother Paulo."

That decided it.

"Let's go." They ran.

Antoine led them through back alleys, moving with the fluid efficiency of someone who'd done this before. He never hesitated, never checked directions. Every turn was deliberate. Behind them, voices shouted in Portuguese.

"Who are they?" Liam gasped as they ran.

"Later," Antoine said.

They emerged onto a side street. A dark sedan waited, engine running. Antoine opened the back door. "In."Elena and Liam tumbled into the back seat. Antoine slid behind the wheel and pulled into traffic.

"Seatbelts," he said, as if they were going for a Sunday drive.

In the rearview mirror, two figures emerged from the alley, scanning the street. One of them locked eyes with Antoine. For a moment, something passed between them. Recognition. Challenge. Antoine turned a corner, and they were gone. Elena's heart was pounding. She looked at Liam, who looked like he might be sick.

"Does someone want to explain...what the hell just happened?"

Antoine's eyes found hers in the rearview mirror. "You opened the satchel." It wasn't a question.

"How do you—"

"Because Brother Paulo is dead. And you could be next." The car's interior suddenly felt tiny.

"Who are you?" Elena demanded.

"Someone who knows what you found." Antoine's jaw tightened. "And I know what it means when the Guardians pursue someone."

Liam's voice cracked. "The Guardians?"

"Yes. A splinter order of the Templars."

Her phone vibrated. She looked down. Another text message, this time, just an image. Her hotel room. Photographed from across the square. The window was clearly visible. And below it, a single line of text:

We know where you sleep—Guiomar.

"Who's Guiomar?"

Antoine glanced over, the first crack of tension showing in his calm. "Isabella Guiomar," he said. "She's not church or state. She runs a rogue breakaway order — calls them the Guild of Shadows. Zealots. They believe the original Templars failed their divine mission and that it's their duty to finish it, no matter the cost."

"Chased by Zealots. Awesome." Liam's voice cracked.

Elena looked up at Antoine in the rearview mirror. His expression was stone-cold.

"Where are you taking us?"

"Somewhere safe." He turned down a narrow street. "But first, you're going to tell me what that fragment says."

"I don't have to do—"

✠ ✠ ✠

The rear windshield exploded. Glass rained down. Liam screamed. Antoine cursed and yanked the wheel hard right. Elena twisted in her seat. Through the shattered window, she saw a motorcycle—black, no plates—weaving through traffic behind them. The rider wore dark leather and a full helmet. In their hands: a pistol with a suppressor.

"DOWN!" Antoine shouted.

Another shot punched through the trunk. Antoine sped up, taking corners at speeds that threw Elena against the door. Liam, hyperventilating beside her.

"Who are these people?" she screamed.

"Not Guardians." Antoine's voice was ice-cold, focused. "Worse."

He yanked the wheel again, cutting through an alley so narrow Elena could hear stone scraping both sides of the car. The motorcycle followed, agile. They burst onto a wider street. Market stalls. Pedestrians scattering. Antoine swerved around a produce truck. The motorcycle gained.

"The satchel!" Antoine barked. "Check the lining—is there anything else in there? Maybe a GPS tracker?"

Elena grabbed her bag with shaking hands and pulled out the satchel. Her fingers found the hidden seam where she'd discovered the fragment. She reached deeper. Her fingers touched something else. Something small. Metallic. She pulled it out. A flash drive. Black. Unmarked.

"No tracker, but there's a—"

"Flash drive, right?" Antoine's voice had changed. "And now I know why they want you dead."

The motorcycle pulled alongside them. The rider's helmet turned toward Elena's window. For one frozen moment, they made eye contact through the tinted visor.

The rider raised the pistol—

Antoine slammed on the brakes.

The motorcycle shot past. Antoine cranked the wheel, reversing direction in a screaming U-turn that left rubber smoking on the cobblestones.

"Hold on!"

They rocketed down a side street, then another. The motorcycle was gone—for now. Two minutes later, Antoine killed the engine in an underground parking garage. Emergency lighting casts everything in yellow. Silence now, except for their breathing.

"What's on the drive?" Elena asked.

Antoine was staring at it as if it were a live grenade. "If I'm right? The locations of all nine fragments."

Liam made a sound between a laugh and a sob. "That's impossible. The fragments have been hidden for centuries."

"Not hidden." Antoine looked at Elena. "Protected. By people who would kill to keep them separate." His eyes dropped to the flash drive. "Until now."

Elena's mind raced. "But if someone wanted us to have this—if they planted it in the satchel—"

"They're not trying to protect the secret." Antoine's voice was deadly quiet. "They're trying to expose it."

"Why?"

Before Antoine could answer, Liam's phone lit up. He looked at the screen and went pale.

"What?" Elena asked.

Liam turned the phone toward her—a news alert. Portuguese, but the photo was clear enough: The municipal archives. On fire.

The headline: INCÊNDIO DESTRÓI ARQUIVO MUNICIPAL—UM MORTO

One dead.

"Oh my God," Liam said. "Senhora Mendes—she was still—"

"They're cleaning up. Destroying evidence." He looked at Elena. "Everyone who's touched that satchel ends up dead."

"Except for us," Elena said.

"Except us." Antoine started the engine and pulled out into the rain, heading for the highway.

"We need to figure out what's on that drive. Find the fragments before they do." He glanced at Elena in the mirror. "And find out who wants them badly enough to start a war."

Elena clutched the flash drive. Her thoughts racing. Brother Paulo. The cipher. The Guardians. Guiomar. The Guild of Shadows. 1 of 9.

Other fragments are hidden somewhere in Tomar.

And someone was willing to burn the city down to find them.

2 - Mors Rubra

The warehouse squatted south of the river, windows punched out, loading dock strangled by weeds. Antoine killed the headlights two blocks away and approached on foot, motioning Elena and Liam to come closer.

Inside, the space was cavernous and cold. Moonlight shafted through broken skylights, sketching bones of shadow across the concrete. Rows of rusting shelving stood like dead trees.

Antoine moved as if he owned the place, clearing corners, testing doors. He led them into a back office—window-less, with a single entrance, lockable from the inside.

"We stay here tonight," he said, dropping a duffel. "No lights. No calls. My hotspot only."

Liam sank onto a crate, trembling. "This is insane."

"Yeah." Antoine passed out bottled water and protein bars with military economy. "Welcome to the club."

Elena set the satchel on a rusted desk. "If we're going to survive, I need to know who you are. Really."

Antoine studied her, then showed his phone—security ID photo, younger face, same cold eyes. "Private protective services. Sometimes artifact recovery when things get...

complicated. Three months ago, I was hired to track criminal activity in Portugal. Anonymous client. Standard job, or so I thought. Then Brother Paulo turned up dead."

"Hired by who?"

"Don't know. Encrypted channels. Payments routed through shell companies. But they knew about the fragments. The Guardians. And what happens if the cipher's ever reassembled."

Elena took out the flash drive. "Let's see what we're dealing with."

Liam had his laptop open before she finished. "May I?"

She handed it over.

For ten minutes, the only sound was keys tapping. Liam hunched in, fear gone, mind on fire.

"WPA2," he said. "Quick and dirty. Like Wi-Fi encryption. Twenty seconds, max...." His fingers flew. The screen flickered. "Got it."

A single folder appeared. Inside: four files with scrambled names—each flagged corrupt.

"Whoever rushed the copy didn't verify it," Liam said.

"How long?" Antoine asked, eyes on the blacked-out glass.

"Just a few minutes." Liam unplugged, re-plugged, and fed a file into a recovery tool. A loading bar crawled. "I can pull chunks—headings, partial text."

Latin spilled in patchwork: half words, broken lines, numbers out of order.

Pestis Prima. Mors Rubra... transmissio per sanguinem...

"Plague number one. Mors Rubra, blood-borne—keep going."

Febris debilitas hemorrhagia oculis, naso, ore...

"Fever, weakness, hemorrhaging from eyes, nose, mouth. Internal organ liquefaction. Mortality: eighty-three percent. Death in eight to twelve days. No treatment recorded. No survivors beyond day six.

✠ ✠ ✠"

Silence.

"That's worse than—" Liam began.

"Ebola," Antoine said, his voice flat. "Filovirus. Or older. I've seen what that looks like—Halabja, 2007. Chemical weapons." He shook his head. "This is worse. Chemicals kill. Biology spreads."

She continued translating. "Pestis Prima Facit — sanguis humanus per salem argenti et radicem mandragorae sub luna nova distillatur; fove in vitro vitali donec rubor sanguinis vivat et se multiplicet."

"This isn't medicine," Elena said. "It's instructions for an engineered pathogen. If this is what the Templars found—what they hid—"

She stopped, breath catching. "There are eight more," she finished for herself.

The recovery tool coughed up a header thumbnail: nine circles surrounding a small tower.

"Not decoration," Elena said. "A count."

She marked nine dots in her notebook—one to nine. "If the icon repeats, it's structural. Nine entries. One symbol."

More text appeared: nine plagues, each meticulously recorded. Every entry ended the same way:

Fragment location: [ENCRYPTED]

At the bottom, a tenth entry stood apart:

Antidotum Universalis — compositum ex Salvia sacra, Myrrha, et Mandragora officinarum; experimentum cum successu limitato contra Pestes Secundam ad Quintam.

An experimental compound derived from sacred sage, myrrh, and mandrake root; tested with limited success against Plagues Two through Five. Preparation: [Appendix].

Elena stared at the words. "An antidote?"

"An experiment," she murmured. "Something they tried—maybe even believed in—for a while."

Antoine leaned against the wall. "They discovered plagues, documented them, made what cures they could—and then buried everything."

"Deliberate fragmentation as security," Elena said. "Nine locations. Unless you have all nine—"

"Can't weaponize them. Can't release them into society," Antoine finished. "Assuming they stay separated."

"We have one fragment. And whoever killed Brother Paulo knows it."

Elena laid the vellum on the desk, angling the laptop's glow across the faded ink. Geometric shapes. Abbreviated Latin. Numbers.

She opened to a new page in her notebook. "Frequency analysis first." The most common symbol appeared seventeen times—a vowel. Secondary patterns suggested consonant clusters.

"Substitution cipher?" Liam asked.

"Layered with positional encoding," Elena murmured. "Same symbol changes by position. And these numbers—" She traced them. "Not values. Keys. Each tells you which layer to apply."

For twenty minutes she worked, Liam feeding dictionaries and Templar forms. Twice the Latin collapsed into nonsense; on the third key, a phrase locked into place:

Sub lapide angelorum flentium.

"Beneath the stone of weeping angels," Elena translated.

"Where the Red River meets the Sacred Hill. The first plague sleeps in darkness, guarded by twelve who know not what they protect."

"A location cipher," Antoine said. "Poetic."

Elena cross-referenced:

Red River. Sacred Hill. Weeping angels.

"Alcobaça," she said. "The Monastery of Alcobaça—fifty kilometers north. 'Red river' is the Alcoa; the monastery sits on the sacred hill, and the tomb of Inês de Castro—" She pulled up images. "—Angels that 'weep blood' cover it, according to the legend."

"Twelve who know not what they protect," Liam said. "Monks."

"Likely." Elena felt gears click. "The Templars hid the first plague there, in a vault twelve monks guard without knowing what's inside."

✠ ✠ ✠

Antoine checked his phone. "Public hours end at six. That gives us fourteen hours to plan entry."

Elena looked at the translation.

Mors Rubra. "Red Death."

Mortality: eighty-three percent.

This wasn't publishable scholarship anymore.

"Doctor Voss?" Liam asked. "What do we do?"

Walk away. Burn the drive. Disappear. If she walked away, someone else wouldn't.

"We find the vault," she said. "Confirm what's there. Then make sure no one ever finds it again."

"And if the Guardians catch us first?" Liam asked.

"Then we prove we're on their side," Elena said. "Because the real enemy isn't them."

Antoine nodded. "Alcobaça. Tomorrow night."

Elena's phone chimed—a telephoto image: their warehouse, shot from across the street—time-stamped twenty minutes ago.

Sleep well, Doctor Voss. We'll see you in Alcobaça—G.

Elena's pulse froze mid-beat. She showed Antoine. His face didn't change; his hand slid to the pistol grip at his waist.

"Pack up," he said. "We're moving. Now."

"But you said—"

"I said we'd stay. I was wrong." He was already stripping the room. "They're not just tracking us."

"They're herding us."

✠ ✠ ✠

3 - The Scarred Man

Elena shoved the flash drive into her backpack—when the skylight shattered. Glass rained down in a crystalline cascade. A rope dropped, a figure rappelled through the opening—fifteen feet, straight down—and landed in a crouch that made no sound. Male. Dark tactical gear. Face obscured by a balaclava. A scar is visible beneath one eye. Cold. Professional. Calm.

Antoine's hand was already going for his weapon—

The man was faster.

He covered the gap in three strides. Antoine twisted, deflected, and countered with a Krav Maga elbow strike that should have connected with the man's temple.

Should have.

The attacker slipped it by millimeters, pivoted, and swept Antoine's legs.

Antoine rolled with the momentum and came up in a Wing Chun fighting stance, launching a series of fierce, rapid fire chain punches to head and body. His expression had changed. No longer the controlled protector. Now something harder. Trained, martial arts mastery. Proficient. Fast

"Run!" he barked at Elena and Liam.

He was already moving.

A Taekwondo *dollyo chagi* roundhouse snapped toward Antoine's head, followed by a tornado kick that forced him to pivot hard. A jab-cross combination tore in—precise, efficient.

Then the clinch—Muay Thai *khao strong* knees to ribs, one after another. A Krav Maga hammer fist whipped toward Antoine's throat—he intercepted it, forearm cutting across in a tight parry that broke the angle.

The intruder flowed straight into the next attack, dropping levels, hooking Antoine's leg, and ripping him toward the ground in a Brazilian Jiu-Jitsu inside trip, already reaching for control as they hit the floor.

For seconds that felt endless, the two men were motion—fluid, brutal, professional. Then the masked fighter shifted, used Antoine's leverage against him, and broke free. They circled again.

Elena couldn't move. This isn't a movie fight scene. This is real. Brutal, efficient, blazing fast.

"Elena!" Liam grabbed her arm. "We need to—"

The intruder's eyes flicked toward them—one instant, one mistake. Antoine seized it. Spinning back-kick to the ribs. Solid hit. The man staggered, recovered, and came harder.

Elena suddenly understood. He wasn't looking at them. He was looking at the desk.

At her notebook.

The intruder broke away, sprinting for the table. Antoine dove, caught an ankle, and dragged him down. They rolled—punches, chokeholds, a steel blade fell onto concrete. The man tore free, lunged for the desk.

Elena dove too. Her fingers closed on the notebook. The man's hand ripped a page free. The tear shrieked through the warehouse.

He turned for the door. Liam stepped into his path.

Then swung his laptop.

The MacBook Air struck the man's head with a sharp crack. He reeled—more surprised than hurt. Liam froze, adrenaline flooding him.

✠ ✠ ✠

Lightweight. Not covered by Apple Care flashed through Liam's mind—absurdly. Then the man straightened, blood darkening his mask. His eyes met Liam's—something flickered there. Not rage. Respect.

Antoine hit him again—elbow, palm strike. Blood sprayed. The man answered with a downward kick to Antoine's knee. The joint folded. Enough.

He bolted through the loading-dock door and vanished into the night. A motorcycle engine roared alive—then faded.

Gone.

Elena clutched her notebook to her chest, heart pounding. Pages bent, spine cracked—but most of it intact. Most.

"What did he get?" Antoine asked, limping back. His voice was level, too level.

Elena flipped through the notebook. Her notes stared back: cipher work, coordinates, translations. Then—the torn edge.

"No," she said. "The last translation. He's got it—the coordinates."

Liam slid down the wall, laptop still in hand. A dent marred the casing. "Did I just hit someone with my computer?"

"You did," Antoine said, testing his leg. "Good instincts."

"I think I'm gonna throw up."

"Later." Antoine slung his duffel. "If he found us—"

"There'll be more," Elena finished.

She turned the page and froze. Indentations. Faint grooves where her pen had pressed through.

"Wait—there's writing underneath." Liam's phone light angled low. Shadows turned into numbers and half-letters.

"It's there," Elena said. "Not all, but enough."

"I'll photograph it," Liam said, snapping shots, brightening them. The outlines sharpened.

"Latitude thirty-nine point five-five-two," she read. "Longitude... last digits missing."

Liam zoomed in on his screen. "Crossmatch with monasteries and—there." He looked up. "Alcobaça. It fits the 'weeping angels' line. That's our site."

✠ ✠ ✠

Elena tore out the marked page and folded it into her jacket pocket. "They'll never get ahead of us."

Antoine watched the door, pistol drawn. "Guiomar knows our next move. Assume she's already planning for it."

"Then we move faster than she expects." Elena shouldered her pack. "How long to Alcobaça?"

"Forty-five minutes." His tone darkened. "If they know, it's a trap."

"Then we spring it on our terms," she said. "Evening Mass at eight. We blend with the congregation, stay behind—"

"Break into a monastery," Liam said sarcastically. "Perfect."

"We're protecting it," Elena said. "Big difference."

Antoine checked his watch. "Three a.m. Five hours till public access. We scout before dawn. Then we plan."

"Plan for what?" Liam asked. "That guy again? Because I'm out of laptops."

"Plan for whoever Guiomar sends next," Antoine said. "And next time, it won't be one person."

Elena looked at the torn notebook, the fragment on the table. Nine plagues. Nine fragments. They'd just decoded the first.

They moved through the warehouse, rain whispering on the roof. The air outside was cold, the street empty. Antoine checked the car, the street, and listened.

"Clear," he said.

They climbed in—Elena up front. Liam is behind, juggling devices. Antoine started the engine.

Elena's phone—inbound text message.

See you there—G.

Then an image. The Monastery of Alcobaça—sunlit, crowded, fresh. In the courtyard, a dark-clad figure waited, blade glinting in hand.

Elena showed Antoine. He stared, jaw tight.

"That's her."

"Guiomar?"

He nodded once. "She's not sending agents now." His knuckles whitened on the wheel. "She's coming herself."

He slipped a hand into his pocket, fingers brushing an old coin—realized it, dropped it.

"How does she know our every move?" Elena asked.

"Her operatives are following us, taking photos. The Guild of Shadows has tremendous power and resources."

Elena thought of the masked man. His precision. His speed. If Guiomar was better—

"Can you beat her?" Liam asked.

Antoine didn't answer. He put the car in gear and drove into the darkness, north toward Alcobaça—toward the tomb of weeping angels and Mors Rubra.

"We're about to find out," he said.

✠ ✠ ✠

Behind them, on a rooftop three blocks away, the scarred man watched their taillights fade. Blood trickled from his nose. His ribs throbbed.

He pulled off his mask. The scar ran from his eye to his ear—old, white, cruel. He touched the torn notebook page in his pocket, then dialed.

Guiomar answered on the first ring. "Report."

"They have the location. Heading to Alcobaça. One's DGSE, the woman's brilliant, the boy's... resourceful."

"Did they see you?"

"Yes. Up close." A dry laugh. "Memorable."

"Good work, Cristiano." Her tone purred with satisfaction. "They know I'm serious now. What about the research?"

He smoothed the torn page. Elena's handwriting gleamed under the streetlight.

"I have the coordinates to the next location."

"Can they continue without it?"

"Yes, more than likely. Voss is smart."

Guiomar's pause was long. "Then let them come. Let them open the vault."

"And?"

Her voice sharpened to steel. "Then we take everything. By whatever means necessary.

And this time, Cristiano—"

She hesitated.

"Make sure the DGSE operative doesn't walk away."

4 - Sacred Ground

The Monastery of Alcobaça emerged from the morning mist like something from a dream.

The parking lot was still empty in the pre-dawn light and Elena felt the weight of seven centuries pressing down on her. The Gothic façade rose before them—limestone weathered to cream and gold, twin bell towers flanking the entrance, rose windows that would catch fire when the sun climbed higher. Beautiful. Sacred. Ancient.

Somewhere inside, hidden beneath stone and prayer, lay a fragment with plague information that could kill millions.

"It's magnificent," Liam said. He had already lifted his camera, the lens catching the pale mist.

"Founded in 1153," Antoine said. "First Gothic building in Portugal. The monks here preserved manuscripts through the Dark Ages—and apparently preserved something else too."

He scanned the perimeter, his movements precise. "Three visible entrances. Probably more on the north side. Cameras are modern but sparse. Motion sensors on the main doors."

Elena opened her damaged notebook. The translation stared back at her:

Beneath the stone of weeping angels, where the red river meets the sacred hill.

The Tomb of Inês de Castro. The murdered queen, buried here beside her lover, King Pedro I. Their tombs faced one another, feet-to-feet, so that they would see each other first on Judgment Day. And beneath that tomb—if her cipher was right—lay the fragment with its encrypted plague information.

Pestis Prima: Mors Rubra. The Red Death.

She closed the notebook, feeling the absence of the torn page like a missing tooth. They had it now. Guiomar knew they were coming.

"We have eight hours until evening Mass," Antoine said. "We use them to scout. Find the tomb, the access points, and plan our entry and exit."

"Or our funeral," Liam said.

"That too."

They waited until six, when the monastery opened to early visitors. A few tourists wandered in—elderly couples, photographers chasing the light. The three of them blended easily.

Inside, the nave stretched long, ribbed arches rising three stories high. Sunlight filtered through the stained glass in pale bands. The air smelled of incense, candle wax, and centuries. Elena's footsteps echoed over marble worn smooth by devotion. This is a place meant for silence. For reverence. And she is here to violate it.

"Dr. Voss?" Liam's voice was soft. "Are you okay?"

She realized she'd stopped walking.

"I'm fine."

But she wasn't.

She recalled Brother Paulo, left for dead in a Lisbon alley—Senhora Mendes, burned in the archives—the weight of what they were chasing pressed heavily on her chest.

Her father's voice surfaced from memory—warm, patient, steady.

She was seven, sitting on his knee, the day he came home from deployment. He smelled like coffee and jet fuel and pulled a roll of Smarties candies from his pocket.

"There's my smartie-pants," he'd said, grinning through exhaustion. "Did you keep being smart while daddy was gone?" He laid the roll of Smarties candies in front of her. A ritual each time he came home from deployment. She'd told him about the Rosetta Stone—how it helped grown-ups read the Egyptian "emojis" they used instead of words.

"Breaking codes at seven," he'd said. "That's my little smartie-pants." He died two years later in Kandahar. She'd kept his last roll of Smarties—a promise she'd never spoken aloud—until now.

"Elena?" Antoine's voice pulled her back.

She nodded. "I'm ready."

They found the Tomb of Inês de Castro in the south transept. White limestone carved with impossible precision—angels, saints, vines, and sorrow frozen in stone. Inês lay serene in death, hands folded, her face turned slightly toward heaven. The surrounding angels seemed to weep.

"There," Elena said, kneeling near the base. "The inscription." Latin worn smooth:

Até ao fim do mundo.

"Until the end of the world," Liam translated.

Across from her, King Pedro's tomb mirrored hers—feet facing feet, waiting for resurrection. "Romantic," Liam said. "If your idea of romance includes... eternal footsie."

"Focus." Antoine examined the floor, the walls, every seam of the marble base.

Elena circled, fingers tracing the carvings. Tourists drifted nearby, whispering. Nothing revealed itself—no seams, no hinges, no hidden door.

"It's here," she murmured. "It has to be. The cipher—"

"Elena," Liam interrupted, voice tight. "We've got company."

Two monks had entered the transept. Young, early twenties, in the white habits of the Cistercian Order. They spoke in low Portuguese, gesturing toward a nearby door marked:

NÃO ENTRE — ÁREA RESTRITA.

Do Not Enter. Restricted Area.

✠ ✠ ✠

Antoine was already moving toward it.

"Antoine—"

Too late. He slipped through the door and vanished into the shadows. The monks hadn't seen him yet.

Elena hesitated, then grabbed Liam's arm. "Come on."

They slipped through after him. The corridor was narrow and cold, lit by a single emergency bulb. Stone walls closed in around them. Antoine stood twenty feet ahead, flashlight in hand.

"Are you insane?" Elena hissed.

"Look." He aimed the beam at the wall.

Carved into the limestone, worn almost smooth—a wheel: broken, nine spokes radiating from its hub. Elena's pulse jumped. "That's the same mark the Guardian drew on the sidewalk in Lisbon. The one I saw in the photos at Oxford during my research."

Antoine nodded. "This is it. The Guardians marked their containment vaults the same way. This corridor leads to the first one."

Voices behind them. Footsteps. The monks had noticed the open door.

"Olá? Há alguém aí?" Hello? Is anyone there?

Liam moved fast. He stepped back toward the door; hands raised in embarrassment. "Oh, thank God! We were looking for—do you speak English?"

The monks appeared, puzzled. One nodded. "A little. You should not be here. This area is—"

"I know, I'm so sorry!" Liam gestured helplessly. "We got turned around looking for the restrooms—thought this was the way."

The monks' suspicion softened into weary amusement—lost tourists. "The restrooms are on the other side," one said. "Left ahead, then right. Please return to the public area."

"Of course. Left, right. Got it. Thank you so much!" Liam backed out, ushering Elena and Antoine with exaggerated mortification.

"Tourists," one said in Portuguese—not unkindly.

Outside, sunlight broke through the mist.

"Lost tourists looking for bathrooms," Elena said, exhaling. "Classic cover story."

Liam grinned. "Worked, didn't it?"

Antoine's gaze drifted back toward the transept doors. "That wheel was confirmation—the Guardian mark from Lisbon. The vault was behind that wall."

And beneath its sanctified floors, the knowledge of *Mors Rubra* waited.

5 - The Vault

The monastery looked different at night. Elena watched from the shadows across the square as the last lights went dark in the upper windows. 9:00 P.M. The monks would be at Compline—the final prayer before silence. Roughly half an hour before they retired.

Beside her, Antoine checked his watch. "We go in at nine-thirty. That gives us until midnight before the system logs any anomalies."

"How do you know about their security?" Liam asked.

"I asked." Antoine's expression didn't change. "The maintenance man was invaluable—for fifty euros."

They'd spent the afternoon in a café three blocks away, timing guard rotations, mapping security cameras. Now, dressed in black, they looked like shadows among the stone facades.

The bells tolled half-past nine.

"Now," Antoine said.

They crossed the square, hugging the blind spots beneath the eaves. Antoine had already marked their entry point: the side access to the cloister, which had only a deadbolt to secure it. He had it open in fifteen seconds.

Inside, the monastery held its breath. Moonlight spilled through stained glass, turning the floor into a mosaic of muted color. From somewhere distant came the low hum of chant—the monks at prayer.

They passed the tomb of Inês de Castro and her weeping angels, heading for the restricted corridor from that morning. A new padlock now barred the door. Antoine knelt, opened his worn leather lock picking kit, and went to work.

"Two minutes," he murmured.

Elena kept watch. Liam's breathing rasped in the stillness. Hyperventilating.

"Are you all right?" she asked.

"Breaking into a monastery to find a fragment with medieval plague information? While being hunted by assassins? I'm thriving," he said.

The lock clicked. Antoine eased the crossbar down without a sound. The door creaked open, revealing the narrow corridor beyond—its walls damp, the air cool and old. He left the door cracked behind them. A way out for later.

✠ ✠ ✠

The passage stretched ahead, low-ceilinged, stone sweating with age.

"There," Elena said.

The Guardian's mark—nine-spoked wheel, fractured rim—carved into the wall, worn smooth by centuries. The same symbol drawn in chalk on Lisbon's pavement. Proof they were following the correct trail.

They pressed deeper. Wooden doors lined the walls—*Archivum, Scriptorium, Bibliotheca*—each filled with the ghosts of manuscripts, at the far end, a door of black iron, its hinges ancient but oiled, its surface bare of any cross or name.

Antoine's picks slid into the mechanism. Click. The iron door groaned open.

Stone steps fell away into darkness. Antoine switched on a narrow-beam flashlight. "Stay close."

They descended—twenty, thirty steps—until the air turned cold enough to see their breath. Below stretched another corridor, older still, the masonry rough-hewn and etched with symbols. The broken wheel repeated, like a warning.

"Templar work," Elena said. "Fourteenth century, or prior." At the corridor's end stood a massive stone door with no handle. Antoine ran his hands along the frame. "There has to be a—"

"Stop!" Elena's voice cut through the dark. A faint line divided the floor before him, misaligned stone.

"Pressure plate," she said.

Antoine crouched. "Counterweight trap. Step on it and something drops—or someone does." He traced the seams. "The entire floor's a grid."

"The cipher mentioned nine." Elena's eyes followed the wall markings. "Every ninth stone."

Antoine tested the count and stepped forward. Nothing. He shifted his weight—still safe. He moved again, mapping a path across the chamber. Elena and Liam mirrored his steps until he reached the door. He pressed against the stone. It rumbled sideways on hidden rollers, revealing a circular vault.

Antoine's beam swept the room—arched ceiling, carved alcoves, the pattern of nine repeating. At the center, on a pedestal beneath centuries of dust, rested a glass case. Inside lay a single sheet of vellum.

Fragment Two.

Elena approached as if entering a chapel. The seal—wax pressed with the broken wheel—had kept air and time at bay. Antoine eased the lid open. Elena lifted the fragment with both hands. Amber vellum, densely scripted, ink faded to rust.

She began to transcribe. Liam hovered near her shoulder; Antoine watched the door.

Symbols unfolded into language:

Pestis Secunda: The Burning.

"Recorded A.D. 1244, after Montségur. Transmission by breath and touch. Incubation: three days. Fever, lesions, hemorrhaging lungs. Mortality rate: eighty-seven percent."

A location cipher emerged, pointing to the plague's location:

"The vessel rests behind stone marked with twelve crosses, fourth from the eastern wall, three cubits high. Remove only in extremis. The corruption sleeps but does not die."

Beneath it: Pestis Secunda Facit — crystallum aeris in vas vitale cum spiritu sulphuris resolvitur; fove sub calore rubenti donec vapor nascatur et in aërem contagiosum vertatur.

Instructions to create a plague that any college-level biochemist could weaponize in a week. One crucible. One furnace. One choice.

Elena turned. There are twelve small crosses etched into a block halfway up the east wall.

"This one."

Antoine joined her. The stone sat deeper than its neighbors, edges loose. Together they pried it free. Behind it waited a narrow cavity and, within, a bronze cylinder bound with corroded wire.

Even sealed, it radiated menace.

"No one opens that," Elena said.

"Agreed."

They slid the stone back into place—then froze. Footsteps echoed from the corridor, fast and sure.

✠ ✠ ✠

"Someone's coming."

"Hide." Antoine drew his pistol and pressed against the wall near the entrance. Elena and Liam melted into the alcoves.

The steps stopped at the threshold. A figure entered wearing a janitor's coveralls. The stitched name tag read *Cristiano.* A scar glimmered beneath his eye. His gaze swept the room. He saw the empty pedestal. Then he saw Antoine.

For a heartbeat, silence.

"You're persistent," Antoine said.

Cristiano drew a curved Damascus blade. "Guns are loud. Monks would notice. We finish this the old way."

Antoine slid his pistol away, drew his knife. "Your call."

Steel met steel. The confined vault magnified every clash. Cristiano attacked with surgical precision—slashing, pivoting, driving Antoine backward. Antoine matched him, knife flashing in tight arcs. An elbow connected; blood flowed. Cristiano reeled—then stepped against an alcove—a faint click.

"Wait—!" Antoine started.

The wall pivoted open. Cristiano fell backward into blackness. The sword skittered away, and his body vanished with a crash.

They crowded the gap. Fifteen feet below lay rubble—and movement. He was alive. Leg twisted at a grotesque angle.

"We're done here," Antoine said. "Move."

They retraced their path, stepping across the safe stones, sprinting up the stairs. The monastery above was waking. Voices. Footsteps. Lights flaring to life.

"Security," Antoine said. "Someone tripped an alarm."

"Windows," he said. "South transept."

They ran. Stained glass loomed ahead—locked.

Liam seized a chair. "Sorry, Saint Francis," he said, and hurled it through.

Color exploded into shards. Antoine cleared the frame and dropped to the cloister garden. Elena followed, then Liam.

The alarm screamed.

They scaled the outer wall and vanished into the narrow streets. Within minutes, they reached the car and tore away as sirens rose behind them.

Elena held Fragment 2 in her lap, fingers trembling. They'd found it—and survived.

"The monks will report the break-in," Antoine said. "We can't stay in the area."

"Where do we go?" Liam asked.

Elena thought of her unfinished translation. There was more—a clue buried deeper.

"North," she said. "Fátima. A priest named Father Miguel. Historian. If anyone can help us interpret the rest, it's him."

Antoine nodded, turning onto the highway.

Far below, in the vault, monks found Cristiano broken but alive. They lifted him from the pit, calling for an ambulance, for police. Pain blurred his vision, but a thin smile curved his mouth.

They had Fragment 2. And through Dr. Voss, they would lead Guiomar to Fragment 3.

Pain was temporary.

Guiomar's plan was eternal.

6 - The Aqueduct

The Aqueduto das Águas Livres stretched across the Alcântara valley like a stone giant's spine—thirty-five arches rising sixty-five meters above the ground, pale limestone catching the late afternoon sun.

Elena stood at the base, neck craned back, Fragment 2 rested in her jacket pocket.

Where stone carries heaven's breath across the valley of sorrow, beneath the arch that drinks the wind, the third corruption waits in silence.

"Stone carries heaven's breath," she'd translated. An aqueduct. It had to be.

Antoine studied the structure with a professional assessment. "Built in the 1700s. But the foundations are older. Roman, or earlier."

"The Templars would have known about it," Elena said. "They controlled water routes throughout Portugal. If there was a Roman aqueduct here in the thirteenth century—"

"They'd have used it." Antoine checked his watch. "It's a public monument. Tourists can walk across the top during daylight hours. But we need to get underneath. Into the structure itself."

Liam pulled up information on his laptop. "The aqueduct's main span has hollow chambers inside the arches. They were used for maintenance access. Most are sealed now, but—" He zoomed in on an architectural diagram. "Here. Arch seventeen. There's a service entrance. Probably locked, but—"

"I can handle locks," Antoine said.

They walked beneath the aqueduct, following the massive stone pillars supporting the arches above. The structure created a perpetual shadow—cool even in the Portuguese heat. The wind funneled through the arches, creating a low, mournful sound.

Liam shivered. "This place is creepy."

"It's called the Arches of Death," Elena said quietly. "Over a hundred people jumped from the top in the 1800s. They had to install barriers."

"That's... not comforting."

They found Arch Seventeen. A small iron door set into the massive stone pillar, rusted with age and marked with a faded sign:

Entrada Proibida—Serviço de Manutenção.

No Entry—Maintenance Only.

Antoine inspected the lock. Old but functional. He took out his picks. "Two minutes."

Elena kept watch while he worked. A handful of tourists walked along the top of the aqueduct, visible as silhouettes against the sky. None looked down. None noticed three people about to break into a national monument.

The lock audibly clicked. Antoine pulled the door open with a groan of metal on stone. Inside, darkness and the reek of old water and limestone.

"Flashlights," Antoine said.

They switched on their lights and stepped inside.

The inside of the arch was hollow—a vertical shaft rising through the massive stone pillar, with iron rungs set within the wall forming a ladder—maintenance access to the water channels above.

But halfway up the shaft, the ladder passed through a small chamber cut into the stone. Not part of the modern construction. Much older.

"There," Elena said, pointing.

They climbed. The rungs were slick with moisture, the air growing colder as they ascended. In the chamber, they stopped.

It was small—barely two meters across. The walls, carved with symbols. Templar symbols. Geometric patterns. And in the center of the chamber, set into the wall: a stone relief of nine concentric circles, like ripples spreading from a central point.

"The cipher," Elena breathed. "It's describing this."

She studied the relief, comparing it to the decoded instructions in Fragment 2. The circles represented something. A sequence. A key.

Antoine explored the chamber's edges with his flashlight. "No obvious hiding place. No hollow stones."

"It's here," Elena said. *"The arch that drinks the wind. This chamber is positioned exactly where wind would funnel through the aqueduct's structure."* She pressed her hand against the relief, feeling the surface. The circles were carved at different depths. Not decorative. Functional.

"It's a combination lock," she said. "Mechanical. Medieval style. You press the circles in a specific order, and—"

She studied Fragment 2's cipher again. The geometric patterns contained a numerical sequence hidden in the spacing between symbols. She'd decoded it as coordinates, but what if it was also instructions?

Third circle. Fifth. First. Seventh. Second.

She pressed them in order, feeling each one give slightly under her fingers with a soft click.

Nothing happened.

"Try reversing it," Liam suggested.

Elena pressed the sequence backward.

Second. Seventh. First. Fifth. Third.

A deeper click. Then a grinding sound—stone on stone, mechanisms that hadn't moved in centuries, waking up.

The central circle of the relief rotated. Sank inward. Behind it, a small hollow space revealed itself.

Inside: a copper tube, sealed with wax. Smaller than the previous fragments' containers, as if the Templars had wanted to minimize its presence.

Fragment 3.

Elena carefully lifted it out, broke the wax seal, and opened the tube. The vellum inside—rolled tight, darker than the others, as if age had stained it more deeply.

She unrolled it carefully. The familiar rust-brown ink. Geometric cipher patterns. But the text seemed denser. More urgent somehow.

"We need to go," Antoine said. "We've been inside too long."

Elena returned the fragment to its container, then slipped it into her pocket.

✠ ✠ ✠

They descended the shaft, emerged from the iron door, and returned to the shadowed base of the aqueduct. The sun had shifted lower. Late afternoon shadows stretched across the valley.

Back at the car, Elena spread Fragment 3 on her lap and began the initial translation. The cipher was like Fragments 1 and 2, but with an additional encryption layer. It took her twenty minutes to break through the first level.

Then the Latin text emerged:

Pestis Tertia: Mors Aeris.

"Plague 3: The Death of Air."

She continued translating, her hands growing cold despite the warm car.

"Recorded in the Year of Our Lord 1263, in the port cities of Marseille and Valencia. Transmission: Airborne aerosolized droplets. Spreads on breath and wind. Incubation period: eighteen to twenty-four hours. Initial symptoms: difficulty breathing, chest constriction. Secondary stage: progressive asphyxiation as lung tissue deteriorates. Tertiary stage: complete respiratory collapse. Victims literally drown in air, unable to process oxygen even as they breathe. Mortality rate: ninety percent."

Pestis Tertia Facit — sanguinem serpentis cum cinere ossium calcinatorum in vas vitale miscetur; fove sub calore moderato donec humor niger gignatur et se multiplicet.

A single vial—two possible outcomes. A formula too elegant to be coincidence—and too lethal to be mercy.

Silence in the car.

"That's worse than Plague two," Liam said quietly.

"They're escalating," Elena confirmed. "Plague one was eighty-three percent. Plague two was eighty-seven. Now, plague three is ninety percent."

"What's Fragment 4 going to be?" Antoine asked.

Elena continued decoding, finding the location cipher for Fragment 4 at the bottom of the text:

Where stone remembers ancient vows, in the house of the first master's rest, the fourth corruption waits beneath the seal.

She cross-referenced the phrases. "House of the first master." That would be a burial church. The first master of the Portuguese Templars was Gualdim Pais. Where was he buried?

She pulled up historical records on the laptop.

Found it.

"Doctor Tavares," she said. "There's a historian in Constância. His family has owned pieces from Templar sites for generations. Fragment 4 might be in a private collection."

"That's not heavily guarded," Antoine said. "Not like a fortress."

"None of them have been easy." Elena secured Fragment 3 with the others in the satchel. Three fragments now. Six more to find.

She thought about Mors Aeris. The Death of Air. A plague that made breathing itself deadly. That spread on wind and breath, killing ninety percent of those infected.

A Medieval bioweapon.

She was beginning to understand why the Templars had hidden these so carefully. Why they'd split the cipher into nine pieces and scattered them across Christendom. Because assembled, these fragments contained the knowledge to end the world.

"Where to next?" Antoine asked, starting the engine.

"We need to find Doctor Tavares," Elena said. "Research his collection. Plan our approach."

"We'll need more than lock picks and luck this time," Liam muttered.

Antoine pulled onto the road, heading north.

Behind them, the Aqueduto das Águas Livres stretched across the valley, its arches carrying nothing now but wind and shadow. The hollow chamber inside Arch seventeen was empty once more, its secret taken, its seven-hundred-year duty fulfilled.

In the satchel under Elena's seat, the fragments rested together.

Pestis Prima: Mors Rubra.

Pestis Secunda: The Burning.

Pestis Tertia: Mors Aeris.

And somewhere ahead, Fragment Four waited.

The hunt continued.

7 - The Diversion

Hours later, more than a hundred kilometers north, they were closing in on Alcobaça when the police lights flared behind them. "Shit," Antoine muttered, eyes flicking to the rearview mirror. "Stay calm. Let me handle this."

He eased the car onto the narrow shoulder. The patrol vehicle slid in behind them, its strobes painting the countryside in rhythmic pulses of blue. Elena's fingers tightened on Fragment 3. They had broken into a monastery, shattered centuries-old glass, left a man bleeding in a vault—and now this.

"What did we do?" Liam whispered from the back.

"Red light," Antoine said. "Back in town. I saw it. Hoped no one else did."

A single officer approached, flashlight slicing the night. Late twenties, crisp uniform. He motioned for Antoine to lower the window.

"Boa noite. Documentos, por favor."

Antoine handed over the license and registration. The officer studied them under the beam, then glanced at Antoine, Elena, and back to the papers.

"French?"

"Tourists," Antoine replied. "Is there a problem?"

"You ran a red light. Very dangerous." The flashlight swept the interior, pausing on Elena's backpack—then the leather satchel at her feet.

"I apologize," Antoine said. "It won't happen again."

The officer's radio crackled. *Mosteirô, vidro partido.* He stepped back, spoke in rapid Portuguese, listened. His posture shifted—alert now, coiled. He returned to the window, hand resting on his holster.

"Please step out. All of you."

Antoine's jaw clenched. "Officer, is this really—"

"Out. Now."

They climbed from the car. The officer positioned them along the hood, hands flat on warm metal. Professional. Cautious.

Elena's mind raced. What did the radio say?

Backup arrived within minutes—two more cruisers, lights strobing. With them came a man in plain clothes. Fifties. Graying hair. Sharp eyes. A detective's badge glinted on his belt. He moved with the quiet authority of someone who had done this a thousand times.

"Doctor Elena Voss?" His English was perfect.

Dread coiled in her gut. "Yes."

"Detective Durand. Porto Criminal Investigation." He studied her face. "I've been looking for you."

"Why?"

"Two days ago, a man was murdered in Tomar. The municipal archives burned. Your names were on the visitor log."

"We were researching," Elena said. "We left before—"

"Before the fire. Convenient." Durand showed her a photograph on his phone of a man in his late sixties with a gray beard and kind eyes. Dr. Marcus Almeida.

Elena's world tilted.

"You know him?"

"That's—" Her voice cracked. "Doctor Almeida. He was my—" She couldn't finish.

"He was found stabbed in a storage room. The fire was set to cover it." Durand's tone was flat. "When did you last speak to him?"

Elena couldn't breathe. Marcus. Her mentor. The man who had guided her after her father's death. Who believed in her when she doubted herself. Dead.

"Doctor Voss?"

"I emailed him three days ago," she managed. "About cipher work. I didn't know..."

Durand watched her reaction. "You didn't know."

"No." The word came out small. "He was my friend."

"Then you'll understand why I need answers. At the station."

"We had nothing to do with it," Antoine said. "We were there earlier. For research. We left."

"Perhaps. But there are irregularities." Durand nodded to the officer. "Search the vehicle."

The officer moved toward the car. Elena's pulse skyrocketed. The fragments. The satchel. The flash drive.

The officer opened the back door and began rummaging through Liam's gear. Antoine's hand shifted—slow, deliberate—toward his jacket.

Durand saw it. His own hand dropped to his weapon. "Hands where I can see them."

The moment stretched, taut as a wire.

Then the world exploded.

A massive concussion rolled from Alcobaça, lighting the sky in a bloom of orange. The shockwave hit seconds later, rattling windows, setting off car alarms for miles.

Everyone turned.

"Meu Deus," the officer whispered.

Durand was already shouting into his radio. Sirens wailed to life.

"All units—explosion in the town center! Multiple casualties—"

✠ ✠ ✠

In the chaos, Antoine met Elena's eyes. One word, silent: *Now.*

They moved.

Back into the car. Antoine is behind the wheel. Engine roaring.

"Stop!" Durand yelled, sprinting toward them. "Do not—"

Antoine reversed hard, tires screaming, and swung the car around. Gravel sprayed.

"Stop, or I will shoot!"

But they were gone, swallowed by darkness. In the rearview mirror, Durand stood in the road, weapon raised but unfired. Duty won. His cruiser spun toward the fireball.

Antoine drove in silence, taking back roads and doubling back, confirming there was no pursuit.

✠ ✠ ✠

"Everyone okay?"

"Define okay," Liam said.

Elena stared at Fragment 3, seeing Marcus's face. His smile. His faith in her. Gone.

"Elena?" Antoine's voice was soft.

"They killed him," she said. "Guiomar. The Guild. To cover their tracks. To send a message."

"Probably both."

"He was just a scholar. A good man." Her fingers tightened on the vellum. "They murdered him. Burned the archives. Killed Senhora Mendes."

"I'm sorry."

"I should destroy this. Let the secret die."

"You could," Antoine said. "Is that what you want?"

She thought of Marcus. Brother Paulo. What would happen if Guiomar won?

"No," she said. "Marcus died protecting this. The least I can do is make his death mean something." She met Antoine's eyes. "We find them all. And we make damn sure Guiomar never gets them."

Antoine nodded. "Then we get off the road. Durand will put out an APB. Every cop in Portugal will be looking."

"Father Miguel," Elena said. "He'll help."

"You're sure?"

"No. But we're out of options."

Antoine turned north, toward Fátima.

Elena hesitated. "Marcus mentioned him once. In an old email. 'Non-institutional repositories.' He wrote:

If you make it to Fátima, ask Father Miguel at Nossa Senhora da Paz about the mourning knight. Local mural—house painter with a scholar's eye. Lance not pious—angle, not posture. Might be nothing. Might be a compass.

"He called me 'Ellie,'" she murmured. "I hated it. Told him to stop. He never did." A tear slid down her cheek. "I'd give anything to hear it again."

Liam reached forward and squeezed her shoulder. Said nothing.

They reached the monastery just before midnight—simple stone exterior, bell tower, olive groves glowing silver under moonlight. A sign read: *Mosteiro de Nossa Senhora da Paz. Private. Visitors by appointment only.* Antoine parked behind the trees.

"Wait here," he said. "I'll check."

He vanished into the shadows. Elena sat with Fragment 3 on her lap, reviewing it again.

Antoine returned. "Someone's awake."

✠ ✠ ✠

They approached the heavy wooden door. Antoine rang the iron bellpull. Footsteps. The door creaked open. A man peered out—sixty, gray-haired, gentle face, oil lamp in hand.

"Yes?"

"Father Miguel?" Elena asked. "Doctor Elena Voss. I was told that you can help me."

He studied them—three exhausted strangers at midnight. Should have refused. Instead, he opened the door wider.

"Come in," he said in accented English. "You look like you need sanctuary."

They stepped into a hall of whitewashed stone. A crucifix hung on the wall. The scent of wax and olive oil. Father Miguel led them to a small sitting room lit by lamps.

"Sit," he said. "I will bring water. Food."

"We don't want to impose—"

"Not at all, please sit and relax."

He left. Liam sank into a chair. "I like him."

"Don't get comfortable," Antoine murmured. "We can't stay long."

Elena studied the mural opposite—a knight in white, shield raised, lance angled. Behind him, a field of graves. Old. Cracked. Fading, but striking.

"That's..."

Father Miguel returned with bread, cheese, and water. "You admire the mural," he said. "A local man painted it. Tony Bongiorno. For my grandfather, also a priest here." Tony was not a professional—he painted houses for a living. But this was his masterpiece. I can't afford restoration, so it fades."

"Don't paint over it," Elena said. Something in her tone made him pause.

A memory surfaced—Marcus's scrawl: *Lance not pious—angle, not posture.*

She stepped closer. The lance wasn't raised in devotion. It leaned—seventeen degrees off true. Exact. Intentional. Pointing.

"Father Miguel," she said quietly, "do you have a map of Portugal? A detailed one?"

"I... yes. In my study. Why?"

"Because," she murmured, eyes tracing the lance's bearing, "I don't think this mural is just a painting."

"I think it's a cipher."

8 - Seventeen Degrees

Earlier that morning, Elena had chased a breadcrumb through digitized archives—a cramped note in a traveler's journal: "Bongiorno—painted knight; parry 17°—Nossa Senhora da Paz." A stray hint, the kind a bored scribe leaves for the curious.

Father Miguel returned with maps—old, detailed, spread across the study table like relics.

"My grandfather's maps," he said. "Templar sites. Roman roads. Medieval fortifications." He smiled. "I keep them, though I understand little of what fascinated him."

Elena stood before the mural. Her flashlight traced Bongiorno's decades-old brushstrokes.

A Templar knight in white. Shield raised. But the lance—angled at seventeen degrees from vertical. Hidden in the brushwork: a tiny compass rose on the knight's shoulder. North aligned with the lance—a bearing.

Above him, a descending sword—Guardian's blade. And an arrow, frozen in flight, struck the knight's shoulder as he parried.

"Oh, my goodness," she whispered.

"Doctor Voss?"

She stepped closer. The background revealed a burning fortress. Flames consumed the towers. In the distance, a boy is running—clutching a scroll.

"This isn't just a painting," she said. "It's a record."

Behind the knight: graves. Hundreds. Thousands. Headstones with dates—the plague years.

"Your father," Elena said, turning to Miguel. "Did he explain this mural?"

"Only that my grandfather told him the story. A legend, I thought. A knight who died protecting a secret." He gestured at the graves. "My father said these were all who died so others might live."

"It's not a legend," Elena said. "It's truth."

She pulled out Fragment 3 and laid it beside the maps. Antoine and Liam watched as she cross-referenced geometric patterns with the mural. The seventeen-degree angle is repeated in the cipher—a maker's mark.

She rotated the map until the painted rose's hairline matched. The parry snapped into a direction. "It's a key," she murmured. "The angle encodes a bearing."

She traced the line. "Seventeen degrees east of north—from Tomar."

Her finger moved across the map. North. Slightly east. It touched a castle icon.

Castelo de Almourol.

Antoine leaned in. "Island fortress. Middle of the Tagus." He removed an old coin from his pocket, rolled it across his knuckles, and returned it. "This city has long memories. So do some people."

"Built by the Templars in 1171," Miguel said. "A museum now. Tourists love it."

Elena was already translating the third fragment's cipher. It made sense now:

Where the river meets the stones of ages, beneath the sleeping fortress, the fourth corruption waits in darkness.

"Almourol," she said with certainty. "Fragment 4 is there—with its plague."

Miguel studied her, "Scholars come for my father's mural. They measure. Photograph. Take notes. None see what you do. What do they miss?"

"A cipher," Elena said. "Your grandfather knew Templar secrets. Passed them through stories. Bongiorno painted what he was told—preserving knowledge without revealing it."

Miguel stared at the mural, seeing it anew. "My grandfather... was he part of something?"

"I think so. An organization protecting these secrets."

"The men who came today. The Guardians."

Elena nodded.

"My grandfather was a good man. If he kept secrets, he had reasons." He looked at Elena. "As do you."

"Yes."

"Will you tell me what you seek?"

Elena hesitated. "Something that could save millions. Or kill them. Depending on who finds it first."

Miguel absorbed this. "Then I will pray you find it first."

Hours passed. Dawn light filled the study with gold. Liam stretched. "I need air. My brain's fried."

"Go," Elena said, eyes on the map. "I'll be here a while."

He stepped outside. Gravel parking area. Olive trees. Children's laughter. Six kids, eight to twelve, playing football with a worn ball and makeshift goals. Liam watched, envying their joy.

The ball rolled toward him. He trapped it—muscle memory from high school.

"*Desculpe!*" a boy called.

Liam smiled, kicked. The ball arced perfectly into the goal. The children erupted.

"*Incrível!*" The boy jogged over. "Do you play?"

"Used to. Not well."

"Better than nothing!" He gestured. "We need one more. Play with us?"

Liam glanced at the monastery. Elena was still working. Antoine is on watch.

"Yeah," he said. "I'd like that."

Inside, Elena stood at the window with the coffee Miguel had brought, watching Liam run with the children.

He struggled at first—American football instincts, using the hands—but the kids laughed and demonstrated. He found a rhythm. Pass. Fake. A shot wide, but they cheered. He was smiling, really smiling.

"He is good with children," Miguel said, appearing beside her.

"He's good with people," Elena said. "Genuine."

They watched in silence as Liam scored—the children mobbing him with high-fives.

"These children have so little," Miguel said. "Poor families. But here, for an hour, they are just children." He smiled. "Your friend gave them joy today. It matters."

Elena felt something loosen in her chest. Amid death and horror—here was this. Liam making children laugh.

Liam attempted a bicycle kick. Failed. Landed on his back. The children collapsed in giggles.

"That's going to hurt tomorrow."

"No doubt," Elena said.

She watched Liam rise, laughing at himself, and wondered how someone could be so decent in a world this dark.

The game ended with church bells for morning prayers. The children thanked Liam and ran to the chapel. He returned, winded, dusty, grinning.

"I think I pulled something," he said. "But those kids are awesome."

"Better than you?" Elena teased.

"Way better. The eight-year-old could go pro." He collapsed into a chair. "Figure out the mural?"

"Yes." She showed him the map, the seventeen-degree line. "Castelo de Almourol. Fragment 4."

Liam's smile faded.

"How far?"

"Ninety kilometers. An hour and a half."

"When do we leave?"

Elena looked at Miguel. "We've imposed enough. We should—"

"Stay for lunch," Miguel said. "You've been running all night. You need food. Rest. A few hours won't matter."

"Father, we don't want to bring trouble—"

"Trouble finds us all. Besides, I have soup. It would be a sin to waste it."

Antoine checked his watch. "We leave at two. Daylight to scout Almourol before entry."

"Agreed," Elena said.

Miguel left to prepare lunch. The moment he was gone, Antoine's posture changed. He checked his phone.

"We have a problem."

"What?"

He showed her the screen. A news alert:

AUTHORITIES SEEKING 3 FOREIGN NATIONALS IN CONNECTION WITH ALCOBAÇA MONASTERY BREAK-IN AND EXPLOSION. AMERICAN WOMAN— EARLY 30s, AMERICAN MAN—LATE 20s, FRENCH- MAN—LATE 30s. CONSIDERED ARMED AND DANGER- OUS.

Police sketches. Close. Very close.

✠ ✠ ✠

"Durand," Elena said.

"He's motivated," Antoine said. "Every cop in Portugal is looking for us now."

"Can we make Almourol?"

"Back roads. No highways. No street cameras." He met her eyes. "But the net is tightening."

Car engines outside. Antoine moved to the window.

✠ ✠ ✠

Two black SUVs are pulling into the courtyard.

"How many?"

"Six or so." He studied them. "Not police."

Doors opened. Men emerged. Dark suits. Coordinated. One looked up—gaze sweeping the windows. Elena pulled back. She knew the walk—the formation.

Guardians.

"They found us," she said.

"How?" Liam asked.

Antoine was already moving. "Doesn't matter. We go. Now."

"Father Miguel—"

"They're not here for him." Antoine checked his weapon. "Back exit. Olive grove. Trees for cover. To the car—"

A knock at the front door. Miguel's footsteps.

"No," Elena hissed. "Don't—"

Too late. The door opened.

Miguel's voice, polite: "Good morning. May I help you?"

"We're looking for three people. They may have come here seeking shelter."

"I am the only one here," Miguel said. "This is a private monastery—"

"May we look around?"

A pause. "I... suppose. Though I assure you—"

Footsteps. Multiple. Entering.

Antoine gestured toward the study's back door. They moved—narrow hallway, storage room, out into the olive grove. Morning sun bright after the dim interior. Trees offered broken cover. They ran, crouched low, using the trunks for cover.

Behind them, voices. Someone found the study. The maps. Elena's notes.

"They were here!" A shout. "Recently!"

✠ ✠ ✠

The hunt was on. Antoine led them deeper into the grove.

Fifty meters.

Forty.

A figure stepped from behind a tree. Guardian. Young. Fit. Weapon holstered, hand ready. He saw them. Eyes widened. Antoine closed the distance in three strides—palm strike to the solar plexus, elbow to the temple.

The Guardian dropped.

"Keep moving," Antoine said.

They reached the car. Antoine hit the gas. In the rearview mirror, two Guardians burst from the grove, weapons drawn. But they were gone—disappearing around a bend, lost in the countryside.

"They knew," Liam said, breathing hard. "How?"

"They're tracking something," Antoine said. "Phones. Car. Or—"

"The fragment, what if it has some sort of a tracker?"

"No," Antoine said. "If they could track it, they'd have taken it already. It's something else."

✠ ✠ ✠

Elena's phone rang.

"Hello?"

A voice. Male. Older. Calm. Slight European accent.

"Doctor Voss. Prefect Valerius. I lead the Order of Guardians."

She put it on speaker.

"I'm listening."

"You have some fragments. You've decoded locations. You are intelligent. Dedicated. Resourceful." A pause. "You are also interfering in matters beyond your understanding."

"I understand enough," Elena said. "You want them hidden. Guiomar wants them found. I want neither of you to have them."

"Noble. Naïve. Impossible." Valerius's voice hardened. "The fragments must remain separated. It is our sacred duty."

"Even if it means murdering innocent people. Brother Paulo. Doctor Almeida—"

"Brother Paulo was a traitor. Doctor Almeida researched forbidden knowledge." No remorse. "Choices have consequences."

"So do I," Elena said. "I could destroy what I've found. End this."

Silence.

"You won't. You want the truth. It's what drives you. What your father taught you." A pause. "Yes, Doctor Voss. We know about Lieutenant James Voss. Died in Kandahar. Duty above all."

Elena's hand tightened.

"He would be ashamed," Valerius said. "Unleashing horrors for curiosity."

"I'm trying to protect—"

"You're helping Guiomar. Every fragment you find brings her closer. And when she has it—millions die."

His voice turned bitter. "We will stop you by any means necessary. Turn yourself in. Give us the fragments. Or we will take them. And you will not survive."

The line went dead.

"Well," Liam said. "That was ominous. They're right—every fragment we find, Guiomar gets closer. She's using us."

"I know."

"So, what do we do?"

Elena looked at the map. The line to Castelo de Almourol. Fragment 3, with its terrible knowledge.

"We find the next one," she said. "Before either of them can. Then we end this."

"How?"

She didn't answer.

She didn't know.

Behind them, Father Miguel stood in his study, staring at the maps Elena had left. The Guardians had questioned him. Searched. Found nothing incriminating. They'd left.

He looked at the mural—the knight locked in a seventeen-degree parry, graves vanishing into shadow. His grandfather had told the stories for years. Legends, he'd thought. Until now.

Dr. Voss had seen something. Understood something. What had his grandfather known? What secret had lived here for three generations, hidden in plain sight?

He couldn't grasp what she chased—but he knew one thing: Dr. Elena Voss was no criminal. She was running from something. Or toward something. And it mattered more than he could imagine.

He turned to the mural—the knight frozen in his parry, Bongiorno's masterpiece, his grandfather's secret in paint on plaster.

"Pray for them," he said to the painted knight.

They're going to need it.

9 - The Island Fortress

Castelo de Almourol rose from a small island in the river's center—a fortress of pale stone, towers, and battlements catching the sun. Medieval. Impregnable. Beautiful. Somewhere inside, Fragment 4 waited.

Elena, Antoine, and Liam stood on the dock at Vila Nova da Barquinha, watching tourist boats ferry visitors to the castle.

"How do we get in?" Liam asked, studying the fortress through binoculars.

"We don't," Antoine said, lowering his own. "Not without being seen. Tourist site by day. Cameras everywhere. At night—locked down. No boat access. No entry."

Elena frowned. "The cipher pointed here. Fragment 4 is inside."

"We don't know that," Antoine said. "Seven hundred years is a long time. Relics get moved—sold, inherited, lost. Maybe it's still there, maybe not."

Liam opened his laptop. "Let's find out...Castelo de Almourol. Templar history..." He stopped. "Here—a private collection. Doctor Henrique Tavares, historian, lives in Constância—across the river. His family has owned Templar artifacts from Almourol for generations."

Antoine glanced at Elena. "If he's got Templar pieces, maybe that's where it ended up."

"Then we pay Doctor Tavares a visit," she said.

By early evening, they reached Constância.

Dr. Henrique Tavares answered the door of his modest estate with visible unease—seventy-two, white hair, cardigan, wire-rimmed glasses—hand trembling on the doorframe.

"Doctor Tavares?" Elena asked. "I'm Doctor Elena Voss. I'm a historian and cryptographer. Researching Templar artifacts once held at Almourol. May we speak?"

He studied them. His eyes flicked to Antoine—military bearing—then back to Elena. "You're not with her." A plea, not a question.

✠ ✠ ✠

"With whom?"

"The woman. Portuguese. Came last week. Asking about my collection. She wasn't asking. She was demanding."

"We're not with her," Elena said. "We're trying to stop her."

A flicker of hope. He hesitated, then stepped aside.

The interior was a museum of quiet devotion: framed manuscripts, coins, maps, relics behind glass. But the reinforced locks, corner security cameras—fear lived here.

Tavares led them to his study. "What are you looking for?"

"A vellum fragment," Elena said. "Templar origin. Symbols or Latin text."

Recognition. Dread.

"The woman wanted the same," he said. "Offered money first. Then mentioned my grandchildren's names, schools, and routes home." His voice cracked. "She never raised her voice. She didn't have to."

"Did you give it to her?" Antoine asked.

"No. I said it was in a bank vault. Needed time. She gave me one week. Tomorrow, she returns."

Elena felt sick. "Then we move it. Tonight."

He studied her. "Who is she?"

"Isabella Guiomar," Elena said. "Leads the Guild of Shadows. Collecting fragments of a Templar cipher—documents describing biological plagues."

Tavares sighed. "And my family has been guarding part of that?"

"I'm afraid so."

He crossed to a locked cabinet, returned with a small wooden box banded in iron, wax seal intact. "In my family for two centuries. Protect it. Never open. Never speak of it. I thought it sacred. But I won't let my grandchildren die for a secret."

He pushed the box toward her. "Take it. Just promise you'll stop her."

✠ ✠ ✠

Elena's throat tightened. "You have my word."

Tavares's hand lingered. "She mentioned a scientist. Said he could make me regret the refusal. A man who builds diseases. Be careful, Doctor Voss. These people are not collectors. They are executioners."

Elena nodded. "Thank you. We'll stop her."

When they left, the box in her lap felt unbearable. Inside lay Fragment 4—the next link in a chain that had already claimed too many lives.

As Antoine drove north through the dark countryside, Elena decoded by flashlight. The cipher was denser; geometry layered with new complexities. But the meaning surfaced.

Pestis Quarta: Morbus Consumens.

"Plague 4: The Wasting."

"Progressive tissue necrosis. Organ failure. Victims wasting away as their bodies consumed themselves from within. Ninety-five percent fatal."

✠ ✠ ✠

She was shaking. "This one's worse. It kills you from the inside out."

"Pestis Quarta Facit — morbus consumens; corpus proprium devorat, caro in pulverem redit, spiritus exhaustus fugat vitam."

The instructions were disturbingly complete—ratios, stages, measurements precise to the drop. A blueprint any biologist could weaponize without ever realizing what they'd built. A design for ruin disguised as a cure.

She turned the vellum—a location cipher.

Where the first master knelt in prayer, beneath the rose that never bloomed, the fifth corruption sleeps in stone.

Her voice hardened. "Fragment Five... is in Tomar. The Convento de Cristo. Inside the Guardian compound."

Antoine's grip tightened on the wheel. "Their headquarters? No way. That's a death wish."

Elena met his eyes. "Yes, it is. That's where we go next."

10 - Eighteen Minutes

The chapter-house basement was colder than the aqueduct. Elena stood perfectly still, letting her eyes adjust to the dim light. A stone corridor stretched in both directions, fluorescent fixtures humming above—modern veins in medieval bones. The sound of electricity was the only life here.

Antoine gave them each a walkie-talkie and an earpiece from his pack. "Let's synchronize our phones. Set a timer for exactly eighteen minutes."

Near the end of the corridor, a grate—locked from above with a keyed padlock. Antoine crouched beneath it, studying the angle.

"I can reach the shackle," he murmured. He slid a pick and tension wrench up through the grate's openings, working blind. Ten seconds. A faint click.

He pushed the lock upward, unhooked it from the eyelets, and drew it back through the grate. Set it aside.

Antoine checked his watch, then his phone: 17:45. Fifteen seconds lost breaching the grate.

He pointed left. They moved—single file, silent. Antoine first, Elena second, Liam last, watching their six. The corridor branched. Antoine consulted the architectural diagram on his screen, made the call, and turned right. Closed doors lined both sides—dark wood, iron hardware. No windows. No second chances.

Elena's earpiece carried only breathing—Antoine's calm, her own too fast. She forced it slower.

A stairwell spiraled upward into shadow. They climbed. The air warmed, tasting of candle soot and age. At the top, another corridor—wider, moonlight filtering through narrow windows. Voices.

Antoine's fist rose. *Stop.*

Two Guardians patrolled thirty meters ahead, moving away, murmuring Portuguese. Antoine waited until they vanished, then signaled forward. They crossed the exposed hall and slipped into an archway.

Elena withdrew Fragment 4 and reviewed the location cipher again by phone light.

Where the first master knelt in prayer, beneath the rose that never bloomed, the fifth corruption sleeps in stone.

Gualdim Pais. Founder of the Convento de Cristo. Where would he have prayed? The chapter-house chapel. It had to be.

"Chapel," she whispered into the mic. "East wing."

Antoine's voice returned, low. "Third floor. Keep tight."

They ascended through a refectory—long tables, candle smoke, echoes of centuries of vows. A noise ahead. Footsteps.

They froze behind a column.

A Guardian appeared—older, heavyset, unarmed but dangerous by posture alone. He passed within arm's reach. Liam's breath caught, a cold sweat beading at his temples.

The man stopped. Looked around. Ten seconds. Twenty. Then moved on. Liam exhaled—then Antoine's radio crackled, a ghost of static. The Guardian turned back.

Antoine gestured: *down.*

They pressed against cold stone. A flashlight swept past.

"Olá? Há alguém aí?"

No one moved. Then, mercifully, a distant shout: *"Marco! Vem cá!"* The Guardian hesitated, then left. A door slammed.

"That was close," Liam whispered.

"Stay sharp. Chapel ahead."

They found it moments later—small, austere. A single crucifix over an ancient altar. Above it, carved in stone: a wilted rose with nine petals, one fallen to the base. "The rose that never bloomed," Elena said.

✠ ✠ ✠

She studied the altar numbers, etched in medieval notation.

Antoine kept watch. "Make it quick."

"It's not decoration," she murmured. The pattern—ratios, geometry—echoed something she'd seen before. Almeida's words returned: *They were mathematicians as much as warriors.*

She decoded the sequence—ratios forming a perfect circle of eight with a ninth displaced. "The fallen petal marks a point beneath the floor."

They rolled the altar on ancient runners. A single tile beneath matched the ratio perfectly. Antoine pried it up. A hollow space. A sealed vellum parcel.

Fragment 5.

Elena unfolded it. Faded ink. A three-by-three grid, repeating. "It's a matrix cipher."

Liam's voice crackled. "A matrix? Seriously?"

"Yes. Ancient mathematical encryption. I need the key. It's carved into the rose."

Roman numerals—II VII VI / IX V I / IV III VIII.

A perfect 3×3 matrix.

"Liam, help me solve it. Now please. I can't do it on my phone. Use your laptop."

"You owe me a coffee for this one."

Liam pulled his laptop from his pack. While he calculated, Antoine scanned the hallway. Shadows moved.

"Guardians converging," he said. "Shift change soon, in the basement. Our exit's there."

"How long do I have?" Liam asked frantically.

"Five minutes, max."

Liam's calculations echoed through the comms.

"Determinant... cofactor... inverse equals negative thirty-seven over three hundred sixty, nineteen over one hundred eighty... minus thirteen over... Done.

Coming back at ya, Elena..." He sent her the inverted matrix through an encrypted email.

She ran the numbers mentally. They worked. Multiplied the cipher blocks by the inverse, line by line. Letters emerged.

Pestis Quinta: Febris Nigra.

"Plague 5. The Black Fever."

"Transmitted through blood contact. Incubation: three days. Initial: high fever, hemorrhaging from mucous membranes. Secondary: internal bleeding, organ failure. Tertiary: complete vascular collapse."

Pestis Quinta Facit — cinis serpentis cum oleo myrrhae et aqua ex fonte benedicta; calefactum donec vapor nigrescat, infunde per nares ad purgationem aut damnationem.

Written as a prayer but measured like a weapon. Even the punctuation marked dosage. A cure for the faithful—or a scourge for the faithless.

"Mortality rate?" Antoine asked.

"Ninety-eight percent."

Elena decoded the location cipher:

Where wisdom sleeps in golden chains, beneath the eyes that never close, guarded by creatures of the night.

"Coimbra," she said. "The Joanine Library. The bats protect the books from insects."

✠ ✠ ✠

Antoine gave a grim nod. "Let's live long enough to reach it."

"Multiple hostiles," Liam warned. "At least a dozen heading downstairs."

They packed the fragment. Moved for the exit—then froze—voices on the stairs above. Antoine cursed. Backtracked into the chapel. A side door. Locked. He pulled his picks.

The tumblers clicked just as flashlights licked the walls outside. They slipped into the sacristy—tiny, air thick with candle wax.

"We're trapped," Liam said.

"Not yet," Antoine said, scanning. "Window. Two-story drop. Climb down."

Outside, the courtyard swarmed with voices.

Elena thought that they would be spotted. "Stay in the shadows." She went first, fingers scraping cold stone. Liam followed, muttering prayers that hardly qualified as Latin. Antoine last.

They hit the ground running. Guardians clustered near the main gate.

"Basement entrance. Far side. Move. Now."

They slipped from shadow to shadow.

Twenty meters.

Fifteen.

A Guardian turned. They froze. He looked past them. Ten meters. The basement door stood open, unguarded.

"Now," Antoine said. They sprinted across the courtyard, dove into the stairwell as shouts erupted behind them.

Down through the basement corridors. The cistern chamber ahead. The aqueduct grate is still open.

"Go!"

Elena dropped first, then Liam, then Antoine. A flashlight beam swept overhead as the grate slammed shut.

Water splashed around their ankles. They ran through the aqueduct's maze, breath echoing off stone. Behind them, the clang of pursuit.

"Left fork!" Antoine barked. They turned. The sound of chasing boots faded.

The rusted exit gate appeared ahead, moonlight bleeding through its bars. They burst through into the open air. Antoine jammed a branch through the latch.

Two hundred meters to the car. They reached it, breathless. The engine caught, headlights slicing through the trees as they tore down the forest road.

All three phones chimed: *0:00.*

Liam started laughing—a release more than joy. "We made it. No time to spare."

Elena clutched the fragment, shaking. "That was way too close."

Antoine's eyes glanced at the mirrors. "Good work, both of you. Especially that matrix solution, Liam. Well done."

"Thanks."

Elena looked down at the vellum, now on her lap.

Pestis Quinta: Febris Nigra. Ninety-eight percent mortality.

Five fragments found. Four to go.

Somewhere behind them, Prefect Valerius stared at the hollow beneath the chapel's altar. A subordinate approached. "They breached through the aqueduct—three intruders—two men, one woman. The woman led. She knew exactly where to look."

Valerius smirked. "Doctor Voss."

"Yes, Prefect."

He studied the empty space, the centuries-old dust disturbed. She'd stolen a fragment from under his nose. That could not happen again.

"Summon the council," he said. "All chapters. Emergency session."

"Sir?"

"She has five fragments now. We can't chase her—we must get ahead of her."

He looked down at a map of Portugal, red markers gleaming like wounds.

"We fortify the likely sites. Set traps. And when she comes for Fragment Six—"

He smiled, a thin blade of satisfaction.

"We'll be waiting."

11 - Coimbra

The highway stretched north through the Portuguese night, dark and empty. Antoine drove fast but not recklessly, eyes flicking to the mirrors. Elena sat beside him; Fragment 5 clutched in her hands. The vellum felt heavier than it should. They now held more than half the cipher.

"Pull over," she said. "Next rest stop. Please."

Antoine glanced at her. "We should put distance—"

"I need to wrap this carefully. Secure it. Five minutes."

He nodded, took the exit.

Elena pulled the satchel from under her seat—Brother Paulo's leather satchel, worn and cracked with age. She had carried it since Alcobaça, hidden in the car through every trial. She opened it, added the latest fragment, wrapping it with the same care as the others. Multiple pieces of vellum, each holding secrets that had survived centuries. A folio of death.

The satchel grew heavy. Physical weight matched the burden she carried. Elena closed it and secured the buckles. She wondered if she was doing the right thing. Thought of her mentor, Dr. Almeida, who had warned that some secrets should stay hidden. No. She couldn't stop now. Not an option. She slid it back under the seat. Not ideal protection, but the best they had while moving.

"We need a different car," Antoine said. "They have our plates."

"How do we get another one?" Liam asked from the back.

"My job." Antoine pulled out of the rest stop, back onto the highway. "City ahead. Leiria. Big enough to get lost in. We ditch this, acquire another."

"Acquire," Elena repeated. "You mean steal."

"I prefer 'borrow without permission.'"

Despite everything, Liam almost smiled. "That's still stealing."

"Would you prefer explaining to the Guardians why we broke into their headquarters?"

Point taken.

Elena studied the decoded information from the latest fragment on her phone, memorizing details.

Pestis Quinta: Febris Nigra. Plague 5. The Black Fever.

Symptoms are worse than anything before—complete vascular collapse. No cure.

Mortality rate: ninety-eight percent. Only two percent survived. Bodies remained infectious for hours after death.

She thought of the plagues in these fragments. Each deadlier than the last. Each plague can kill millions if released.

Somewhere, Guiomar hunted them. Getting closer with every fragment Elena decoded. She shook her head, subconsciously.

"Are you okay?" Antoine asked, seeing her expression.

"No." Elena put her phone away. "But I will be. Once we stop her."

Leiria was mid-sized—urban enough for cover, not so large they'd stand out. Antoine found a shopping mall parking garage: multilevel, plenty of vehicles, minimal cameras in older sections. He parked on the third level, in a corner with a broken light.

They gathered gear. Elena slung the satchel over her shoulder and grabbed her backpack; Liam grabbed his camera bag and laptop bag. Antoine chambered a round in his Beretta and tucked it into his waistband.

They moved through the garage like ordinary shoppers—unhurried, invisible. Found the stairwell. Descended to ground level. At the exit, Antoine paused, scanning the lot.

"That one," he said, pointing to an older sedan. Portuguese plates. Common model. Nothing memorable. Within thirty seconds, the door was open; he worked the ignition.

The engine turned over. Antoine adjusted the seat and checked the mirrors. "Get in."

They were moving again, in an unfamiliar car, harder to track. "How long before the owner reports it stolen?" Liam asked.

"A few hours. By morning, we'll be in Coimbra." Antoine merged into traffic, just another car on the road. "We have time now."

✠ ✠ ✠

They reached Coimbra at two in the morning. The city was beautiful even in darkness—built on hills overlooking the Mondego River, medieval architecture mixed with university buildings. The oldest university in Portugal, one of the oldest in Europe. Somewhere within it, the

Biblioteca Joanina. Among the most magnificent baroque libraries in the world.

Fragment 6 waited.

Antoine found a small hotel on the outskirts—the kind that took cash, asked no questions. Two rooms. They'd sleep in shifts; one awake. Watching.

Elena took first watch while Antoine and Liam collapsed, exhausted from days of running. She sat by the window, looking at the sleeping city, satchel at her feet. She pulled out her notebook, reviewed the fragment's cipher for the next location:

Where wisdom sleeps in golden chains, beneath the eyes that never close, among the words that cage the truth, the sixth corruption waits in silence.

Golden chains: the Joanine Library kept rare books chained to prevent theft—literal golden chains for the most valuable texts—now more decoration than security.

Eyes that never close: the library's trompe-l'oeil ceiling—painted to look three-dimensional, angels and figures whose eyes seemed to follow you.

Among the words that cage the truth: the books themselves. Thousands of volumes containing knowledge, preserving truth and hiding it in layers of text.

Fragment 6 is hidden in that library, among 60,000 books, gilded shelves, baroque splendor.

✠ ✠ ✠

Elena knew she couldn't just walk in. Heavily monitored. Guided tours only. No unsupervised access to restricted sections. She needed help. Someone with access who understands rare books and historical research. Someone she could trust.

She opened her laptop and searched the Coimbra University faculty. Medieval studies. Cryptography and historical linguistics. Found a name: Dr. Sophia Reyes. PhD from Cambridge. Specialization in medieval Portuguese manuscripts and cryptographic analysis. Teaching at Coimbra, published extensively on Templar documents.

Elena read her publications. Research papers. Approach to historical puzzles. Dr. Reyes was brilliant. Thorough. The kind of Professor Elena would have been if her life hadn't taken this violent detour.

She checked the time. 2:30 A.M. Too early to call. They needed an ally. Someone to get them into that library. Someone who understood hidden knowledge. Dr. Sophia Reyes might be it.

Elena called at 7:00 A.M.

The phone rang three times. A woman's voice, groggy. "Sim?"

"Doctor Reyes? I'm Doctor Elena Voss—a researcher from Oxford. I'm in Coimbra on a time-sensitive project related to Templar cryptography. I desperately need expert consultation. Any chance we can meet today?"

A pause. Then, more alert: "Doctor Voss? Elena Voss? I've read your work. Your dissertation on medieval cipher systems was exceptional."

Elena felt slight relief. Academic credentials still mattered, even in chaos. "Thank you. I know this is sudden, but—"

"Are you the Doctor Voss in the news? The monastery incident at Alcobaça?"

Elena's heart sank. Of course. Police sketches. The manhunt.

"Doctor Reyes, I can explain. The reports aren't accurate. I'm not a criminal. I'm trying to protect something important. I need help from someone who understands Templar documents."

Another pause. Longer.

"Where are you?"

"Coimbra. I can meet you anywhere. Your office, a café—wherever you're comfortable."

"Café Santa Cruz. Across from the university. Nine a.m." Reyes's voice was cautious but curious. "I'll hear you out. But if you're wasting my time or putting me in danger—"

"I'm not. I promise."

"Nine a.m. Doctor Voss. Don't be late." The line went dead.

Antoine appeared in the doorway, freshly showered, alert. "Do we have a contact?"

"Yes. Doctor Sophia Reyes. Medieval studies professor. Knows my work. Willing to meet."

"And if she's with the Guardians? Or Guiomar?"

"Then we'll find out soon enough."

12 - The Joanine Library

The Biblioteca Joanina stood like a jewel within the University of Coimbra campus. Baroque façade in pale stone, ornate columns, coat of arms of King João V—eighteenth-century grandeur. But the building's beauty hid its age. Built on older foundations. Medieval structures. Templar structures, some researchers believed.

Dr. Reyes led them through the main entrance, past clusters of tourists waiting for the morning tour. She showed the guard her faculty credentials and gestured toward Elena.

"Research assistant. We need access to restricted collections."

The guard checked his list, nodded, and waved them through.

Antoine and Liam remained outside, blending with the crowd. Early warning if trouble came.

✠ ✠ ✠

Inside, the library was magnificent. Lamplight gilded leather spines: a faint river of dampness hung in the air. The room smelled of dust, oil, and old glue—history held close.

Three interconnected rooms, each more spectacular than the last. Walls rose floor to ceiling, gilded and painted in wood. Thousands of leather-bound volumes, many still chained to shelves. The ceiling was a masterwork of trompe l'œil—painted architecture and figures so real they seemed to watch her pass.

"The eyes that never close."

"This way," Reyes said, voice low, steering Elena past the public viewing area through a door marked *Privado*. Fewer tourists here. Climate-controlled cases protected the oldest, most valuable manuscripts.

Reyes locked the door behind them. "We have an hour or so before someone questions why we're here. What are we looking for?"

Elena pulled out her notebook. "Fragment 6 should be hidden somewhere in this building. The cipher places it among books— 'among the words that cage the truth.' I need to narrow it down."

"The cipher must contain specifics. Show me."

Elena turned to the page with Fragment 5's decrypted information. Reyes studied the page, then tapped her phone, muttering as she searched—half to Elena, half to herself.

"Okay—these sequences look like shelf ticks, not dates. Try 125.3, Shelf C, third room, theological tranche, thirteenth century." She smiled, amused. "A modern catalog overlays it now, but old marks survive in the bindings. If I cross-reference with historical records—"

Her fingers flew across the screen, turning dry data into running commentary. Elena watched, impressed.

"Here," Reyes said. "The catalog number matches a specific shelf in the third room. The section is dedicated to thirteenth-century Portuguese theological texts."

"Templar period."

"Perfect."

They moved deeper into the library, past the second room with its painted ceiling, into the third—the oldest section, where the earliest books resided. The theological corner lay behind a locked gate. Reyes produced a card key. "Perks of faculty access."

She held the proximity card near the sensor, and the gate clicked open.

Inside, shelves narrowed; books were older, bindings worn. Many volumes remained chained, though chains appeared polished, maintained for appearance more than function.

Reyes checked the catalog number. "This shelf. Theological treatises, 1250–1280."

Elena looked over the spines: Latin titles, faded leather, books unopened in years. She pulled out notes from Fragment 5's location cipher and compared geometric patterns to the shelf arrangement. Templars used architectural encoding—the placement of objects forming part of the cipher itself. She counted books. Looked for patterns. Found it.

One book was bound differently than the others. While others were coarse calfskin, this one gleamed with tight-grained goatskin, color unnaturally even—preserved by oils no medieval scribe could have made. Templar work. The spine read:

Tractatus de Medicina Sacra. Treatise on Sacred Medicine.

"This one," Elena said.

Reyes eased the book free, opened it, and examined the pages. "It's authentic. Thirteenth century. But this is cataloged—researchers can access it. Why would—"

"Check the binding," Elena said.

Reyes turned the volume over. "Someone replaced the back cover recently."

"Someone rebound it. But why? Who would know centuries-old rebinding techniques?" Elena ran her hand along the back cover, feeling the subtle thickness beneath the goatskin. "We need to open it."

"That's destruction of a historical artifact—"

"Doctor Reyes. If I'm right, what's inside is more valuable than the book."

Reyes hesitated, then produced a small penknife used for delicate restoration work. "I'll do it."

She made a precise incision along the inner edge of the back cover, worked the blade gently between layers, and revealed a thin compartment. Inside: a folded piece of vellum sealed with wax.

Fragment 6.

✠ ✠ ✠

Reyes held the book out. Elena's hands trembled as she lifted the fragment free. Its seal bore a Templar cross pressed into red wax.

"My God," Reyes said. "You were right."

Elena unfolded the vellum. The same rust-brown ink, but the structure more complex—interlocking patterns, recursive loops, impossible symmetry. Each fragment is more sophisticated. "We need to get out," Elena said. "Now. Before—"

Footsteps sounded in the outer room. Both women froze. Voices—multiple, Portuguese. Through the gap in the gate, Elena could see two men enter the third room.

"Guardians."

"Who?"

"Let's go Sophia. Now please! I'll explain later."

Elena tucked the new fragment inside her jacket pocket and slipped the hollowed book back onto the shelf. "Is there another exit?"

"The service door. Through the archives. But it's alarmed—"

"Better than capture."

They moved toward the back of the restricted section. Behind the oldest stacks, a metal door: *Saída de Emergência.*

The voices grew louder.

"Doctor Reyes? Are you back here?" a voice called, feigning politeness.

Reyes pushed through the emergency door. The alarm screamed—loud and piercing.

"Run!"

✠ ✠ ✠

They fled through a narrow service corridor of concrete and pipes, the alarm echoing around them. Shouts followed. They burst into daylight and blended into a stream of students moving between classes. Antoine materialized almost at once, already moving toward them.

"Guardians," Elena gasped.

"This way." Antoine guided them into the crowd, using students as cover. Liam appeared from another direction, camera bag bouncing. "What happened?"

"Later. Move."

They merged with a group of students heading for the main campus entrance—just four more faces in a crowd, nothing notable.

Behind them, Guardians spilled from the library, scanning the square. Too many people, too much motion. By the time they focused, Elena's group had turned a corner and vanished.

They didn't stop until they'd left the campus, cutting through side streets to put distance between themselves and the library. In a small park blocks away, they paused to catch their breath. Reyes leaned against a tree, still breathless. "That was insane. How did they know we were here?"

"They're watching likely locations," Antoine said. "Universities, libraries—anywhere Templar documents might be stored."

"They knew about the library," Elena added. "Not about Fragment 6, but they expected us."

Reyes looked at Elena, at the bulge in her jacket. "I'm happy to have helped you find it."

"Thank you."

"Don't thank me yet. I just became an accessory to... whatever this is." She didn't sound angry—she sounded exhilarated. "Can I see it? The fragment?"

✠ ✠ ✠

Elena hesitated, then drew it out, unrolled the vellum across her palm. The script shimmered faintly in the light. Reyes leaned closer. "It's beautiful—and terrifying. Knowing what it contains."

"Can you read it? Now?"

"Some of it. The full translation will take hours."

"Then give me the short version."

Elena scanned the opening lines. The structure was like the others, but with additional layers of complexity. Still, she could extract the essentials: designation, symptoms, mortality.

Pestis Sexta: Mors Lenta.

"Sixth Plague. The Slow Death."

"What does it do?"

"It's easy to mistake for a common illness. But it leads to progressive respiratory failure, then complete lung collapse."

Pestis Sexta Facit — solutio neurotoxini diluta ad decimam partem; infunde lente in vena cubiti donec respiratio deficit.

A recipe for death—born in someone's mind, written with intent.

"Mortality rate?"

"Ninety-eight point five percent."

Reyes closed her eyes. "Higher than the others?"

"They're getting worse. Each fragment records a deadlier plague."

"How many more?"

"Three fragments left. Three more terrible plagues."

"And someone wants to use them as weapons?"

"Yes."

"Why not give them to the police?" Reyes asked.

"By then, it will be too late. Guiomar will find the rest before the police can—if the police even look."

"What's your next step?"

"I decode Fragment 7's location. We keep moving. Stay ahead."

"You'll need help. Research access. Someone who knows the Portuguese academic system."

"Doctor Reyes, you've already done enough. You're at risk—"

"I'm already involved, Doctor Voss. I'm not walking away. This is the discovery a historian dreams about. Even if we never publish it." She managed a slight smile. "And you need someone who can get you into places without triggering every alarm in Portugal."

Elena looked to Antoine. He shrugged. "Your call. Local knowledge helps."

"Partners?"

"Partners." Reyes extended her hand.

Elena took it, but something in her grip felt off. Too eager, perhaps.

They moved to a different safe house—an Airbnb on Coimbra's outskirts, paid with cash withdrawn from Reyes's account to leave no digital trail. Elena spread Fragment 6 on the table and began the complete translation. Reyes watched, fascinated, as Elena worked through substitution patterns, geometric keys, medieval encryption.

"How long to learn this?" Reyes asked.

"Years. My dissertation focused on Templar cryptography. But I've never seen a system this sophisticated. The Templars were more than warriors—engineers, linguists, advanced cryptologists, and philosophers."

Elena kept at it. Hours passed. Antoine fetched food. Liam scoured historical databases for patterns.

As evening fell, Elena stopped typing. Her eyes tracked the final alignment across the screen. "It's done."

They gathered around the table.

"Fragment 6's location cipher," she said. "It describes a place: 'Where stone bears witness to faith's betrayal, beneath the cross that fell to earth, the seventh corruption sleeps in darkness.'"

"Stone bears witness to faith's betrayal," Reyes repeated. "Poetic and vague."

"Cross-reference with Templar history," Liam said. "Oh—I know."

"October thirteenth, 1307," he said. "Friday the thirteenth. Philip IV ordered mass arrests of Templars. It was the beginning."

"But this is Portugal," Reyes pointed out. "Many Templars were protected here. King Dinis helped them, renamed them the Order of Christ."

"True. But some fled here from France seeking sanctuary."

Elena studied the cipher. "A place of stone. A church? A burial site?"

"There's a church near Tomar—Igreja de Santa Maria do Olival—the burial place of Templar masters. Knights buried there after they fled France."

"Stone bears witness to faith's betrayal," Elena said. "A burial church for betrayed Templars. That fits."

"And 'beneath the cross that fell to earth'?" Liam asked.

"A fallen cross or grave marker." Reyes pulled up images. "The church has a crypt with medieval tombs and carved stone crosses."

The pieces clicked. "The next fragment is in the crypt of Igreja de Santa Maria do Olival. Beneath a Templar grave."

"That's Tomar," Antoine said. "We were there already."

"We have to go back." Elena looked at Fragment 6, then at the satchel where the others waited. "Six down. Three to go."

✠ ✠ ✠

Reyes studied a map. "The crypt's closed. We'd need permission."

"Can you get it?" Elena asked.

"I know the parish administrator. I could claim research—"

"No," Antoine said. "A formal request creates a paper trail. The Guardians will notice."

"Then what?" Liam asked.

Antoine smiled. "We wait until night. We improvise."

"You mean break in," Reyes said.

"I prefer 'conduct unauthorized historical research,'" Antoine said. Elena almost laughed. Almost. The weight of Fragment 6 settled behind her ribs: ninety-eight point five percent mortality. Fragment 7 would be worse.

In Tomar, Prefect Valerius stood before a map of Portugal. Red pins marked the places Dr. Voss had been spotted: Alcobaça, the monastery, Almourol, and now Coimbra. Minutes earlier, his men had been close enough to the library to catch a glimpse; she'd escaped again.

"She found Fragment 6," Valerius said.

His lieutenant nodded. "We believe so."

"And she had help. A university professor."

"Doctor Sophia Reyes. We're running background now."

Valerius studied the map. She has six fragments now. Dr. Voss was proving resourceful.

"She'll decode the next location soon," he said. "Where will she go next?"

"We don't know. The cipher suggests several locations."

"Then we cover all of them. Double presence at every Templar site within two hundred kilometers." Valerius turned from the map. "Doctor Voss has been lucky. But luck runs out. When it does, we'll be there."

"And?"

"Take her alive if possible. The fragments are useless without her translations." Valerius's voice tightened. "But if she refuses to cooperate, if she tries to destroy them—"

"Sir?"

"Then we stop her. Permanently."

In a safehouse in Lisbon, Guiomar's men watched from a distance. Present at every site—Coimbra, the library—and Guiomar knew Elena retrieved another fragment.

She smiled.

Dr. Voss was exceeding expectations. She has several fragments now. Each location decoded, each cipher solved. Soon she'll have them all.

Cristiano entered, still limping but healing.

"How are you feeling, Cristiano? Our guild has some of the finest doctors in all of Portugal; you'll heal fast," Guiomar said with the soft assurance she used on those who needed comforting.

"I'm fine. They injected something to help it heal faster."

"Good."

"Doctor Voss is moving faster than expected," Cristiano added.

"Let her do the work. Let her solve the puzzles." Guiomar closed her laptop. "We'll take the fragments when the time is right."

"When is that?"

"When she has them all." Guiomar crossed to the window.

"Patience, Cristiano. Doctor Voss thinks she's protecting humanity. Soon she'll understand the truth."

"Truth?"

Guiomar looked at him. "That protection requires sacrifice. Humanity must be cleansed to be saved. Those nine fragments contain the means."

She did not see herself as a murderer. She was the surgeon who cuts to heal.

"Let her find the rest. Then—" She smiled. "Then we give humanity its rebirth."

The planet was a body in fever, and she—its surgeon—would burn away the infection before it killed the host. Compassion, she told herself, demanded it.

13 - Beneath The Cross

They returned to Tomar after dark. Elena understood the irony—back to the city where they had escaped the Guardian chapter house two days before. Back to the heart of Templar territory, where Valerius and his forces were almost certainly watching.

Fragment 7 was here. In the Igreja de Santa Maria do Olival. They couldn't afford to wait.

Antoine drove them past the church twice, studying the surroundings. The building sat in a quiet neighborhood, away from the main tourist areas. Medieval stone construction, simple compared to the splendor of the Convento de Cristo up the hill.

"Security?" Elena asked.

"Minimal. It's a church, not a fortress. Probably locked at night. There could be an alarm on the main doors." Antoine pulled into a side street and parked in the shadows. "The crypt entrance will be inside. We go in, find what we're looking for, and get out. Thirty minutes maximum."

"And if someone sees us?" Reyes asked. She had been quiet during the drive, processing what she had gotten herself into.

"Then we move fast and don't get caught," Antoine checked his watch. "It's two a.m. The neighborhood's asleep. We should go right now."

They exited the car and walked through dark streets. The church loomed ahead, bell tower silhouetted against the night sky. At the main entrance, Antoine examined the lock. Old but functional. He pulled out his picks and worked silently. Elena stood watch, scanning the street. No movement. No cars. Just crickets and distant dogs.

The lock clicked. Antoine opened the door, testing for alarms. Nothing. Just darkness and the smell of old stone and candle wax. They slipped inside and closed the door behind them.

Inside, the church was simple. Stone columns. Wooden pews. A modest altar. No baroque decoration like the monastery or library—this was a functional space, built for worship, not display. The floor—marked with gravestones. Dozens of them, set into the flagstones, carved with crosses and Latin inscriptions. Templar graves.

"The crypt entrance should be near the altar," Reyes said, leading them forward with a small flashlight. "Churches like this typically have stairs leading down to burial chambers." They found it behind the altar—a heavy wooden door, worn smooth by centuries, set into the floor at an angle. Stone steps descended into darkness beyond.

Antoine tested the door. Unlocked. "Stay close. Watch your footing."

They descended single file.

The stairs were steep, narrow, and uneven. It grew colder and damper as they descended—a change in the smell—earth, stone, age. At the bottom, they found themselves in a vaulted chamber with a low ceiling. Stone walls lined with alcoves containing sarcophagi and burial niches.

Reyes swept her light across the space. "This is it. The Templar crypt. Some of these graves date back to the fourteenth century." Elena pulled out Fragment 6 and studied the cipher by flashlight *beneath the cross that fell to earth.*

She examined the graves, looking for something specific. A fallen cross. A marker that had collapsed or was damaged. Most tombs were intact. Stone lids carved with crosses and knights' effigies. But in the far corner, one alcove was different. The stone lid had cracked, shifted. The carved cross on its surface had broken, one arm fallen away, lying on the ground beside the tomb. A cross that fell to earth.

"There," Elena said.

The tomb was older than the others, the carving more worn. The inscription read:

Hic iacet frater Guillermus, miles Templi, qui mortuus est anno Domini MCCCVII.

"Here lies Brother William, Knight of the Temple, who died in the Year of Our Lord 1307."

"He died the year the Templars were arrested," Reyes said. "One of many who fled France."

"Betrayed," Elena said. "Stone bears witness to faith's betrayal. This is it."

Antoine examined the broken lid. "We need to move it. See what's inside."

"That's desecration of a grave—" Reyes began.

"Doctor Reyes, we've already broken into a church and a library. I think we're past worrying about protocol." Reyes took a breath, then nodded. "Alright. But these stones are fragile." Together, Antoine and Elena lifted the broken section of the lid and set it aside. Beneath, darkness. Elena shone her light into the tomb.

Not a body. At least, not anymore. Dust had long since consumed whatever remained. But resting on the stone floor of the burial niche, wrapped in sealed oilcloth: a rectangular package.

Fragment 7.

Elena reached in and lifted it free. The oilcloth crackled in her hands, dry and ancient. Beneath it lay vellum, ink dark as dried blood, geometric symbols drawn with obsessive precision.

"You found it," Liam said. He had been keeping watch at the stairs but couldn't resist looking.

"The seventh fragment," Elena said. "Two more to go."

✠ ✠ ✠

A sound from above. They all froze. Footsteps. On the church floor. Multiple people, moving with measured cadence.

"Crap," Antoine said. "Someone's here."

"Guardians?"

"Or police. Doesn't matter." Antoine was already moving toward the stairs. "We need another exit."

"There isn't one," Reyes said. "This is the only way out."

The footsteps were getting closer. Elena wrapped up the fragment and tucked it inside her jacket.

"How many people?"

Antoine was at the base of the stairs listening. "Four or so. Probably armed."

"Can we get past them?"

"Not without a fight. And fighting in a church will bring every cop in Tomar."

"Then we hide," Liam suggested. "Wait them out."

"Where?" Reyes gestured at the crypt. "This is an empty room with stone tombs. There's nowhere to—"

"The alcoves," Elena said. "The burial niches. They're deep. We could—"

"You want us to hide in graves," Liam said.

"You have a better idea?"

The footsteps reached the crypt door.

"Now," Antoine ordered.

They scattered. Elena and Reyes went into one alcove, sliding behind a sarcophagus. Liam into another. Antoine positioned himself near the stairs, ready to intervene if necessary.

The crypt door opened. Flashlight beams swept the chamber. Elena pressed herself against the cold stone. She could see part of the room through a gap between the sarcophagus and the wall.

Two men descended. Not Guardians. Police uniforms. Local cops, responding to a silent alarm or a neighbor's report. One officer spoke into a radio. *"Na cripta. Nada ainda."* In the crypt. Nothing yet.

The other officer moved through the chamber, shining his light into alcoves, checking corners. He was getting closer to Elena's hiding spot. She could hear his footsteps. See his shadow on the wall.

Five meters. Four.

He paused at Brother William's tomb. Noticed the displaced lid.

"João. Vem cá." João. Come here.

The second officer joined him. They studied the broken grave, the moved stones.

"Alguém esteve aqui." Someone was here.

"Recentemente?"

The first officer touched the stone lid. *"Ainda está quente do toque."* Still warm from touch.

They were going to search more thoroughly, check every alcove. Elena's hand moved to her jacket, where the fragments rested. If they were caught, if the police took the fragments—

A sound from the stairs. A third person descending. But not a cop. The two officers turned, surprised. A figure in dark clothing emerged from the stairwell. Moving fast. Professional.

A Guardian.

Before the officers could react, the Guardian struck. Two quick movements—one officer dropped, unconscious. The second reached for his radio but never made it.

Silence.

✠ ✠ ✠

The Guardian stood over the fallen officers, speaking in English. "Doctor Voss. I know you're here. Come out. We need to talk." Elena recognized the voice. Valerius. The Prefect himself. No one moved.

"Doctor Voss, I've just incapacitated two police officers to prevent your arrest. That makes me complicit in whatever you're doing here." Valerius stepped into the chamber, scanning the alcoves. "I'm not here to hurt you. I'm here to talk. To explain what you don't understand."

Antoine appeared from behind a pillar, weapon drawn. "Stay back." Valerius didn't seem surprised. He kept his hands visible, non-threatening. "I'm not armed. See?" He opened his jacket and showed them. "I came alone."

Elena glanced at Antoine, who nodded with confirmation.

"Why help us?"

"Because we want the same thing, Doctor Voss. To protect the fragments."

"By killing people? By hunting us?"

"By preventing worse outcomes." Valerius moved. "You think we're the villains. We're not. We're the guardians. It's literally in our name."

"You murdered Brother Paulo. Doctor Almeida—"

"I've told you already that Brother Paulo was a traitor and Doctor Almeida was researching knowledge that could destroy nations. Neither died by Guardian hands, though I won't pretend we mourn them."

"Then who—"

"The Guild of Shadows. Guiomar's people. They've been killing anyone who knows about the fragments. We've been trying to protect the people you've been endangering."

Elena felt the ground shift beneath her. "You're lying."

"Am I? Doctor Voss, you're brilliant. Surely, you've noticed. The deaths don't fit our methods. We're surgical. Precise. Guiomar is brutal. Sends messages. Makes examples of people."

Elena thought of Brother Paulo. Stabbed. Left to bleed out. Of Almeida's death—violent, angry. Not the work of disciplined soldiers. The work of criminals.

"Even if that's true," she said, "you still hunt us. You still want the fragments."

"To protect them. Not to weaponize them." Valerius gestured at the tomb. "You found another one. How many do you have now?"

"Why would I tell you?"

"Because you need to understand what you're dealing with. Those aren't plague descriptions, Doctor Voss. They're something else entirely."

Elena's heart skipped a beat. "What do you mean?"

"The fragments don't describe how to create plagues. They describe how to cure them."

✠ ✠ ✠

A radio crackled upstairs—two short bursts. Flashlight beams sliced across the stairwell.

Antoine said, "They're sweeping the nave. Two more minutes."

Valerius kept his voice low. "Latin flips on context. You read *facit* as 'causes.' In these texts, it also means 'cures.' The knights recorded the disease to describe the cure's reach." Valerius watched her face. "You didn't know."

"That's... no. That makes no sense. The symptoms, the mortality rates—"

"Think of the fragments again—swap 'causes' for 'is cured by,' and see what it yields." Elena did it in her mind. Not a recipe for ruin. A boundary of protection.

Medieval medicine named treatments after the afflictions they addressed. "Valerius took a step closer. "The Templars didn't create bioweapons. They stole medical knowledge that the Church had suppressed. Knowledge that could save millions."

Elena's mind raced. The fragments and descriptions. Latin phrasing that had seemed so clear—But Latin was ambiguous. Verb forms that could mean both "causes" and "cures." Context-dependent grammar. Had she been wrong from the beginning?

"If that's true," she said, "why hide them? Why not use them?"

"Cures can be twisted into tools of destruction. Therefore, we protect them. The fragments must never be reunited because once assembled, once the complete cipher is known, someone will weaponize them."

"Guiomar," Elena said.

"Yes. And she's close. Closer than you know. She's been following you, letting you decode the locations, waiting for you to do the hard work." Valerius looked at each of them. "Give me the fragments. Let us protect them. Let us end this before Guiomar takes them all."

Antoine kept his weapon trained. "And we're supposed to trust you?"

"No. You're supposed to make the smart choice. You're one man protecting three people and a collection of artifacts that could end civilization. We're an organization with resources, training, and centuries of experience protecting dangerous knowledge." Valerius spread his hands. "You can't win this alone. But together, we might stop Guiomar."

Elena thought of the fragments in her jacket. At Reyes emerging from hiding, at Liam watching from his alcove, at Antoine's steady aim. Valerius was offering protection. Resources. An end to the running. But could she trust him?

"I need time," she said. "To think about this."

"You don't have time, Doctor Voss. Guiomar knows you're here. Her people are already moving in." Valerius gestured at the unconscious officers. "We need to leave. Now. Before more police arrive."

"Then we leave separately," Antoine said. "You go your way. We go ours."

Valerius sighed. "You're making a mistake, but I understand. Trust must be earned." He moved toward the stairs. "When Guiomar comes for you—and she will—remember this conversation. Remember that I offered help." He paused, then turned.

"One more thing. The next fragment. I know where it is. Guiomar doesn't. Not yet. If you want it before she finds it, you'll need to move fast." He looked back. "Monsanto. Two hours east. There is a fragment in the castle chapel. You have about twelve hours before Guiomar decodes that location too."

"Why tell me this?"

"Because I'd rather you have it than her. At least you're trying to protect them." Valerius climbed the stairs. "Good luck, Doctor Voss. You'll need it."

He disappeared into the church above.

✠ ✠ ✠

For a moment, no one moved. Then Antoine lowered his weapon. "We need to go. Now. Before those officers wake up."

They ran up the stairs, through the church, out into the night. The street was still empty. No sign of Valerius. No sign of police backup. They ran for the car, piled in. Only when they were kilometers away did anyone speak.

"Do we trust him?" Liam asked.

"No," Antoine said. "Never trust someone who knocks out cops and offers you a deal in a crypt."

"But what he said about the fragments," Reyes began. "About them being cures, not plagues. Could that be true?"

Elena pulled out Fragment 7, studied it in the passing streetlights. The Latin text. The descriptions she'd translated as plague symptoms.

But if Valerius was right, if the phrasing was ambiguous—

"I am not sure now," she said. "I need to retranslate everything. Compare all the fragments. Look for patterns I might have missed."

"And Monsanto?" Liam asked. "The castle. The next one."

"Could be a trap," Antoine said.

"Or it could be real," Elena countered. "Either way, we need to know. If another fragment is there, we can't let Guiomar get it first."

"So, we go to Monsanto?"

"Yes," she agreed.

Elena looked at Fragment 7. Seven pieces now. Two left and a growing suspicion that everything she thought she knew was wrong.

She thought about Valerius's words. About cures and weapons. About ambiguous Latin and seven-hundred-years of misunderstanding. Had she been hunting medicine all along? Or was Valerius manipulating her, trying to make her doubt herself? She didn't know.

In the Guardian chapter house, Valerius returned to find his lieutenant waiting.

"How did it go?"

"She doesn't trust me yet. But I planted the seed." Valerius removed his jacket. "I told her about the cures. About the next fragment's location."

"You gave her Monsanto? Why?"

"Because she'll go to Monsanto to take what she thinks is history. We will be there when she arrives. Not to bargain, not to parley—to stop her before she desecrates another grave.

We must protect what the dead entrusted to us," he said.

"Tonight, she will collect her last fragment."

14 - Monsanto

They drove until dawn, putting distance between themselves and Tomar, taking back roads through the Portuguese countryside.

Elena sat in the passenger seat, Fragment 7 spread across her lap, her notebook beside it. Reyes and Liam dozed in the back seat. Antoine drove in focused silence.

"Talk to me," he said, eyes on the road. "What's Fragment 7 telling you?"

Elena rubbed her eyes. She'd been translating for two hours straight, exhaustion catching up. "The plague designation is:

Pestis Septima: Pestis Omnium.

'Plague 7: The Plague of All Pathways.'"

"Transmission through multiple vectors: respiratory droplets, direct contact, bodily fluids. Like combining the worst aspects of several diseases into one."

She continued reading, her expression growing darker.

"Incubation period: seven days. Initial symptoms: fever, respiratory distress. Secondary stage: hemorrhagic complications, organ failure. Tertiary stage: complete systemic collapse."

"Initial symptoms sound a little like COVID-19," Antoine said.

"Transmission-wise, similar. But far deadlier."

She continued, "Pestis Septima Facit — combinatio aerosolium, fluidorum, et serum sanguinis; stabilis in ambitu, replicatio automatica per corpora viva."

The fragment wasn't just an instruction—it was a choice disguised as chemistry.

Elena's voice was flat. "Mortality rate: ninety-nine percent."

"Wow."

"Yes. Scary."

They drove in silence for several kilometers. Then Antoine asked the question he'd been avoiding. "What Valerius said. About the fragments being cures, not plagues. Do you believe him?"

Elena looked at Fragment 7. At the Latin text she'd been translating for weeks. The descriptions she'd read were of plague symptoms.

"I just don't know," she admitted. "The Latin is ambiguous. Verb forms that could mean 'causes death' or 'prevents death' depending on context. I translated them one way because that's what made sense, given the cipher's structure. But—"

"But if he's right, you've been wrong from the beginning."

"Yes."

"Or he's manipulating you. Making you doubt yourself, so you'll hand over the fragments."

"Yes." Elena closed her notebook. "I need to retranslate all seven fragments. Compare them systematically. Look for patterns that confirm or refute what Valerius said."

"How long will that take?"

"Hours. Or even days."

✠ ✠ ✠

"We don't have days. If Valerius gave us Monsanto's location, either it's real and we need to get there before Guiomar, or it's a trap and we're walking right into it. Either way, we decide now."

Elena looked back at Reyes and Liam, both sleeping. Then, at the satchel under her seat, containing all seven fragments. Seven pieces of a nine-piece puzzle. Almost complete. So close to understanding the full cipher. But at what cost?

"Let's go to Monsanto," she said. "But we have to be careful. We scout first. If it looks like a trap, we abort."

"And if it's not a trap? If Fragment 8 is there?"

"Then we take it. Before Guiomar does."

Antoine nodded. "Monsanto it is."

They stopped at a rest area outside Castelo Branco to refuel and regroup. The sun was up now. While Antoine filled the car's tank, Elena bought coffee and pastries from a roadside vendor—basic fuel for bodies that had been running on adrenaline for days.

Liam woke, groggy and disoriented. "Where are we?"

"About an hour from Monsanto," Elena said, handing him coffee. "We're going after Fragment 8."

"Based on intel from the guy who's been hunting us?" Liam rubbed his eyes. "That seems smart."

"It's what we have." Elena sat at a picnic table, studying a map on her phone. "Monsanto is a fortified village. Medieval. Built into a granite hillside. The castle ruins are at the top. Small, remote. A tourist attraction but not heavily visited."

Reyes joined them, gratefully accepting a cup of coffee. "I know Monsanto. I visited once for research. The castle is in ruins now. The chapel is still standing but not maintained. No electricity. No security."

"Which makes it perfect for hiding a fragment in plain sight," Liam said. "But also perfect for an ambush."

Antoine returned from paying for gas. "We approach from above—park outside the village. Hike in through the ruins. Scout the chapel before committing."

"How do we know Valerius isn't already there waiting?" Reyes asked.

"We don't. But if he wanted us dead, he could have killed us in the crypt." Antoine leaned against the car, arms crossed. "He wants the fragments. Which means he needs us alive to find them. At least for now."

"Comforting," Liam said.

Elena studied the map, calculating distances and timing. "If Valerius is setting a trap, he'd need time to position people. Get resources in place. He only left the crypt a few hours ago. We might get there before he's ready."

"Might," Antoine emphasized. "No guarantees."

"There are never guarantees." Elena finished her coffee and stood. "But we can't stop now. Seven fragments aren't enough to understand the complete cipher. We need all nine."

"Why?" Reyes asked. "If these are bioweapons, why do we need the complete set? Why not destroy what we have and stop?"

It was a fair question. One Elena had been asking herself.

"Because Guiomar already knows we have seven fragments," she said. "She's been tracking us, learning from our discoveries. If we stop now, she'll just continue the hunt without us. At least if we find them first, we control them."

"Control them how? We're four people being hunted by multiple organizations. We can't protect seven fragments indefinitely, let alone all nine."

Elena knew she was right.

Monsanto Village–The Next Day

Monsanto looked like something out of a fairy tale. A granite hill with medieval ruins, and the village clung to the slopes with houses built around boulders. They parked at the base of the hill, hidden among trees. The village above was quiet—a handful of residents, a few tourists exploring the cobblestone streets.

Antoine checked his weapon. "We'll hike up. Stay off the main paths. Use the boulder field for cover."

They began the climb. The terrain was brutal—steep, rocky, the massive granite formations creating a natural maze. But it also provided cover. They moved from boulder to boulder, ascending toward the castle ruins at the summit. Halfway up, they rested. Elena looked back at the valley below—beautiful, peaceful, seemingly untouched by the chaos they carried with them.

Liam pointed upward. "There."

The castle ruins emerged from the granite—crumbling walls, a single tower still standing, and a small chapel nestled against the hillside with a mostly intact roof.

"That's where Fragment 8 should be," Elena said.

They continued climbing, slower now, more careful. Antoine scouted ahead, checking for watchers, for any sign of Guardian presence. Nothing. The ruins were deserted.

They reached the chapel's entrance—a simple stone archway, the wooden door long since rotted away. Inside, the space was small, bare. Stone walls. Dirt floor. An altar stone is still in place but stripped of any decoration;

centuries of weathering had reduced the interior to its essential elements.

"Where would they hide it?" Liam asked.

Elena looked at Fragment 7 again, studying the cipher for Fragment 8's location:

Where stone remembers ancient oaths, beneath the mark of the broken sword, the eighth corruption waits in silence.

She examined the chapel walls, tracing the light of her flashlight across the carvings. Dozens of Templar crosses appeared—small, shallow, carved by different hands over centuries. Each one a vow. A confession. A brother's mark left before battle.

"Here," Elena said.

She studied the marks more closely. Some overlapped, others faded into the stone. But one set stood apart: nine crosses arranged in a perfect circle, each smaller than a coin.

At the center of the circle, a single gouge, vertical and deliberate—as if a blade had once struck the wall and split the symbol in two.

"The mark of the broken sword," she said. "Not a carving—a strike."

Antoine stepped beside her.

"You think someone hit it?"

"Not someone. A knight. A vow carved in ritual. Where stone remembers ancient oaths, the oath itself is the key."

She pressed her hand over the nine small crosses, feeling the faint vertical groove—subtle, almost imperceptible—a seam. The wall wasn't solid stone at all, but a series of precisely fitted blocks.

Antoine took out his knife, sliding the tip into the groove. "There's space behind it."

They worked together, prying the circular stone plate loose. Dust fell away, revealing a narrow recess cut deep into the masonry. Inside, something glinted faintly—a thin sliver of metal catching the beam of her flashlight.

Elena reached in and drew it out. Not a sword. A broken piece of a Templar dagger, its blade etched with Latin words worn almost smooth:

Non Deficimus—We do not falter.

She turned it over. The dagger fragment was hollow. A compartment sealed with wax. She cracked the seal and slid the parchment free.

✠ ✠ ✠

Fragment 8.

Wrapped in oiled leather, in pristine condition. Elena stared at it. "Eight fragments now. One more to go."

"I love the mystery, but the stress..."

Liam noticed her hands trembling and touched her shoulder from behind, a small comforting gesture. She turned, smiling.

"I couldn't do this without you guys. We make a great team."

"No doubt," Antoine said as he scanned the chapel through the narrow beam of his flashlight. "They wouldn't make it this easy. Valerius gave us this location—so where's the trap?"

✠ ✠ ✠

As if in answer, voices echoed up the hill—footsteps on stone.

Antoine moved to the doorway, peered out, and drew back. "Guardians," he said. "Six of them. Surrounding the chapel."

"Can we get past them?" Reyes asked.

"Not without a fight."

"Then we fight. Six against four," Elena said.

Antoine shook his head. "No offense, but not a chance in hell."

"Then what do you suggest?"

Before Antoine could answer, a voice called from outside. Valerius.

"Doctor Voss. I know you're in there. And I know you have Fragment 8. I helped you with the location." No one moved. "You can't escape." A pause. "Come out. Bring the fragments. Let's end this peacefully."

Elena looked at Antoine. "Options?"

"Run. But they're blocking the only exit."

"Surrender. Give him the fragments."

"Also, not part of the plan."

"Or?"

Antoine smiled. "We're getting pretty good at improvising."

He moved to the back wall of the chapel and examined the stones. Found what he was looking for—a section of wall that had partially collapsed, leaving a gap just wide enough for a person to slip through.

"The boulder field continues behind the chapel. If we can reach it, we can lose them in the maze." He looked at Elena. "But we have to move fast. And we might have to split up."

"I don't like splitting up."

"Neither do I. But it's our only option."

Outside, Valerius spoke again. "Doctor Voss, I'm giving you thirty seconds. Then we come in. And I can't promise my men will be gentle."

"Let's go," Elena said. "Now."

They moved through the gap one at a time. Elena first, clutching the satchel to her chest. Reyes next. Liam. Then Antoine, covering their exit.

The boulder field behind the chapel was dense—massive granite formations creating a labyrinth of passages and hiding spots. They ran. Behind them, shouts. The Guardians had spotted their escape.

"Split up," Antoine ordered. "Meet at the car. Go!"

Elena and Reyes went left, diving between boulders. Liam and Antoine went right.

Elena ran, scrambling over rocks, the satchel bouncing against her side. Reyes stayed close, moving surprisingly well for an academic unused to this kind of chaos—footsteps behind them. Guardians pursuing.

"This way," Reyes gasped, pointing to a narrow gap between two massive boulders.

They squeezed through. Emerged on the other side to find—a steep rocky slope covered in loose scree and scrub brush.

"We have to jump," Reyes said. "There's brush—it'll break the fall."

"That's still going to hurt—"

"Or we get caught."

The footsteps were getting closer. Elena looked at the drop, then the satchel.

"On three. One. Two. Three."

They jumped.

The fall was terrifying—five meters of empty air, the ground rushing up at them—they hit hard. Elena rolled, tumbling, the satchel swinging wildly. Branches tore at her clothes, and rocks bruised her ribs. She slid to a stop just before hitting a large boulder, gasping. Beside her, Reyes groaned, clutching her ankle. "I think I twisted it."

"Can you move?"

"Yes. But not fast."

Above them, voices. The Guardians at the ledge, looking down.

"They jumped. Circle around. Find them. Now!"

Elena grabbed Reyes and helped her up. Reyes limped, putting weight on her injured ankle, but she could still move. They stumbled forward, using boulders for support, descending the hillside as fast as Reyes's injured ankle allowed.

The village was below them. The car was just beyond the sparse line of trees. They had to reach it before the Guardians cut them off.

Elena's phone chimed. A text from Antoine:

At the car. Where are you?

Coming. 2 mins. Reyes got hurt.

Hurry.

They reached the tree line, ducked into the shadow. Elena could see the car ahead, ten meters away. Antoine was behind the wheel, engine running. Liam is in the back seat, watching for pursuit.

"Run," Elena urged Reyes.

They ran—Reyes limping, Elena supporting her.

They jumped into the car. Doors slamming. Antoine hit the gas. Behind them, Guardians emerged from the trees, weapons drawn. Too late. They were gone, speeding down the narrow road, leaving Monsanto and Valerius behind.

Antoine drove for ten minutes before anyone spoke.

"How bad is it?" he asked, glancing back at Reyes.

"Sprained." Reyes winced as she tried to rotate it. "I can still walk, but not fast."

"We need to get you some ice," Liam said.

"And rest," Reyes added. She looked at Elena. "You have eight fragments now. Just one more, right?"

"Yes."

"Then you'll need to move fast. I'm sure Guiomar already knows that you have Fragment 8—you have to keep moving." She adjusted her injured ankle and grimaced. "I'll only slow you down like this."

Elena started to protest, but Reyes continued.

"Drop me somewhere safe—a hotel. I can research remotely, help decode locations, and provide information. But I can't keep running on this ankle. I need to go to an Urgent Care."

Antoine caught Elena's eye in the rearview mirror—a silent question—*your call.*

Elena looked at Reyes's injured ankle and at the genuine pain on her face. "Alright," she said. "We'll find you a safe place. You rest, recover. Stay in contact. Help us remotely."

"Thank you." Reyes leaned back, relieved. "I'm sorry. I wanted to see this through to the end."

"You still will. Just from a distance."

They found a small hotel in Castelo Branco—quiet, unremarkable, paid cash. Elena helped Reyes inside and got her checked in under a false name.

"I'll start researching Fragment 9's location tonight," Reyes said, settling onto the bed with visible relief. "Send me photos of Fragment 8 when you can. I'll cross-reference with historical databases, look for patterns."

"Thank you, Sophia. For everything."

"We're partners, remember?" Reyes smiled. "Now go. Find the last fragment. I'll be here when you need me." Elena left, watching Reyes limp to close the door.

✠ ✠ ✠

Back in the car, Antoine pulled onto the road. "She'll be safe there. There's also a hospital nearby called Amato Lusitano. She'll be fine."

"I hope so," Elena said.

"What now?" Liam asked.

"We decode Fragment 8. Find Fragment 9. Keep moving."

Elena pulled out Fragment 8 and began studying it. Soon, Fragment 9 would reveal its location. One more to find. Then they'd have them all.

Then what? Destroy them? Give them to Valerius? Turn them over to the police? Trust that the right people would protect them. She didn't know. She knew one thing, though—Guiomar would never get her hands on them. Ever.

But first, they had to find the last one.

Twenty minutes later, Liam was reading something on his laptop in the back seat. He'd set up a police scanner app days ago—monitoring Portuguese law enforcement frequencies, news alerts, anything that might give them a warning if Durand was closing in.

Detective Durand was still hunting them. Still convinced they were criminals responsible for the Alcobaça break-in and explosion. Only if someone proved that Guiomar's people committed Almeida's murder, and not them, would that be resolved. Until then, they were fugitives.

Liam scrolled through the alerts, half-listening to the police chatter. Then he stopped. Went still.

"Elena."

Something in his voice made her turn around. "What?"

"You need to see this."

She leaned back to look at his screen. A police alert. Posted fourteen minutes ago.

Anonymous tip received regarding American fugitive Dr. Elena Voss. The caller reported sighting at Monsanto castle ruins. Local police dispatched. Suspects fled before arrival. Timestamp: 10:20 A.M.

Elena checked her watch—11:01 A.M.

They'd left Monsanto at 10:30.

The tip came while they were still there. While they were in the chapel. While Reyes was still with them. Elena felt ice in her stomach.

"Only a few people knew we were going to Monsanto," she said.

✠ ✠ ✠

Antoine's eyes flicked to the rearview mirror. He understood immediately. "Could have been Valerius," Liam suggested. "He knew we'd be there."

"Valerius wanted to capture us himself," Antoine said. "Why call local police? That would just complicate his operation."

"Then who—"

Elena thought about the timeline. The four of them climbing the hill, finding Fragment 8. The Guardians arriving. And before that, at the rest stop, when they'd discussed the plan. Reyes had excused herself and gone to the bathroom. She'd been gone for... how long? Five minutes? Long enough to make a call.

"Sophia," Elena said. The name tasted bitter.

"You think she called it in?" Liam asked.

"Who else?" Elena pulled up the hotel address on her phone. Looked at it. "We just dropped her off. Told her where we'd be and what we were doing."

"She's injured," Liam protested. "She couldn't even walk."

"Or she's an excellent actress."

Silence in the car.

Antoine's hands tightened on the wheel. "If she's reporting to someone—"

"Then she's been doing it since Coimbra," Elena finished. "Since the library. Maybe longer."

"Since the moment she agreed to help you."

Elena thought about their conversations. Reyes's questions about the fragments, about their methods, about where they were going next. Not curiosity. Intelligence gathering.

"Guiomar," Elena said. "Reyes is working for Guiomar."

"We don't know that for certain—" Liam began.

✠ ✠ ✠

A text arrived on Elena's phone. Perfect timing.

Doctor Reyes has been invaluable. She tells me everything. Thank you for making this so easy—G.

Elena stared at the screen. Showed it to Antoine. "We need to move. If Reyes knows where we're going—"

"She doesn't," Elena said. "We haven't decoded Fragment 8 yet. She doesn't know Fragment 9's location."

"But she will. She expects you to call her for help to figure it out." Antoine took the next exit, heading away from their planned route. "We can't communicate with her anymore. Can't let her know our plans."

"She's our research support," Liam said.

"She's a spy," Antoine corrected.

Elena looked down at the message once more. The single letter '*G*' at the bottom seemed to burn through the screen.

Guiomar knew everything. She'd been inside their circle since Coimbra. None of them had seen it coming.

And somewhere in Lisbon, the surgeon of humanity prepared her next cut.

15 - The Price

Around midnight, they found an abandoned textile factory on the outskirts of Lisbon—three stories of empty industrial space, windows broken, machinery long since stripped away. The kind of place that had died with Portugal's manufacturing economy decades ago.

Antoine had scouted it out—multiple exits. Clear sightlines. Far from main roads. Safe.

Elena was translating Fragment 8, the vellum spread on an old workbench. Liam was setting up his laptop nearby, checking news feeds and police scanners. Antoine stood watch at a broken window overlooking the street.

"How's the translation coming?" Liam asked.

"Slowly. This cipher is much more difficult."

"Company," Antoine said. His tone made them both freeze.

"How many?"

"Six. Tactically advancing. Guardians."

"How did they find us?"

"Probably followed us from Belém. I should have seen it." Antoine's voice was tight with self-recrimination. "Get the fragments. Back exit. Now."

Elena grabbed the satchel and placed Fragment 8 inside with the others. Liam closed his laptop. But before they could move, the factory's main entrance exploded inward. Not blown—kicked. Professional breach. Six men in dark tactical gear poured through. Moving with military precision.

"Go!" Antoine shoved Elena and Liam toward the back stairs. But two more Guardians emerged from that direction, blocking the exit. Trapped.

Antoine positioned himself between the Guardians and Elena. Pulled his collapsible baton from his pocket—snapped it to full extension with a sharp crack. "Stay behind me," he ordered.

The lead Guardian stepped forward. Older, commanding presence. Valerius. "Doctor Voss. You've been difficult to corner. I'm impressed." He gestured to his men. "But this ends now. The fragments. All of them. Hand them over."

"No," Elena said.

"Then we take them forcibly." Valerius nodded to his team.

Four Guardians moved forward, drawing weapons—swords—short blades designed for close combat. Antoine dropped into a fighting stance.

"Last chance. Walk away."

"I don't think so."

The Guardians attacked.

Antoine met the first one head-on—baton deflecting the sword strike, using the Guardian's momentum to spin him off-balance—a sharp strike to the knee. The man went down. Three more are already moving in.

Antoine fought like a trained killer who'd spent years in close-quarters combat. His baton cracked against sword blades, against knees, against ribs. He used speed and angles, never letting them close in on him. But there were too many.

A sword got through his defense and sliced his shoulder. Shallow but bleeding. Another Guardian grabbed his baton arm. Antoine twisted, drove his elbow into the man's face, and broke free.

But in that moment, one Guardian slipped past. Going for Liam.

"Liam, look out!" Elena screamed.

Liam saw the Guardian coming. Saw the sword and raised his hands in self-defense.

"No—" Antoine started. Too late.

The Guardian's pommel strike caught Liam in the temple—a precise, brutal blow. Liam dropped like a puppet with its strings cut.

"LIAM!" Elena screamed.

Antoine tried to reach him, but two Guardians blocked his path. He fought desperately—knife out now, no more restraint—but they kept him back. He watched, helpless, as two Guardians lifted Liam's unconscious body.

Valerius spoke into a radio: "Target secured. Exfil now."

A black van screeched to a stop outside the factory. Rear doors opened. They threw Liam inside like cargo.

"NO!" Elena cried out, struggling against the Guardian holding her. Antoine broke free, running toward the van—But it was already moving. Accelerating. Gone.

The remaining Guardians retreated in tactical order, covering each other's withdrawal. Valerius was the last to leave. He looked at Antoine, then Elena.

"We have your friend. If you want him back alive, you know what we want. The fragments. All of them." He paused. "You have forty-eight hours. Then we start asking him questions. And the Guardians have very effective interrogation methods." He left.

The factory fell silent except for Elena's ragged breathing. She stood there, staring at the empty doorway where they'd taken Liam. Then her legs gave out. She collapsed to her knees, sobbing. Wrenching gasps. Months of pressure, fear, and exhaustion broke through all at once.

"He's gone. They took him. Oh no, they took him—"

✠ ✠ ✠

Antoine checked the street—empty now—then moved to Elena. Put a hand on her shoulder.

"We'll get him back."

"How?!" Elena looked up at him, tears streaming. "How do we get him back? We can't assault a Guardian compound. We don't even know where they're holding him. We don't have—"

Antoine's voice was calm. Professional. But Elena could see the pain beneath it—the guilt.

"I know."

"Then what do we do?!"

Antoine was silent.

Elena stood, paced, her mind racing. "Guiomar. She's been watching us. Following us. Her people are everywhere. She MUST know where the Guardians are holding him."

"No. Absolutely not."

"Then what's your plan?!" Elena's voice rose, desperate. "Liam is being held by people who will torture him for information we can't let them have! Every minute we waste—"

"Guiomar uses people. She's not an ally. She won't help without a price."

"I don't care about the price!"

"You should. Because with Guiomar, the price is always higher than you can afford."

"I don't care!" Elena was shaking. "Liam is my friend. Our friend. I'm not leaving him with those people."

Antoine looked at her for a prolonged moment, then his shoulders sagged. Defeated. "There is one way," he said.

Antoine rubbed the edge of that same old coin again in his pocket, like he'd been carrying the choice for years. He seemed to decide on something and nodded to himself.

"What?"

"A protocol. From years ago. A mission in Macau. Guiomar and I weren't allies. But we established an understanding."

"What kind of understanding?"

Antoine pulled something from his pocket. A coin. Old, worn, with markings Elena didn't recognize.

"A challenge coin. From Macau. We were both hunting the same target—different reasons, different employers. We kept crossing paths. Nearly killed each other twice." He turned the coin over. "But there was... respect. Between professionals. We had dinner one night." Elena's gaze searched him. "We became..."

Antoine looked away. "We made a pact," he said. "In case either of us needed—"

"She gave you that?"

"Yes. And I kept it. Swore I'd never use it." Antoine looked at the coin. "But Liam's life is worth breaking that promise."

"What do you do with it?"

"There's a place—a dead drop. Guiomar grew up here, and I lived with her for a short time—that's long over, but it's how we decided on the drop's location. If either of us placed our coin there, it meant mayday. Everything on the line."

"Where?"

"Padrão dos Descobrimentos. The monument at Belém. There's a specific spot—a crack in the stone at the base, north side. Small enough that no tourist would notice. We'd leave the coin there."

"How will she know? How can you be sure she'll see it?"

Antoine met her eyes. "Because Guiomar's been following us this whole time. We've been too lucky. Too many narrow escapes. She's been letting us succeed. Letting you decode the fragments. We're doing her work for her.

Her people are ghosts—I've only seen traces. Movements in crowds. Vehicles that appear too often. She's been waiting for us to complete the cipher." He held up the coin. "When I place this, her people will see. They'll tell her. And she'll come."

"And she'll want payment?"

"Yes."

Elena thought of Liam. Unconscious. In Guardian's hands. Being taken somewhere to be questioned. Perhaps even tortured.

"Then we pay her price," Elena said. "Whatever it is."

✠ ✠ ✠

"Elena—"

"Antoine. I don't care what she wants. He protected me. We are not abandoning him." Antoine studied her face. Then nodded.

"Alright. I'll place the coin. But you need to understand—once we invoke this protocol, once we owe

Guiomar, there's no walking away. She'll collect. And it won't be a small transaction."

"I understand."

"Do you? Because Guiomar doesn't work for money. She works for power. For leverage. And the only thing we have that she wants—"

"Is the complete cipher," Elena finished. "All the fragments."

"Yes."

Elena looked at the satchel.

"Then we give it to her," she said. "We find Fragment 9. We complete the cipher. And we trade it for Liam's life."

"You'll be handing her the tools to kill millions."

"I know. But Liam is real. He's here. He's ours. The millions are... theoretical. Possible futures. Liam is now."

Antoine paused. Then he pocketed the coin. "Let's go. The monument isn't far."

✠ ✠ ✠

They drove to Belém as night fell.

The Padrão dos Descobrimentos rose against the darkening sky—a massive monument shaped like a ship's prow, carved with figures of Portuguese explorers. At this hour, the tourist crowds were gone. Antoine parked at a distance. They approached on foot.

"North side. Stay close."

They walked around the monument's base. Antoine's eyes swept the area—looking for watchers, for Guild operatives. No one.

He found the spot. A crack in the stone, weathered by decades. Invisible unless you knew what to look for. He pulled out Guiomar's coin. Looked at it one last time.

Then placed it into the crack. Pushed it deep enough that it wouldn't fall but could be retrieved.

"Done," he said. They walked away. Didn't look back.

Somewhere in the shadows, someone was watching and soon, Guiomar would know.

In a nearby café, a man in a windbreaker spoke into his phone.

"The Frenchman placed the coin. Mayday signal confirmed." On the other end, Guiomar listened.

"Interesting," she said. "After all these years, Antoine needs me. How wonderful... and unexpected."

"Orders?"

"I'll retrieve the coin myself. I know where it is." She smiled. "And prepare a team. If Antoine invoked the protocol, something significant has happened. Find out what."

"Yes, ma'am."

Guiomar hung up. Looked at her reflection in the window. Antoine never broke promises. Never showed weakness. Never asked for help until now. Dr. Voss was desperate, which meant opportunity.

Guiomar left her apartment, drove to Belém herself. Some things required personal attention. She found the monument. The crack in the stone. The coin. She pulled it out, examining it in the streetlight. Her coin. Returned after so many years. A warrior's bond invoked. She pocketed it and pulled out her phone.

"Where are they?"

"Warehouse district. East side. Waiting."

"Tell them I'm coming. And that I'm... intrigued." She walked back to her car.

Dr. Voss had already decoded most of the fragments in record time—only one more to go. Now she was desperate enough to invoke a blood debt with the Guild of Shadows.

Perfect.

Guiomar had been patient—watching, waiting for the right moment; that moment had just arrived.

✠ ✠ ✠

Antoine and Elena waited in the abandoned building—a warehouse, concrete and steel, with clear sightlines—no more surprises.

An hour passed. Then two.

"Maybe she's not coming," Elena said.

"She'll come. Guiomar will honor the oath. It's the one thing you can trust about her."

"The one thing?"

"The only thing."

Footsteps echoed in the warehouse. Antoine's hand moved to his knife. But when the figure emerged from the shadow, he recognized her.

Guiomar.

She looked the same as he remembered—mid-forties, athletic build, dark hair pulled back. Cold eyes that missed nothing. She wore practical clothes and moved with economical grace. Two operatives flanked her. Silent. Professional.

She stopped ten meters away. Studied Antoine. Then Elena.

"Antoine. It's been eight years."

"Seven," Antoine corrected.

"Has it? Where does the time go?" Her English was perfect—Portuguese accent. "You invoked the protocol. That's not something you'd do lightly."

"It's not."

Guiomar lifted something between two fingers, letting the light catch on old metal—the coin.

She rolled it once across her knuckles—his old trick—and smiled. "You gave me a promise, Antoine. Not a souvenir."

His thumb found the ghost of where the coin should be in his pocket and met only fabric.

"You always collect, don't you?" Antoine asked.

"Always," she said. "You know that."

"So." Guiomar's eyes moved to Elena. "This must be Doctor Voss. The brilliant cryptographer who's been hunting Templar fragments across Portugal. I've been following your progress with great interest."

Elena stepped forward. "Where is Liam?"

Guiomar smiled. "Direct. I appreciate that. Your friend—the young photographer—is being held by the Guardians. North of Lisbon. A facility in Sintra. Old monastery, heavily guarded."

"Can you get him out?"

"Of course."

"Then do it. Please. They have him. They're going to torture him for information. I can't let that happen."

"You can't. But I can." Guiomar tilted her head. "For a price."

"What do you want?"

"You know what I want, Doctor Voss. You're too intelligent to pretend otherwise." Guiomar stepped closer. "The complete cipher. All the fragments. When you find Fragment 9—and you will—you bring them all to me."

"You'll weaponize them. Kill millions."

Guiomar tilted her head, her eyes narrowing slightly as she studied Elena's face.

"I'll restore balance..." She paused, letting the words hang in the air like a threat. "There's a difference."

"There's not."

"That's a philosophical debate for another time. Right now, you have a choice. Your friend's life, or your conscience. Which matters more?"

Elena looked at Antoine. He said nothing. This was her decision. She thought of Liam. Stepping in front of that Guardian. Taking the blow meant for her.

"I'll do it," Elena said. "I'll get the last one and bring you the complete cipher. Just get Liam back. Alive."

Guiomar studied her face. Then nodded.

"You have my word. I'll extract your friend from the Guardian facility. Alive and relatively unharmed—though I can't guarantee his mental state, depending on what they've already done to him."

She pulled out her phone, made a call, speaking in rapid Portuguese. Then looked back at Elena. "My team is moving now. You'll have your friend back within twelve hours."

"Thank you—" Elena started.

"Don't thank me. This is a transaction. You owe me a debt, and I plan on collecting."

Guiomar turned and paused at the dock. "One last thing. Don't try to run and don't even think about destroying the fragments. I've spent too much on this hunt. Betray me and there will be consequences."

Guiomar left with her operatives, disappearing into the shadows as smoothly as she'd arrived. Elena stood there, shaking.

"I just made a deal with the devil," she said.

"Yes. You did."

"And Liam's alive because of it."

"For now."

"But millions may die."

"Probably."

Elena looked at him. "How do you live with choices like this?"

"You make them. You live with the consequences. And you pretend there were no better options." Antoine checked his weapon. "Come on. We need to move. If Guiomar's hitting a Guardian facility, this entire area will crawl with police soon."

They left the warehouse. Behind them, in the darkness, the weight of Elena's choice settled like a stone. One friend's life. For the tools to end millions. There were no good choices left. Only terrible ones. And she'd just made hers.

The Guardian Facility—Sintra

Liam hung by his wrists. Leather cuffs secured to a beam above, keeping his arms extended above his head. His toes barely touch the floor—just enough contact to prevent his shoulders from dislocating, but not enough to take any actual weight off his arms. A hood covered his face. Heavy fabric. Claustrophobic.

Dissonant noise blasted from large nearby speakers. Frequencies designed to disorient, to prevent sleep. He didn't know how long he'd been here. Hours. Or days. Time became meaningless in darkness and noise.

The hood lifted. Bright light. Blinding after so long in darkness. Liam squinted. Saw Valerius standing in front of him.

"Mr. Hayes. You're awake. Good."

Liam said nothing. Couldn't. His mouth was too dry. Water appeared. Valerius held it to Liam's lips. Let him drink. A small mercy. Or a tactic. Liam didn't know which.

"I'm going to ask you some questions," Valerius said. "And you're going to answer them. This can be easy or very difficult. Your choice."

Liam's voice came out as a croak. "I won't tell you anything."

"Everyone says that." Valerius gestured to a table against the wall. Instruments laid out. Pliers. Knives. Electrical equipment. "Do you know what these are for?"

"Torture."

"Persuasion. There's a difference."

Valerius picked up a pair of pliers.

"The human body has many sensitive areas. Fingernails. Teeth. Joints. The pain is... considerable. But the interesting thing about pain is that the anticipation is often worse than the reality. The mind imagines horrors. And imagination is infinite."

He put the pliers down. Picked up a knife. "Where is Doctor Voss?"

"Don't know."

"Where is she taking the fragments?"

"Don't know."

"How many fragments does she have?"

Liam closed his eyes. "Don't know."

"I think you do." Valerius stepped closer. "You've been with her from the beginning. You've helped her decode locations. You know everything she knows."

"I'm just the photographer."

"No. You're more than that. You're loyal. That's admirable."

Liam watched as Valerius turned toward the hearth. A small brazier glowed inside—coal stacked like black teeth, flames licking through wax that hissed and smoked, burning hotter than firewood ever could. He set the knife down in it, the steel flashing orange as the heat took hold.

"But loyalty," he said, watching the blade darken, "has limits. Pain has a way of clarifying priorities."

He nodded to a Guardian standing near the door. The hood went back over Liam's face. The noise started again. Louder now.

"We'll start with sleep deprivation," Valerius's voice came through the noise. "Forty-eight hours. No rest. No relief. Then we'll revisit our conversation. See if your priorities have shifted." Footsteps. A door closing.

Liam hung there in darkness and sound. His shoulders screamed. His wrists burned. Exhaustion pulled at him, but the noise and the position made sleep impossible. He thought of Elena. Of the fragments.

Don't tell them. Don't give them anything. Even if they hurt him. If they broke him. He wouldn't betray his friends. He couldn't. Too much at stake.

Forty-Eight Hours Later

Liam had lost track of time. The noise had stopped. Started. Stopped again. Or was it continuous, and his mind was fragmenting the sound? He'd tried to sleep standing. Couldn't. His body wouldn't allow it. Tried to shift weight. The cuffs prevented it. Tried to focus on anything—memories, songs, counting breaths—but the exhaustion scattered his thoughts.

The hood lifted again. Valerius. Still calm. Still patient.

"How are you feeling, Mr. Hayes?"

Liam couldn't form words. Just stared.

"Forty-eight hours without sleep does interesting things to the mind. Hallucinations. Paranoia. Psychosis." Valerius offered water again. Liam drank desperately.

"Where is the next fragment's location?"

"Don't... know..."

"Doctor Voss decoded the latest one. She knows where to go next. She would have told you. Where is it?"

"Didn't tell... me..."

"I don't believe you." Valerius picked up the pliers again. "Perhaps we should make this more... interesting?"

He stepped forward. Liam tensed, preparing for pain—

Gunfire. Distant but unmistakable. Automatic weapons. Then closer. Shouting. Valerius spun toward the door.

"What the—"

An explosion. The building shook. The door burst open. A Guardian rushed in. "We're under attack! Multiple hostiles! Heavily armed!"

"How many?"

"Unknown! They breached the north wall—"

More gunfire. Much closer now.

Valerius looked at Liam. Then at his men. "Fall back. Defensive positions. Hold this facility."

"Sir, they're using explosives. Professional grade. This isn't the police—"

"Then who?!"

The answer came in the form of three figures in tactical gear crashing through a side entrance.

Guild of Shadows operatives.

They moved with brutal efficiency—suppressed weapons. Precise shots. Two Guardians dropped.

Valerius drew his sidearm, fired—

One Guild operative went down. But the other two kept advancing. The fight was brief and vicious. Valerius retreated through a back exit, taking his surviving men with him.

One of the Guild operatives moved to Liam. Cut his cuffs with a knife. Liam collapsed to the floor. Couldn't stand. Couldn't process what was happening.

"We've got him," the agent announced into his radio—Portuguese accent. "Target secured. Exfil now."

They lifted Liam. He tried to resist, too confused and exhausted to understand he was being rescued.

"Easy," the agent stated. "We're getting you out."

"Who... are you...?"

"Shut up and walk. We'll explain later."

They half-carried him through the facility. Past dead Guardians. Past structural damage from the breaching charges. Outside, a van waited. They threw him in the back—not gently, but not cruelly either. Professional.

The van accelerated. Liam lay on the cold metal floor, shaking from adrenaline, exhaustion, and shock. Someone wrapped a blanket around him.

"You're safe," a female voice said. "We're taking you somewhere secure."

"Who are you?" Liam managed.

"Friends of a friend. That's all you need to know."

The van drove for what felt like hours but might have been minutes. When it finally stopped, Liam smelled salt air—heard water. They pulled him out. He saw a boat—a trawler, old but functional. They took him aboard. Laid him on the deck. Placed a tarp over him to hide him.

"Stay here. Rest. Someone's coming for you." Then they were gone. Liam lay there, trembling. The boat rocked gently—the sound of water against the hull.

He closed his eyes and slept.

The Docks - 2 Hours Later

Elena ran.

Antoine had gotten the message: Liam was secure. Offshore. Coordinates provided. They'd driven to the docks, rented a small boat, and navigated to the trawler's location. Elena climbed aboard, her heart racing as if she had just run a marathon.

"Liam!" No answer.

She found him under the tarp on the deck. Curled up. Shivering despite the blanket. No visible injuries. But when she touched his shoulder, he flinched.

"It's me," Elena said. "It's Elena. You're safe now."

Liam's eyes opened. Unfocused. Exhausted beyond measure.

His voice trembled as he spoke. "Elena?"

"I'm here. You're safe. We got you out."

"The Guardians—"

"They don't have you anymore. You're with us."

Liam closed his eyes. A tear slid down his face.

"Didn't tell them anything," he said. "Didn't... betray you..."

Elena's own tears came. "I know. I know you didn't." She held him while he shook. While he cried. While the trauma broke through the exhaustion. Antoine stood nearby, watching the horizon for threats.

Footsteps on the dock. Antoine's hand moved to his weapon—Guiomar.

Walking toward the trawler with calm purpose. She stopped at the dock's edge. One of her operatives approached, speaking in Portuguese. "Two dead. Three wounded."

Guiomar nodded once, dismissing him. Elena overheard. She looked up from Liam. "I'm... I'm sorry. Your people—"

"For the greater good," Guiomar said. Her voice was icy. Flat. No emotion. No grief.

Elena said nothing.

Guiomar's eyes moved to the trawler, to Liam wrapped in the blanket, to Elena holding him.

"How touching," she said softly. "You have your friend back. Alive. As promised."

Her tone hardened. "Now you owe me the fragments. All of them. The complete cipher. Don't make me come looking for it." She turned and left. Elena watched her go. Then she looked down at Liam, still shaking, still traumatized. He was alive. But the price. The price was the end of the humanity. And Elena would pay it willingly.

16 - Two Days

The trawler rocked gently as Guiomar's operative untied the mooring lines.

"Wait," Elena said. "How do we get back to—?"

The operative looked at her with flat eyes. "Not my problem. We delivered your friend. The debt stands. That's all that matters." He climbed onto the dock and walked away without looking back. Elena watched him disappear into the pre-dawn darkness, on a military raft.

They were alone. On a boat they didn't own. With Liam almost unable to stand. One half mile from shore.

"We need shelter," Antoine said. "Liam needs some rest."

Elena thought about their options. Abandoned buildings—too cold, too exposed. The car is too cramped. Hotels required ID, which meant risk. But Liam shivered despite the blankets. His eyes were hollow, dark circles beneath them like bruises. He needed warmth. Safety. Recovery.

"I have a credit card," Elena said. "I haven't used it since Oxford."

"Using it leaves a trail."

"I know. But look at him." She gestured to Liam. "We can't keep running him ragged. He'll collapse."

Antoine studied Liam's face. The exhaustion. The trauma. "OK, a small place," he said. "Off the main roads. Cash only. We stay two nights. Three at most. Let him recover."

"Agreed."

They helped Liam into the small boat that Antoine rented, rowing back to shore. The sky was lightening with dawn as they arrived at the car. Liam slumped in the back seat, asleep before Antoine started the engine.

They drove north into the hills outside Sintra. The roads grew narrower, quieter. Small villages passed. Stone houses with terracotta roofs. Gardens overgrown with bougainvillea.

Antoine spotted a sign: Quinta da Rosa - Quartos - Rooms Available.

A family-run guesthouse, set back from the road. Old stone building, two stories, with a garden and a view of the valley below. Peaceful. Remote. Perfect.

The owner—a woman in her sixties with kind eyes and graying hair—asked no questions when Elena paid cash for three nights.

"Breakfast at eight," she said in accented English, handing over keys. "You look tired. Rest well."

"Thank you."

They climbed the stairs to the second floor—two rooms, connected by a shared bathroom. Clean beds. Windows overlooking the garden. The smell of lavender and old wood. Liam made it to the nearest bed and collapsed fully clothed. Elena pulled a blanket over him and watched him for a moment. His breathing is shallow. Hands twitched in sleep—dreams or memories, she couldn't tell.

"He'll be okay," Antoine said from the doorway. "Give him time."

"Time." Elena's laugh was bitter. "We don't have time—Guiomar's waiting. The Guardians are hunting us. And we owe a debt we can't pay without dooming millions."

"Then we rest while we can. Tomorrow, we figure out the next move." Antoine moved to the window, checked the view, and the approaches. Old habits. "Get some sleep, Elena. You need it."

She nodded and went to her own room. Fell into bed without even removing her shoes. She slept.

Elena woke later, thirsty. The room was dark. She slipped out, tiptoeing downstairs in bare feet.

The kitchen light was on. Faint. Just the small lamp over the sink. Senhora Rosa stood with her back to the stairs, phone pressed to her ear, speaking in low, careful English.

"...yes, I understand. Enough to renovate the entire place?" Rosa's voice filled with desperate hope. "That would be so wonderful. The roof alone needs—yes, yes, I can do that. No problem at all. Just thirty seconds of work and... I have one handy that will fit. Tomorrow morning, when they're at breakfast. Thank you so much, Miss—"

She turned. Saw Elena frozen on the stairs. Rosa's face went white. She ended the call immediately.

"Doctor Voss! I didn't hear you come down."

"I was just getting some water," Elena said, studying Rosa's expression. Fear. Guilt. Both trying to hide behind a smile.

"Of course, of course." Rosa moved to the sink, filled a glass, and handed it to Elena, trembling.

"I was just—someone called about helping renovate this old place—a benefactor. Very generous. You know how it is, trying to keep an old building like this running. Everything needs repairs."

"At three in the morning?" Elena asked.

"She's calling from—from London. Business hours there."

Elena sipped the water. Watched Rosa over the rim of the glass. Something was wrong. The fear in Rosa's eyes. The way she'd cut off that name. *Miss—who, Guiomar? No. Impossible. Rosa was just a guesthouse owner. Sweet. Harmless. There was no way—*

"Everything okay, Senhora Rosa?" Elena asked.

"Yes! Yes, of course. Just excited about the renovations. This place could really use a facelift, you know?" Rosa laughed, but it sounded forced.

"You should get back to sleep, Doctor Voss. You look exhausted."

"You're right. Goodnight."

"Goodnight."

Elena paused on the stairs, a chill running through her. *"Miss who?"* But exhaustion won; she pushed the thought away. Probably nothing. Paranoia. She was exhausted, seeing shadows where none existed. Still, something felt wrong. She made a mental note to tell Liam and Antoine about the conversation in the morning—just in case. She'll check her satchel tomorrow to make sure all the fragments are accounted for and tell Liam to review his photographs on the camera.

She would forget.

She shouldn't have.

✠✠✠

Elena woke the next morning to sunlight streaming through the window and the smell of coffee brewing— Starbucks Pike Place, dark and rich, carrying that mix of toasted caramel and smoke that always reminded her of airports and early mornings. She closed her eyes, letting the warmth cut through the cold in her chest.

For a moment, she didn't remember where she was. Then it came back—the trawler, Liam's rescue, the guesthouse. She checked her phone.

10:00 A.M. She'd slept for almost twelve hours.

She found Antoine downstairs in the small dining room. He sat at a table near the window, coffee and pastries in front of him, a Portuguese newspaper open but unread.

"Morning," he said.

"Morning." Elena poured herself a cup of coffee from a pot on the sideboard. "How long have you been up?"

"Since six."

"Any sign of trouble?"

"None. We're off the grid here. For now." Antoine gestured to a plate of fresh bread, cheese, and fruit. "The owner—Senhora Rosa—she's been bringing food. Says we look too thin."

Elena smiled despite everything. "She's not wrong."

She ate. Fresh bread still warm from the oven. Local cheese. Olives. Orange juice that tasted like actual oranges, not concentrate. It was the best meal she'd had in weeks.

"How's Liam?" she asked.

"Still sleeping. I checked on him an hour ago. He's okay. Just exhausted."

They ate in companionable silence for a while. Then Antoine turned on the small television in the corner—news, volume low. The anchor was speaking in Portuguese, but the images told the story—a police press conference. Detective Durand is at a podium.

"Turn it up," Elena said.

Antoine found the remote and raised the volume.

The subtitles appeared in English:

New evidence in the Marcus Almeida murder investigation. Dr. Elena Voss is wanted for questioning but has been cleared of all suspicion in Dr. Almeida's death.

Elena set down her coffee.

The screen showed security footage of someone in dark clothing entering Almeida's building. Not her. Not Antoine. Someone else.

Police have identified this individual as a person of interest.

Cristiano's photo.

Interpol has issued an alert. Dr. Voss is no longer considered a suspect in the murder.

The camera cut to Durand at the press conference. He looked tired. Thoughtful.

A reporter asked a question in Portuguese.

Durand answered in English, for the international press:

"Doctor Voss is cleared of murder charges, yes. However, she and her companions are still wanted for questioning regarding multiple incidents of breaking and entering at historical sites across Portugal. We don't believe Doctor Voss is a danger to the public, but we believe she has information about activities that may be connected to organized criminal elements."

Another reporter shouted a question.

Durand held up a hand. "We ask that Doctor Voss contact us voluntarily. For her own safety as much as anything else. We want to understand what's happening."

The broadcast cut back to the studio, local weather.

Elena stared at the screen. "He knows," she said.

"Knows what?"

"That we're not criminals. That something else is happening. That there's more to this than theft." She looked at Antoine. "He's a good cop. He wants to understand before he acts."

"Good cop or not, he'll still arrest us if we cross paths."

"He's... waiting. Giving us space." Elena turned off the television. "At least we're not running from murder charges anymore."

"Just breaking and entering. Destruction of historical property. Evading arrest." Antoine smiled. "Minor stuff." Despite everything, Elena laughed. It felt good. Like being human again, even for a moment.

✠✠✠

Liam appeared in the doorway around noon, moving stiffly. He'd showered—his hair was damp—and changed into clean clothes from his bag. However, his eyes still looked haunted. The kind of look that wouldn't fade for years.

"Hey," Elena said.

"Hey." His voice was hoarse. "Is that coffee?"

"Fresh pot. Help yourself." He poured a cup with shaking hands and sat at the table. Ate mechanically—bread, cheese, fruit. Not tasting it, just refueling.

They didn't push him to talk. After a while, he said, "I didn't tell them anything."

"I know," Elena said.

"They asked about the fragments. How many you have. Where we are going next. I said nothing."

"Liam, you don't have to—"

"I need to say it." He looked at her, his eyes red-rimmed. "They hung me up. Leather cuffs. For hours. Maybe days. I lost track of time. The blaring noise and the hood. The anticipation. They showed me things. Tools. Told me what they'd do."

Elena reached across the table and put her hand on his. "But they didn't hurt you."

"Not physically. But up here—" He tapped his temple. "I kept thinking they were about to start. That the next time the hood came off, they'd do it. The waiting was... it was worse than I thought pain could be."

"But you held out," Antoine said. "You didn't break. That takes strength most people don't have."

"I didn't feel strong. I felt terrified."

"Courage isn't about not being afraid. It's about being afraid and doing the right thing anyway." Antoine met his eyes. "You protected us. You protected the fragments. You could have told them everything and made it stop. You didn't. That's courage."

"Thanks."

They sat together, the three of them, in the quiet guesthouse dining room. Outside, birds sang in the garden. The morning sun warmed the old stone walls. For a moment, they weren't fugitives or cryptographers or soldiers—just three people who'd survived something terrible together.

✠✠✠

That afternoon, Elena spread Fragment 8 on the table in her room—perfect lighting from the window. Perfect space. Correct tools—her notebook, pencils, and reference books on Liam's laptop. He'd done an incredible job compiling information. For the first time since this started, she could work without rushing. Without the nausea from reading in a moving car.

She examined the vellum. This one would take a while. More symbols and letters than the previous fragments. Each piece is designed to challenge the decoder's dedication to the solution. She worked methodically. Identifying patterns. Cross-referencing with the other fragments and searching for consistency in the encryption methods.

On her laptop, the decryption app whirred to life. Lines of symbols and numbers streamed across the screen—green, then red. Gibberish. She adjusted the key length. No change. Shifted the language profile—Latin, Old Portuguese, and even phonetic roots. Still nonsense. She reversed the sequence. Split it into halves. Merged again. Each run ended the same way: Gibberish.

The cipher refused to yield as the sun moved across the room.

Antoine brought her coffee. Liam sat nearby, recovering in his own way—sorting gear, scanning news feeds, wordless but present.

Afternoon light turned golden. Elena leaned back, eyes burning, fingers stiff.

Then the stream of text froze. The symbols stopped.

In green text: Decryption complete.

"Ah ha," she whispered. "There you are, you sneaky little..."

Liam and Antoine moved to the table. Elena's notebook showed the decoded text.

"Fragment 8," she said, her voice tired.

Pestis Octava: Morbus Prion.

"The Prion Disease."

"What's a prion?" Liam asked.

"Misfolded proteins. They're responsible for diseases like Creutzfeldt-Jakob, mad cow, and even fatal familial insomnia." She traced the decoded text, frowning. "They're terrifying because you can't kill them—prions aren't alive. They're just malformed proteins that trigger others to misfold, a chain reaction that eats the brain from the inside out."

"How does it work?"

"A prion disease that's been modified. Engineered. Transmission: airborne. The prions are aerosolized and stable in air for extended periods. You breathe them in. They cross the blood-brain barrier. The cascade begins."

"Symptoms?"

Elena's expression darkened. "Incubation period: fourteen days. Initial symptoms: headaches, confusion, and memory loss. Secondary stage: dementia, loss of motor control, seizures. Tertiary stage: complete neurological collapse. The brain literally develops holes. Spongelike. Until there's nothing left. Mortality: ninety-nine point seven percent."

"Whoa," Liam said.

"And there's no cure. Prions can't be killed because they're not alive. Heat doesn't destroy them. Radiation doesn't work. Disinfectants are useless." Elena looked up. "Once you're infected, you die. It's just a matter of time."

"Pestis Octava Facit — proteina misfoldita per contactum neuralem; transit sine febre, sine dolore, donec mens ipsa colliquat."

"Used one way, it could regenerate damaged neural tissue," Elena said. "Used another, it could erase a mind completely."

"Is it possible to aerosolize it? Or worse yet, release it from a plane?"

"According to this, yes. The fragment describes stabilization methods. Delivery mechanisms. It's designed for mass deployment." Elena set down her pen. "This isn't a natural disease. This is a weapon. Engineered specifically to spread and kill."

Elena closed her eyes. "She gave us Liam's life in exchange for the reassembled cipher."

"We haven't found the last fragment yet."

"We will. And when we do, we hand Guiomar the keys to genocide." Elena's hands wouldn't stay still. "How do we live with that?"

"We don't hand them over," Liam said.

"She has leverage and will come for them. She'll use whatever means necessary. She'll hurt the people we love."

"Then we destroy them first," Antoine said.

Elena nodded. "That's what we'll do. We find the remaining fragment. We make sure we understand what we're dealing with. And if they are weapons—or cures that can become weapons—we destroy them. All of them. Before Guiomar can take them from us."

"She won't let us walk away from the debt," Antoine warned.

"I know. But destroying them is how we pay for it. We promised her the cipher. We didn't promise her it would be intact." Elena turned from the window. "We fulfill the letter of our agreement. Then we deal with the consequences."

"The consequences might be lethal."

"Better that than millions, possibly billions dead."

✠✠✠

That evening, they ate dinner together in the guesthouse's small dining room. Senhora Rosa had prepared bacalhau—salt cod with potatoes and olives. The smell of roasted garlic and olive oil filled the air. Simple food. Comfort food. They ate, savoring each bite. Finally, a table that wasn't a workbench or a car hood, or the floor of an abandoned building.

"Tell me about Macau," Elena said to Antoine. "About Guiomar. How you know her."

Antoine decided how much to share.

"It was seven years ago," he said. "I was still with DGSE, French Special Forces. We'd been tracking an arms dealer—Russian, with connections to terrorist networks. The op was supposed to be surveillance only. Gather intel, pass it up the chain." He paused, sipped water.

"But Guiomar was tracking the same target—for different reasons. The arms dealer had something the Guild of Shadows wanted. We kept crossing paths. Watching each other watch him."

"Did you work together?" Liam asked.

"Not officially. But there was an understanding. We were both professionals. Good at what we did. There was mutual respect. There was an attraction between us. Fatal attraction. We were..." he changed the subject.

"One night, the arms dealer made his move. Tried to leave the city with whatever Guiomar wanted. She hit his convoy. I was watching. Could have called it in, let my team handle it. But..."

"But?"

"But she was outnumbered. Four of her people against twelve of his. I watched them fight for a few minutes, then I joined in."

"You helped her?" Elena asked.

"She needed me. Even if they weren't on my side. It was..."

"What happened?"

"We took down the arms dealer's people. Guiomar got what she came for. I didn't ask what it was. She didn't tell me. But afterward, we sat on a rooftop, drinking Chinese whiskey, one thing led to another... the next morning, we watched the sun come up over Macau. And we made a pact."

"The challenge coin," Elena said.

"Yes. We exchanged coins. If either of us ever needed the other, no questions asked, we'd honor it. A mayday protocol. Last resort." Antoine looked at his hands. "I never thought I'd use it. Never wanted to."

"But you did. For Liam."

"Absolutely." Antoine met Elena's eyes. "And now we owe her."

They sat in silence.

"Something happened to Guiomar over the years," he said. "She's not the same person. She's deranged. Wants to kill people to establish some sort of new world Order."

Outside, night fell over the hills. Stars emerged. The guesthouse settled into quiet.

"I'll start decoding the next fragment's location tomorrow," Elena said.

"One more day. Let Liam continue recovering. Let us all recover. We'll need our strength for what's coming next."

Elena nodded. "OK, one more day." They finished dinner. Said goodnight. Went to their separate rooms.

✠✠✠

The next morning, Elena woke early. She made coffee, brought her notebook and laptop to the table, and spread-out Fragment 8 again. This time, she was looking at the cipher for the next location.

Elena studied the patterns, marveling at the precision. These weren't the crude encryptions of medieval scribes—they were equations, layered like code.

The Templars hadn't been warriors alone; they were centuries ahead of their time. In hidden halls, they'd mastered what the Church condemned: calculus, physics, electromagnetics, scripture, languages, chemistry, biology, and medicine. Knowledge buried under vows of silence—power disguised as faith.

Antoine joined her an hour later and watched in silence.

Moments later...

"There it is. The location of the next fragment."

"Great. Where is the next one?" Antoine asked.

Elena showed him the decoded text:

The saint who guards the city, whose bones travel between shadow and light, carries a seal within his golden prison.

"Cryptic. And a little spooky," Antoine remarked.

Elena smiled as she pulled up historical references on her laptop. "That's Saint Vincent. Lisbon's patron saint. His remains are kept in the cathedral."

"And what about that phrase— *'bones travel between shadow and light'*? What's that supposed to mean?"

"The annual procession. They carry his reliquary from the cathedral through the city to the waterfront. From shadow to light—stone and incense giving way to open air and sea. It happens every year."

"When?"

Elena checked the calendar. Her face drained of color. "The Procession of Saint Vincent is tomorrow. That's not nearly enough time to—"

"And Fragment 9" Antoine interrupted.

"*Carries a seal within his golden prison.* The reliquary. It's not a fixed site—it moves. The next fragment isn't hidden at Saint Vincent's Cathedral. It's inside his reliquary. It travels with the saint's remains during the procession."

"You must be kidding. That's fucking impossible," Antoine said. "Let me get this straight—you're saying we need to steal from a saint's reliquary? During a public procession? In front of thousands of witnesses?"

"C'mon, Antoine. You love a challenge. And we're not stealing—we're just borrowing... sort of... indefinitely."

Elena pulled up an image of the reliquary: ornate gold and silver, roughly the size of a large chest. "But yes. That's exactly what I'm saying."

"That's insane."

"That's why the Templars hid it there. Who would dare desecrate a saint's reliquary during a holy procession?" Elena zoomed in on the reliquary base in the photograph. "But look here. See these decorative medallions on the base? I think they're not just decorative. I think they're a locking mechanism."

"Can you open it?"

"If I can decode the rest of the cipher. There's more here—a second layer. Not just the location, but instructions for accessing it." She returned to her notebook and studied the geometric progressions. "Give me a few hours. I'll figure it out."

Liam joined them at the table mid-morning, looking better rested. The haunted look lingered in his eyes, but he seemed steadier now. Stronger.

He scanned Elena's notes. "The next one is..." He hesitated, then looked up. "Saint Vincent's reliquary?"

"You heard?"

"Hard not to. These walls are paper-thin." He studied the images on the screen.

"The Procession of Saint Vincent. I photographed it two years ago for a travel magazine. Massive event. Thousands of people. Church officials, security, and police for crowd control."

"What's it like?" Elena asked.

"Formal. Religious. Six priests carry the reliquary in ceremonial robes. They process from the cathedral through the old city to the waterfront. Takes about an hour. Crowds line the entire route."

"Security?"

"Heavy. Not just church security—city police, crowd control barriers, news trucks, cameras everywhere. It's a major public event. And a holy one. Any disruption would be... problematic."

Antoine leaned forward. "We're going to need more than a distraction. We need chaos. Something that scatters everyone. Makes the priests set down the reliquary."

"What kind of chaos?" Liam asked.

"I'm working on that," Antoine said.

Elena heard them, but she focused entirely on the second layer of Fragment 8, on the geometric progressions that hadn't yet resolved. There was more here. Instructions. A key.

She worked through the afternoon, cross-referencing symbols, testing different substitution patterns and encryption methods, and following the mathematical progressions.

The others gave her space. Antoine disappeared for several hours—she didn't ask where. Liam organized equipment, checked escape routes on maps, and prepared for whatever came next.

As the sun set, Elena figured it out.

"It's a two-layer lock," she said, her voice tight with exhaustion and excitement. Antoine returned. They gathered around her.

"The medallions on the reliquary base—there are six of them. Each one rotates and has twelve symbols carved around it. But it's not just about finding the right symbols. You have to turn them in a specific order."

"What do you mean?" Liam asked.

"Look at these geometric patterns." She pointed to the fragment. "They encode two things. First: which symbols to align. Cross, Crown, Sword, Chalice, Star, Lamb. Second: in what order the medallions need to be turned.

Not 1, 2, 3, 4, 5, 6. But 4, 2, 6, 1, 5, 3."

"Why does order matter?"

"Even if someone knew the exact number of turns and the correct direction to align the medallions, they'd still fail if they turned them in the wrong sequence. The internal mechanism only releases when all three factors align—the right number of turns, the right direction, and the correct order."

She pulled up the photograph of the reliquary's base and zoomed in on the six medallions arranged in a circular pattern around it.

"I have to remember which medallion is one, two, three... what symbol each must align to, the sequence to turn them, and how many rotations each needs to reach the right mark."

"Almost like the lock on a safe?" Liam asked. "That's complex."

"That's the point. This one's the most protected. The Templars wanted to be sure only someone who fully decoded the cipher could access it."

Elena studied her notes again. "I need to practice—visualize it. Memorize every step."

"How long will it take you?" Antoine asked. "When you're actually doing it?"

"If I've practiced enough? Two minutes, give or take. Less if everything goes perfectly."

"And if you get one medallion wrong?"

"The mechanism doesn't release. We don't get the fragment. And we've just desecrated a saint's reliquary in front of thousands of witnesses for nothing."

The weight of that settled over them.

"Then you practice," Antoine said. "As much as you need. We have until tomorrow morning."

Elena sat at the table, eyes closed, hands moving through empty air, visualizing the base of the reliquary. Six medallions arranged in a circle.

- *Fourth medallion—bottom right position—rotate counter-clockwise seven clicks—chalice symbol.*
- *Second medallion—top center—rotate clockwise three clicks—crown symbol.*
- *Sixth medallion—bottom left—rotate counter-clockwise four clicks—lamb symbol.*
- *First medallion—top right—rotate clockwise two clicks—cross symbol.*
- *Fifth medallion—center right—rotate counter-clockwise six clicks—star symbol.*
- *Third medallion—center left—rotate clockwise five clicks—sword symbol.*

Repeatedly. Until her hands knew the movements without conscious thought and could feel the phantom resistance of the rotating medallions. She must burn the sequence into muscle memory.

Liam watched for a while, then left to give her space.

Antoine stayed, standing by the window, keeping watch as always. "You'll get it," he said after an hour. "I have faith."

"This is different," Elena said, not opening her eyes. "This isn't decoding in a library. This is doing it under pressure. In chaos. With Guardians trying to stop me."

"Then we make sure they can't reach you. That's my job."

"What if there are too many? What if—"

"Elena." Antoine's voice was firm. "You do your part. I'll do mine. Trust that."

She opened her eyes and looked at him. "I do trust you. I just... this is it. After this, we'll have them all. And then everything changes."

"Yes. It does."

"Are we doing the right thing? Destroying them?"

"Not sure, but it's the best choice we have. And sometimes that's all there is—the least terrible option."

Elena nodded, closing her eyes again. Returning to the practice.

Fourth medallion. Second. Sixth. First. Fifth. Third.

The sequence played in her mind like music. Tomorrow, she'd have one chance. In smoke and chaos and panic. With one hundred twenty seconds on the clock. And the fate of millions riding on whether her hands remembered the sequence. No pressure.

Elena stood at her window, looking out at the moonlit landscape. Stars scattered across the sky like fragments of light. A beautiful night, disguising what would come tomorrow.

She thought about her father. About what he'd said before his last deployment: *Sometimes the right choice is the hard choice.* He'd been talking about leaving his family to serve, about duty versus comfort.

But perhaps he'd been talking about something bigger. About choices where no good option existed. Where you had to choose the least terrible path and live with the consequences.

She thought about Fragment 9—the last piece. If the pattern held, it would be the worst of all. Higher mortality. More contagious. More devastating.

Behind her, the door creaked open. Antoine stepped into the room. "Couldn't sleep either?"

"Too much thinking."

He joined her at the window.

"You should reconsider," he said. "We could stop. Leave Fragment 9 hidden. Just walk away."

"And Guiomar?"

"We'll deal with her. Without giving her anything."

Elena shook her head. "She'll hunt us down. We can't run forever."

"So, we give her what she wants?"

"No, we get to choose how this story ends. We hold all the cards. She has nothing yet. We'll destroy them."

"She won't accept that. She'll see it as betrayal."

"So, Beit. But we don't hand her the tools to kill millions of people. Not for Liam. Not for anything, or anyone."

Antoine nodded. "Alright. We do this your way. Find the fragment. Understand the truth. Make the hard choice."

"Together?"

"Together."

Tomorrow, they'd go to Lisbon.

Steal from a saint.

And when the sun rose, destiny would find them waiting—ready or not.

17 - The Reliquary

Elena woke before dawn, her hands already moving through the sequence in half-sleep. Fourth medallion, second, sixth, first, fifth, third. The movements were automatic now, burned into muscle memory through hours of practice.

She dressed and found Antoine already awake in the common room.

"Ready?" he asked.

"As I'll ever be."

They woke Liam and gathered their equipment. Minimal gear—nothing that would draw attention. Elena carried her notebook and a small tool kit. Antoine, his concealed weapons. Liam brought his camera equipment—legitimate cover as a journalist.

Senhora Rosa made them breakfast, seemingly oblivious to the tension radiating from her guests. Or perhaps she'd seen enough in her years to know when not to ask questions.

They ate, thanked her, and left.

The drive to Lisbon took an hour. Morning traffic was light. The city woke, golden light spreading across terracotta roofs and white stone buildings. They parked in Alfama, the old Moorish quarter. Narrow streets. Steep hills. Easy to disappear if necessary.

"I have an errand," Antoine said. "I'll meet you at the cathedral in two hours."

"Where are you going?" Elena asked.

"Better you don't know. If something goes wrong, you can honestly say you weren't involved."

"Antoine—"

"Two hours. Trust me." He left before she could argue.

✠✠✠

Elena and Liam walked toward the Sé de Lisboa—Lisbon Cathedral. The procession would begin there at 10:00 A.M. They needed to scout the route, identify the best location for their intervention, and understand the timing.

"He's getting explosives," Liam said as they climbed the steep streets.

"I know."

"That's a line we haven't crossed yet. Creating an explosion in a crowded area. Even if no one gets hurt—"

"I know," Elena said again. "But we're out of clean options. A minor distraction won't work. People won't scatter. The priests won't set down the reliquary for anything less than genuine panic."

"And if someone gets hurt?"

Elena stopped walking and looked at him. "Then we live with that. The same way we'll live with destroying nine cures. Or live with Guiomar weaponizing them. There are no clean choices left, Liam. Only terrible ones."

They continued in silence.

The cathedral was already busy with preparations. Clergy in ceremonial robes moved through the interior. Workers set up crowd control barriers along the procession route. Police checked security positions.

Elena and Liam entered as tourists, camera ready, guidebooks in hand.

The reliquary sat in a side chapel, where Elena had seen it in photographs—gold and silver, ornately carved, about the size of a large steamer trunk. It rested on a wooden platform with six carrying poles extending from its base. Two priests stood nearby, preparing the ceremonial vestments for the carriers.

"That's it," Elena said.

She moved closer, pretending to photograph the chapel's vaulted ceiling while studying the reliquary's base. There are six circular medallions, each about five centimeters across, arranged evenly around the perimeter. To most eyes, they were just decoration, tiny icons of saints and angels. Elena knew better.

She couldn't get close enough to see the individual engravings without drawing attention, but she'd memorized their layout from photographs.

Still, something nagged at her. Every photo she studied showed the view from the procession aisle, which was the opposite side of where she stood now. If the design were symmetrical, it wouldn't matter.

But if the medallions were directional, her entire sequence could be reversed—a mirror image of what she'd practiced—wasting valuable time. She told herself it didn't matter. Geometry was geometry.

She visualized the medallions, the turns, the pressure, the sequence her hands knew by heart.

Ready.

✠✠✠

At 10:00 A.M., church bells rang across Lisbon. The procession emerged from the cathedral. First came the altar boys in white robes carrying incense and candles. Then the clergy in ceremonial vestments. Then the choir, singing hymns in Latin. Then, local officials. Church elders. Representatives from various religious orders.

Then the reliquary.

Six priests in gold-threaded robes carried it on their shoulders, moving with practiced synchronization. The reliquary gleamed in the morning sunlight—gold and silver, ornate carvings, centuries of devotion made manifest in metal and faith.

Inside, the bones of Saint Vincent, Lisbon's patron saint.

And hidden in the base:

Fragment 9.

The crowd pressed forward, people crossing themselves and reaching out as if proximity to the saint's remains could bring a blessing. The procession moved ceremonially down the cathedral steps. Into the street. Elena tracked its progress. Estimated speed. Calculated timing. At this pace, the reliquary would reach the target point in approximately eighteen minutes. She sent the timing to Antoine and Liam. Both confirmed receipt.

The procession continued.

Hymns echoed off stone buildings. Incense smoke drifted. Children threw flower petals. Elena's heart pounded. The fear had crystallized into focus.

Fifteen minutes.

The reliquary turned onto Rua Augusta. The crowd here was densest. People packed shoulder to shoulder behind barriers. Police monitored from strategic positions.

Elena spotted them—Guardians—four of them. Spread through the crowd. Not in uniform, but she recognized the way they moved—the way they watched. Valerius stood near the front, close to the barriers. He was scanning the crowd and looking for them. She turned, letting the crowd conceal her.

She sent a quick text to Antoine:

Guardians present. At least four. Valerius is here.

Noted. Proceeding.

Ten minutes.

The procession advanced. The priests carrying the reliquary showed no strain, but Elena could see the careful choreography of their steps. The way they adjusted for the street's slight incline. The weight they carried—not just physical, but spiritual. They were about to set that weight down in panic and chaos. Elena pushed the guilt away. Focused.

Five minutes.

The reliquary was now forty meters from the target point. Then thirty. Then twenty. Then ten,

Valerius shifted position. He'd seen something or sensed something. His eyes swept the crowd again. Elena froze. She was too far for him to identify clearly, but if he looked directly at her—He moved on. Scanning other faces. Other positions.

The reliquary reached the target point.

Elena's hand moved to her phone. She sent a single word to Antoine:

Now.

The explosion was perfect. Not large. Not devastating. But loud. Sharp. A crack that echoed off buildings and sent pigeons erupting from rooftops in panicked flight. Smoke billowed from the trash receptacle. Gray and thick.

Then a flashbang—brilliant white light, a second concussive boom that left ears ringing.

The crowd erupted. Screaming. Running. Parents grabbed their children and fled. Older people stumbled, pushed forward by the surge. Police shouted orders that no one could hear over the panic and the ringing.

The six priests carrying the reliquary froze for a split second—training battling instinct.

Then survival won.

They set down the reliquary—and scattered like everyone else. Toward doorways. Away from the smoke and noise. Seeking cover.

The reliquary sat alone in the middle of Rua Augusta.

Smoke swirled around it. People ran past it in both directions. No one was looking at it. Everyone was looking toward the explosion, toward the threat, toward escape routes.

Elena stepped through the smoke, moved to the reliquary's far side—the wall side, where the angle would hide her from most sight lines. Knelt beside it. Her hands found the base. Six medallions. The world around her was chaos, noise, and motion. But here, beside the reliquary, in the concealing smoke, there was only the sequence.

- *Fourth medallion—bottom right. Her fingers found it.*
- *Rotate counterclockwise. Seven clicks. Chalice.*
- *Second—top center. Clockwise. Three clicks. Crown.*
- *Sixth—bottom left. Counterclockwise. Four clicks. Lamb.*
- *First—top right. Clockwise. Two clicks. Cross.*
- *Fifth—center right. Counterclockwise. Six clicks. Star.*
- *Third—center left. Clockwise. Five clicks. Sword.*

Nothing moved.

No release. No hidden gears waking. Just the roar of the crowd and smoke thinning by the heartbeat. She froze. Had she miscounted a click? Or—

The mirror. They had taken the photos on the opposite side. From here—on the wall side—left and right were inverted. On mirrored medallions, the rotation directions would also reverse. She'd solved the puzzle from the wrong side.

"Move!" a voice shouted through the haze—Guardian cadence, close. A barrier clattered. Somewhere behind her, a woman screamed, and Liam's voice cut through the noise from the balcony, pitched for panic: "Gas! Gas leak—move back!"

Elena forced air into her lungs and remapped the circle in her head: swap left and right, invert the turns on the mirrored positions.

Reset. Calm.

Bottom left—now the true fourth on this face.

Clockwise seven to Chalice.

Top center—second stays second.

Counterclockwise three to Crown.

Bottom right—now sixth.

Clockwise four to Lamb.

Top left—now first.

Counterclockwise two to Cross.

Center left—now fifth.

Clockwise six to Star.

Center right—now third.

Counterclockwise five to Sword.

The panel hesitated—then gave a tired, ancient click. Internal pins withdrew. A hidden cam rotated.

It worked.

Elena pulled it open. The hidden compartment was small, no larger than her palm.

Inside, a sealed copper cylinder. Smaller than the others. Green with verdigris. As if even the Templars wanted to minimize the physical presence of what it contained.

Fragment 9.

Elena grabbed the cylinder, shoving it deep into her jacket pocket. Zipped the pocket. Now close the compartment. The panel clicked back into place. Rotate the third medallion one position out of alignment. Lock it. Done. Seventy-two seconds in total. She stood, turned away from the reliquary, and walked calmly toward the opposite curb.

The smoke was clearing. Police were establishing a perimeter around the explosion site. Shouting for everyone to stay back, stay calm.

The priests emerged from doorways, from behind barriers. Shaken but unhurt. They moved back toward the reliquary, checking it for damage. But Elena was already gone and had disappeared into the crowd on the opposite side of the street. Just another panicked festival goer. Nothing unusual. Nothing suspicious.

She walked—not running, that would draw attention—through a side street. Then another. Away from the procession route. Away from the chaos.

✠✠✠

Her phone dinged—inbound text message.

Liam: *Clear. Heading to the car.*

Antoine: *Clear in five.*

Elena kept walking. Forced herself to breathe normally. To not touch the pocket where Fragment 9 sat like a burning coal. She'd done it, stolen from a saint. In front of thousands of witnesses. And no one had seen.

Behind her, on Rua Augusta, the priests examined the reliquary.

"Any damage?" the lead priest asked.

They checked the gold and silver surfaces. The carved details. The carrying poles.

"No. It seems intact."

"Thank God. Let's get it back to the cathedral. Now. Before anything else happens."

They lifted the reliquary and began carrying it back the way they'd come. The procession was over. Safety was more important than tradition.

One of the younger priests ran his hand along the base of the reliquary. "Should we check inside? Make sure the saint's remains are undisturbed?"

The lead priest shook his head. "The seals haven't been broken. Everything is intact. We'll have it examined back at the cathedral."

They carried Saint Vincent back to safety. Never knowing that the decorative medallions on the base had been turned. Never knowing that a seven-hundred-year-old secret compartment had been opened and that Fragment 9—the most dangerous piece of a deadly cipher—had just been stolen in front of their eyes.

✠✠✠

Elena approached the car. Liam placed his camera equipment into the trunk. Antoine arrived five minutes after that, moving casually, just another local going about his day. They got into the car and drove off, saying nothing until they were out of central Lisbon, heading back toward Sintra. Elena pulled the copper cylinder from her pocket.

Fragment 9 inside.

"We have them all," she said. "I almost blew it. I worked the sequence from the wrong side—the photos I studied were mirror images. I had to invert the turns on the fly."

Antoine glanced at it in the rearview mirror. "Any heat?"

"Don't think so. No one saw me. The priests took the reliquary back to the cathedral. They think it's undamaged."

"And the explosion?"

"Police are investigating. Probably think it's terrorism or a protest. But there were no casualties. No injuries. Just smoke and noise."

"Durand?" Liam asked.

"He'll hear about it. An explosion during a religious procession. He's smart. His instincts will tell him we're involved."

"But no proof," Antoine said.

"No proof. Just suspicion." Elena looked at the cylinder again. "Wow, I can't believe we got it."

They drove in silence. Fragment 9 sat in Elena's hand. The last piece of the cipher. Now they just had to decode it. And discover what the Plague of Babel really was all about.

In his office at Polícia Judiciária headquarters, Detective Durand watched the news footage for the third time. The explosion at the Procession of Saint Vincent. Smoke. Panic. Crowds scattering. No injuries. No structural damage. Just chaos.

The explosive device had been small, professional. Designed to frighten, not to kill.

"Terrorism?" his lieutenant asked.

Durand shook his head. "I don't think so. Terrorists want casualties. Want to make a statement. This was surgical. Precise. Created maximum chaos with minimum harm."

"Then what?"

Durand pulled up the file on Dr. Elena Voss. Her pattern. The historical sites and break-ins. The systematic search for something.

"A distraction," he said. "Someone needed the crowd to scatter. Needed everyone's attention somewhere else."

"For what?"

"That's the question." Durand looked at the footage again. The reliquary sat alone in the street. Smoke swirling around it. "Was anyone seen near the saint's reliquary during the chaos?"

"We're reviewing footage. But the smoke makes it difficult. And everyone was running. Hard to identify individuals."

Durand leaned back in his chair. His instincts—honed over twenty years of police work—were screaming at him. Dr. Voss. The historical sites. The pattern. And now, an explosion at a religious procession.

She was still hunting, still searching. And whatever she was looking for, she'd just found another piece of it.

"Keep reviewing the footage," he said. "Focus on the reliquary. Anyone who moved toward it instead of away. Anyone who didn't run."

"You think Voss was involved?"

"Wherever these incidents happen, she's nearby. Finding whatever she's looking for." Durand closed the file.

"Should we issue another alert?"

"No. She's cleared of murder. And we have no evidence she was involved in this. Just..." He paused. "Keep watching. She'll surface again. And when she does, I want to know why. What is she hunting? What's worth all this risk?"

His lieutenant left. Durand sat alone, staring at the frozen image on his screen—the reliquary in the smoke. Something had happened there. He could feel it.

But what—and why?

18 - Babel

They drove back to Sintra in silence. The copper cylinder sat in Elena's lap, warm from her body heat.

Fragment 9. The last piece.

Antoine kept checking the mirrors—looking for pursuit, for Guardians, for police. But the roads were empty. They'd disappeared cleanly.

Liam stared out the window, processing what they'd just done. Stolen from a saint. Terrorized thousands of people. All for a fragment of ancient vellum sealed in corroded copper.

"We crossed a line today," Liam said.

"We've been crossing lines since Oxford," Elena replied.

"This was different. Those were historians. Tourists. Regular people. We scared them. Made them think they were under attack."

"I know." Elena's voice was tight. "But we're out of clean options. We have been for a while."

They pulled into Quinta da Rosa just after 1:00 P.M. Senhora Rosa greeted them with her usual warm smile and asked if they'd enjoyed the festival.

"Beautiful," Elena lied. "Very moving."

They climbed the stairs to their suite. Locked the door.

"This is it," she said. "After this, we'll know everything. All nine plagues. The complete cipher."

She picked up the cylinder. It was smaller than the others, the copper darker with age. The seal was intact—black pitch, cracked but unbroken for seven centuries. Elena opened it. The pitch crumbled. She unscrewed the cap—threads worn but functional.

Inside: vellum. Rolled tight. Darker than the other fragments, as if the copper's oxidation had stained it over the centuries. She unrolled it on the table.

The text was dense. Exponentially more complex than Fragment 8. As if the Templars had saved their most sophisticated encryption for the most dangerous knowledge.

"How long?" Liam asked.

"Several hours. This is more complex than anything I've ever seen. They didn't want anyone to decode this easily."

"Then we let you work."

Elena pulled out her notebook, reference materials, and laptop. The other eight fragments lay beside her for comparison. And then she began.

The afternoon unfolded in focused silence.

She worked methodically, layer by layer—identifying cipher keys, cross-referencing geometric patterns, testing substitutions.

On the laptop, decryption software parsed each sequence in real time: green to red. Failure. Then another line. Again. And again. Nothing.

Liam brought her coffee at three. She barely looked up. The sunlight crawled across the room—gold to amber, amber to red. Dust drifted through the beams like ash. At six, Antoine brought dinner. She ate without tasting it, eyes fixed on the vellum.

By eight, the cipher began to yield. Latin words surfaced through the haze of code—clinical, cold. Transmission vectors. Mortality statistics. Controlled infection.

At ten, the pattern completed itself.

Elena stopped typing. The monitor's glow lit her face, pale and motionless.

"Elena?" Liam's voice was soft, unsure.

She didn't answer. Not at first. Her pen slipped from her fingers and rolled across the table, the sound impossibly loud in the stillness. When she finally spoke, her voice was barely above a whisper.

"It's worse than I thought," she said. "Worse than all of them combined."

They looked over her shoulder. Elena's notebook showed the decoded text. Her handwriting was tight and controlled, but her hands had been shaking as she wrote.

"Fragment 9," she said, her voice hollow.

Pestis Nona: Resonantia Babel.

"The Plague of Babel."

"What does it do?" Antoine asked.

Elena read from her translation: *"It's a DNA resonance pathogen. Activated by electromagnetic frequencies. When triggered, it..."* She paused, reading her own notes as if seeing them for the first time.

"It rewrites the human genome into noise. The body's instructions become a language it can no longer understand—cells wait for meaning that never comes. Within hours, the heart forgets its beat. The blood fails to clot. The body collapses into silence.

The Plague of Babel doesn't just kill. It unteaches life."

The room was silent.

Liam sat down heavily. "WHO THE FUCK..."

Elena glanced at Liam, then back at the fragment.

"Mortality rate?" Antoine asked.

"Ninety-nine point nine percent." Elena looked at the fragment. "One in a thousand *might* survive. But even survival would mean... what? A body that doesn't remember how to function?"

Liam leaned forward now, regaining his composure. "There's no *facit*, like the others had? No cure listed. Anything?"

"No," Elena said. "Nothing about a cure."

"And it's EM-activated?" Liam asked.

"Electromagnetic frequencies trigger it. Radio waves. Cell towers. Wi-Fi. Anything broadcasting on the right frequency." Elena traced the technical specifications in her notes. "Once deployed, it stays dormant in the population. Days. Weeks. Then the activation signal is broadcast. And everyone exposed..."

She didn't finish. She didn't need to.

Aerosolized," Elena said. "But it wouldn't need aircraft like Plague 8. No fleets or missiles. It could ride the same systems already in place—geoengineering planes, atmospheric research programs. The world's trying to cool itself with aerosols in the upper atmosphere. Replace those compounds with this, and you'd seed the planet in days."

"You mean climate control planes," Antoine said. "Stratospheric injection."

She nodded. "Exactly. Babel isn't about disease. It's about hubris. We built the perfect delivery system ourselves.

"And you think that Guiomar has the resources to do this kind of Stratospheric injection into the atmosphere?"

"Yes. I believe that she does. The Babel plague alone could end human civilization. The other plagues are just... variations. Different methods with varying mortality rates. But Babel is extinction-level."

They sat in silence.

Outside, night had fallen. Stars emerged over the hills. The guesthouse settled into quiet.

Elena looked at Fragment 9 again. "I don't care if they could save lives. I don't care if they're the greatest medical discovery in history. If Guiomar gets them, she'll turn them into weapons, and I won't be responsible for that."

"She'll come for us," Antoine warned. "We owe her the complete cipher—"

"Then she comes for us." Elena's voice was sure. Hard.

Elena sat at the table long after Antoine and Liam had gone to their rooms, staring at the nine fragments spread before her. Nine pieces. A complete cipher describing diseases that could end civilization. But why? Why would the Templars hide these? Why preserve them?

She picked up Fragment 1 again and read the Latin text.

Pestis Prima: Hemorrhagia Fulminans — fatis...

"Plague 1: Hemorrhagic fever."

Fatis could mean to cause... or to cure, depending on context. Her mouth went dry. She'd always translated it as *causes hemorrhagic fever*. But it could just as easily mean *cures hemorrhagic fever*.

She stood and paced to the window, mind racing. Valerius had told her—they weren't weapons. She'd dismissed him. She had been wrong.

The fragments weren't describing plagues at all. They were describing cures—medical knowledge preserved by the Templars, hidden from a Church that feared its power. Knowledge that could heal the world or destroy it.

Elena looked down at the fragments again. All nine pieces. She felt the weight of a terrible choice.

I'm sorry, she thought—sorry to the Templars who hid this, sorry to her father, to Almeida, to everyone these cures could have saved.

But she knew what she had to do.

✠✠✠

The night faded to morning. Elena had slept for only a few hours. Her dreams were fragmented with disturbing faces dissolving into static languages she couldn't place. The Tower of Babel collapsed as she watched.

She sat at the table and looked at the fragments again. Antoine found her there at seven that morning.

"You figured something out," he said. It wasn't a question.

"They are cures, as we suspected. I worked all night." Elena said. "All of them. The fragments don't describe plagues. They describe antibodies, treatments—medieval medicine that could save millions of lives."

For almost a millennium, the pieces had been separated and protected. Now, for the first time since Brother Martin of Troyes cut them apart in 1307, they would be reunited.

She cleared the table and laid out a large sheet of archival mounting board—plain, white, clean—a blank canvas for history.

"How do they fit together?" Liam asked.

"Like a puzzle. Look at the edges." Elena positioned Fragment 1 in the center. "See these irregular cuts? They're not random. Each piece connects to specific others."

She worked carefully. Fragment 2 aligned against the right edge of Fragment 1. Fragment 3 aligned next to it. Fragment 4 beneath. Piece by piece, the pattern emerged—a circular design, nine fragments forming a single whole.

When Fragment 9—the Plague of Babel—slotted into place, the original parchment revealed itself. Not perfect: gaps where material had been removed, edges darkened with age. But recognizable. One document. One cipher. Split apart and now reunited.

"That's what Brother Martin held," Elena said. "Before he cut it. Before he hid the pieces."

Nine cures. Or nine weapons.

The difference depended on who held them.

Elena secured each fragment with archival corners—small triangular holders that kept the vellum in place without adhesive. Then she rolled the mounting board into a scroll and tied it with simple twine. The complete cipher. Portable. Ready.

"What now?" Liam asked.

On Elena's phone—an inbound text message.

"Doctor Voss," Guiomar said, her voice measured. *"It's time to pay your debt."*

"I know."

"Bring me the complete cipher. All nine fragments. Assembled as they are meant to be."

"Where?"

"Cais do Sodré. Dock seven. Eleven tonight." Guiomar paused. *"And please don't be late. Tardiness is unacceptable."*

"And if I refuse?"

"Then I make good on my other promises. And people you care about suffer. Your choice. But time is not on your side."

The line went dead.

Elena looked at Antoine and Liam. "We have until eleven."

Antoine checked his watch. "Five hours. We should prepare. If Guiomar brings her Guild operatives—"

"She will," Elena said. "But she won't attack until she sees the cipher. After that..." She met Antoine's eyes. "After that, we run."

✠✠✠

At ten forty-five, they drove to Cais do Sodré. The waterfront was quieter at night. Bars still glowed, music drifted from open doors, but the crowds had thinned. The docks smelled of salt and diesel—industrial, utilitarian, built for work, not spectacle.

Dock 7 sat at the far end—isolated, poorly lit. Perfect for a clandestine exchange. Antoine parked three blocks away. They walked the rest.

Elena carried the scroll. Antoine had his knife, baton, and pistol hidden beneath his jacket. Liam brought his camera—habit more than plan.

They reached the dock at 10:58 P.M. Guiomar was already there. She stood near the edge of the pier; five Guild operatives spaced around her. Professional formation. Clear sight lines. Hands resting near weapons.

Not an ambush—a message: *I'm in control.*

Elena, Antoine, and Liam approached. Water slapped against the pilings. Ships groaned in the current, mooring lines pulling taut, then easing again—in a slow, unspoken rhythm. Lisbon's lights shimmered across the black tide. They stopped ten meters from Guiomar.

"Doctor Voss," Guiomar said. "You kept your appointment. I'm impressed."

"I keep my promises."

"Do you? Then you have the complete cipher."

Elena held up the scroll. "Right here. All nine fragments. Assembled. Complete."

"Show me."

Elena unrolled the mounting board. The nine vellum pieces gleamed under the dock lights—a mosaic of history, whole for the first time in seven centuries.

Guiomar studied them, eyes moving with clinical precision. "Beautiful," she said. "Brother Martin would be proud. You've completed his work."

"His work was hiding them," Elena said. "Not revealing them."

"Semantics." Guiomar stepped forward. "Now hand them over. Your debt is paid in full. You go free."

"No."

Elena drew a lighter from her pocket.

Guiomar's gaze narrowed. "What are you doing?"

"Fulfilling our agreement. You wanted the complete cipher. Here it is." She thumbed the lighter. A flame bloomed. "You can have what's left after I burn it."

"You wouldn't."

"Watch me."

Elena struck the lighter. The tiny flame flickered in the night air—fragile, trembling, alive.

She touched it to Fragment 1. The vellum caught instantly, curling black, the ink bleeding into flame. Fire raced like veins of lightning across the surface.

Fragment 2. Fragment 3.

Each piece fed the growing inferno, centuries of guarded knowledge collapsing into heat and smoke. The flames hissed as they consumed the ink—words and symbols that had outlived empires. The air filled with the scent of burning parchment and old oil, a library dying one page at a time.

Flames danced around her fingers. She didn't flinch. Not once. Elena fed the fire, feeding them everything the Templars had preserved. Cures mistaken for weapons, secrets too dangerous to endure.

The fire reflected in her eyes, gold and merciless. Her hands shook, but she didn't stop.

"They can't be used for evil," she said. "Not now. Not ever."

Flames coiled higher, wrapping her in their feverish glow; the smoke clung to her hair and clothes. It stung her throat, but the pain anchored her—proof that she was still choosing, still fighting. She was ending what centuries of zealots, Templars, Guardians, and soldiers had protected.

Fragment 4. Fragment 5. Fragment 6.

Smoke rose into the night.

Fragment 7. Fragment 8.

Then Fragment 9—the Plague of Babel. The copper-stained vellum caught instantly, curled, vanished.

Elena dropped the burning fragments to the dock and stepped back. The last light guttered out. Ash drifted on the wind. It was done. Mission accomplished. A wave of relief flooded her—all that stress, now in the past.

She looked up, expecting fury. Instead, Guiomar smiled.

"How dramatic," she said. "Very noble. Very heroic."

She reached into her jacket and drew a small rectangle of plastic—a memory card.

Elena's stomach turned.

"Did you really think I needed the originals?"

Liam grabbed his camera from the bag, checked the slot, went pale. "You have to be kidding me...how the—"

"What?" Elena asked, though she already felt the dread.

"This isn't my memory card," he said. "Mine was 128 gigabytes. This one's 32 gigs. Empty."

"When?"

He met her eyes. Thinking. "The guesthouse this morning during breakfast. Senhora Rosa."

Elena flinched. "No. She—she helped us—"

"Helped herself," Guiomar said, holding up the memory card. "Enough money to renovate her entire property. To retire. A good investment for thirty seconds of work." She smiled. "Don't judge her too harshly. She's practical. And I make very persuasive offers."

Elena thought of the coffee, the bread, the warmth. All of it a lie—the early morning phone call—she'd forgotten to have Liam check the memory card.

"Your photographer was meticulous," Guiomar said. "High-resolution images, multiple angles, every cipher captured in exquisite detail." She slipped the card into a memory card holder, then into her pocket. "Everything I need to synthesize the cures—and weaponize them."

"You're off your rocker," Liam said.

"I'm a visionary." Guiomar gestured toward the ashes. "Your sacrifice was touching. But I have perfect digital copies of all the fragments. I don't need the physical parchment. Everything is right here in my hands. Thanks to your photographer. Such a team player!

"And now my own cryptographers will work tirelessly to decode them. It won't take them long, although they don't have your skill set, Doctor Voss. You could make it easier on us all and just tell me what they say. Hand over your notes."

A pause.

"Okay, I suppose not. It doesn't matter. We will decode them, and we have all the time in the world to do so. You can't stop us. No one can."

Elena couldn't move. Couldn't speak.

Guiomar turned and walked away, her operatives closing around her. No fight. No need. She had already won.

Elena, Antoine, and Liam stood amid the ashes— black and gray ghosts of what had been.

"I'm sorry," Liam said. "I thought we'd need records. For research. I didn't—"

"It's not your fault," Elena said. "She'd have found another way."

Antoine's jaw tightened. "Then we find a way back. We have to."

"What's left to fight with?" Elena asked. "We have nothing."

"Then we learn how to win with nothing," he said. "Because giving up—is not an option. We have come too far to get defeated now. Not like this."

Elena looked at the ashes, then toward the dark city where Guiomar carried away the stolen cures. Nine fragments. Nine cures. Nine engineered plagues.

They drove to the guesthouse in silence. Senhora Rosa was in the kitchen, cleaning up. She smiled when she saw them—until she saw their faces. Elena walked past without a word. Liam followed.

Antoine paused in the doorway.

"How much?" he demanded.

Rosa froze. "I don't—"

"How much did she pay you?"

A long silence. Then: "Enough. Enough to save this place. To retire. To send my grandchildren to private school." Her voice trembled. "I'm sorry. It was only a small favor. She said it wouldn't hurt anyone."

"That small favor might end the entire world," Antoine said.

"I didn't know—"

"It doesn't matter." He turned for the stairs. "We're leaving in the morning. Don't expect payment for tonight."

Rosa stood alone in the kitchen, surrounded by dishes and guilt. Upstairs, Elena sat at the window, watching the hills fade into darkness.

At 2:00 A.M., a knock came at her door.

Antoine.

"I spoke with Liam earlier. He's tearing himself apart. Blames himself for documenting everything."

"It's not his fault."

"Tell him that."

"I have. But he doesn't listen."

They sat in silence. The kind that fills a room like smoke.

"We failed," Elena said at last. "We did everything we could, and we still failed. Guiomar has the complete cipher. She'll kill innocent people."

"Maybe."

"Not maybe. Definitely. You know her. She's not bluffing."

"We can still stop her."

"How? We have nothing—no fragments, no leverage, no plan. Just..." She gestured helplessly. "Just guilt and ashes."

"We have one thing Guiomar doesn't."

"What?"

"We know we can't win by playing her game. She's always ten steps ahead, always has contingencies, always controls the board." He looked at Elena. "We change the game. Stop trying to take her pieces away. Flip the board."

"I don't understand."

"Neither do I. Not yet."

He stood, one hand braced on the doorframe, his silhouette caught in the half-light.

"But we've got some time. Guiomar still has to synthesize the cures—turn them into something usable. She'll need to weaponize them, build a delivery system. Aerosolize the compounds, stabilize them outside the lab. That's not her specialty."

Elena looked up. "So, she'll need help."

"A rogue biochemist, someone with the experience and the lab space to do what she can't. That kind of partnership always leaves a trail—money, logistics, movement of materials.

And if there's a trail, we can find it." Antoine said.

"She's won the battle, not the war. We can still stop her."

Elena nodded, exhausted but resolute. "Then we find her scientist. Follow the trail back to her. Tell the cops. She needs to go to jail for a very long time."

Antoine's expression softened. "Get some sleep, Elena. Tomorrow, we plan."

When he was gone, Elena stayed by the window for a while longer—thinking about guilt. About impossible choices. About the moment a single act of mercy—or pride—could doom the world. Wondering if there was any way—any way at all—to stop what was coming.

The Black Chalice. The end of everything.
Born from nine cures she had helped assemble.
Enabled by photographs she never knew existed.
Paid for by an older woman's dream of a better life.

Now unstoppable—Or was it?

19 - The Hidden Message

Elena sat in her room as dawn broke over the hills. She hadn't slept. Couldn't sleep. The ashes on the dock haunted her. Seven hundred years of knowledge. Burned. And for nothing. Guiomar had won. She now had the complete cipher and would weaponize it, releasing the plagues.

Elena's laptop sat on the table, still open to Liam's cloud backup folder. The photographs he'd taken. Every fragment. Every location. Every detail. The same photographs Guiomar now had on the stolen memory card.

Elena had been staring at them for hours. Looking for... what? Some weakness? Some flaw in Guiomar's plan? There was nothing. The cipher was complete. The fragments were documented perfectly. Game over.

But something nagged at her. A detail she couldn't quite identify. A pattern just beyond recognition. She opened the images again. All nine fragments. Arranged them digitally on the screen, recreating the pattern she'd used on the mounting board when she'd assembled them physically.

Fragment 1 in the center. Then 2, 3, 4, 5, 6, 7, 8, 9 around it in the circular arrangement. The complete cipher—exactly as Brother Martin of Troyes had held it before cutting it apart. Elena zoomed out, viewing it whole. A pattern emerged. She leaned closer to the screen.

The edges. The places where Brother Martin had made his cuts. They had... markings. Tiny symbols. Decorative elements written into the borders of each fragment. She'd noticed them before and assumed they were just ornamental. Medieval flourishes. Meaningless decoration. But now, looking at all nine fragments arranged together...

The edge symbols were all connected. The symbols formed... letters. Latin letters.

Elena examined the edges and traced the connecting symbols. They weren't decorative. They were text. Hidden text. Written into the borders of each fragment. Meaningless when separated, but when all nine pieces were assembled correctly, the edges formed words. A message.

Elena grabbed her notebook and started transcribing. The letters were small, archaic, and difficult to read. But they were there.

Sigillum nonum frangit linguam, sed clavis silentii vivit ubi Petrus servat volumina. Quaere Codicem Babel in domo falsae salutis.

Her hand shook as she wrote the last word. She read it again. Translated carefully.

"The ninth seal breaks the tongue, but the key to silence lives where Peter keeps the scrolls. Seek the Babel Codex in the house of false salvation."

Elena sat back, her mind racing. The ninth seal. Plague 9. The Plague of Babel. But the key to silence—how to stop it or activate it—wasn't in the fragment itself. It was somewhere else.

Where Peter keeps the scrolls.

The Vatican. St. Peter's keys. Its Secret Archives. The Babel Codex. "Holy shit," Elena whispered.

Antoine knocked at her door.

"Hey, what's going on?" She opened the door. He took one look at her face. "What happened?"

"There's something else." Elena pulled him by the arm over to the laptop. "Look at this. The edges of the fragments. When all nine are assembled, they reveal a hidden message." She showed him the screen. The connected edge symbols formed Latin text. Antoine leaned close, studying it. "How did we miss this?"

"Because we never had all nine fragments assembled physically long enough to examine them properly. We were always running. Always moving. I only had them together for maybe an hour before the meeting with Guiomar. I was focused on the main cipher text, not the borders."

"What does it say?"

Elena showed him her translation. "'The ninth seal breaks the tongue, but the key to silence lives where Peter keeps the scrolls. Seek the Babel Codex in the house of false salvation.'"

"The Babel Codex," Antoine repeated.

"Fragment 9 describes the Plague of Babel. But it's incomplete. The fragment shows what it is—a DNA resonance pathogen, EM-activated, but not the complete specifications. Not the exact frequencies or the synthesis protocols." Elena pulled up her notes on Fragment 9. "I thought the fragment was comprehensive. But look at this section. The electromagnetic activation. It gives frequency ranges, but not precise values. Variables, but not constants."

"Why would the Templars leave it incomplete?"

"They split the cipher into nine pieces to protect it. But even if someone found all nine pieces, they still couldn't fully weaponize Plague 9 without the master document. The Babel Codex." Elena looked at him. "It's a fail-safe. Multiple layers of security."

"And it's at the Vatican?"

"'Where Peter keeps the scrolls'—that's the Vatican Secret Archives. The library. Restricted section. 'House of false salvation'—that's how the Templars viewed the Church after their persecution."

"Are you sure?"

"I'm sure." Elena stood and paced. "The Templars hid the cipher in nine pieces across Portugal. But they hid the master key—the Babel Codex—in the one place their enemies controlled. The Vatican. Because that's the last place anyone would look."

"And Guiomar?"

"She has the nine fragments digitally, on the memory card, but she doesn't have this." Elena gestured to the hidden message. "She doesn't know the edges contain text. Doesn't know about the Babel Codex. Not yet."

"Yet?" Antoine asked.

"But she will soon enough. She's too intelligent not to figure it out. When she examines the fragments closely and studies the edges, she'll see the hidden message. And then..."

"Then she goes after the Codex."

"Yes."

They were silent for a moment.

"We have a window," Antoine said. "Before she figures it out. How long?"

"Days. Maybe a week if we're lucky. Guiomar needs to synthesize the plagues first—her priority—and then start the weaponization process. She'll be focused on that. But eventually, she'll notice the activation frequencies in Fragment 9 are incomplete. She'll look for answers. And she'll find the hidden message."

"Then we need to move fast." Antoine checked his watch. "Can we get to the Vatican before her?"

"Maybe. We'd need access to the Secret Archives. That's not open to the public. It's restricted. Requires papal authorization, academic credentials, specific research proposals..."

"Or we break in."

Elena looked at him. "Break into the Vatican? The most secure location in Europe? You must be insane!"

"You have a better idea?"

She didn't. There was a soft knock. Liam, looking exhausted but awake.

"I heard you guys talking. What's up?"

Elena showed him the hidden message. Explained about the Babel Codex. Liam studied the screen. "Guiomar has nine fragments. But there's a tenth fragment—the master key—at the Vatican."

"Not a fragment. A codex. A separate document." Elena corrected. "Brother Martin cut one parchment into nine pieces, as we know from history. But the complete medical knowledge—the source material the fragments were based on—was kept separately. At the Vatican. The Church had it when they persecuted the Templars. They probably didn't even know what they had and just locked it away with thousands of other confiscated texts."

"And it's been sitting there all this time?"

"Yes."

"Can we access it legally?" Liam asked. "I mean, if we make a formal request—"

"That takes months," Elena said. "Applications. Reviews. Approvals. We'd need institutional backing, detailed research proposals, and letters of recommendation. By the time we got access, Guiomar would have already figured out about the Codex and taken it."

"We steal it," Liam said simply.

"From the Vatican," Elena emphasized. "One of the most protected locations on Earth. Security. Cameras. Guards. The Swiss Guard, for God's sake."

"We've stolen from everywhere else," Liam pointed out. "Monasteries. Cathedrals. A saint's reliquary during a public procession. Why not the Vatican?"

"Because those were in Portugal. Small security. Local police. The Vatican is different. It's a sovereign nation. An international incident if we're caught. And we'd be caught—there's no way we could—"

"We have to try," Antoine interrupted. "Because if we don't, Guiomar gets the Babel Codex and combines it with the nine fragments. She then has everything she needs to deploy the Plague of Babel. Ninety-nine point nine percent mortality. Potentially billions, dead."

Elena closed her eyes. He was right. They had no choice.

"Then we plan a Vatican heist," she said. "Figure out how to access the Secret Archives. Find the Babel Codex. Get it before Guiomar does."

"And then?" Liam asked.

"Then we destroy it. Make sure no one can ever weaponize Plague 9." She looked at the hidden message on the screen again.

Quaere Codicem Babel in domo falsae salutis.

"Seek the Babel Codex in the house of false salvation."

Brother Martin of Troyes had written this message into the edges of nine fragments. Hidden it so only someone who found all nine pieces—someone dedicated, smart, and worthy enough—would discover it. He'd left them a trail. A final test. And a warning: *The cipher is incomplete without the Codex.*

Elena had failed to protect the fragments and failed to stop Guiomar from copying them. But maybe she could still win if they reached the Vatican first and found the Babel Codex before Guiomar. It was a desperate plan. Nearly impossible. But it was worth a shot.

✠✠✠

They spent the morning researching. Elena pulled up everything she could find about the Vatican Secret Archives. The layout, security, access procedures, and cataloging system. Liam researched the physical structure. Floor plans. Entry points. Guard rotations. Antoine studied tactical approaches. How to infiltrate and get back out again. By noon, they had a rough picture.

The Vatican Secret Archives—officially called the *Archivum Secretum Apostolicum Vaticanum*—contained over 85 kilometers of shelving. Fifty-three miles of documents. Papal bulls. Letters. Records going back twelve centuries.

Access was severely restricted. Only accredited researchers with certain credentials were allowed. Applications took months. Even then, you could only request specific documents by catalog number. You couldn't browse or explore freely. And the Babel Codex?

If it existed in the Archives, it would be in the restricted section. The documents confiscated from the Templars during the 14th century. Cataloged under heretical texts. Sealed. Forbidden.

"How do we even find it?" Liam asked. "We can't just walk in and start searching fifty-three miles of shelves."

"The catalog," Elena said. "Everything is indexed. If we can access the Vatican's digital catalog system, we can search for Templar-related documents from the early 1300s. Narrow it down."

"Can we access the catalog remotely?"

"No. It's internal only. Protected network. We'd need to be physically inside the Vatican to access it."

"Then we go inside," Antoine said. "During business hours. Maybe as tourists again—it worked last time. Then find a way to access a terminal."

"And after we find the catalog listing?" Liam asked. "We still need to physically retrieve the document from the Archives. Which are locked. Guarded. Under surveillance."

"One problem at a time," Antoine said.

✠✠✠

They drove back to Lisbon that afternoon and checked into a small hotel near the airport. Not Quinta da Rosa. They'd never go back there. Never trust another "safe" location again.

Elena couldn't stop thinking about Senhora Rosa. The betrayal. How Guiomar had bought her for the price of a renovation. She wondered how many others Guiomar had compromised with the promise of money? How deep did her network go? Trust no one. That was the lesson.

They ate dinner in their rooms. Pizza delivery. Anonymous. Safe. Elena spread the images of the fragments across her laptop screen again. Studied the hidden message one more time.

The ninth seal breaks the tongue, but the key to silence lives where Peter keeps the scrolls.

The Plague of Babel. The cure that could become an extinction weapon. It was somewhere in the Vatican, buried in the Archives, the master key to making it work. Or stopping it. "Which is it?" Elena murmured to herself.

"Does the Codex show how to weaponize Babel? Or how to neutralize it?" Maybe both.

Maybe the Templars had preserved the complete knowledge—creation and destruction, cure and weapon—hoping future generations would be wise enough to choose correctly. Elena hadn't been wise enough. She'd burned the fragments. But Guiomar had copies anyway. Maybe this was her second chance.

Get the Babel Codex. Study it. Understand what Plague 9 really was. And then decide—destroy it or find a way to neutralize Guiomar's weaponized version.

There was a knock at her door. Antoine and Liam, looking grim. "We need to talk," Antoine said. They came in and closed the door.

"We can't do this alone," Antoine said. "The Vatican is too big. Too secure. We need help."

"From whom?" Elena asked. "We can't trust anyone. Guiomar has people everywhere. Money buys loyalty. We've learned that."

"Not everyone can be bought," Liam said quietly.

Elena looked at him. "Who are you thinking of?"

"Durand." The name hung in the air.

Detective Inspector Durand. The Portuguese police detective who'd been tracking them all this time. He cleared them of murder but still wanted them for questioning.

"He'll arrest us," Elena said.

"Maybe," Antoine said. "Or maybe he'll listen. He's a good cop. Smart. He knows we're not criminals. Knows something else is going on."

"And if we tell him about the fragments? About Guiomar? About the Vatican?"

"Then maybe he helps. Or maybe he doesn't. But we need an ally," Antoine said. "I can infiltrate buildings and handle security, but the Vatican. That's beyond my skill set and way above my pay grade. We need someone with resources. Connections. Authority."

Elena thought about Durand. About his press conference, in which he said she was no longer a suspect in Almeida's murder but still wanted for questioning regarding the break-ins at historical sites. Could they trust him? Could they afford not to?

"If we contact him," Elena said slowly, "we're putting ourselves in his hands. He could arrest us. Turn us over to Interpol. We'd lose everything."

"Or he could be the ally we need," Liam said.

Elena looked at the laptop. At the hidden messages and fragments that had consumed her life for months. Brother Martin had trusted that someone would find his hidden message and understand what needed to be done. Maybe it was time for Elena to trust too. "Alright," she said. "We contact Durand. Tell him everything and see if he'll help."

"What if he arrests us?" Liam asked.

"Then at least we tried." Elena closed the laptop. "And maybe from a jail cell, we can still warn someone about what Guiomar is planning." It wasn't much of a plan.

✠✠✠

The next morning, Elena drafted an email.

To: Inspector Durand, Polícia Judiciária
From: Dr. Elena Voss
Inspector Durand,
I know you've been looking for me and have questions. I'm ready to answer them. But first, I need you to listen. Not as a police officer. As someone who wants to prevent a catastrophe.

What I've been searching for—what you've been tracking me searching for—is real. It's dangerous. And it's now in the hands of someone who intends to weaponize it. I can explain everything. But I need your help. And I need you to trust me.

If you're willing to listen, meet me tomorrow. 3 PM. Jardim da Estrela, Lisbon. Northeast corner, near the lake. Come alone.

I know you have no reason to trust me. But I'm trusting you with this. With everything. Please. —Elena Voss

She showed it to Antoine and Liam. "It's good," Liam said. "Personal. Honest."

"He'll bring backup," Antoine warned. "Police don't meet suspects alone."

"Then we watch for backup. If he brings a team, we don't show. If he comes alone, we talk."

Elena took a breath. Hit send. The email disappeared into the void. Now they waited to see if Durand would respond. Could one good cop help them stop Guiomar's insane plan to start a new world Order?

Outside, Lisbon woke to another beautiful day. Tourists walked cobblestone streets. Vendors sold pastéis de nata. Trams climbed steep hills. Normal life. Oblivious life. None of them knew that somewhere in the city, a woman with a memory card held the keys to their extinction. And somewhere in the Vatican, a centuries-old document held the final piece.

The Babel Codex. The key to silence. Or the key to the apocalypse.

20 - The Alliance

Elena checked her email for the hundredth time. Nothing. It had been eighteen hours since she'd sent the message to Durand. Eighteen hours of waiting. Watching. Wondering if he'd respond or if the police would kick down their hotel room door instead.

Antoine sat by the window, methodically cleaning his weapons. Liam paced, nervous energy radiating from every movement. "Maybe he's not going to respond," Liam said.

"He'll respond," Antoine said without looking up. "The question is how."

An email arrived—her heart jumped. She opened it.

From: Inspector Durand, Polícia Judiciária

To: Dr. Elena Voss

I'll be at Jardim da Estrela tomorrow at 3 PM. Northeast corner, as you specified. Alone. I hope you're prepared to explain everything.

– Durand

Short. Professional. No promises. No threats. But he was coming. Elena exhaled slowly. "He's meeting us. Tomorrow. Three p.m."

"Alone?" Antoine asked.

"He says alone."

"Saying and doing are two different things. He's a cop. He'll have backup somewhere close by."

✠✠✠

The next day arrived quickly. They took separate routes to Jardim da Estrela, arriving at different times from different directions.

The park was beautiful—manicured gardens, a lake with ducks, and families with children playing. Normal life. Oblivious life.

Antoine positioned himself near the park entrance, watching approaches. Liam took a bench with a view of the lake. Both had phones ready to warn Elena if they spotted backup. Elena arrived at 2:55 P.M. Five minutes early. She walked to the northeast corner, near the lake. Found a bench. Sat. Waited.

At exactly 3:00 P.M., Detective Inspector Durand appeared. He walked alone. No visible backup. He wore civilian clothes—jeans, jacket, sunglasses. Trying to blend in, but his posture gave him away. Police stance. Alert. Assessing. He spotted Elena and walked over. Sat on the bench beside her, leaving a professional distance between them.

"Dr. Voss."

"Inspector."

They sat in silence for a moment. Watching the lake. The ducks. The families. "I came alone," Durand said finally. "As promised."

"Thank you."

"Don't thank me yet. I'm here to listen. Not to promise anything." He turned slightly, looking at her. "You said you're ready to answer questions. Let's start with the obvious one, what have you been searching for?"

Elena took a breath. This was it. All in.

"Medical knowledge. A cipher split into nine fragments. Hidden across Portugal by the Templars in 1307." She kept her voice low, calm. "Each fragment describes a cure for a deadly disease. Hemorrhagic fever. Respiratory plague. Prion disease. Nine cures in total."

"Cures," Durand repeated. "Not weapons?"

"Both. That's what makes them dangerous. They're medieval medicine. Antibodies. Treatments. But if you know how to cure a disease, you know how it works. You can reverse engineer it. Enhance it. Weaponize it."

"And someone wants to weaponize them."

"Yes. A woman named Isabella Guiomar. She runs an organization called the Guild of Shadows. She's been tracking us—letting us do the work of finding and decoding the fragments. And now she has them. All nine. Perfect digital copies."

Durand was quiet, processing.

"Where are the real fragments?"

"I burned them," she admitted. "I had to. Guiomar couldn't have them—at any cost."

"I should arrest you right now, Doctor Voss." He paused. "But there are larger fish to fry. I'll deal with your having destroyed priceless artifacts later."

A long pause.

"The murder," he said finally. "Dr. Almeida. You were cleared—we identified the real killer. A man named Cristiano Rocha. Portuguese national, military background, suspected ties to organized crime. He disappeared after the murder."

"He works for Guiomar. A Guild operative. My associate—Antoine—fought him earlier. We thought Cristiano had died. Apparently not."

"So Guiomar had Almeida killed. Why?"

"Because Almeida was helping me. He had information about some of the Guild's members. She eliminated him and made it look like I did it."

"And the break-ins? Alcobaça, Tomar, Coimbra, Monsanto, Belém Tower, the Procession of Saint Vincent?"

"Searching for the fragments. Each one hidden in a different location. Protected by Templar engineering—by puzzles and traps. Seven hundred years of concealment."

Elena met his eyes. "I know it sounds insane, but it's real. And Guiomar now has the complete cipher. She's going to weaponize it—release the plagues—and kill millions, maybe billions."

"And exactly how did Guiomar get the digital copies of the nine fragments?"

"She stole the memory card from Liam's camera. He was taking pictures of them—for posterity, and for evidence."

"Evidence?" Durand smirked. "You'll need all the evidence you can get for your trial—if this blows up on you."

Durand removed his sunglasses and studied her face. "It sounds like a Hollywood movie," he said quietly. "Ancient conspiracy. Deadly plagues. Secret organizations. Too dramatic to be real."

"I know."

"But your actions suggest you believe it. You've risked everything. Your career. Your freedom. Your life." He gestured around the park. "You're meeting with a police inspector who could arrest you right now. That's not the behavior of a criminal or a fantasist. That's the behavior of someone who's desperate to stop something terrible."

"I am desperate. Because it's real. And I failed to stop it. Guiomar has the fragments. But there's one more piece. A master document hidden at the Vatican. The Babel Codex. It contains the activation codes for Plague 9—the deadliest one. Without it, the ninth fragment is incomplete. Theoretical. But with it..." Elena's voice tightened. "With it, Guiomar can deploy a DNA resonance pathogen. Ninety-nine point nine percent mortality. Extinction-level."

"The Vatican."

"Yes."

"And you want to break into the Vatican Secret Archives. Steal this Codex before Guiomar finds it."

"Yes."

Durand leaned back on the bench. Looked at the sky.

"If you're lying," he said, "if this is some elaborate hoax or delusion, I'm about to destroy my career by helping you. I'll be the fool who believed a conspiracy theory and aided international criminals."

"I'm not lying."

"But if you're telling the truth..." He looked at her. "If you're telling the truth, and I don't help, potentially billions could die. And I'll have to live knowing I could have prevented it."

"Yes."

He was silent for a long time.

"Ok. Show me your evidence."

✠✠✠

Elena pulled out Liam's laptop. Opened the photographs. All nine fragments. The decoded text. The hidden message written into the edges. She walked Durand through each piece. Plagues 1 through 9. The escalating mortality rates, transmission methods, and technical specifications.

"This is Plague 9," she said, showing him her translation. The Plague of Babel. It rewrites the human genome into noise. The body's instructions become a language it can no longer read. Within hours, the heart forgets its beat. The blood forgets to clot. The body collapses into silence.

Durand read the translation. His face was unreadable.

"And this hidden message?" He pointed to the edge symbols. "These point to the Vatican?"

"Yes. *Where Peter keeps the scrolls*—the Vatican Secret Archives. 'The Babel Codex'—the master document. It contains the electromagnetic frequencies needed to activate Plague 9. Without it, the plague is incomplete. But with it..."

"Guiomar can weaponize it."

"Yes."

Durand closed the laptop and handed it back.

"I want to not believe you," he said. "I want to think this is paranoia or delusion. But..." He gestured to the computer. "That's real research and precise medical terminology. You're not making this up."

"I'm not."

"And Guiomar? The Guild of Shadows? They're real too?"

"Very real. She has resources. Money. Operatives across Europe. She's been ten steps ahead of us the entire time." Elena's voice was bitter. "We thought we were protecting the fragments. But we were just collecting them for her. Doing her work."

"So why hasn't she gone after this Babel Codex yet?"

"Because she doesn't know about it. Not yet. The hidden message is only visible when all nine fragments are assembled. We only discovered it yesterday. But she's smart. She'll figure it out. When she does, she'll go to the Vatican. And if she gets the Codex before we do..."

"Then she has everything she needs."

"Yes."

Durand stood. Paced a few steps. Turned back.

"How can I help?"

"We need information. Maps. Access codes." Elena stood too. "We can't break into the Vatican alone. We need intelligence. Guard rotations. Security systems. Any information we can get our hands on."

"I'm a police inspector. I can't help you commit international crimes."

"I know. But—"

"But," Durand interrupted, "I can provide some information. Share a little intelligence. Introduce you to contacts who might have knowledge about Vatican security." He met her eyes. "Unofficially. Off the record. If you happen to use that information to plan an infiltration, that's your choice. Not mine."

Elena felt a surge of hope. "You'll help?"

"I'll provide what I can. But if you're caught, I was never involved. My contacts were never involved. You planned and executed everything alone. Understood?"

"Understood."

"Because if the Vatican discovers I helped, it's an international incident. Portugal's relationship with the Holy See is complicated. I can't be the one who destroys it."

"We won't mention you. Ever."

Durand nodded slowly. "I have two contacts in the Vatican Gendarmerie. The Vatican's police force. Good men. I met them at an Interpol conference three years ago. We've stayed in touch professionally."

"Will they help?"

"They'll provide information. Guard schedules. Security layouts. Things that aren't classified but aren't public either." Durand's expression was serious. "But they won't be actively involved. If you're caught, they'll deny everything. And I'll back them up."

"Fair enough."

"They're sworn to duty. To protect the Vatican. They won't approve of what you're planning. But they also won't stop you if they don't know about it in advance." He pulled out his phone. "I'll reach out to them today. Tell them I'm consulting on a sensitive case. Ask about Vatican security protocols. Hypothetically."

"And they'll share?"

"Professional courtesy. One law enforcement officer to another." Durand pocketed his phone. "What you do with that information is your business."

Elena extended her hand. "Thank you, Inspector."

He shook it. "Don't thank me yet. You're about to attempt something nearly impossible. The Vatican Secret Archives is one of the most secure locations on Earth. The Gendarmerie patrols constantly. The Swiss Guard may be ceremonial, but they're also trained soldiers. And if you're caught..." He didn't finish.

"We won't get caught."

"Everyone says that." Durand turned to leave, then paused. "Dr. Voss. One more thing. If this is real—if Guiomar really has these plagues and intends to weaponize them—then you're not just stopping a crime. You're preventing genocide."

"I know."

"Which means the stakes are too high for pride or hesitation. If you need help or something goes wrong, contact me. Immediately. Career be damned. Understood?"

Elena felt tears welling up in her eyes. "Understood."

Durand walked away through the park. Elena sat back down on the bench. Let out a shaky breath. They had an ally. A reluctant, pragmatic ally who was risking his career on the word of a woman he'd been tracking for months. But an ally, nonetheless.

Antoine appeared from behind the trees, Liam following. "He came alone," Antoine said. "I watched the whole area. No backup. No surveillance. He actually trusted you."

"Or he's very good at hiding his backup," Liam said.

"No. He really came alone." Elena looked at where Durand had disappeared. "He believes us. Or wants to. Either way, he's helping."

"What did he offer?" Antoine asked.

"Vatican contacts. Two men in the Gendarmerie. They'll provide intel. Guard schedules. Security systems. Layouts."

"That's it? Just information?"

"That's everything. Without it, we're infiltrating blind. With it, we at least have a chance."

They walked out of the park together.

"I can't believe that we're really doing this," Liam said. "We're breaking into the Vatican."

"Yes."

"When?"

"As soon as Durand gets us the intelligence. Days. Maybe a week." Elena stopped, looked at them both. "This is it. The last piece. The Babel Codex. If we get it, we can stop Guiomar. If we fail..."

"We won't fail," Antoine said simply.

They walked back to the hotel. Clouds pressed low, and the air carried that unmistakable scent—the cool, earthy breath before rain. Elena breathed it in.

Somewhere in Lisbon, Guiomar was synthesizing the plagues. Building her weapons. And somewhere in Rome, in the deepest vaults of the Vatican Secret Archives, a seven-hundred-year-old codex waited. The key to silence. Or the key to the apocalypse. The race was on.

Two days later, Durand sent an encrypted file—Vatican security intelligence. Everything his contacts could provide without directly implicating themselves.

Elena opened it on Liam's laptop.

Guard Rotation Schedule

- Shift changes: 6 A.M., 2 P.M., 10 P.M.
- Weakest coverage: 2–3 A.M. (skeleton crew, four guards total)
- Archives patrol: One guard per hour
- Rounds take approximately twelve minutes
- Forty-eight-minute window between checks

Security Systems

- Cameras: Main entrance, primary corridors, restricted-section entrance
- Blind spots: Storage areas, older wings (pre-1960s construction)
- Alarms: Magnetic locks on restricted doors; motion sensors in vault areas
- After hours: All alarms active, remote monitoring from the security office

Physical Layout

- Detailed map of Vatican City annotated with security positions
- Archives building: Four levels, eighty-five kilometers of shelving
- Restricted section: Basement level, east wing
- Templar documents: Catalog section Ordines Militares Suppressi 1307–1314
- Access: Vatican ID or special permission (almost never granted after hours)

Access Procedures

- Scholars: Appointment only; credentials verified; always escorted
- Staff: Vatican employee ID cards; biometric scanners at restricted areas
- After hours: Emergency access only, requiring authorization from the Director of Archives

Emergency Exits

- Three marked exits from the Archives building— alarmed but functional—leading to the Vatican gardens and service areas. Not monitored continuously. Budget cuts; older system.

Note from Durand:

This is everything they could provide without breaking their oaths. Use it wisely. You have one chance. After this, I can't help you anymore. If you're caught, I was never involved. Neither were my contacts. Good luck.

—Durand

"This is good," Antoine said, looking over her shoulder. "Very good. With this, we can plan an infiltration."

"When?" Liam asked.

"We need to scout the location first. Physically. Verify this intelligence." Antoine pointed to the map. "These emergency exits. The blind spots. We need to see them ourselves."

"So we go to Rome," Elena said.

"We go to Rome," Antoine confirmed. "Scout for two days. Plan for one. Execute on the fourth night. 2 A.M. In and out before dawn."

"And if we're caught?"

"We're not getting caught." Antoine's voice was flat. Certain. "Because if we fail, Guiomar gets the Babel Codex. And failure is not an option."

Elena looked at the file again. At the detailed intelligence Durand's contacts had risked their careers to provide. At the map of the Vatican. The guard schedules. The security systems. One chance. That's all they had. One chance to break into the Vatican Secret Archives and find the Babel Codex.

And to stop the Black Chalice before it consumed the world.

"Book the flights," she said.

"We leave for Rome tomorrow."

21 - The Eternal City

The flight to Rome took just under three hours. Elena sat by the window, laptop open, reviewing Durand's intelligence packet for the hundredth time. Guard rotation schedules. Security camera placements. The layout of the Vatican Secret Archives. The restricted section where Templar documents were stored. Somewhere in that basement vault, the Babel Codex waited. If it was still there. If it hadn't been moved. If seven centuries of cataloging errors hadn't misplaced it. Too many ifs.

The flight attendant stood in the aisle, demonstrating the oxygen mask procedure with practiced grace. Liam glanced up, watching the demonstration half-heartedly. *She's cute,* he thought, then looked back at his seat-back tablet, pretending to follow along.

Across the aisle, a child began to cry. Her mother murmured softly, trying to soothe her, but the sound carried above the drone of the engines. Elena glanced over and smiled. When the child peeked through her tears, Elena crossed her eyes and puffed her cheeks. The girl blinked, then giggled.

The exchange continued for a few seconds—faces, smiles, laughter—until the tension in the row dissolved. Elena gave the mother a reassuring nod, then turned back to her laptop, her reflection flickering in the darkened screen as she resumed typing.

Liam sat in the middle seat, his own laptop open to the cloud backup of his fragment photographs. He'd triple-checked them since the memory card incident. Backed them up to three different servers. Paranoid, maybe. But justified.

Antoine had the aisle seat, reading through the Vatican Gendarmerie patrol patterns. His expression was thoughtful. Calculating. He'd fought in worse situations—smaller teams, worse odds, less intelligence. But those had been military operations with backup and extraction plans. This was three people breaking into a sovereign nation with no support and no way out if things went wrong.

"The emergency exit on the east side," Antoine said quietly, pointing to the map on Elena's screen. "Durand's contact marked it as alarmed but functional. What kind of alarm?"

"Magnetic lock. Connected to the security office." Elena focused on the architectural drawing. "When the door opens, it triggers a silent alarm. Guards respond within two to three minutes."

"Then we have two minutes to get inside and disable it."

"Can you disable a magnetic lock?" Liam asked.

"If I have the right tools. And if it's a standard system. If it's custom..." Antoine shrugged. "We'll find out."

"Comforting," Liam muttered.

A flight attendant appeared in the aisle beside them—young, maybe Liam's age, dark hair pulled back in a neat bun. Her name tag read Sofia.

"Can I get you anything?" she asked in accented English.

"I'm good, thanks," Elena said without looking up.

"Water, please," Antoine said quietly.

"Coffee, please," Liam added.

Sofia smiled and moved off. When she returned a few minutes later, she set the drinks down carefully. Her hand brushed Liam's as she handed him the coffee.

"Thank you," he said.

She hesitated, lowering her voice and leaning in towards Liam. "You might want to close that laptop for a while. The man three rows back has been watching your screen since takeoff. Dark jacket. Scar on his left cheek."

Liam froze, pulse kicking up. "You're sure?"

"I've worked long-haul flights for six years. I know when someone's just curious—and when they're not." She straightened, forcing a polite smile back onto her face. "Enjoy your flight," she said, and moved on.

Antoine leaned forward slightly. "Scar on the cheek?" Liam nodded. "Row twenty-three." Antoine's tone turned low and cold. "Cristiano."

Liam and Elena shut their laptops. "How the hell did he get on this plane?"

"Doesn't matter," Antoine said. "He's not here for a joy ride. Eyes forward. We act normal until landing."

The plane began its descent thirty minutes later. Elena closed her laptop and looked out the window at Rome spreading below them. Ancient and modern, layered on top of each other. Terracotta roofs. White stone. The Tiber River cut through the city. And in the distance, barely visible through the haze, the dome of St. Peter's Basilica.

The Vatican.

Where the Babel Codex waited. One document. Hidden for centuries. The key to stopping Plague 9. Or the key to perfecting it. Elena's stomach tightened. They were really doing this—breaking into the Vatican, stealing from the Holy See, committing a crime that would make international headlines if they were caught.

"You okay?" Antoine asked quietly. He noticed her clenched fists.

"Not really," Elena said. "But we're doing it anyway."

"That's the spirit."

✠ ✠ ✠

The plane touched down at Fiumicino Airport at 4:15 P.M. They collected their bags—minimal luggage, just essentials—and moved through customs. The Italian immigration officer barely glanced at their passports and stamped them through. Tourists. Just three more tourists visiting Rome.

They walked through the terminal toward the exit. Sofia was at the gate, saying goodbye to passengers as they deplaned. She spotted Liam and smiled. He pulled a cocktail napkin from his pocket—he'd scribbled his phone number on it during the descent—and walked over.

"I know you have another flight tonight," he said. "But if you're ever in Lisbon. Or if I'm ever back in Rome." He held out the napkin.

Sofia took it and looked at the number. Then at him. "Liam Hayes," she read from what he'd written. "Professional photographer. Or possibly an international art thief if the security consultant's comment was real."

"That would be a much more interesting story," Liam said.

"It would." Sofia laughed, pocketing the napkin. Her smile was genuine. Warm. "Have a wonderful time in Rome, Liam. All of you."

"Thanks," Elena said.

They walked out of the terminal into the heat of Rome. Dry. Intense. The smell of espresso, exhaust, and ancient stone in the air. "She's going to call you," Antoine said as they found a taxi.

"Probably not," Liam said. "But it was nice to pretend normal life exists for a minute."

They climbed into the taxi. Antoine gave the driver an address in Prati—a neighborhood northwest of Vatican City. Small hotels. Residential. Easy to disappear. The taxi wound through Roman traffic, aggressive and chaotic, drivers treating lanes as suggestions.

Elena watched the city pass. Cafés. Shops. People living normal lives. Not knowing that three people in this taxi were about to commit one of the most audacious thefts in modern history. Not knowing that the Babel Codex was about to be stolen from the Vatican Secret Archives.

The taxi turned a corner. And there it was. St. Peter's Square. The Basilica. The Vatican walls were smaller than Elena had expected. More contained. A nation within a city. 44 hectares. 121 acres. The smallest country on Earth. But one of the most secure.

"There," Antoine said quietly, pointing to a building east of the Basilica. "That's the Archives." Elena looked. Four stories. Renaissance architecture. Windows barred. Guards visible at the entrance. Somewhere inside that building, in the basement restricted section, the Babel Codex waited. Cataloged under *"Ordines Militares Suppressi 1307-1314."* The Templars. One document among thousands. Buried. Forgotten. Hidden in plain sight for centuries. Until now.

"We're really doing this," Liam said.

"We're really doing this," Elena confirmed.

The taxi continued past the Vatican and into the residential streets of Prati. Tonight, they would scout.

Tomorrow, plan. And in the early morning—2 A.M.—they'd infiltrate.

One chance. That's all they had. One chance to reach the Babel Codex before Guiomar did—before she could weaponize what it contained.

Elena looked back as the Vatican disappeared behind the rows of ocher buildings.

"We're coming back for you," she whispered.

22 - Reconnaissance

They woke early. The Rome sun was already warm through the hotel windows by 7:00 A.M. Elena showered, dressed in tourist clothes—jeans, comfortable shoes, a light jacket despite the heat. Liam did the same. Antoine wore dark pants and a polo shirt; sunglasses clipped to his collar. They looked like any other tourists visiting Rome. Unremarkable. Forgettable.

They ate breakfast at a café two blocks from the hotel. Cornetti and espresso. Elena's mind was already at the Vatican, calculating distances, memorizing guard positions from Durand's intelligence packet.

"We're just tourists today," Antoine reminded them. "Curious. Relaxed. Nothing suspicious. We walk the perimeter. Take photos. Observe. That's it."

✠ ✠ ✠

"And tonight?" Liam asked.

"Tonight, we find my friend Marco and get the equipment we need."

They finished breakfast and walked toward Vatican City. The streets were already filling with tour groups, vendors selling religious souvenirs, and tourists with cameras and guidebooks. The energy was chaotic but purposeful—thousands of people drawn to the smallest nation on Earth.

St. Peter's Square opened before them. Massive. The colonnade embraced the space like arms. Bernini's architecture, centuries old, and still breathtaking. Tourists posed for photos. Priests in black cassocks moved through the crowds. Swiss Guards in their Renaissance uniforms stood at attention near the Basilica entrance.

"There," Antoine said quietly, gesturing with his phone as if checking directions. "On the east side. The Archives building."

Elena looked. Four stories. Renaissance stone. Barred windows. The Apostolic Vatican Secret Archives— though they'd dropped "Secret" from the official name in recent years, trying to seem less mysterious. But the building itself still radiated *keep out* energy.

Two Gendarmerie officers stood at the main entrance. Vatican police, not Swiss Guard. These were the real security—trained law enforcement with modern weapons and communication equipment.

"Cameras?" Liam asked, taking photos like a tourist.

"Three visible from here," Antoine said. "Main entrance, above the doorway. Southeast corner. And there—" He pointed casually. "—northwest corner, covering the side approach."

Elena memorized the positions. Durand's intelligence indicated that five cameras were on the Archives building. Three visible meant two were hidden or positioned where they couldn't be seen from this angle. They walked the perimeter slowly. Staying with the tourist flow. Stopping to take photos. Reading plaques. Acting interested in history while studying security.

The east side emergency exit was exactly where Durand's map had shown it. Unmarked door. Steel. No visible camera directly above it, but there would be alarms. Magnetic locks. Silent alerts to the security office when opened.

"Two minutes," Antoine murmured. "That's our window. From the time we open that door to when guards arrive. We need to be inside and past the alarm in two minutes."

"Can we do that?" Liam asked.

"We'll find out."

They continued walking. Noted the guard shift change at 10:00 A.M.—exactly as Durand's schedule indicated. Six Gendarmerie officers rotating positions. Professional. Alert. Not ceremonial, like the Swiss Guard.

Elena watched them move. Their communication style. How they checked doors. How often they walked the perimeter. Every fifteen minutes one guard circled the building. The pattern was predictable. That was good. Predictable meant exploitable.

By noon, they'd walked the entire Vatican perimeter twice. Identified all visible security. Confirmed Durand's intelligence was accurate. The Archives building was accessible—barely—but it would require precision timing and specialized equipment.

"We need Marco," Antoine said as they left Vatican City. "Without his equipment, this doesn't work."

✠ ✠ ✠

They found lunch at a trattoria in Trastevere. Quiet corner table. Antoine made a call, speaking in rapid French. Elena caught enough to understand he was setting up a meeting.

He hung up. "Tonight. Eight p.m. Marco will meet us."

"Where?" Elena asked.

"The restaurant backroom. Trastevere. He's being cautious—wants to make sure we're not being followed, not working with police."

"Are we sure we can trust him?"

"No. But we don't have any other options." Antoine leaned back. "Marco was a Carabinieri—Italian military police—for twenty years. Retired five years ago. Now he brokers security equipment. Mostly corporate espionage, some government work. He's expensive but reliable."

"How do you know him?"

"NATO operation. Syria, 2015. He provided intelligence on Russian movements. We worked together for three months. He's solid. Professional and discreet."

"But he's a criminal now," Liam said.

"He's a businessman in a gray market. There's a difference." Antoine checked his watch. "We have six hours. Let's rest for a while, review the plan one more time, and then meet Marco. Tomorrow night—2 a.m.—we infiltrate."

Elena felt her stomach tighten. Tomorrow night. They're really doing this.

The restaurant was small. Family-run. Checkered tablecloths and wine bottles lining the walls. The owner—a heavyset man in his sixties—greeted Antoine with a nod and led them through the kitchen to a back room.

Marco was already there.

Mid-fifties. Lean. Salt-and-pepper hair cut military short. Sharp eyes that assessed them in seconds. He wore jeans and a casual button-down, but his posture was pure law enforcement. Decades of training that never quite left.

"Rousseau," he said, shaking Antoine's hand vigorously. "It's been a while."

"Too long. Thanks for meeting on short notice."

"Your message said it was urgent." Marco gestured to the table. "Sit. We have privacy here. The owner is a friend." They sat. Marco studied Elena and Liam.

"Dr. Elena Voss," Antoine introduced. "Cryptographer. Medieval studies. And Liam Hayes. Photographer and tech specialist."

"Interesting team." Marco's eyes lingered on Elena. "I looked you up after Rousseau called. You've been busy. Portugal. Multiple break-ins. Historical sites. Police think you're art thieves. But you're not stealing art, are you?"

"No," Elena said.

"What are you stealing?"

"That's our business."

Marco smiled slightly. "Fair enough. But I need to know enough to help you. Rousseau said you need equipment. Vatican-level security bypass. That's specialized stuff. Expensive. And risky for me to provide."

"What do you need to know?" Antoine asked.

"Where you're going. What you're taking. How long you'll be inside."

Elena hesitated. Looked at Antoine, who nodded.

"Vatican Secret Archives," she said. "Restricted section. Medieval documents. We'll be inside thirty to forty-five minutes."

Marco's expression didn't change. "That's suicide. You know that, right? Vatican Gendarmerie doesn't mess around. If you're caught, it's an international incident. Prison. Possibly worse."

"We know."

"And you're doing it anyway."

"We don't have a choice."

Marco leaned back, considering. "What do you need from me?"

"Magnetic lock bypass for the east side emergency entrance. A camera loop device. Updated guard schedules. Anything else you think we may need." Antoine pulled out Durand's intelligence packet and spread it on the table. "We have good information. But we need equipment that we can't get on our own."

Marco studied the documents. His eyes moved across the floor plans, the security layouts, the guard rotation schedules. Professional assessment.

"This is good intelligence," he said finally. "Very good. Where did you get it?"

"Portuguese police contact. His friends in the Vatican Gendarmerie."

"Durand? Inspector Durand?" Marco smiled. "He helped you? That's interesting. He's a good cop. Honest. Must really believe in what you're doing."

"He does."

Marco tapped the emergency exit on the map. "Magnetic lock. Standard system, but Vatican-grade hardware. You'll need a bypass that works on their specific frequency. I have one. It'll give you ninety seconds—that's how long before the system realizes it's been tampered with and triggers the alarm, anyway."

"Ninety seconds to get inside and disable the internal alarm?"

"Yes. Can you do it?"

"We'll have to."

Marco nodded. Pointed to the camera positions. "Camera loop device. It'll freeze the feed for two to three minutes. Long enough for you to move past covered areas. But you can only use it once—after that, security will notice the glitch and investigate."

"Understood."

"Let me find the Guard schedules," Marco said as he glanced at his phone. "I have current rotations. More recent than what you have there. The schedule shifted two weeks ago, due to budget cuts and reduced night staff. You have a slightly larger window than you thought."

"How much larger?"

"Fifteen minutes, maybe. Instead of a four-guard night shift, they're down to three. That means longer patrol loops, more gaps in coverage."

Antoine smiled grimly. "Budget cuts are good."

"Sometimes bureaucracy helps criminals." Marco set down his phone. "So. Here's what I have for you: a bypass device, camera loop, current schedules, and maps showing security blind spots I've marked from my own sources. Everything you need to get in and out."

"What's the cost?" Elena asked.

Marco looked at her for a long moment. "Information. I want something in return."

"What kind of information?"

"There's a document in the Vatican Archives. Modern section, third floor. Not where you're going. But close enough." He pulled out a photograph of an old catalog card. "This. I want you to photograph it while you're inside."

Elena took the photograph. Read the catalog reference. *Correspondence - Banco Ambrosiano - 1982 - Restricted.*

"Banco Ambrosiano," she said quietly. "The Vatican Bank scandal."

"Yes. My client is Sofia Marchetti. Her father was Antonio Marchetti, a banker with Banco Ambrosiano in the 1980s. He was found dead in 1982 under Blackfriars Bridge in London. Ruled a suicide. But Sofia believes the Vatican had him killed."

"Why?"

"Because he knew too much. Vatican Bank corruption. Money laundering. Connections to organized crime. The usual." Marco's expression hardened. "Sofia has spent forty years trying to prove her father was murdered. The Vatican has stonewalled her. Destroyed evidence. But this document—correspondence between Vatican Bank officials dated June 1982, days before Marchetti died—could give her answers."

"What's in it?"

"Not sure exactly, but according to my sources, it discusses 'resolving the Marchetti situation. Permanent solutions.' It's not a signed confession, but it's evidence that Vatican officials knew something was going to happen to him."

Elena studied the catalog reference. Third floor. A different section from the basement where the Babel Codex would be. It would add time. Add risk.

"This is in a different part of the Archives," she said. "We'd have to access two areas instead of one."

"I know. It adds ten to fifteen minutes to your infiltration. But you're already breaking in. You're already taking the risk. What's one more photograph?" Marco leaned forward. "Sofia Marchetti doesn't want money. She wants the truth. She wants to know what happened to her father. Wouldn't you want the same?"

Elena thought about her own father—how he'd died serving in Kandahar, how she'd grown up trying to make sense of his sacrifice. There'd been no mystery, only a silence that duty had left behind. But the need to understand—to honor—was the same.

"Yes," she said quietly. "I would."

"Then help her."

Antoine shook his head. "It doubles our exposure time. We planned for thirty minutes inside. Now you're asking for forty-five. That's a long time to avoid detection."

"I'm asking you to help a daughter learn the truth about her father's death." Marco looked at Elena. "The Vatican buried this for forty years. They don't want anyone to know what they did. Are you really protecting them by refusing?"

Elena hated that he had a point. She looked at Antoine, at Liam. "We'll do it," she said. "But we hit the third floor first. Get Marco's document before we go to the basement for our objective. It's along the way, sort of."

"Elena—" Antoine started.

"It's the right thing to do. And we need his equipment." She looked at Marco. "We photograph your document. You give us everything we need for the infiltration. No payment. No debt. A clean transaction."

Marco extended his hand. "Deal."

✠ ✠ ✠

Elena shook it. Felt the weight of another impossible promise. But they needed the equipment. And Sofia Marchetti deserved answers. Just like Elena had deserved them.

"Good," Marco said. He pulled a duffel bag from under the table. "Let me show you what you're working with." The equipment was professional. Military-grade. Marco laid it out piece by piece.

The magnetic lock bypass looked like a small black box with two leads. "Attach it to the door's magnetic sensor. Press this button. It creates a counter-frequency that tricks the system into thinking the door is still closed. Ninety seconds before the backup system catches it."

The camera loop device was even smaller—a USB drive with a wireless transmitter. "Plug it into any network port inside the building. It'll hijack the camera feed and loop the previous three minutes of footage. Gives you two to three minutes of frozen video before monitoring catches the glitch."

Marco also provided updated floor plans with hand-written notes. Guard positions. Blind spots. Patrol timing. "This is current as of last week. Memorize it. Don't bring paper inside—if you're caught, you don't want evidence of premeditation."

Antoine studied everything carefully. Asked technical questions. Tested the bypass device on a practice lock Marco had brought. Satisfied himself that it would work.

"One more thing," Marco said. He handed Antoine a small radio earpiece. "Emergency contact. If something goes catastrophically wrong and you need extraction help, this connects to a secure frequency. I'll be monitoring. I can't come get you—that's too much risk—but I can create a distraction to buy you time."

"Why would you do that?" Elena asked.

"Because I like Rousseau. And because if you get caught, you might talk. Might mention where you got the equipment. I have a vested interest in your success." Marco smiled slightly. "Call it insurance."

They spent the next hour reviewing the plan. Entry point, east side emergency exit, 2:00 A.M. Ninety seconds to bypass the magnetic lock and get inside. Disable the internal alarm panel—Antoine's job. Plant the camera loop device—Liam's job. Navigate to the third floor, find Marco's document, and photograph it. Then to the basement restricted section to find the Babel Codex and take it. Exit the way they came. Total time, forty-five minutes if everything went perfectly.

"It won't go perfectly," Marco warned. "Something always goes wrong. When it does, adapt. Don't panic. And don't get caught."

"Comforting advice," Liam muttered.

Marco packed up the equipment and handed the duffel to Antoine. "Good luck. You're going to need it."

They left through the kitchen. The restaurant owner didn't look up from his cooking. Professional discretion.

Outside, Rome was alive with nightlife. Couples walking the cobblestone streets. Tourists finishing late dinners. Music drifting from open doorways. Normal life. Oblivious life.

Tomorrow night, Elena thought. Tomorrow night they'd break into the Vatican. And after that, everything would change.

Back at the hotel, Elena sat at the small desk, reviewing her notes on the Babel Codex one more time. The hidden message written into the fragments' edges. The catalog reference: *Ordines Militares Suppressi 1307-1314 - Codex Babel.* She'd memorized it weeks ago, but she read it again, anyway. Focusing. Preparing. This was it. The last piece. The key to stopping the Plague of Babel. Or the key to perfecting it.

There was a soft knock. Antoine sat on the edge of the bed. "You can quit right now. We could walk away. Let Guiomar figure out the Babel Codex on her own. Maybe she never finds it."

"She'll find it. She's too smart not to." Elena closed her notebook. "And then she'll have everything she needs to create her new world Order."

"Or we could give her the Codex. Trade it for peace."

"There is no peace with Guiomar. Only temporary truces before the next demand." Elena looked at him. "We must get it first. We have to keep it from her. It's the only leverage we have left."

Antoine was quiet for a moment. "You've changed. Since this started. You were an academic. Now you're planning heists. Breaking into the Vatican. Dealing with black market arms dealers."

"I know."

"Does it bother you?"

"Every single day." Elena's voice was soft. "But the alternative is worse. If I do nothing, Guiomar wins. Everything ends. I'll do what I must. Even if it means becoming someone I don't recognize."

"For what it's worth," Antoine said, "your father would be proud. You're fighting for something bigger than yourself. That's what he did too."

Elena felt tears building in her eyes. "I hope so."

Antoine stood. "Get some rest. Tomorrow's going to be a long day. And tomorrow night..." He didn't finish.

Tomorrow night they'd find out if they were good enough, lucky enough, or just desperate enough to pull off the impossible.

"Goodnight, Antoine."

"Goodnight."

He left. Elena sat in the darkness, looking out the window at Rome. Ancient city. Eternal city. Built on layers of history, each generation adding to what came before.

Tomorrow night, they'd add their own layer. One more crime. One more secret. One more desperate act in the service of something larger.

She finally lay down. Closed her eyes. Tried to sleep. But all she could see was the Vatican. The Archives. The Babel Codex waiting in its vault. One document. Hidden for centuries.

Tomorrow night, she'd hold it in her hands.

If they didn't get caught first.

23 - The Infiltration

The alarm on Elena's phone vibrated at 1:00 A.M. She woke instantly, adrenaline already coursing through her veins. No grogginess. Just a sharp awareness that this was it. The big day. Make or break.

She dressed in dark clothes. Black jeans. Dark blue long-sleeve shirt. Running shoes with a good grip. No jewelry. No reflective surfaces. Nothing that would catch light or make noise.

Antoine and Liam were already awake in the adjoining room. Antoine wore tactical pants and a dark jacket. Liam had chosen all black—probably too much, making him look like a burglar in a movie—but it would work. They looked at each other without speaking. There was nothing left to say. They'd reviewed the plan a dozen times. Now they just had to execute.

Antoine opened the duffel bag Marco had provided. Laid out the equipment again. Magnetic lock bypass. Camera loop device. Updated floor plans were memorized but not brought along. Liam's camera with a fresh 128 GB memory card. Flashlights. Lock picks. Wire cutters. Basic tools. Gloves to avoid fingerprints. And the emergency radio earpiece, which Antoine fitted into his ear. "Marco, you there?" A crackle. Then Marco's voice, quiet. "I'm here. Monitoring Vatican security frequencies. You're clear so far. No alerts. No increased patrols."

"Good. We're moving in fifteen."

"Be careful. And Rousseau? Don't get caught."

"Not planning on it."

They left the hotel at 1:30 A.M. The streets were quiet. A few late-night stragglers stumbling home from bars. A taxi passed by. But mostly empty. Rome was sleeping.

They walked separate routes toward Vatican City. Antoine first. Elena, five minutes later. Liam last. If one of them was spotted, the others could abort. Standard surveillance evasion. Elena's heart pounded as she walked. Every shadow seemed to hide a threat. Every footstep behind her might be Gendarmerie. But the streets stayed quiet. No one followed. No one watched.

She reached the meeting point at 1:50 A.M.—a small piazza three blocks from the Vatican. Antoine was already there, standing in a shadow near the closed café. Liam arrived two minutes later.

"Clear?" Antoine asked.

"Clear," Elena confirmed.

"Clear," Liam said.

"Let's go. Stay close. Stay quiet. If I signal, we abort immediately. Understood?" They nodded.

Antoine led them through narrow side streets toward the Vatican's east side. Away from the main entrance. Away from St. Peter's Square. Into the residential areas that bordered the smallest nation on Earth.

The Vatican walls appeared ahead. Ancient stone. Fifteen feet high. Security cameras at intervals. But there were gaps. Dark spaces between cameras where budget and architecture created blind spots. Antoine stopped at one such gap. Checked his watch. 1:58 A.M. Two minutes.

"Wait here," he whispered.

He moved forward alone, staying in the shadows, approaching the east-side emergency exit they'd identified during reconnaissance. The unmarked steel door and its magnetic lock. A silent alarm would trigger the moment it opened. Unless Marco's bypass device worked.

Elena watched from thirty feet away. Her breath shallow. Her gloved hands clenched. This was the first test. If the bypass failed, guards would respond. Everything would be over before it even started.

Antoine attached the bypass device to the door's magnetic sensor. Two leads clipped to the lock mechanism. He pressed the button. A tiny green light appeared on the device. Ninety seconds. That's all they had. Antoine pulled the door open. No alarm sounded. He waved them forward. Elena and Liam ran across the open space. Reached the door. Slipped inside. They were in.

The Vatican Secret Archives. The most audacious theft of their lives had just begun.

✠ ✠ ✠

Antoine closed the door behind them. They stood in a service corridor. Concrete walls. Fluorescent lights dimmed for night hours. The smell of old paper and musk filled the air.

"Internal alarm panel," Antoine whispered. "Thirty seconds. Liam, the camera loop." Liam pulled out the USB device. Found a network port on the wall and plugged it in. The green light flickered briefly, then held steady. "The loop is active," Liam said. "We have two to three minutes before monitoring notices."

Antoine located the alarm panel around the corner and opened it with a screwdriver. Found the main circuit.

Cut it. The panel went dark. "Alarm disabled. We're clear."

Elena checked her watch. Two minutes inside. Forty-three minutes remaining in their window. They had to move fast.

"Third floor first," she said. "Marco's document." They found the stairwell—concrete, industrial, lit by emergency lights. They climbed quickly but quietly. Their footsteps echoed slightly. Elena winced at every sound; certain someone would hear. But no one came. They reached the third floor. The modern documents section. Correspondence. Financial records. Recent Vatican history. Less historically protected than the medieval basement, but still restricted.

The corridor stretched before them. Rows of filing cabinets and archive boxes. Organized by date and subject. They needed Banco Ambrosiano. 1982. Correspondence.

"There," Liam whispered, pointing to a section labeled *Finanze - 1980-1985*.

They moved down the aisle and found the subsection: *Banco Ambrosiano - Corrispondenza - 1982*. Three boxes. Elena pulled the second one—June 1982, the month Marchetti had died. Inside were folders, dozens of them. Organized by date. She found the one dated June 10, 1982. Five days before Marchetti's death. Opened it carefully.

Letters. Memos. Internal Vatican Bank correspondence. All in Italian. Elena's Italian was functional but not fluent. She scanned quickly, looking for keywords.

Marchetti. Situazione. Soluzione.

There. A memo from a Vatican Bank official to another. Dated June 11, 1982. Four days before Marchetti died.

Regarding Marchetti situation - recommend immediate resolution. Permanent solution advised. Coordinate with contacts in London. Minimize exposure.

Elena felt cold. This was it. Not a confession. Not explicit. But damning enough. Vatican officials discussing a "permanent solution" and "minimize exposure" days before Marchetti turned up dead. "Liam, photograph this. Every page." Liam pulled out his camera. No flash—the low-light capability would have to be enough. He photographed the memo. The letterhead. The signature. Every word.

"Got it," he said after thirty seconds.

Elena returned the folder to the box. Closed it. Put everything back exactly as they'd found it. "Marco's mission complete," she said. "Now ours."

✠ ✠ ✠

They left the third floor and returned to the stairwell. Descended to the basement. The restricted section. Where the oldest, most protected documents were stored. Where the Babel Codex waited.

The basement was different. Older. Stone walls instead of concrete. Vaulted ceilings. The air was cooler, drier—climate-controlled to preserve ancient parchments. It felt like descending into history itself.

They found the restricted section door. Heavy wood. Modern lock. A small sign:

Accesso Limitato—Autorizzazione Richiesta.

"Access Limited—Authorization Required."

Antoine pulled out his lock picks and worked on the mechanism. It was a good lock—Vatican-grade security—but not impossible. After two minutes, the lock clicked. The door opened. Inside, rows of shelving. Dim lighting.

Documents in protective boxes, organized by subject and date. Medieval. Renaissance. Enlightenment. Centuries of secrets preserved in controlled darkness.

Elena consulted her mental map. They needed:

Ordines Militares Suppressi 1307-1314.

Suppressed Military Orders. The Templars.

"This way."

They moved through the aisles. Reading labels. Passing papal bulls. Inquisition records. Excommunication decrees. The Vatican's hidden history laid bare in thousands of documents. And there. At the end of the aisle. A section labeled exactly what they needed.

Ordines Militares Suppressi - Templarii - 1307-1314.

Elena's hands trembled as she scanned the boxes. There were dozens. Confiscated Templar documents. Interrogation transcripts. Financial records. Evidence from trials.

And one box, smaller than the others, with a catalog card that read:

Codex Babel - Documenta Medica - Originem Incerta.

The Babel Codex. Medical documents. Origin uncertain. Elena pulled the box from the shelf and set it on a nearby reading table. She opened it.

Inside, a single book. Small. Bound in dark leather that had aged to almost black. About the size of a hand-held Bible, maybe twelve pages. The leather was soft with age and the binding was intact despite centuries of storage. The cover was unmarked except for a small symbol pressed into the leather—a tower with flames at its base.

The Tower of Babel.

Elena opened it. The pages were vellum. Thin but surprisingly durable. The text was dense. Latin. Medical terminology mixed with technical specifications. Diagrams showing cellular structures that shouldn't have been visible to medieval scholars. Electromagnetic frequency charts that predate Maxwell by six centuries.

This was it. The Babel Codex. The master document describing the plague with complete activation protocols. The frequencies needed to trigger the DNA resonance pathogen. Instructions for synthesis. Everything Guiomar would need to perfect it. And everything Elena would need to stop it.

For the first time, she wondered if the pursuit of truth could be as dangerous as the lies it uncovered. She turned the pages slowly. Twelve pages total. Each one filled with text and diagrams. The Codex was brilliant. Terrifying. It described the plague with scientific precision that seemed impossible for its time. As if whoever wrote it understood modern genetics, molecular biology, and electromagnetic theory. Knowledge that shouldn't have existed in the 14th century. Or earlier, because the Codex's age was uncertain. It might be medieval. Or it might be far, far older.

Liam readied his camera to take pictures.

"No. We're taking it," Elena said.

"What?" Liam asked.

"We're taking the original. Not photographing it. Taking it." Elena looked at Liam. "If we leave it here, Guiomar will come for it. She's smart enough to figure out the hidden message on the fragments' edges. She'll decode the location just like we did. And then she'll have everything."

"The Vatican will notice it's missing," Antoine said.

"Eventually. But not immediately. This section isn't accessed frequently. It could be days. Maybe weeks before they realize it's missing." Elena carefully closed the Codex. "And by then, we'll be long gone."

"They'll investigate. Issue alerts. We'll be wanted for stealing a Vatican artifact."

"We're already wanted for breaking into half of Portugal's historical sites. What's one more charge?" Elena slipped the Codex into her inside jacket pocket. It fit perfectly. Barely noticeable unless someone searched her. "We can't let Guiomar get this. That's all that matters."

Antoine considered for a moment. Then nodded. "Agreed. We take it."

Elena returned the empty box to the shelf. Left everything else exactly as they'd found it. No evidence they'd been here except one small document missing from one small box that might not be checked for months.

✠ ✠ ✠

"Let's go. Before—"

Footsteps.

From the corridor outside the restricted section.

Guards.

Antoine grabbed Elena and Liam, pulled them behind a row of shelving. They crouched in darkness. Elena's hand instinctively went to her jacket pocket, where the Codex rested. If they were caught now, with a stolen Vatican artifact on her person, there would be no explaining it away.

The footsteps grew louder. Two guards. Their voices speaking Italian. Casual conversation. A routine patrol that happened to reach this section.

The restricted section door opened.

Flashlight beams swept across the room.

Elena held her breath, pressed against the shelving. Beside her, Liam was frozen. Antoine had his hand on his baton, ready but hoping not to need it.

The guards entered. Walked down the main aisle. Their flashlights played across boxes, shelves, and shadows.

"Sembra tutto normale."

"Everything looks normal."

"Questi vecchi documenti mi mettono i brividi."

"These old documents give me the creeps."

"Come se i fantasmi vivessero qui sotto."

"Like ghosts live down here."

"Non essere superstizioso. Sono solo carte."

"Don't be superstitious. Just papers."

They walked the length of the main aisle. Checked the reading area. Shone their lights into corners.

The Codex in her pocket felt like it was burning. Screaming its presence. If they were found—if the guards searched them—

The first guard's flashlight beam swept past their hiding spot. Six feet away. Five feet. Then stopped.

"Aspetta. Hai sentito qualcosa?"

"Wait. Did you hear something?"

"Cosa?"

"What?"

"Un suono. Come... un movimento."

"A sound. Like... movement."

Elena didn't breathe. Didn't move. The Codex pressed against her chest. Centuries old. Priceless. Stolen. Becoming a shadow among shadows.

The guard stepped closer. His flashlight beam inched toward their position. Four feet away. Three feet. Then his radio crackled.

"Unità Tre, raggiungi l'ingresso principale. Abbiamo una possibile violazione del perimetro sul muro nord."

"Unit Three, report to the main entrance. We have a potential perimeter breach on the north wall."

The guard stopped.

"Ricevuto. Sto intervenendo."

"Copy that. Responding."

Both guards turned and walked quickly back toward the door. Their footsteps receded. The door closed behind them. Silence.

Elena exhaled slowly. The Codex was still safe in her pocket.

"That was close," Liam whispered.

"Too close. We need to leave. Now." Antoine checked his watch. "We've been inside thirty-two minutes."

They moved quickly back through the basement. Up the stairs. Elena's hand stayed on her jacket pocket, protecting the Codex. Through the corridors toward the exit.

"Wait," Liam said as they reached the service level. "The camera loop device. We left it plugged in."

"Get it. Quickly." Antoine was already moving back toward where they'd entered. "I need to retrieve the bypass device from the door too. We can't leave any equipment behind."

Liam ran to the network port where he'd planted the USB camera loop. Unplugged it. Pocketed it. Ran back.

Antoine was at the emergency exit, carefully detaching the magnetic lock bypass device from the door mechanism. Two leads disconnected. Device pocketed. He pulled the duffel bag from where he'd stashed it near the door—empty when they left it, now holding all their equipment again. Lock picks. Wire cutters. Flashlights. The bypass device. Everything.

"Camera loop?" he asked Liam.

"Got it." Antoine confirmed.

"Each of you, put your gloves in this plastic bag. Nothing left behind. No fingerprints, no equipment they can trace." Antoine slung the duffel over his shoulder. He opened the door carefully and checked outside. "Clear. Let's go."

He removed his gloves, placing them inside the duffel. They slipped out into the cool night air. Away from the Vatican walls. Into the dark spaces between streetlights.

They didn't run. Running would draw attention. They walked quickly but calmly. Three people heading home late. Nothing unusual. One of them was carrying the most dangerous document on Earth in her jacket pocket. Another was carrying a duffel bag of illegal equipment over his shoulder. The third had unauthorized photos of secret Vatican documents on his camera.

They reached the piazza where they'd started and kept walking in separate directions again. Meeting back at the hotel.

Elena's legs felt weak. Her heart—still racing. But the Codex was safe in her pocket. Guiomar couldn't get it now. The Vatican didn't know it was missing yet. They'd done it. They'd broken into the Vatican Secret Archives and stolen the Babel Codex. The actual document. The original. And somehow gotten away with it.

Back at the hotel, they gathered in Antoine's room. The adrenaline was fading, leaving exhaustion in its wake. Elena carefully pulled the Babel Codex from her jacket pocket. Set it on the table. The small leather-bound book that held the keys to Plague 9.

"We actually stole from the Vatican," Liam said, staring at it.

"Yes. We did." Elena ran her hand over the cover. The leather was soft. Ancient. The tower symbol pressed into it.

"Marco's document?"

"Got it. Clear images. Every page is readable." Liam showed them the photos on his camera. The Vatican Bank memo. June 1982. Evidence of what happened to Marchetti.

"Send them to Marco. We fulfilled our end of the deal." Liam created an encrypted email. Attached the photos. Sent them to the address Marco had provided. Thirty seconds later, Marco's reply:

Received. Thank you. Sofia will finally have answers. Good luck with whatever you're trying to stop. And Rousseau, we're even. But if you ever need equipment again, you know how to reach me.

Antoine's emergency radio crackled. Marco's voice, "Nice work. Saw you exit clean. No pursuit. Guards are still investigating that false perimeter alarm I triggered on the north wall. You're clear."

"Thanks, Marco. For everything."

"Stay safe. And whatever you took—" Marco paused. "—I hope it's worth the risk."

"It is."

"Good. Marco out."

The radio went silent. Elena looked at the Babel Codex on the table.

"What now?" Liam asked.

"Now I translate it. Every word." Elena opened the Codex carefully. The first page showed the tower symbol again, larger. And beneath it, Latin text:

"Hic liber continet clavem ad silentium vel ad finem mundi. Lege cum timore."

"What does it say?" Antoine asked.

Elena translated, "This book contains the key to silence or to the end of the world. Read with fear."

They stared at the text. The key to silence. Or to the end of the world.

"Get some rest," Antoine said quietly. "Tomorrow, we figure out what we have. And what we do with it."

Elena nodded. But she didn't move. She sat staring at the Codex. At the warning written centuries ago by someone who understood what they were creating.

Read with fear. She was afraid. More afraid than she'd been breaking into the Vatican. More afraid than she'd been fighting Guardians or confronting Guiomar.

Because now she held the end of the world in her hands. And she had no idea how to stop it.

24 - The Translation

Elena woke at 9:00 A.M., to sunlight streaming through the hotel window. For a moment she forgot where she was; then it slammed back: Rome. The Vatican heist. The Babel Codex.

She sat up, pulse climbing. The small leather book still rested on the nightstand where she had placed it at four in the morning, after collapsing from exhaustion. Compact, ancient, deceptively harmless. Inside lay knowledge that could end civilization.

She ran her fingers over the tower symbol pressed into the cover. They had actually done it—stolen from the Vatican Secret Archives. One of the most audacious thefts in modern history, and the Vatican did not know yet.

A knock. Antoine.

"Morning. You look terrible."

"Thanks." Elena rubbed her eyes. "What time is it?"

"Nine. I let you sleep. Liam's still out—he collapsed the moment the adrenaline left him." Antoine's gaze settled on the Codex. "Ready to see what we stole?"

"Coffee first, then translation."

They found a café two blocks away and took a table outside in the morning sun. Tourists and locals passed by, oblivious to what the people at a corner table had done the night before.

Elena ordered a double espresso, the caffeine cut through the fog.

"We need to leave Rome," Antoine said quietly. "Soon. When the Vatican realizes the Codex is missing, they'll investigate. Check footage. Even with the camera loop, something might surface. We should be gone before that happens."

"Agreed. But I need time to translate this first—to understand what we have." Elena slid the Codex onto her lap, shielding it from view. "A few hours, then we leave."

"Where to?"

"Somewhere we can think and plan, far from the Vatican and Guiomar."

"That might not exist."

"Then somewhere harder to find." Elena opened the Codex to the second page. "Let me work. I'll translate what I can before we go."

Antoine nodded, ordered more coffee, and kept watch on the street while Elena worked.

The Codex's Latin was intricate and archaic, yet the author casually referenced ideas discovered only centuries later: genetics, electromagnetic theory, molecular biology. The contradiction jarred—like reading a script written in two centuries at once.

Page two laid out the basic mechanism of the Babel plague. Elena's translation was rough, but the meaning was unmistakable:

The agent infiltrates through respiratory pathways, crossing cellular barriers via engineered protein markers. Once within, it targets the transcription mechanism—the process by which genetic instructions are read. It does not destroy; it confuses. Adenine becomes cytosine. Guanine becomes thymine. The code becomes noise. The cell speaks—but the body no longer understands.

The Babel plague didn't kill directly.

It scattered meaning.

It made life itself forget its language.

Page three listed exact electromagnetic frequencies—numbers, wavelengths, activation protocols. This was what Guiomar still needed. Without these, Plague 9 remained theoretical. With them it became an extinction-level how-to manual.

Elena photographed the page and uploaded it to her encrypted cloud. If the physical Codex was lost, the frequencies would survive.

Pages four through seven were synthesis protocols—step-by-step instructions for culturing the pathogen from the antibody formula in Fragment 9, complete with protein sequences and optimal growth conditions. Everything required to weaponize the cure.

Pages eight through eleven, however, offered something else: neutralization protocols.

Elena read more slowly, translating word by word. A counteragent. A way to disrupt the electromagnetic activation. A method to repair corrupted DNA before cellular collapse became irreversible.

It was possible—if someone acted fast enough, had the resources, and understood the science.

"The Codex only counters the Babel plague," she said, looking up. "Nothing here neutralizes the others. The Templars built it as a failsafe for the master plague. The other eight... we can only prevent their release or contain the damage after the fact."

Page eleven gave brutal neutralization effectiveness rates: ninety-eight percent within six hours of exposure, seventy percent within twelve, twenty percent within twenty-four. After that, irreversible.

Page twelve—the final page—showed a circle with nine points, each marked by a different plague symbol, all radiating from a center containing text in a language Elena did not recognize.

She stared, trying to parse it, and failed. Older than Latin. Older than medieval scholarship. Something the author had copied without fully understanding.

"What does it mean?" Antoine asked, leaning over her shoulder.

"I don't know. Not Latin, Greek, or Arabic. Something much older."

"How much older?"

"No idea. Weeks, maybe months of work with the right tools and linguists." Elena closed the Codex. "But I have enough. I understand how Babel works, how to activate it, and how to stop it—if we're fast."

"Can we stop Guiomar?"

"If we act now. Intelligence. Surveillance. Durand's contacts. Maybe even Valerius and the Guardians—they want her stopped too." She stood. "First, we leave Rome."

Antoine nodded. "Geneva. WHO headquarters. If Plague 1 deploys, they'll be the first to respond. We need to be there when the alarm goes out."

"That's assuming we don't stop the deployment."

"We try. But if we fail..." Elena slipped the Codex into her jacket pocket. "At least we'll be ready to minimize casualties."

✠ ✠ ✠

They returned to the hotel, woke Liam, packed in minutes, and checked out. Three tourists cutting their Roman holiday short. Nothing suspicious.

The taxi driver asked if they had enjoyed Vatican City.

"Enlightening. They're very good at keeping secrets." Elena smirked. Liam nudged her knee with his own, in response.

The drive to Geneva took nine hours. They stopped twice for food and fuel; otherwise, straight north through Italy and into Switzerland. Mountains rose on either side of the highway; lakes gleamed in the afternoon sun. Beautiful, peaceful country that had no idea what was coming.

Elena spent the journey translating the remaining pages, documenting frequencies, neutralization protocols, and synthesis instructions—everything Guiomar would need to perfect the plague.

By the time they reached Geneva, eleven of the twelve pages were done. Only the final page—the strange symbol and ancient text—remained a mystery.

They checked into a small hotel near Lake Geneva and paid cash.

Antoine immediately began making calls—Durand, Vatican contacts, anyone who might have intelligence on Guiomar's movements. No one had answers. She had gone dark.

✠ ✠ ✠

Elena sat at the desk with the Codex open to the last page, staring at the nine-pointed symbol. Something vital was hidden there. The author would not have included it without reason.

An inbound text arrived on her phone.

Dr. Voss, I know you have the Babel Codex now. Congrat-ulations. But you're missing something. The final page contains the key to everything. Meet me tomorrow, 2:00 PM, Parc des Bastions. Come alone. I can help you understand—V.

Valerius.

Antoine read it over her shoulder. "It's a trap."

"Maybe. But he claims he can translate the final page, and we're running out of time. If he knows anything that helps us stop Guiomar..." Elena looked at the symbol. "We need every advantage we can get."

"He tried to kill us."

"He tried to stop us from collecting the fragments. Now we have the Codex. Maybe that changes things."

Antoine was quiet a moment. "If you go, I'm coming too. Armed. Close."

"The email says alone."

"Then I'll be invisible."

Elena typed:

I'll be there. 2 PM. But if this is a trap...

Instant reply:

It's not a trap, Dr. Voss. I'm trying to save the world. Same as you. Tomorrow you'll understand.

She set the phone down and looked out at the calm lake. Geneva—the city of treaties and humanitarian law—was about to become the nerve center of a war against nine ancient plagues.

Tomorrow she would meet the man who had once ordered her death, hoping he held the final piece of the puzzle.

"This is insane," Liam said from the doorway.

"I know."

"But we're doing it anyway."

"We're doing it anyway."

They were out of time, out of options, and out of safe choices.

Tomorrow Elena would discover whether the Guardians were allies or enemies—and finally learn the meaning of the last page of the Babel Codex.

She hoped it would be enough to stop what was coming.

Twenty-four hours until Mors Rubra went live. Then people would die.

Unless they could stop it.

The clock was ticking.

25 - The Guardian

Parc des Bastions sits in the heart of Geneva's old town. Chestnut trees lined the pathways. University students lounged on benches. Tourists photographed the Reformation Wall—a massive stone monument to Calvin, Farel, Beza, and Knox, reformers who had once changed the world.

Elena walked through the park at 1:50 P.M., ten minutes early. Antoine was somewhere nearby—she had spotted him twice, keeping distance, watching. Armed and ready.

The park felt peaceful, safe. International Geneva, where diplomacy happened and wars were prevented through dialogue rather than violence. But Elena knew better. Violence was coming. Mors Rubra—Plague 1. Thousands would die unless they stopped it.

She found an empty bench near the Reformation Wall and sat. At exactly 2:00 P.M., a man approached.

✠ ✠ ✠

Mid-fifties. Gray hair. Lean build. Khakis and a light jacket—casual, forgettable. But his eyes were sharp, the eyes of someone who had seen too much and trusted too little. Valerius.

"Doctor Voss," he said, sitting beside her at a respectful distance. "Thank you for coming."

"You said you could help."

"I can. But first, I owe you an apology." Valerius looked at the Reformation Wall. "My people tried to kill you. The mental torture of your friend... that was excessive. We believed you were working with Guiomar, that you intended to weaponize the plagues from the fragment information."

"I burned them."

"I know." Valerius smiled faintly. "That took courage—or desperation."

"Both."

"And now you have the Babel Codex. Stolen from the Vatican. Very impressive." He turned to her. "May I see it?"

Elena hesitated, then pulled the small leather-bound book from her jacket pocket, keeping it in her own hands. Valerius leaned closer, studying the cover without touching it. The tower symbol. "Remarkable. I've spent twenty years guarding its secret, and you uncovered the Codex itself in weeks."

"Guiomar will find it too, eventually. She'll figure out the hidden message on the fragments' edges, decode the location, and break into the Vatican just like we did."

"Perhaps. But the Vatican knows now. As of this morning they realized the Codex was missing. The shelving has built-in weight sensors—like those grocery self-checkouts that know when you remove an item. The system recorded the book's removal and replacement down to the second. They've tightened security and changed every access protocol. If Guiomar tries again, she'll be caught."

"Good."

"But you don't understand what you have, do you?" Valerius gestured to the Codex. "You've translated most of it—the activation frequencies for Plague 9, the neutralization protocols. But the final page—the symbol, the ancient text—you haven't been able to read it."

"No. It's proto-Sumerian or something older. I don't have the expertise."

"The Guardians do. We've studied this symbol for decades—Babylonian tablets, pre-dynastic Egyptian fragments. Always the same nine points radiating from a center, always tied to plague, to extinction." Valerius pulled out a small notebook and opened it to a page covered in coordinates and city names. "Three years ago, we finally decoded it."

He didn't hand her the notebook yet. "If the tower's nine points are literal, tell me what the northeast spoke would be in modern terms." A test.

Elena stared at the symbol in the Codex, sketched it quickly, then overlaid a mental compass rose. "High latitude, far right... Tokyo."

Valerius handed her the notebook. "Good. Now look."

Nine sets of coordinates. Latitude and longitude. Beside each, a city name in Valerius's cramped handwriting.

"The nine points aren't symbolic," he said. "They're literal GPS coordinates. Each marks a location chosen for maximum-impact deployment—population density, transportation hubs. Whoever created these plagues picked the optimal sites for pandemic spread."

Elena stared at the list:

Point 1: 2.3°S, 28.8°E – Central Africa (Kivu region)

Point 2: 50.9°N, 6.9°E – Cologne, Germany

Point 3: 51.5°N, 0.1°W – London, United Kingdom

Point 4: 40.7°N, 74.0°W – New York City, USA

Point 5: 35.7°N, 139.7°E – Tokyo, Japan
Point 6: 1.3°N, 103.8°E – Singapore
Point 7: 19.4°N, 99.1°W – Mexico City, Mexico
Point 8: 55.8°N, 37.6°E – Moscow, Russia
Point 9: 31.2°N, 121.5°E – Shanghai, China

Nearby, a cyclist clipped the curb and skidded hard. People shouted. Elena flinched, half rising; Antoine appeared from nowhere, hand inside his jacket, then relaxed when the rider stood, embarrassed but unhurt.

Valerius never looked over. "Distractions are a common Guild technique. Stay with me, Doctor Voss."

"Point 1," Elena said, her voice hollow. "Central Africa. Kivu region."

"Yes. Mors Rubra has already been deployed there. A remote village. Testing delivery method. Proving the plague works. Four hundred dead."

"Oh my God—no! Those poor people. Innocent lives... the children." Tears welled in her eyes. She forced herself to stay composed.

Valerius pointed to Point 2. "Cologne. That's next. Plague 2."

"How do you know?"

"Guardian intelligence. We've tracked her operatives. Intercepted communications three days ago. Cologne Christmas market. Sunday late afternoon or early evening. Peak crowd density." Valerius closed the notebook. "She's following the map point by point, building toward Point 9—Shanghai. Plague 9. The Plague of Babel deployed in the world's most populous metropolitan area."

"Then potential worldwide release of the Plague of Babel. How exactly and when we're not yet sure. But Shanghai will be its beta test site, and she won't stop there."

✠ ✠ ✠

Elena felt a shiver climb her spine. Nine cities. Nine plagues. Millions, potentially billions, dead. Guiomar was working methodically, testing each plague, perfecting deployment protocols, building her new world order.

"We know the cities," Elena said, "but not the exact locations within them. Cologne is big. Where in Cologne?"

"The coordinates give a few-kilometer radius. We've narrowed it to the cathedral district, probably the Christmas market. Best guess."

"It's not enough. We need to find her operative and stop the deployment."

"That's why you need institutional support—the WHO, Interpol, German authorities. Surveillance. Intelligence networks. Resources we don't have."

Valerius pulled out his phone and showed her a photograph: a woman, mid-thirties, dark hair, professional appearance.

"Codename Marlene. Former bioweapons researcher. East German background. She'll carry Plague 2—aerosolized dispersal device. Probably disguised—camera, hairspray canister. Inside purse or pocket."

Elena angled her phone and photographed his screen—Marlene's face, the coordinates, the list of cities. Evidence for the WHO.

"How did you decode the symbol?" she asked. "What does the proto-Sumerian text say?"

"A warning. Roughly translated:

'Nine plagues for nine nations. When the ninth falls, the tower crumbles, and voices cease forever.'

"It's not a metaphor. It's a literal instruction set. Deploy these nine plagues at these nine locations. When the ninth falls in Shanghai, humanity loses the ability to function at the cellular level. Mass extinction."

"Then we stop her. We prevent Plague 2. Break her momentum."

"That's the plan. But even if you stop Plague 2, Guiomar has redundancies—backup operatives, alternative methods. She's planned for interference. Stopping one plague won't stop her. You'll need to stop all of them."

"One at a time. Starting with Cologne."

Valerius stood and handed her a business card with a handwritten number on the back. "If you need Guardian support, call this. We have operatives worldwide. Intelligence networks. Resources. We may not agree on everything, but we agree on one thing: Guiomar must be stopped."

Elena took the card. "Why help us now, after trying to kill us?"

"The Guardians were founded to protect the fragments—to keep them separated forever. We never knew where each one rested, only that they existed, hidden through misdirection, bloodlines, and silence. That was our task." His eyes grew distant. "We failed. She has them now and is turning cures into bioengineered plagues. Our only hope is to work with you and your team."

Valerius started to walk away, then turned back. "Dr. Voss. When you present to the WHO tomorrow, show them this." He tapped the notebook. "Nine coordinates. Nine cities."

He rapped Point 1 with his knuckle. "Two weeks ago, a village clinic at 2.3° S, 28.8° E logged forty-three hemorrhage cases in one night. No power. No press. We pulled the nurse's paper ledger ourselves. That's proof. The WHO will have to respond."

"Thank you."

"Don't thank me yet. Thank me when we stop Plague 9." Valerius walked away and disappeared into the park's winding paths.

Elena sat alone on the bench, the Babel Codex in her hands, Valerius's coordinates on her phone. Nine cities. Nine plagues. And they had already lost one.

Her phone vibrated. A text from Antoine:

Clear? Any problems?

All clear. Heading back. I have new intel.

✠ ✠ ✠

She stood and walked back through the park, realizing Valerius and Guiomar were two sides of the same vow—guardians of knowledge, one protecting by concealment, the other by release. Maybe she was no different. Maybe every conviction, carried far enough, became its own kind of madness.

Students still lounged. Tourists still photographed monuments. Normal life continued, unaware that ten thousand people in Cologne would soon be exposed to a weaponized plague unless someone stopped it.

But now they had a map. Nine cities. Nine targets. And proof that Guiomar was following ancient coordinates with terrifying precision.

Back at the hotel, Elena found Antoine and Liam waiting. "What did Valerius say?" Liam asked.

Elena pulled up the photograph on her phone and showed them the nine coordinates. The nine cities.

"Oh, shit," Liam whispered. "London. New York. Tokyo. She's targeting the world's biggest population centers."

"Plague 2 is Cologne. But now we know the pattern. We know where she'll hit next."

Elena opened the Babel Codex to the final page. The nine-pointed symbol. "Each point is a GPS coordinate. Valerius decoded them. Point 1 was Central Africa—a village where four hundred innocent people died—"

"We were too late for Plague 1. Fuck!" Antoine interrupted, a rare flash of emotion. He looked down at the table, then recomposed himself. "Who created this map? How could they have known all this back then?"

"I don't know. But whoever they were, they understood population dynamics and transmission vectors. They chose the optimal sites for maximum pandemic spread. And Guiomar is following their playbook exactly."

✠ ✠ ✠

Antoine studied the list. "If we stop Plague 2 in Cologne, she moves to London for Plague 3. Then New York. Then Tokyo. We're playing defense across the entire planet."

"Then we go on offense. We find Guiomar and stop her before the next deployment."

Elena's phone rang. Durand. "Elena. The WHO wants to meet with you. Tomorrow morning. Geneva headquarters. Bring everything you have: the Codex, the coordinates, all your evidence."

"They believe us?"

"They're taking it seriously. I told them about the African village—four hundred dead from hemorrhagic fever, no known pathogen. That got their attention. When you show them the coordinates match Point 1 exactly, they'll have to respond."

"What about Cologne? Can they mobilize in time?"

"If you convince them tomorrow, yes. The WHO has rapid-response protocols. German authorities will cooperate. But you need to make the case. Show them this isn't a conspiracy theory, that Guiomar is real, the plagues are real, and Plague 2 will be deployed next."

"I will."

"Good luck, Elena. Remember, tomorrow you're presenting to the Director-General, to epidemiologists who've handled Ebola, SARS, COVID. They've seen pandemics, but they've never seen weaponized medieval plagues deployed according to ancient, planned coordinates. Make them believe." He hung up.

"Tomorrow morning. WHO headquarters. We present everything—the Codex, the coordinates, Valerius's intelligence, the operative's photograph. Everything we have."

"And if they don't believe us?" Liam asked.

"Then we go to Cologne ourselves. Find Marlene. Stop Plague 2 however we can," Elena continued. "The WHO is our best chance. They have resources, authority, the ability to mobilize governments. If they believe us, we can stop not just Plague 2, but all of them."

✠ ✠ ✠

"That's a big if," Antoine said.

The clock was ticking.

Now they had to convince the World Health Organization that eight more ancient plagues were about to be deployed across eight remaining densely populated metropolitan areas.

That four hundred people in Africa were just the beginning, and that Guiomar was following a centuries-old map aimed at worldwide extinction—a "cleansing," she called it.

The WHO either believed them, or it didn't.

Tomorrow they would find out if the world's leading health organization could stop what was coming.

26 - Synthesis

The World Health Organization Headquarters
Geneva, Switzerland
Elena stood outside the conference room; the Babel Codex tucked inside her jacket like a second heart.

Inside waited the Director-General, chief epidemiologist, bioterrorism coordinator, Interpol, German BKA, Swiss police—and Inspector Durand, who had made this meeting possible.

Antoine stood beside her. Liam hovered behind, laptop ready with every fragment photograph backed up and encrypted.

"You ready?" Antoine asked.

"No. But we're doing it anyway."

"That's becoming our motto."

Elena drew a breath and stepped inside.

The room was large, glass-walled, world maps glowing on perimeter screens. Fifteen people watched her, deciding if she was credible or insane.

"Doctor Voss," Director-General Rajesh Kumar said—older, Indian accent, kind eyes, hard expression. "Inspector Durand has briefed us. Your claims are extraordinary. Medieval plagues. Ancient coordinates. Weaponized cures. We need proof. Concrete and verifiable."

Elena set the Codex on the table. "Yes. I can give you that." She connected Liam's laptop. The main screen filled with nine ancient fragments.

"Six weeks ago, a courier left a leather satchel at my hotel in Lisbon. Inside the lining I found this."

Fragment 1 appeared—an ancient vellum, Latin text, medical formulas.

"At first, I thought it described a medieval bio-weapon. Hemorrhagic fever. Synthesis instructions. Nine fragments hidden across Portugal. Each seemed to describe a deadlier plague. Each contained a riddle leading to the next fragment. I decoded them all."

She displayed the nine fragments side by side.

"Nine plagues. Or so I believed—until Valerius, leader of the Guardians, told me the truth."

"What truth?" Kumar asked.

"They were cures." Elena let it land. "Nine medical breakthroughs centuries ahead of their time. Hidden by the Templars, protected by the Guardians ever since."

Dr. Sarah Chen leant forward. "Cures?"

"Yes. Fragment 1 contained the cure for hemorrhagic fever. Fragment 2 cured respiratory plague, continuing all the way to Fragment 9, which cured a DNA transcription plague. Someone in the Middle Ages understood molecular biology better than we do today."

"Then why are people dying?" Kommissar Bauer asked.

"Because Isabella Guiomar is using the information contained within the fragments to create biological weapons. She leads the Guild of Shadows. They murdered my mentor Doctor Almeida of Oxford when he got too close. Then someone—still unknown—sent me the first fragment, and I collected the rest. When I realized what they Guiomar intends to do with them, I burned the originals."

"But?" Kumar prompted.

"But Guiomar already had perfect digital copies—stolen from Liam's camera memory card." Elena gestured to Liam; he stared at the floor, guilt raw. "She is turning medicine into bioweapons. Cure becomes pathogen."

She displayed the African village photographs—bodies in biohazard bags.

"Two weeks ago, four hundred died in the Kivu region. Hemorrhagic fever. Unknown pathogen. Dr. Chen, your team investigated."

Chen nodded slowly. "We never identified it."

"It was Plague 1. Deployed exactly where this map predicted." Elena opened the Codex to the final page—the nine-pointed symbol.

"This is the deployment map. Hidden on the fragments' edges. Visible only when all nine are assembled. Nine GPS coordinates. Chosen centuries ago, for maximum pandemic impact and spread."

She overlaid Valerius's list. Point 1 matched the village precisely.

"That is proof."

The room erupted in low, urgent conversation.

"Where did the map come from?" Kumar asked.

"The last page of the Babel Codex. Stolen from the Vatican Secret Archives. I stole it two days ago." Elena showed the physical book. "It contains the deployment plan—and the only known counteragent for Plague 9."

Gasps. The Interpol representative half-rose. "You stole from the Vatican? You should be arrested—"

Durand cut in. "Please. We need her help to catch Guiomar, then we can investigate the other related crimes."

Elena displayed the nine cities:

Point 1: Central Africa

Point 2: Cologne, Germany
Point 3: London
Point 4: New York City
Point 5: Tokyo
Point 6: Singapore
Point 7: Mexico City
Point 8: Moscow
Point 9: Shanghai

"Point 1 already happened. Four hundred dead, exactly where the map predicted. Point 2 is next. Cologne."

The room fell silent.

"How do you know?" Bauer asked.

"Guardian intelligence. The organization that's been protecting these fragments has been tracking Guiomar. They intercepted communications. Cologne. The Christmas market. Roughly thirty-six hours from now. Peak crowd density." Elena pulled up the photograph Valerius had given her.

"This woman. Codename Marlene. Real name possibly Anneliese Vogel. Former East German. Biochemistry background. Formerly with the BND biodefense program before she disappeared three years ago. She's the operative assigned to the Cologne deployment."

Bauer studied the photograph. "We can work with this."

"She'll be carrying an aerosol canister," Elena continued. "Probably disguised as something innocuous. Perfume. Hairspray. Something that wouldn't attract attention. She'll spray it into the crowd. Maximum foot traffic. Optimal dispersal. Then she disappears as quickly as she came."

"Casualties?" Dr. Chen asked.

"Potentially ten thousand initial infections within twelve hours. Respiratory plague. Airborne transmission.

Incubation: six hours. Symptoms: twelve hours. Death: forty-eight hours."

"Treatment?"

"There isn't one. The formula was designed to evade an immune response. Guiomar made them resistant to the very antibodies they were designed to create." Elena opened the Codex to the middle pages, the content on neutralizing the Babel Plague. "This is our only hope. A counteragent that can reverse DNA transcription corruption. But it only works for Plague 9. The worst one. Not the others."

"If Marlene successfully deploys Plague 2—"

"We can't cure it. We can only contain it. Quarantine. Try to prevent secondary transmission." Elena looked around the room. "That's why we must stop the deployment. Because once Plague 2 is released, thousands of people will die. And there's nothing we can do to save them."

Inspector Durand stood. "I've worked with Doctor Voss for three weeks and have investigated Doctor Almeida's murder. I've verified her research. The Vatican confirms the Babel Codex was stolen—this evidence is real. Portuguese police can confirm the break-ins where fragments were recovered. The African village outbreak matches Point 1 on this map exactly. This isn't theory. Four hundred people are already dead. And potentially ten thousand more will die unless we act now."

Dr. Kumar looked around the room. At his staff. At Interpol. At the German BKA. At Elena.

"If we mobilize and you're wrong, we waste resources and money. Create panic. Damage the WHO's credibility." He paused. "But if we don't mobilize, and you're right, thousands of people die. Maybe more."

He turned to Bauer. "Can German authorities secure the Cologne Christmas market? Increase surveillance? Prepare for a potential bioterror event?"

"Yes. Additional police presence. Undercover surveillance. Facial recognition at market entrances. If this operative is there, we'll find her."

"Do it." Dr. Kumar looked at Dr. Chen. "The Rapid Response team deploys to Cologne immediately. Doctor Voss and her colleagues go with you. If deployment occurs despite prevention efforts, we'll need their expertise."

"Understood."

Dr. Kumar stood. "We mobilize. Full protocols. This is a credible bioterror threat. If Doctor Voss is wrong, we've been overly cautious. If she's right..." He looked at the nine-pointed symbol on the screen. "If she's right, this is only the second of nine plagues. And we're already behind the eight ball."

He looked at Elena. "You decoded nine cures that became nine weapons. Now help us stop them before it's too late.

"I will."

"Let's go to Cologne."

En Route to Cologne

Three WHO vehicles left Geneva in convoy: two marked SUVs, one unmarked van carrying containment gear and a mobile lab.

Elena rode in the lead vehicle with Dr. Chen, Antoine, and Liam.

Chen gripped the wheel. "Walk me through Plague 2. Symptoms. Progression."

Elena opened her notebook. "*Pestis Secunda—Respiratoria.* The Burning."

"Initial infection is respiratory. Inhalation of an aerosolized pathogen. The particles are engineered to penetrate deep into lung tissue and cross into the bloodstream within minutes. Six hours post-exposure: patients are asymptomatic but highly contagious through respiratory droplets. Twelve hours: fever, cough, difficulty breathing—pneumonia-like onset. Twenty-four hours: acute respiratory distress, lung tissue degradation, internal bleeding. Forty-eight hours: death in ninety-eight percent of cases."

Chen grabbed the steering wheel tighter. "And we can't treat it?"

"No. The pathogen was originally designed as a cure to interact with specific immune markers. But Guiomar's scientist reversed it. Made it attack instead of healing. By the time antibodies form, the damage is irreversible." Elena closed her notebook. "The only hope is prevention. Stop deployment. Or if deployment succeeds, immediate quarantine. Prevent secondary transmission. Contain the outbreak to the initial exposure victims."

"Ten thousand people," Chen said. "That's extensive containment."

"I know."

They drove in silence for a while. The Swiss countryside passes. Mountains. Lakes. Villages. Normal life continued, unaware that three vehicles were racing to prevent a plague deployment.

"Why Cologne?" Liam asked from the back seat. "Why that specific city?"

"The coordinates," Elena said. "Whoever created the nine-pointed map chose optimal sites for pandemic spread. Cologne is a major transportation hub. Rail. Air. River traffic on the Rhine. Dense population. International tourism. If you wanted to deploy a respiratory plague in Europe, Cologne is the place to do it. And the Christmas market maximizes exposure. Thousands of people in enclosed spaces. Cold weather means closed environments. Perfect conditions for airborne transmission."

"And Guiomar is following the map exactly," Antoine added. "She's not improvising. She's executing a plan that's centuries old. Maybe millennia old."

"Which means we know where she'll hit next," Chen said. "London. Point 3. When?"

"We don't know the timeline. Plague 1 was two weeks ago. Plague 2 is tomorrow. That's roughly fourteen days between deployments. If she maintains that pace, London would be fourteen days after Cologne. But her scientist is likely accelerating production, since we stopped Plague 2's deployment. She could deploy Plague 3 within days."

"Then stopping Plague 2 doesn't end this."

"No. It just buys us time. Time to find the laboratory. Time to destroy the source. Time to stop Guiomar before she reaches Shanghai." Elena looked out the window. "Plague 9. The Plague of Babel. If that deploys, it doesn't kill a city. It kills a species."

Chen was quiet for a moment. "The neutralization protocol in the Babel Codex. Can it be synthesized? Produced at scale?"

"Theoretically, yes. But it requires specific protein sequences. Electromagnetic activation frequencies. Laboratory synthesis could take weeks. Mass production, months. And it must be administered within hours of exposure to be effective." Elena shook her head. "If Plague 9 deploys in Shanghai—twenty-four million people— we'd need to synthesize and distribute neutralization faster than any pharmaceutical company has ever moved in history. We'd save some. Not everyone."

"Then we don't let it get to Shanghai."

"That's the plan."

The vehicles crossed the border into Germany. Highway signs in German now. Karlsruhe. Mannheim. Cologne. 280 kilometers remaining. Elena checked her watch.

The countdown continued. Every minute brought them closer to Cologne. Every minute brought Marlene closer to deployment.

On Elena's phone—a text message arrives.

Dr. Voss.

I hope you're ready for tomorrow. Cologne will be the proof. The second drop from the Black Chalice. Sleep well—G.

Guiomar.

Elena showed the message to Chen and Antoine.

"She knows you're coming," Chen said.

"She's taunting us," Antoine added.

"She's confident," Elena replied. "She thinks we'll fail."

"Then we'll prove her wrong."

Elena stared at the message. The casualness of it. The certainty. Guiomar wasn't worried about the WHO mobilizing. She wasn't concerned about the German police. She believed Marlene would succeed. Because she'd planned for everything. Backup operatives. Contingencies. Redundancies. Stopping one plague wouldn't stop Guiomar. But it was a start. Elena put away her phone. Tomorrow, they'd find out if it was enough.

Cologne, Germany

Population: 1.1 Million

Saturday morning.

The city was beautiful. Medieval architecture lit up for Christmas. The cathedral's twin spires rising against the darkening sky—Gothic stone that had stood for centuries. The Christmas markets sprawled around it. Wooden stalls selling ornaments, food, and mulled wine. Lights strung everywhere. Festive music. Families walking.

Children excited. The smell of roasted almonds and sausages.

Thousands of people are moving through the markets. Laughing. Shopping. Living. Not knowing that tomorrow, death would walk among them.

The WHO convoy pulled into a secure facility—BKA regional headquarters, two blocks from the cathedral. Kommissar Bauer met them at the entrance. Early fifties. Dark hair, military cut. The look of a man who'd dealt with terrorism before.

"Doctor Voss. Doctor Chen. Welcome to Cologne. We have a command center set up. Surveillance teams are deploying across the market area. Facial recognition is active at major entrances. If your operative enters the markets, we'll find her."

They followed Bauer inside. Upstairs, into a large room filled with monitors. Live feeds from dozens of cameras utilizing thermal imaging. Radio chatter from undercover teams. A dozen BKA analysts are working on computers. Coordinating.

A map of the cathedral district covered one wall. The Christmas market stalls are marked in red. Entrances highlighted. High-traffic zones circled. "She'll probably strike here," Bauer said, pointing to the cathedral entrance area. "Maximum foot traffic and optimal dispersal. If I were deploying an aerosol pathogen, that's where I'd do it."

"How many people pass through there daily?" Chen asked.

"During the Christmas season? Fifteen thousand. More on weekends."

"And tomorrow is Sunday."

"Yes. Peak attendance." Bauer pulled up surveillance footage. Crowds moving through the markets. Families. Tourists. Locals. "We have forty officers in the markets currently. Undercover. Watching. Tomorrow, we double that number. Eighty officers plus the facial recognition. Our mobile response units are positioned around the perimeter. If Marlene appears, we'll have her within minutes."

"She won't come alone," Antoine said. "Guild operatives typically work in teams. Backup. Countersurveillance. If you move on her, others will intervene."

"Then we'll be ready for that too." Bauer gestured to the screens. "We've coordinated with Interpol. They've flagged known Guild associates. If any appear in Cologne, we'll know."

"Why not just shut down the entire Christmas market?" Liam asked. "Better that than people dying, right?"

"I wish it were that easy," Antoine said. "Guiomar would just choose another site for the deployment—and then we'd have no idea where the new one was."

Liam nodded. "At least if she follows the map, we have a chance at stopping her. A small one, but still a chance."

"Yes. We do."

Elena studied the map. The cathedral, markets, and crowds. Tomorrow, Marlene would walk into this area carrying death in her pocket. Ten seconds. One spray. Ten thousand deaths.

"I want to walk the market," Elena said. "Tonight. See the layout. Understand the space. If I'm going to help tomorrow, I need to know what we're working with."

Bauer nodded. "I'll assign protection. Two undercovers, you won't see them, but they'll be close."

"Thank you."

Elena, Antoine, and Liam left the command center and walked toward the cathedral. The Christmas market was still open and would be until midnight. They moved through the crowds. Stalls selling ornaments. Wooden toys. Candles. Hot chocolate. Gingerbread houses. Music playing. Children laughing. Normal. Peaceful. Beautiful. And tomorrow, it would become a plague site.

Elena stopped near the cathedral entrance and looked up at the Gothic spires, black against the clouds. Construction had begun in 1248 and taken more than six centuries to complete.

It had survived wars and plagues. It had withstood fire and catapulted stones. It had endured bombs that fell from the heavens and kings that fell from their thrones. It had stood while empires rose—and it had stood when they turned to dust.

And tomorrow, death would rise again in its shadow.

It would survive.

People would not.

"We're going to stop this," Antoine said beside her.

"I hope so."

"We will. Tomorrow, we find Marlene. We stop Plague 2. And then we find the laboratory. End this before Plague 3 is disbursed." Elena wanted to believe him. But she'd seen Guiomar's precision. Her planning. Her resources.

She turned from the cathedral and walked back through the markets. Vendors were closing stalls. Families heading home. The crowds were thinning.

Tomorrow, they'd return. Thousands of them. For one more day of Christmas shopping. One more day of normal life. Elena would be there too. Hunting a killer in a crowd. Racing to stop a plague before it began.

Elena spent the night at the command center reviewing surveillance footage. Studying Marlene's photograph. Memorizing her face, her walk. The way she held herself. The intelligence Valerius had provided described her as disciplined. Patient. Trained. She wouldn't make mistakes. Which meant they had to be perfect. The markets open today at 11 AM. Marlene would come sometime between then and late evening. Peak crowds. Maximum exposure.

Elena drank coffee and stared at the screens. She watched as early-morning street cleaners prepared the market area. Vendors setting up stalls. A beautiful city was about to become a horrible nightmare.

Dr. Chen entered the command center. She'd slept for about three hours. More than Elena. "Surveillance teams are in position. Facial recognition is active. BKA has two hundred officers deployed—half in markets, half in mobile response units. All are waiting for Marlene's appearance."

"And if she doesn't show?" Liam asked. He'd managed a few hours of sleep too. He looked slightly more human than Elena felt.

"Then either our intelligence was wrong, or she's better at evading detection than we anticipated." Chen looked at the screens. "Either way, we'll know soon enough."

✠ ✠ ✠

Elena's phone —text message.

The Black Chalice tips. The second drop falls. Watch closely, Dr. Voss. You might learn something—G.

Elena showed it to Chen and Bauer. "She's watching us," Bauer said. "She knows we're here and knows we're waiting."

"Then she knows we're serious," Elena replied. "Maybe that makes her reconsider."

"Or maybe it makes her more determined."

Antoine appeared in the doorway. He'd been checking perimeter security with the BKA teams. "Guiomar won't back down. If anything, our presence confirms she's winning. She's forcing us to react—to mobilize—to watch her victory."

"Then we take away her victory," Elena snapped. "Let's find Marlene. Dammit! No more chasing her shadow. I'm sick of this cat-and-mouse game."

The sun rose over Cologne. Light spreads across the cathedral. Across a city that didn't know what was coming.

Crowds poured in—families, tourists, locals. Thousands moved through the wooden stalls, buying ornaments, tasting roasted almonds, eating gingerbread cookies and smoked sausages. Children playing.

A saxophone played in the distance—*O Come, All Ye Faithful*. The air was rich with the scent of roasted chestnuts and toasted pretzels. For a moment, it felt like New York City—street vendors in winter, the hum of the city dressed for Christmas—decorated store windows.

Here in Cologne, people are laughing. Enjoying Christmas. They didn't know that somewhere in this crowd an assassin walked among them. Elena stood in the command center, watching dozens of screens. Each one shows a different angle of the markets. BKA officers are in position. Undercover. Watching for Marlene.

The Facial recognition software was scanning every face. Comparing images to Marlene's photograph. Thousands of people per hour. Millions of data points. Algorithms searching.

Nothing yet.

"She could already be in position," Bauer said. "Arrived early. Found a spot. Waiting for peak crowd density."

"Then we keep watching," Elena said.

The hours crawled. Crowds growing. More families. More tourists. The markets are packed now. Shoulder to shoulder. The smell of food. The sound of music. Christmas in Cologne. Beautiful.

The light was fading. Evening was approaching. The crowds were at their peak. Fifteen thousand people crowded the cathedral district. The optimal deployment window.

If Marlene were coming, it would be soon.

Elena's eyes burned from staring at screens. Coffee had stopped helping hours ago. But she couldn't look away. Couldn't miss the moment.

"Wait," one of the BKA analysts said. "Camera 7. Near the cathedral entrance." The screen zoomed in. A woman. Mid-thirties. Dark hair. Wearing a gray winter coat, moving through the crowd. Confident. Purposeful. The facial recognition software flagged her with an 87% match to Marlene's photograph.

"That's her," Elena said.

Bauer was already on the radio. "All units. Suspect identified. Camera 7. Cathedral entrance. Dark hair. Gray winter coat. Move to intercept. Do not let her reach the deployment zone."

On the screens, undercover officers rapidly converged, moving hastily through crowds. Closing in. Marlene stopped near a wine stall, reaching into her coat pocket.

"She's going for the canister," Chen said.

"Stop her," Bauer ordered. "Now!"

Two officers moved in. Fast. Professional. They grabbed Marlene from behind and restrained her. She struggled and fought, but they held her. Other officers surrounded them and created a perimeter, moving the crowd back.

Bauer spoke into his radio. "Suspect in custody. Secure the device. Biosafety protocols." A hazmat team moved in quickly and carefully removed the canister from Marlene's pocket, placing it in a containment case. Sealed it.

The markets continued with festivity around them. Most people hadn't noticed, it was just another drunk tourist being escorted out. Security handling a problem. They had no idea they'd just avoided dying a horrific death.

Elena continued watching the screens. She watched Marlene being led away in restraints while the hazmat team secured the canister. People continuing to shop. They'd done it. They'd stopped Plague 2's deployment, *Pestis Secunda: Respiratoria.*

"We got her," Liam said. Disbelief in his voice. "We actually got her."

"We got one operative," Antoine corrected. "Guiomar has more."

"True. But today we saved thousands of lives—men, women, children, grandchildren."

Elena looked at the nine-pointed map on the wall. Point 2. Cologne, a bright red X over it now. Stopped. But seven more points remained. Seven more deployments. London. New York. Tokyo. Singapore. Mexico City. Moscow. Shanghai.

Elena's phone vibrated again, with a text message.

Well done, Dr. Voss. You saved Cologne. Enjoy your victory. London deploys in three days. Let's see if you can stop that one. I love a good game of cat and mouse, so much fun! —G.

They both wanted to save the world—one by curing it, one by burning the sickness out of it.

Three days until Plague 3 is deployed.

Guiomar was accelerating the timeline.

The race had just begun.

27 - The Prisoner

Saturday, 5:15 PM — BKA Regional HQ, Cologne
72 hours until Plague 3 deploys in London

Marlene sat in the detention cell, hands cuffed behind her back. Two guards were outside the reinforced door. She hadn't spoken since her arrest forty-five minutes ago. Hadn't resisted beyond the initial struggle. Just silence. Compliant. Professional.

The silence worried Elena more than any outburst would have.

In the observation room Elena stood with Dr. Chen, Kommissar Bauer, Liam, and Antoine, watching through one-way glass while officers processed the prisoner: fingerprints, photographs, DNA swab, biometric scans.

They emptied her pockets and laid each item on the metal table. A folded respirator, a fake ID, and a white unlabeled pill bottle with six chalky tablets. Nothing looked innocent.

"She's not afraid," Elena said quietly.

"She should be," Bauer replied. "German law lets us hold her forty-eight hours without charges. After that we need evidence, or she walks."

"The canister—"

"Is at the WHO lab. Until they confirm what's inside, we have almost nothing. Her lawyer will claim it was perfume. That we panicked."

Elena pictured the market again—the woman with the red scarf who had thanked her for a dropped glove, the boy licking ice cream, the blind man with his German shepherd. Ordinary lives that would have ended in days. Faces, not numbers.

Bauer's jaw tightened. "Forty-eight hours to build an airtight case, or the Guild sends a very good lawyer and she's free."

"She expected capture," Antoine said. "This doesn't surprise her."

"Guild operatives train for it," Chen added. "Interrogation resistance. Legal protocols. They stay silent until extraction or release."

"Then we make her talk," Bauer said. "Find the laboratory. The scientist. The next deployments." He turned to Elena. "Doctor Voss, I want you in the room. You understand the plagues better than anyone. You might catch something she lets slip—or doesn't."

✠ ✠ ✠

Elena nodded and followed him out.

The interrogation room was small, gray, the table bolted to the floor with four bright bolts. A camera recorded everything.

"Geneva Convention protocols are clear: no coercion, no torture. We ask questions—nothing more. Everything stays by the book." Bauer insisted, as they entered the room.

Marlene sat uncuffed now—a gesture of goodwill. Her hands rested calmly on the table. Bauer sat opposite. Elena took position against the wall.

"Ms. Fischer," Bauer began. "Or should I say Anneliese Vogel?"

No reaction.

"You were apprehended at 4:42 PM today at the Cologne Christmas market. In your possession: an aerosol canister containing an unknown substance. You were observed reaching for that canister in a crowded public space. Explain."

Silence.

"We believe the canister contains a weaponized pathogen intended to kill thousands. Were you planning to deploy it?"

Marlene's eyes stayed flat.

"Who is Isabella Guiomar?"

Nothing.

"Where is the laboratory synthesizing these plagues?"

No answer.

Marlene spoke one word, calm and clear.

"Lawyer."

Bauer leaned back. "You have that right. But you also have an obligation—"

"Lawyer," she repeated, louder this time.

"Ms. Vogel, over fifteen thousand people were present at that Christmas market. Families. Children. You were going to kill them. Help us understand why."

Bauer's voice caught on *children*. Elena saw his hand tremble once before he clenched it beneath the table. Even a seasoned detective wasn't immune to imagining the faces.

Marlene looked at him—eyes flat, empty. "I want a lawyer. Until then, I have nothing to say."

Bauer stood. Gestured to Elena. They left.

Back in observation, Bauer slammed a fist on the desk. "She'll give us nothing until counsel arrives. Then she'll give even less."

How long?" Antoine asked.

"An hour. Maybe less. The Guild doesn't waste time." Bauer stared at Marlene through the glass. She sat perfectly still, meditative. "Eighteen hours minimum for the WHO analysis. If we can't prove the canister is a bioweapon, Steiner gets her released."

Elena watched Marlene. The woman believed she would walk. That meant the Guild had contingencies—legal, extraction, both.

"She's ideological," Elena said. "Not a mercenary. Revenge for her father. The state that killed him. Money won't turn her. Reduced sentence won't. She's ready to die for this."

"Then we build the case without her," Chen said. "The pathogen will talk. Synthetic biology leaves signatures."

Bauer nodded. "I'll push the lab again. And we tear her life apart—every record, every contact."

"I'll help," Antoine said.

✠ ✠ ✠

Bauer gestured toward a side office. "I know you're former DGSE. I spoke with Colonel Laurent Delacroix, your former commander at the Directorate. You have clearance. The intelligence terminal is through there—it's a secure network. You'll have access to Interpol, BND, and Europol databases. Pull everything on Anneliese Vogel—aliases, known associates. Build me a file I can use in court."

Antoine left. Elena and Liam stayed, watching Marlene through the glass.

Dr. Chen stood beside them, glancing at Elena. "You're thinking about London."

"Guiomar mentioned three days. If Marlene was the Plague 2 operative, someone else is the operative for Plague 3. Elena pulled out her phone and reviewed the nine-point map. "London is Point 3. Where in London? Trafalgar Square? Piccadilly? The Tube?"

"We'll coordinate with British authorities. MI5. Scotland Yard. Warn them."

"Will they believe us?"

"Yes, they'll believe us, and they'll mobilize. But London is a lot bigger than Cologne. Nearly ten million people live and work there, not even including the visitors. Finding one operative in a city that size..." She shook her head. "It's going to be much more difficult."

"We need to find the lab and stop Plague 3 from leaving wherever it's being made."

"Yes. We should analyze that canister and identify the scientist who synthesized it. We track them down before London."

Elena turned from the glass. "Marlene won't talk. But the pathogen will. Synthetic biology always leaves signatures. Whoever created Plague 2 left clues in their work—we just need to find them."

At the BKA Intelligence office, Antoine started the search for information, "Birth records," He mumbled to himself. "Build the profile from the beginning. Everything about Anneliese Vogel. Who she was. How she became Marlene."

He typed: VOGEL, ANNELIESE. BERLIN, GERMANY. FEMALE. APPROXIMATE AGE: MID-30s.

The database processed the query. A list of matches appeared—five names, one flagged by Interpol cross-reference. He opened it.

Date of birth: 15 March 1988. Berlin. The file expanded: official records, school transcripts, medical history—everything the German government had ever logged about her.

Antoine opened the first file. Birth certificate.

Name: Anneliese Vogel Born: March 15, 1988
Birth Location: East Berlin, German Democratic Republic
Father: Klaus Vogel
Mother: Petra Vogel (née Schmidt)

Liam walked in, glancing over his shoulder.

"You're not supposed to be in here." Antoine said.

He shrugged. "East Berlin. Born before the wall fell."

"Barely. She was eighteen months old when it came down, but old enough to remember the chaos afterwards."

Antoine pulled up the father's file. Klaus Vogel. "Stasi officer. Secret police. One of the worst."

The file detailed Klaus Vogel's career. Surveillance operations. Interrogations. Disappearances. He'd been responsible for monitoring dissidents. Suppressing opposition. Enforcing the regime's control. When the Berlin Wall fell in November 1989, the Stasi collapsed. Officers were arrested and tried for crimes against humanity. Klaus Vogel was among them.

Arrested: January 1991
Charges: Crimes against the state (West Germany), unlawful detention, torture
Trial: Pending
Outcome: Died in custody, April 1993
Cause of death: Suicide by hanging

"Official cause: suicide," Antoine said. "But look at this." He pulled up an investigative report from 1993. Journalists questioning the death. Witnesses claiming Klaus Vogel had been beaten by guards and that his death wasn't suicide but murder.

"They killed her father," Liam said quietly.

"Or he killed himself. Either way, Anneliese lost him when she was only five years old. She never believed the official story."

Antoine pulled up psychiatric reports from Anneliese's teenage years, along with school-counselor notes. Behavioral flags.

- *Age 13: Persistent anger toward authority. Marked difficulty with trust.*
- *Age 15: Submitted an essay titled "The Lie of Justice"— explicit themes of state corruption.*
- *Age 17: Academically exceptional; socially isolated. Counselor recommends continued monitoring.*

"She was brilliant," Liam said, scrolling through her academic records. "Top marks in chemistry, biology, mathematics. Leipzig International gave her a full scholarship."

"Humboldt University too," Antoine added. "Biochemistry. Graduated summa cum laude. Her thesis was on synthetic pathogens."

He opened the abstract. "Listen to this:
'Modern biological defense requires understanding offensive capabilities. This thesis explores reverse-engineering pathogen synthesis to better develop countermeasures.'"

"She was learning how to build bioweapons while claiming she wanted to stop them."

"Maybe she did want to stop them." Antoine switched windows. "But the Guild noticed her potential." He opened BND recruitment logs. "German intelligence picked her up straight out of her PhD program in 2013. Biodefense division. Her job was identifying engineered pathogens and neutralizing biological threats."

"What happened?"

"She excelled—for five years. Exceptional performance reviews." Antoine pulled up a psychological evaluation stamped 2017.

Subject displays growing anti-authoritarian sentiment. Unresolved questions regarding father's death persist. Recommend monitoring for radicalization risk.

"They saw it coming," Liam said.

"But they didn't stop her. Or couldn't." Antoine scrolled to 2018.

"She attended a biodefense conference in Prague. August 2018. Never returned to work. BND launched an investigation and found nothing.

She'd simply disappeared."

"The Guild took her."

"Or she went willingly." Antoine pulled up Interpol sightings with unconfirmed photographs.

Moscow, 2019. Belgrade, 2020. Istanbul, 2021. "She was being trained. Learning about operational security and how to evade surveillance. Along with how to deploy biological agents offensively instead of defensively."

"And then she became Marlene."

"First use of the alias was 2021. Guild operations. Weapons trafficking in Eastern Europe. Nothing biological yet, just groundwork, gaining expertise. Making her almost invisible."

Antoine pulled up the most recent file. "Flagged as a Guild operative in 2022. High-priority target. But no confirmed locations. No sightings, until today."

Liam leaned back. "She spent her whole life preparing for this. Her father's death drove her. Her education gave her skills. The BND gave her access. And the Guild gave her purpose."

"Revenge," Antoine said. "That's what this is. She's not killing for ideology alone. She's killing for her father. For the injustice she believes the state committed.

Cologne wasn't just a deployment.

It was punishment."

He compiled the files. Organized them chronologically. Birth. Childhood. Education. Recruitment. Disappearance. Radicalization. Guild training. Present day. A complete profile of how Anneliese Vogel became Marlene.

✠ ✠ ✠

"Will this help Bauer build a case?" Liam asked.

"It proves she has the skills and the motive, along with the training. Combined with the canister, it's enough to hold her." Antoine saved the files. "But it won't make her talk. She's committed, and nothing we show her will change that."

The lawyer arrived a short time later—tall, mid-forties. Swiss accent. Expensive. Confident.

"He's, her lawyer?" Elena asked.

"Yes. Dr. Heinrich Steiner," Bauer said. "Zurich-based. International law specialist. He defends high-profile terrorism cases, and he's very good. The Guild sent him."

Dr. Steiner entered the interrogation room, speaking quietly to Marlene in German. He opened his briefcase, pulling out documents. Legal briefs. Case precedents. After ten minutes, Steiner stood and walked to the door. Knocked. Bauer entered.

"Kommissar," Steiner said. "My client is invoking her right to silence under Article 6 of the European Convention on Human Rights. She will not answer any questions without verifiable evidence of wrongdoing. You have detained her without formal charges, with no proof that the item confiscated poses any danger to the public. I'm demanding her immediate release."

"She was carrying a canister containing an unknown substance ready to deploy it in a crowded public space—"

"Unknown substance," Steiner cut in. "Meaning you don't know what it is. You have no proof it's dangerous. For all you know, it's perfume. Hairspray. An inhalable steroid for asthma. You've detained my client for carrying an aerosol canister. That's not terrorism, Kommissar. That's overreach."

"We have reason to believe—"

"Belief is not evidence. Analyze the canister. Prove it's dangerous. Until then, my client is being unlawfully detained.

Steiner returned to the interrogation room and sat beside Marlene, whispering something into her ear. She nodded.

Bauer walked back into the intelligence office and fixed his eyes on Antoine. "Tell me you found something. Anything."

Antoine handed him a tablet. "It's all here—birth records, her father's death, education, BND recruitment, disappearance, Guild training. She has the skills, the motive, and the connections. This proves she's capable of deploying a bioweapon."

Bauer scrolled through the profile, jaw tightening. "It's good. Excellent. But capability isn't proof. Steiner will argue she was at the market to shop. That the canister is harmless. That we're profiling her based on her past." He set the tablet down. "We need the pathogen analysis. It's the only thing that holds up."

"Then we wait," Elena said.

"And pray the WHO works fast."

✠ ✠ ✠

Marlene sat alone in her cell, eyes closed, breathing steady. She had been trained for this. The Guild always had extraction plans. She believed she would walk.

She pictured London. Plague 3 on schedule.

Cologne had been stopped. London would not.

Elena sat in the command center staring at Marlene's empty cell feed while others slept on cots.

London was coming.

A text message arrived.

You stopped Marlene. Well done. But there are others. London will not be stopped so easily. Enjoy your small victory, Dr. Voss. Because it's the only one you'll have—G.

Elena closed her eyes and saw them—the street musician with his saxophone, the food vendor with the hot pretzels, a girl clutching a balloon from the market stall. All breathing the same invisible death.

28 - The Laboratory

Sunday, 10:00 AM
WHO Mobile Laboratory Unit, Cologne

The mobile laboratory was a sealed fortress: negative-pressure chambers, HEPA filtration, BSL-4 protocols glowing red on every door. HEPA filtration. BSL-4 protocols. The kind of space designed to contain the world's deadliest pathogens.

Dr. Sarah Chen stood in the airlock, already suited—blue positive-pressure hazmat, face shield fogging faintly. Beside her, Dr. Klaus Hoffmann and Dr. Yuki Tanaka, veterans of Ebola, SARS, and COVID. They had opened lethal packages before. Never one like this.

Elena watched from observation, Antoine and Liam at her sides. Liam documenting everything with his camera. Standard procedure. Record the analysis. Preserve evidence.

The matte-black canister sat on the stainless table. Eight centimeters tall. Forty milliliters of clear death.

"Beginning external examination," Chen said, voice calm through the speakers. "Standard commercial dispenser. No markings, no serials."

She picked it up carefully. Examined it under magnification. "Intentionally anonymous."

"Fingerprint analysis?" Elena asked through the intercom.

"Already completed by BKA forensics. Three sets of prints. Primary set matches Marlene Fischer slash Anneliese Vogel. Secondary set unknown—possibly the manufacturer. Tertiary set partial, unusable."

Chen positioned the canister inside a sealed glass containment box. She reached through the box's built-in gloves and gripped the canister. Slowly twisting the top. It opened easily.

Elena held her breath.

Chen carefully removed the aerosol mechanism. Set it aside. Lifted the canister. Tilted it slightly. Clear liquid inside. No color. No visible particles. Like water.

"Liquid appears stable," Chen said. "No immediate off-gassing. No odor detectable through equipment." She transferred a small sample—one milliliter—into a sterile vial. Sealed it. "Sample secured for analysis.

Beginning microscopic examination."

Chen placed the drop on the slide, lowered the cover slip, and slid it under the electron microscope.

"Low mag first," she murmured.

A soft click as the system engaged.

First jump—5,000x.

A grainy landscape came into view: scattered particulate, dried structures, the faint suggestion of viral density.

"Mid-level." She increased magnification.

Second jump—20,000x.

Spheres emerged. Too uniform. Too regular.

Elena leaned closer.

"One more," Chen said.

Final jump—120,000x.

The image bloomed. Capsids snapped into crisp focus—perfect geometry, engineered symmetry, protein coats like machined shells. A flurry of activity shimmered across the screen: structures flexing, proteins binding, replication nodes firing in coordinated bursts.

✠ ✠ ✠

"A point-five–micron particle," Chen whispered. "Optimized for aerosol transmission. Deep lung penetration. This isn't natural."

A living storm—designed.

"Can you identify it?" Antoine asked.

"Not yet. Running comparative analysis now." Chen transferred the sample to a genomic sequencing machine. "This will take approximately six hours. But initial visual examination suggests this is entirely novel. Not in any database. Not related to any known pathogen. This was created from scratch."

"How is that possible?" Liam asked.

"Synthetic biology," Elena said. "Whoever made this didn't modify an existing virus or bacteria. They built it. Molecule by molecule. Using the medieval formula from Fragment 2 as a blueprint."

"That requires extraordinary expertise," Chen added. "And resources. You can't synthesize a pathogen like this in a basement laboratory. This requires industrial-grade equipment. Bioreactors. Gene synthesis capabilities. Clean room facilities. This is state-level bioweapons program sophistication."

"Or someone who used to work in one," Antoine said.

"Exactly."

While the genomic sequencing ran, Chen prepared for the next phase of analysis. Lethality testing. Transmission modeling. Comparing Plague 2 to known pathogens.

She'd requisitioned laboratory animals. Mice. Standard protocol for pathogen analysis. The WHO ethics committee had approved expedited testing given the severity of the threat. Ten thousand human lives had nearly been lost. Understanding the weapon was worth the cost.

Chen prepared eight mice. Divided into groups. A control group—no exposure. Test groups—with varying exposure levels to the pathogen.

The exposure was done in sealed chambers. Aerosolized pathogen delivered through a mouse cage ventilation system. Mimicking real-world dispersal.

Elena watched from the other room. This was the part she hated, the animal testing. But it was necessary. Better to understand the pathogen's lethality here, in a controlled environment, than to wait for human casualties.

The aerosolized pathogen was introduced into the test chambers. Microscopic particles. Invisible. The mice continued their normal behavior. Eating. Grooming. Unaware.

Ten seconds later. "Exposure complete," Chen said. "Now we wait. Based on the fragment's decoded specifications, symptom onset should occur within six to twelve hours. We'll monitor continuously and record the outcome."

"What are you expecting?" Elena asked.

"Respiratory distress. Fever. Rapid progression to organ failure. The fragment described this as a cure for respiratory disease—which means when weaponized, it becomes a respiratory plague. Attacks lung tissue. Prevents oxygen absorption. Causes systemic collapse." Chen checked the biosensors. "If the medieval formula is accurate, ninety-eight percent mortality will occur within forty-eight hours."

Elena woke in a chair to Antoine's hand on her shoulder. "You need to see this." She sat up. Groggy. Looked at the screens.

The test mice were dying. It had been four and a half hours since exposure. The biosensors showed elevated heart rates. Rapid respiration. Dropping oxygen levels. Through the cameras, Elena could see the mice struggling. Labored breathing. Lethargy.

"Symptom onset at four hours," Chen said, reviewing the data. "Faster than predicted. Fever spiking. Respiratory rate tripling normal baseline. Blood oxygen saturation is dropping. This is very aggressive."

By hour six, three of the four exposed mice were in severe distress. Barely moving. Gasping. Blood visible around their noses—internal hemorrhages already underway.

By hour eight, all four test mice were dead.

✠ ✠ ✠

The control group—unexposed—remained healthy. Active. Normal.

Chen's autopsy robots worked inside the chambers. Results streamed across the screens.

"Alveolar collapse. Cytokine storm. Lungs liquefy. The immune system destroys its own tissue trying to fight the infection."

Mortality table:
- Seasonal flu: 0.1 %
- COVID-19: 2–3 %
- SARS: 10 %
- Ebola: 50 %
- Weaponized anthrax: 85 %
- Plague 2: 98 % – death in $\leq$48 hours

"The most lethal pathogen I've ever seen," Chen said quietly. "Faster and deadlier than anything in nature."

"Can you create an antidote?" Liam asked.

"Not quickly. Creating a countermeasure would require understanding the pathogen's complete mechanism. How it binds to cells. How it evades immune response. It's mechanisms for replication. Then we'd need to design a neutralizing agent. Synthesize it. Test it. Optimize it. Mass-produce it. That's months of work. Maybe years."

"Then prevention is our only option," Elena said.

"Yes. Stop the deployment. Secure the operative. Prevent exposure. Once Plague 3 is released, people will die. And won't be able to save them."

Sequencing complete. Chen called them back.

"The pathogen's genome has been fully sequenced," Chen said. "And it confirms what we suspected. This is entirely synthetic. Artificially created. Man-made. No natural evolutionary markers. No relationship to any known virus or bacteria. Someone built this from scratch using advanced genetic engineering, just as we suspected." She pulled up the sequence on screen.

"But there's something else. The sophistication of this design..." Chen highlighted sections of the genome. "This pathogen is optimized. Replication mechanisms are highly efficient. Immune evasion strategies are elegant. Whoever created this understands molecular biology at a level I've rarely encountered. This isn't amateur work. This is mastery."

"How many people could do this?" Antoine asked.

"In the world? Maybe fifty. Perhaps fewer. You'd need advanced training in synthetic biology. Virology. Genetic engineering. Access to expensive equipment. Years of experience. And most importantly—" Chen looked at them "—you'd need to have worked in bioweapons research. This kind of optimization, this level of lethality... you don't learn that in academia. You learn it only by creating weapons."

"Former bioweapons program scientists," Elena said.

"Yes. Soviet. American. British. Chinese. During the Cold War, every major power had bioweapons programs. Some official. Some secret. Most were shut down or mothballed after international treaties were signed. But the scientists who worked in those programs didn't disappear. Some retired. Some moved to civilian research. And some..." Chen paused. "Some went rogue. Sold their expertise to the highest bidder."

"Like the Guild of Shadows."

"Exactly."

Elena pulled out her phone and opened her notes. "We need a list. Every bioweapons scientist who's gone missing or gone rogue in the last decade. Someone with the capability to create this."

"I'll coordinate with Interpol," Antoine said. "They can track known bioweapons experts and cross-reference the data with disappearances. Known criminal associations. Travel patterns. Financial irregularities. We'll find candidates."

"Do it fast," Chen said. "If we don't stop the source, we're just playing defense. Catching operatives. Stopping deployments one at a time. But the plagues will keep coming."

Sunday, 2:00 PM
BKA Intelligence Office

Antoine sat at the secure terminal with Kommissar Bauer. They'd been working for two hours. Pulling files from Interpol. CIA databases. MI6 intelligence. FSB records.

Cross-referencing known bioweapons scientists with activity patterns over the last ten years.

The initial list was overwhelming—more than two hundred names. Scientists who'd spent their careers inside the world's most secretive bioweapons programs.

Soviet: Biopreparat.

American: USAMRIID.

British: Porton Down.

Chinese: Institute of Military Medicine.

French: DGA.

Programs that officially didn't exist. Programs shuttered on paper, but never in reality.

They filtered. Narrowed. Applied criteria with clinical precision:

- Still alive: reduced to 180
- Ages forty to seventy—experienced, active: reduced to 120
- Advanced synthetic biology expertise: reduced to 60
- Disappeared or gone rogue: reduced to 10
- Capability to create Plague-2-level sophistication: reduced to 8

Antoine studied the final names. "Eight scientists," he said quietly. "Any one of them could be building plagues for Guiomar."

"We need to narrow the list further," Bauer replied. "Eight is too many to investigate simultaneously. Look for recent activity—financial transfers, travel data, intercepted communications. Anyone creating plagues needs resources. Equipment. Laboratory access. Those things leave breadcrumbs."

They dug deeper.

Four of the eight had recent, documented activity: civilian research roles, academic appointments, pharmaceutical work. Unlikely candidates for weaponizing medieval plagues.

That left four.

Bauer examined the files again—slowly, methodically—and crossed out another.

Three names remained.

Three possibilities.

One of them was creating the plagues.

✠ ✠ ✠

He printed the summary sheets, stacked them, and stood. "We need to brief the others," he said. "We have our suspects."

Elena, Dr. Chen, Liam, and Kommissar Bauer gathered in the conference room. Antoine entered, carrying three folders, and set them on the table. "We have three primary suspects," Antoine said. "Bioweapons scientists with the capability to create Plague 2. All three have disappeared or gone rogue. Each has connections to a criminal organization or unknown funding source. Any one of them could be working for the Guild." He opened the first folder.

"Suspect One: Dr. Pascual Gomez." A photograph appeared on the screen. Hispanic man. Graying hair. Intense eyes. "American. Age fifty-two. PhD in synthetic biology from MIT. Worked for the CIA's bioweapons defense program from 2001 to 2018. Based at Fort Detrick, Maryland. Specializes in aerosolized pathogen delivery systems. Developed countermeasures for anthrax, plague, and tularemia. But also studied offensive capabilities—how to weaponize pathogens for maximum lethality."

Antoine clicked through intelligence files.

"In 2018, his classified project was shut down. Budget cuts. Political pressure. Gomez protested. He argued that the program was essential for national security. He was overruled and resigned in 2019. Disappeared shortly after. Last confirmed sighting: 2020, Prague. Interpol issued a red notice in 2021. No subsequent sightings. No financial activity under his name. No communications traced."

"Motive?" Bauer asked.

"Ideological. Gomez believed the U.S. government had abandoned biodefense research. Left the country vulnerable. He may have gone rogue to prove his point. Create a crisis that forces governments to take bioweapons seriously again. Or..." Antoine paused. "Financial. The Guild could have paid him. Five million. Ten million. Enough to disappear and work in private."

"Capability?" Chen asked.

"Extremely high. Gomez published over fifty papers on synthetic biology before his work became classified. Pioneered techniques for rapid pathogen synthesis. If anyone could translate medieval medical formulas into modern bioweapons, it's him."

Elena studied the photograph. Gomez looked serious. Driven. The kind of man who'd dedicate his life to a cause. Or to revenge.

"Suspect Two," Antoine continued.

He opened the second folder.

"Dr. Nigel Ashford. British man. Late fifties. Thin. Sharp features. Wire-rimmed glasses. PhD in microbiology from Cambridge. Worked at MI6's biomedical division from 1995 to 2015. Twenty years developing countermeasures for Soviet bioweapons. He traveled extensively in Eastern Europe during the Cold War. Gained access to former Biopreparat facilities. Studied their work. Learned their techniques."

Antoine pulled up incident reports.

"In 2015, Ashford had a dispute with MI6 leadership. Details are classified, but intelligence suggests it involved a breakthrough in pathogen detection technology. Ashford claimed the discovery was his. Leadership reassigned credit to another team, then buried the project so deeply his name vanished from it entirely. His life's work—erased. His legacy—gone."

Elena exhaled. "They stole it from him."

"More than that," Antoine said. "They shut the project down, sealed the files, and promoted the scientist who took credit. Ashford filed a grievance. It went nowhere. He grew increasingly hostile, refused reassignment, and was dismissed for insubordination in 2015. A year later, he disappeared. Last confirmed sighting: 2017, Belgrade. Interpol issued a red notice in 2018. No trace since."

"Motive?" Elena asked.

"Personal betrayal. MI6 destroyed his reputation and buried his discovery. He may want vindication...or revenge. And Ashford has known connections to arms brokers. It's possible he sold his expertise to whoever could offer him a chance to finish the work he believes was stolen."

"Capability?"

"Very high. Ashford spent twenty years reverse-engineering Soviet bioweapons. He understands weaponization at an expert level. He also has connections in Eastern Europe—where a secret laboratory could be established without scrutiny."

Elena looked at the photograph on the screen. Ashford's expression was cold. Calculating. A man who'd spent decades in shadows. Who knew how to disappear. Who'd been pushed until something broke.

"Suspect Three," Antoine said.

He opened the final folder.

"Dr. Konstantin Volkov."

Russian man. Early sixties. Gray hair. Weathered face. Hard eyes.

Elena stared at the photograph. Something about him.

The precision.

The coldness.

This was a man who'd created death for decades and felt nothing.

"A former Soviet Biopreparat scientist. Worked from 1985 to 1995. Created weaponized anthrax, plague, smallpox. One of the Soviet Union's most prolific bioweapons engineers. After the USSR collapsed, he continued working for the Russian government until 2020. Then disappeared. An Interpol red notice was issued in 2022. No confirmed sightings since."

Antoine pulled up intelligence files.

"Volkov is different from the others. Gomez and Ashford are ideological. They have motives beyond money. But Volkov..." He paused. "Volkov is a mercenary. He doesn't care about politics or revenge. He works for whoever pays the most. And he's the best. Twenty years in Biopreparat. He created pathogens that killed thousands in Soviet testing. He understands lethality better than any scientist alive."

"Capability?" Chen asked, though the answer was obvious.

"The highest. If I had to choose one person on Earth capable of creating Plague 2, it would be Volkov. He has the experience. The expertise. The moral flexibility. And he disappeared at exactly the right time—2020, shortly before the Guild would have begun recruiting for this operation."

Elena studied Volkov's photograph. The dead eyes. The weathered face. A man who'd spent his life creating weapons. Who'd killed thousands through his work. And felt nothing.

"It's him," she said quietly.

"We don't know that," Bauer replied. "All three are viable suspects."

"But Volkov is the most likely. The others have an ideology. Motives. Complications. Volkov is simple. He's a craftsman. He creates bioweapons because that's what he does. The Guild needed the best. They hired the best." Elena looked at Antoine. "It's Volkov."

"Interpol is investigating all three," Antoine said. "The CIA is tracking Gomez. MI6 is tracking Ashford. FSB—is tracking Volkov. We'll know more soon."

"London is in forty-five hours from now. If we don't find the laboratory before then, Plague 3 deploys. And more people die."

"Then we prioritize Volkov," Bauer said. "If Dr. Voss is right—if he's our scientist—then we focus resources there. FSB has informants in Eastern Europe. Black market contacts. If Volkov is operating a laboratory, someone knows something. Someone has seen equipment shipments. Chemical purchases. Personnel movements. We lean on FSB and we find him. Fast."

"And if we're wrong?" Chen asked. "If it's Gomez or Ashford?"

"Then we've wasted time chasing the wrong suspect." Bauer looked at Elena. "But instinct matters in intelligence work. If Dr. Voss believes it's Volkov, that's worth pursuing."

Antoine closed the folders. "I'll coordinate with Interpol. Priority on Volkov. But keep Gomez and Ashford under investigation. We can't afford to be wrong."

Sunday, 5:00 PM
BKA Detention Center

Marlene sat in her cell. Dr. Steiner had returned and informed her of the pathogen analysis results. The canister contained a weaponized biological agent. Confirmed lethal. Her fingerprints are on it. Evidence sufficient to charge her with terrorism. Attempted mass murder. She would not be released.

Dr. Steiner had argued. Challenged the evidence. Suggested contamination. Planted evidence. Coercion. But the science was clear. The canister was real. The pathogen was real. Marlene had been carrying it in the crowded Christmas market. She was going to prison. For life. Maybe worse. But Marlene wasn't afraid.

The mission had succeeded in one way; it had bought time. Cologne had delayed the WHO's response. Forced them to mobilize. Made them focus resources on Germany, and while they were focused on Cologne, the Guild had prepared London. Tokyo. New York. Planning the remaining plague deployments.

Plague 2 had been stopped. But Plague 3 was ready. And this time, the WHO wouldn't be able to stop it. This time, the operative would succeed.

Marlene closed her eyes, thinking of her father. Klaus Vogel. Stasi officer. Dead in a cell like this. But his death had meant nothing. Her death—or her imprisonment—would mean something. She would be part of something larger.

Elena stood in the command center. Looking at the three photographs on the screen. Gomez. Ashford. Volkov. One of them was creating the plagues. One of them had synthesized the pathogen that nearly killed ten thousand people in Cologne. One of them was preparing Plague 3 for London. But which one? Her instinct said

Volkov. The cold professionalism and decades of experience. A moral emptiness that would allow someone to create extinction-level weapons without hesitation. But instinct wasn't proof. And if she was wrong, if she'd focused resources on the wrong suspect, people would die in London.

"We'll find him," Antoine said beside her. "Interpol is coordinating with every intelligence agency. FSB. CIA. MI6. BND. Everyone. If Volkov is operating a laboratory, we'll find it."

"Before London?"

"I don't know."

Elena looked at the countdown timer on the screen. *Forty-two hours.*

Not enough time to find a hidden laboratory in Eastern Europe.

Not enough time to stop Plague 3 from being deployed.

They'd stopped Cologne—but Cologne had been reactive. Defensive. Catching an operative in the act.

London needed to be proactive.

They needed to find the source.

Find the laboratory.

Destroy the plagues before they left.

Before operatives carried them into cities.

A new text message arrived.

Dr. Voss. You stopped Cologne. Impressive. But London won't be so easy. My operative is already in position. Already infected. Even if you catch him, the plague spreads. You can't win this time—G.

Elena felt the words drop into her stomach like stone.

Already infected.

Guiomar's operatives weren't couriers anymore.

They were suicide vectors—intentionally infected before deployment. Capture meant nothing. Containment meant nothing.

Their breath, their touch, their presence was the weapon.

The Guild had adapted.

Learned from Cologne.

Evolved.

"Antoine," Elena said quietly. "Look at this."

He read the message. His jaw tightened. "If the operative is already infected..."

"Then we can't just capture him," Elena finished. "We have to treat him as biohazard-positive from first contact. Full containment protocols. Isolation. And even then..."

She looked at the screens.

"...even then, he could infect people before we reach him."

"We warn MI5," Antoine said. "Scotland Yard. WHO response teams. Anyone who might encounter him treats him as a live biological threat."

"And pray we find him before he deploys."

Elena turned back to the screens.

To the three suspects.

To the timer.

To the narrowing hours bleeding away.

Plague 3 waits—less than two days remain.

And she was running out of time to stop it.

29 - The Contagion

Monday, 7:00 AM
London, United Kingdom.

Thirty-six hours until Plague 3 deploys.

London was grey. Rain threatening. Ten million people hurrying through the damp toward the Tube, toward routine.

Elena stood at the MI5's command center. Vauxhall Cross. The headquarters building rises like a fortress on the Thames. Inside screens. Surveillance feeds. Radio chatter. Intelligence analysts are coordinating with Scotland Yard's Counter Terrorism Command.

Dr. Chen stood beside her. Antoine and Liam are nearby. They'd flown from Cologne six hours ago. Red-eye flight. No sleep. Just coffee and adrenaline and the knowledge that somewhere in this city of ten million people, a Guild operative was carrying death in a canister.

"We have significantly less intelligence than Cologne," said Commander Sarah Mills, MI5's lead on the operation. Mid-forties. Eyes like flint. Twenty years in counterterrorism. "No photographs of the operative. No confirmed location. Just the coordinates from your map." She pulled up a display. Point 3. London. "That's a five-kilometer radius. Central London. Trafalgar Square.

Piccadilly. Leicester Square. Covent Garden. Tourist areas. High foot traffic. Any of them could be the target."

"What about the suicide protocol?" Elena asked. "Guiomar texted me. Said the operative is already infected. That even if we catch him, the plague spreads."

"We're treating this as a biological hazmat threat from first contact," Mills said. "All officers have been briefed. Containment protocols. No one approaches without biohazard gear. If we identify the suspect, we isolate them immediately. Same protocols you used in Cologne."

"Cologne worked because we had a photograph," Antoine said. "We knew who to look for. Here, we're searching blind."

"Not completely blind." Mills pulled up intelligence reports. "We've been monitoring travel into London over the past seventy-two hours. Flagging anyone with connections to Eastern Europe, the Middle East, and known Guild territories. Unusual travel patterns. Financial anomalies. We have five persons of interest. All under surveillance."

She displayed photographs. Three men. Two women. Various ages. Various nationalities.

"Any of them could be our operative. Or none of them."

Elena studied the faces. Which one? Or was it someone else entirely? Someone they hadn't identified. Someone is already in position.

"Where would you deploy?" Mills asked Elena. "If you were the operative. Where in London?"

Elena thought. Population density. Maximum exposure. Enclosed spaces for aerosol dispersal. "The Tube. Underground stations. Enclosed. Crowded. Air circulation spreads the pathogen efficiently. Rush hour. Thousands of people in minutes."

"That's our primary concern," Mills agreed. "We've increased police presence at major stations. King's Cross. Liverpool Street. Waterloo. Victoria. Leicester Square. Plain clothes officers. Watching for suspicious behavior."

"The operative will look normal," Antoine said. "Marlene did. Tourist. Commuter. Blending in. The only tell is the canister. And even that looks innocent."

Mills nodded grimly. "Then we watch everyone. And hope we get lucky."

Monday, 11:00 AM
Thirty-two hours until Plague 3 deploys.

The morning rush had passed. Midday crowds now. Tourists. Shoppers. Business lunches. London is moving at its usual pace.

Elena watched endless feeds, searching faces for something—anything.

"This is impossible," Liam said, standing beside her. He'd been quiet since Cologne. Since watching Marlene nearly deploy Plague 2. "Cologne, we had a photo. A specific market. A timeline. Here? We have nothing. Just hope and surveillance."

"MI5 is good at this stuff," Elena said. "If the operative is here, they'll find them."

A text message notification chirped.

Dr. Voss. Enjoying London? My operative is closer than you think. Already infected. Already in position. You can't stop what's already begun. Tomorrow evening. Rush hour—G.

Elena showed it to Mills.

"She's telling us when," Elena said. "Why?"

"Because she's confident that we can't stop it even knowing when." Mills pulled up Tube station maps. "We lock down surveillance at every major station. Deploy every available officer. Biohazard teams on standby. Armed response positioned nearby. If her operative shows, we take him down before he sprays."

"And if we don't find him in time?" Antoine said.

"Then we minimize casualties. Save who we can."

Mills began coordinating. Radio commands. Deployment orders. MI5 and Scotland Yard are mobilizing for tomorrow evening.

"Why don't we just close down the Tube?"

"Guiomar will just pick another location. As much as I hate to do it, we must let this play out but we will be fully prepared for every possible scenario."

Elena just nodded, staring at the screens. London goes about its day. Unaware that death would walk into a Tube station tomorrow evening.

Tuesday, 6:30 PM
Thirty minutes left.

Every major Tube station in central London was flooded with plain-clothes officers. MI5. Counter Terrorism Command. British Transport Police. Armed response units positioned nearby. Biohazard teams are ready in unmarked vans outside stations.

Elena was stationed at King's Cross. The busiest station. Eight Tube lines converge. Hundreds of thousands of passengers daily. If she were deploying a plague, this is where she'd do it.

Dr. Chen was with her. Biohazard containment gear ready.

Antoine was at Liverpool Street.

Liam is at Leicester Square.

Other WHO and MI5 teams were scattered across the city. They waited.

Commuters flood into stations. Pressed together on platforms. Perfect conditions for aerosol transmission.

Elena watched the crowds through surveillance feeds. Scanning faces. Looking for anything unusual.

Radio chatter is increasing. Officers reported from every station. Nothing yet. No suspects. No unusual activity. Maybe Guiomar was lying. Maybe the intelligence was false. Maybe—

"Possible contact," a voice crackled over the radio.

Liam's voice.

"Leicester Square station. Northern Line platform. Male. Thirties. Middle Eastern appearance. Dark jacket. Carrying a messenger bag. Moving through the crowd. Something about his positioning... he's scanning the platform. Looking for cameras. Looking for police."

Mills responded immediately. "All units converge on Leicester Square. Do not approach until the biohazard team is in position. Maintain visual surveillance."

Elena's heart raced. "I'm moving to Leicester Square. Three minutes away." She ran out of King's Cross, into a waiting MI5 vehicle. Sirens. Racing through London streets. Traffic parting.

Liam's voice on the radio. Calm but tense.

"Subject is moving toward the center of the platform. Away from exits. Away from walls. Optimal aerosol dispersal position. He's reaching into his bag."

"The Biohazard team is entering the station now," Chen said over the radio. "Thirty seconds to platform level."

"Subject has his hand in the bag. I can see something. Cylindrical. Small. He's pulling it out—"

Elena's vehicle screeched to a stop outside Leicester Square station. She jumped out. Ran inside. Down the escalators. Toward the platform. Pushing past people.

Radio: "He's got the canister! Small. Black. Aerosol dispenser. It's in his hand!"

Chen's voice: "LIAM, DO NOT APPROACH! WAIT FOR BIOHAZARD—"

But Liam was already moving.

Elena reached the platform level. Saw it happening thirty meters away.

The man—dark jacket, thirties, Middle Eastern features—stood in the center of the platform. Commuters around him. Hundreds of people are waiting for trains, unaware. The man raised the canister above the crowd—thumb moving toward the spray button.

Liam was ten meters away. He'd been documenting. Camera in his hands, recording surveillance for evidence. He saw the canister. Saw the man's thumb. And didn't think.

He dropped his camera and ran.

The man's thumb was on the button when Liam crashed into him. Full tackle. Both went airborne for a split second, then hit the concrete. Hard.

The canister flew from the man's hand.

Spinning.

Tumbling.

It struck the platform's edge—concrete—at the perfect angle.

A crack.

Not a shatter.

Not an explosion.

Just a single fracture along the side.

A seal breaking.

For two seconds—maybe less—a thin aerosol pulse escaped. A whisper of mist, barely visible, drifting upward in a soft bloom before dispersing into the air.

Then the pressure equalized. The leak stopped. The canister rolled, depressurized, the remaining liquid still sealed inside.

But those two seconds.

That brief pulse.

Forty people stood within arm's reach.

Curious. Alarmed by the sudden tackle.

They edged closer, phones out, filming, streaming live.

"What's going on?"

"Is that a terrorist?"

"Someone call the police!"

They didn't know. Couldn't see.

They had no idea that they were standing inside an invisible cloud of death—a pathogen engineered to kill quickly. Efficiently.

And it was already in their lungs.

Liam pinned the man to the ground.

The man thrashed beneath him, coughing—wet, deep, violent. Blood flecked his teeth. Hour twenty of infection. Suicide protocol. He was dying, and he knew it. Hours left—maybe less.

A martyr for Guiomar's cause.

For the new Order.

He looked up at Liam and smiled through the blood. "You die too now—stupid American."

The words were broken. Thick with accent.

Almost gleeful.

He gathered saliva—ropey, red—and *spat*.

It hit Liam across the face.

Warm. Viscous. A smear of crimson.

Liam froze.

Slowly, he touched his face. His fingers came away wet. Red. Contaminated.

Chen saw it happen.

"BIOHAZARD PROTOCOL!" Dr. Chen shouted as she arrived on the platform with her hazmat team. "LIAM'S BEEN EXPOSED! EVERYONE BACK! BIOLOGICAL HAZARD! NO ONE MOVES!"

Everything happened at once.

The WHO hazmat team swarmed.

They grabbed Liam. Pulled him away from the operative. Stripped off his outer clothes right there on the platform. Jacket. Shirt. Shoes. Everything that was potentially contaminated.

A portable decontamination shower was deployed. Chemical wash. Liam was immediately doused.

Eyes. Face. Mouth. Hair. Everything.

The crowd panicked. Started backing away. Running toward exits.

"STOP!" Mills appeared on the platform. MI5 badge raised. Armed officers flooded in behind her.

"NO ONE LEAVES! This is a biological containment situation! Everyone within fifty feet of that canister—you've been exposed! You need to be quarantined!"

"What," A businesswoman gasped, phone in hand, recording. "Exposed to what?"

"A weaponized pathogen. Potentially lethal. You need to come with us, please. Right now."

Panic.

Real panic.

People are trying to push toward the exits. Police blocking them. Arguments. Shouting. Someone screaming.

"LISTEN TO ME!" Mills shouted.

"You were exposed to an aerosolized pathogen briefly. Most of you will be fine, but we need to test and temporarily quarantine you to monitor for symptoms. If you leave now and go home to your families, you could infect them. Is that what you want?"

That stopped them. The realization that they might be carrying death home to loved ones. Might infect their children. Their spouses. Their parents.

The crowd settled.

There are forty-three people. Counted and verified. All within fifty feet of where the canister had cracked open. All potentially exposed to those two seconds of aerosol pulse. Hazmat suits were distributed. Emergency biohazard gear. Passengers suited up.

Awkward. Terrified. Some crying.

Others are silent, in shock.

Liam was already in a full isolation suit. He looked at Elena through the plastic. Eyes wide. Terrified. She wanted to say something, to reassure him everything was going to be okay. But what could she say? He'd been spit on by an infected operative. He might be dying.

The operative—the man Liam tackled—was also being suited. Restrained. Two officers in hazmat gear lifted him from the ground where he had been tackled. He was laughing. Coughing blood but laughing. An eerie laugh. *Some will die.*

His mission—partially accomplished.

"Too late," he said in broken English to the officer walking with him. "I already infected. Dying. Take me with you. Who cares. Many people die. Spread it. You stop nothing."

The operative coughed again and collapsed. Officers carried him toward the exit. Toward a biohazard transport vehicle waiting outside.

Elena watched as Liam was escorted off the platform. He walked slowly—shuffled really, barely able to move in the isolation suit—toward another transport vehicle. The suit, now his prison. Liam didn't look back. Just kept moving. One foot in front of the other.

Dead man walking.

The forty-three exposed passengers were being organized. Lined up. Escorted toward buses converted for biohazard transport. They'd all go to the quarantine facility. Blood tests. Monitoring. Forty-eight hours minimum.

Mills coordinated the wider lockdown. "Seal the station! No trains enter this platform! Passengers on approaching trains will be held at previous stations. Anyone within three hundred feet of this platform needs to be screened. Temperature checks. Contact information collected. No one leaves until cleared."

Two hundred more people stood on adjacent platforms. Near the escalators. All are being detained. Questioned. Tested. It would take hours.

Nearby, the biohazard evidence bag with the cracked container lay on the ground—sealed. The WHO would analyze it and confirm it was Plague 3. But they already knew. The operative's symptoms. The suicide protocol. This was Guiomar's handiwork.

"How bad?" Antoine asked, arriving on the platform. He'd come from Liverpool Street. Fifteen minutes passed while in traffic.

"Forty-three people were exposed to the aerosol pulse after the container hit the ground, after Liam tackled the guy. Liam was spat on by the operative, who was already infected—the operative is dying. Hour twenty or so of his infection is my guess."

"And Liam?"

"In quarantine for forty-eight hours. We'll know if he's infected by tomorrow morning. Symptoms would appear within six to twelve hours if the viral load was sufficient."

"And if he is infected?"

Elena didn't answer because they both knew. Liam would die forty-eight hours from now. Coughing up blood. Lungs collapsing. Like the mice in the lab test. Like the operative, who would die later this evening.

"He saved thousands," Antoine said quietly. "If that canister had deployed fully. If the operative had sprayed into the crowd... this would be exponentially worse."

"Forty-three people exposed. Maybe more. How many will get sick? Any estimates?" Elena asked Dr. Chen.

"Depends on their proximity to the point of release. It was a brief pulse, just a couple of seconds. Maybe half of them won't get infected because they were far enough away and the exposure was short. Maybe more. We won't know for several hours."

Elena looked at the crowd being loaded into transport buses. Forty-three people. Most of them had been recording on their phones when the canister cracked. Curiosity, wanting content for social media. Moving in close to see what the commotion was all about. And now they might die just for being curious.

"Leicester Square is locked down," Mills said, approaching Elena and Antoine. "The station will be closed for a minimum of forty-eight hours. Full decontamination protocol. The wider perimeter—three hundred feet—we've screened two hundred twelve people. Temperature checks. No symptoms yet. We will hold them until we are certain they have not been infected. Contact information collected. In 12 hours, they'll be released if no symptoms are present, with instructions to self-monitor for fever, cough, and respiratory distress. If symptoms appear, they're to call the WHO emergency services immediately. Don't go to the hospital directly. We'll come to them."

"And the trains?"

"Northern Line service is suspended between Camden Town and Kennington. Trains that were approaching Leicester Square have been diverted. Passengers on those trains are being held at adjacent stations. Screened. Cleared. Service should resume in six hours once we're certain there's no secondary exposure risk."

Elena nodded. Efficient and professional. MI5 had handled this well. But it didn't change the fact that forty-three people had been exposed.

That Liam might be dying.

That they'd stopped a catastrophe, but not perfectly. Never perfectly.

Elena's phone buzzed with a new text message.

Only forty-three were exposed. Not bad, Dr. Voss. You're getting faster. But not fast enough. Now your friend is infected. I watched it all from my operative's body cam. About two seconds of aerosol disbursement. That's enough for now. Some of those forty-three will die, and you'll get to watch it all. Your young friend stopped thousands from dying today. A valiant act of heroism. But he didn't stop everyone. Six plagues remain. Six more cities. How many will you fail to save next time? —G.

Elena looked at the platform from a distance. The spot where Liam had tackled the operative and the empty space where hundreds of commuters had been standing, just minutes ago, were now evacuated. Everyone quarantined. Detained. Lives disrupted. Lives potentially ended.

They'd stopped Plague 3. Mostly.

But at what cost?

Tuesday, 8:00 PM
The WHO Quarantine Facility, London

The facility was a converted hospital wing. Built after COVID for pandemic preparedness. Now housing forty-four people potentially infected with Plague 3.

Liam was in Room 1. Still in the isolation suite. Sitting on a bed. Vitals being monitored remotely. Blood drawn every two hours. Tests are running continuously.

The operative—identified as Reza Ahmadi, an Iranian national aged 34—was in Room 2. Separated by reinforced walls and showing severe symptoms already. Hour twenty-two of his infection. Fever. Coughing blood. Respiratory distress. Dr. Chen had intubated him. Mechanical ventilation. But it was just delaying the inevitable.

The other forty-three exposed passengers were in a separate wing being monitored. For at least six more hours.

Elena stood in the observation room, looking through the glass at Liam. He sat motionless. Staring at the wall. The helmet of the isolation suit was still on. He hadn't moved since arriving two hours ago.

Dr. Chen entered the room, talking to Elena, "Blood tests are negative so far. No pathogen detected. But it's only been two hours. Incubation is about six hours. We won't know until then."

"And if he's infected?"

"Then we keep him comfortable. Manage symptoms as they appear. Hope his immune system can fight it." Chen paused, "The lab mice. Reza now. Hour twenty-two and he's already critical."

"I know."

They stood in silence. Watching Liam through the glass. He finally moved, slowly removing the helmet. He set it aside, then ran his hands through his hair. Touched his face where the spit had landed. Closed his eyes, wondering if he was going to die.

Antoine appeared in the doorway. "Reza is deteriorating. Dr. Chen, they need you in Room 2."

Chen left. Elena and Antoine were alone now in the observation room, looking at Liam.

"He saved lives," Antoine said quietly. "If Reza had sprayed into the crowd, fully emptying the container's contents...thousands could have been exposed. Liam stopped that."

"By getting himself exposed."

"He didn't think, he just acted. He saw the canister and moved. That's who he is." Antoine looked at Liam through the glass. "He's a good man. A brave man. He doesn't deserve this."

"No one does."

"But especially not him. He's a photographer. He documents things. He shouldn't be tackling bioterrorists."

A tear rimmed Antoine's eye—a rare breach in a man forged by combat. He looked away for a moment, blinking hard, regaining himself.

"He should be taking photos in Lisbon right now, not sitting in quarantine waiting to die."

"He chose to come. No one forced him."

"I know, but still." Antoine touched the glass. "If he dies... I don't know if I can keep doing this. This one hits close to home." Elena understood. They'd already lost so much. Seen so much death. If they lost Liam too...She couldn't think about it.

"We wait," she said. "Six hours until we know. Then twelve until symptoms would appear, if he's infected. Then forty-eight until..." She didn't finish. They both knew. Forty-eight hours. If Liam were infected, he'd be dead in two days. Just like Reza.

Elena hadn't left the observation room. Couldn't. Just watched Liam through the glass. He'd finally laid down. Curled on his side. Not sleeping. Just staring at the wall. Silent.

Reza was getting worse. Hour twenty-five of his infection. Severe respiratory distress. Blood oxygen is dropping despite mechanical ventilation. Multi-organ failure is beginning. The plague was killing him. Systematically. Just like it was designed to do.

Mills entered the observation room. "We've processed all forty-two passengers from the exposure zone. Contacted their relatives. Blood tests are running. So far, all negative. But it's early. Chen is still monitoring them."

"How are they handling it?"

"Scared. Angry. Some are threatening lawsuits. Others are just... numb. They were waiting for a train. And now they're in quarantine, wondering if they're going to die."

Mills looked at Liam.

"He's the real hero here. Tackled an armed terrorist. Prevented mass casualties. Saved thousands of people. We're recommending him for commendation. Civilian honor. Something."

"He won't want it. He just wants to go home."

"After this? Can he?"

Elena didn't answer. Because even if Liam survived, even if he wasn't infected, she didn't know if he could go home. Not really. Not after everything he'd seen. Everything he'd done. The nightmares would haunt him, along with the guilt and fear. That was the cost of being a hero. You saved lives. But you paid for it. Forever.

Six hours. Incubation period complete. If Liam were infected, the pathogen would be replicating now. Spreading through his bloodstream. Reaching his lungs.

Blood test results appeared on the screen.

Dr. Chen studied them—too long. Silence stretching. Running numbers again.

Elena went still, every instinct bracing. "What is it?"

Chen exhaled slowly. "Negative. No pathogen detected."

Elena blinked. That wasn't what she expected.

"At hour six," Chen continued, looking up, "if he were infected, we'd see replication markers. Viral load. Something. But there's nothing."

"Are you sure?"

"I'm rerunning the panel three more times to confirm," Chen said. "But preliminary results...he's clean."

Elena felt something break inside her. Relief. Overwhelming. Like a dam bursting.

"Why? Reza was infected. He spat on Liam. Why isn't he infected?"

"Two factors," Chen said.

"First: the saliva must have landed only on Liam's skin—not in his eyes, nose, or mouth. Skin is an effective barrier unless there are cuts or abrasions. No entry point means no infection."

"Second: timing," Chen continued. "Reza was at hour twenty-two when he spat. Early enough in his infection that the viral load in his saliva may still have been relatively low. By hour thirty or forty—when he's fully contagious—respiratory droplets are saturated with pathogen and—" She stopped herself.

Elena understood anyway.

"Liam got lucky."

"*Extraordinarily lucky.*" Chen looked at him through the glass. "But we're not releasing him yet. We'll monitor for a full forty-eight hours—complete incubation cycle. We make certain." She exhaled. "He's going to survive."

Elena pressed her forehead against the glass and closed her eyes.

Thank God.

Thank You, God.

In Room 2, Reza was dying.

In Room 1, Liam was going to live.

Two men. Separated by glass, thin walls, and fate. One had chosen death. The other had been lucky enough to avoid it.

Wednesday, 5:47 PM
Reza: Hour 28 post-exposure.

Reza died at 5:47 PM. Hour twenty-eight of his infection. Respiratory arrest. Despite mechanical ventilation. Despite everything. Dr. Chen performed the autopsy via remote robotic systems. Tissue samples collected. Pathogen isolated.

"Plague 3 is similar to Plague 2," Chen reported to the others in the command center. "Same mechanism. Far more lethal. We estimate a ninety percent mortality. Forty-eight-hour kill time. It also appears to be significantly more contagious. It's optimized for enclosed spaces." She paused. "That's why Guiomar chose it for the Tube."

"The forty-two passengers exposed to the aerosol pulse?" Elena asked.

"Eighteen are showing symptoms," Chen said. "Hour twelve post-exposure. Fever. Cough beginning. We've isolated them in separate rooms. Treating symptomatically. But..."

She didn't need to finish.

Eighteen people were going to die.

Because they'd been standing on a Tube platform at 7:00 P.M. on a Tuesday.

Because they'd leaned in to see a commotion.

Because they were curious.

Mills stepped forward. "Liam saved thousands. If that canister had released at full pressure... if Reza had stayed on his feet another ten seconds... if the seal hadn't cracked when it hit the ground..." She exhaled sharply. "We'd be facing a mass-casualty event. Conservative estimate? Five thousand exposed. Two thousand dead within forty-eight hours."

She tapped the model on the screen—curves rising steeply. "By ninety-six hours, second-wave infections from family members, commuters, hospital waiting rooms... four to six thousand dead. That's the *conservative* projection."

Elena knew he was right. But eighteen wasn't just a number. It was eighteen lives.

Eighteen families who would get calls tonight—or tomorrow—telling them there was no cure.

Telling them to say goodbye now, while there was still time.

"The other twenty-four?" Antoine asked. "The ones not showing symptoms?"

"Hour twelve and asymptomatic. We're cautiously optimistic. We'll monitor for another thirty-six hours, but if they're not symptomatic by hour twenty-four, they're probably clear."

Twenty-four people were saved by luck. By standing slightly farther away. By being upwind. By random chance. Eighteen people are dying despite everything.

"Liam?" Mills asked.

"Still negative. Hour twenty-eight. No symptoms. No pathogen. If he were infected, we'd know by now." Chen smiled slightly. "He's going to make it. We'll release him tomorrow morning. Once the full forty-eight-hour observation is complete."

"And then what?" Mills asked. "Does he go back to his life? Pretend this didn't happen?"

"I don't know," Elena said quietly. "But I don't think he'll be the same. None of us will."

Thursday, 8:00 PM
Liam: Hour 48 post-exposure.

Liam was cleared. He was escorted out of quarantine. Decontaminated one final time. Given clean clothes. Released.

Elena met him outside the facility. He looked terrible. Hadn't slept.

Two days thinking he was dying.

Two days of listening to Reza cough up blood in the next room. Hearing the medical alarms. Knowing that could have been him.

"Hey," she said softly.

"Hey." His voice was hoarse from disuse. "I'm alive."

"You're alive."

He laughed. Hollow. Empty. "I thought I was dead. For forty-eight hours. Every hour, I waited for the fever. For the cough. For my lungs to start collapsing. And it never came. And I don't know if I feel relieved or just... empty."

"You feel traumatized. That's normal. You went through hell."

"I tackled him and didn't think twice about it," Liam said. His voice was raw. "I just saw the canister coming out of his bag and I moved. And then we hit the ground, and it cracked—and eighteen people..." He swallowed. "Dr. Chen told me. Eighteen people got sick from the aerosol that escaped when the canister cracked. Eighteen people are dying right now because I was two seconds too slow. Because I didn't tackle him before he pulled it out of his bag."

"You weren't too slow," Elena said. "You were incredibly fast. If you'd been two seconds slower—if that canister had deployed fully—*thousands* would be dying. Not eighteen. Thousands."

"But eighteen *are* dying."

"I know." Her voice softened. "And that's not your fault. That's Guiomar's fault. That's Reza's fault for agreeing to deploy it. That's the Guild's fault for weaponizing these plagues. But it's not your fault."

Liam looked at her—eyes red, exhausted, haunted. "Then why does it feel like it is?"

Elena had no answer. Because she felt it too—that terrible arithmetic of disaster, the weight of lives saved versus the lives they couldn't save. They'd stopped a catastrophe...but catastrophe was relative. For the families of those eighteen people, the world had ended. *Their* world. And nothing Elena or Liam or anyone else said could change that.

"What now?" Liam asked quietly.

"Now you go home," Elena said. "Rest. Recover. Let us handle the rest."

He shook his head. "I can't do this anymore, Elena. I can't keep tackling bioterrorists. I can't keep thinking I'm going to die. I can't keep watching people die because I wasn't fast enough, or smart enough, or lucky enough."

"Liam—"

"I'm done. I'm out. Find someone else." He turned away. Started walking toward the street where taxis waited.

Elena watched him go. Didn't stop him. Didn't argue. He'd earned the right to walk away. Had earned it the moment he tackled Reza. Had earned it during forty-eight hours of hell in quarantine. Had earned it by saving thousands of lives. He didn't owe them anything more. But the plagues didn't care. Six remained. And Guiomar wouldn't stop until they were all deployed.

Or until someone stopped her.

Mills pulled up the final casualty report: "Eighteen confirmed infections from Leicester Square. All in isolation. Symptomatic. Prognosis: poor. Based on Plague 3 analysis, a ninety percent mortality rate. We'll lose seventeen of them. Maybe all eighteen."

"And the others?" Antoine asked. "The twenty-four exposed but not symptomatic?"

"Hour thirty-six post-exposure and still clear. We're releasing them this afternoon with instructions to monitor for symptoms over the next week. But if they were going to get sick, they'd be symptomatic by now. They're safe."

Elena looked at the numbers.

Eighteen dying.

Eighteen families.

Eighteen funerals in the coming weeks.

"Guiomar is adapting faster than we are," Chen said. "Cologne: clean operative, we caught her before deployment. London: infected operative, partial deployment before we stopped him. Next time? Multiple operatives. Multiple deployment sites simultaneously. Backups and redundancies are both used in sequence. She learns from every failure."

"Then we learn faster," Mills said. "We improve our intelligence gathering. Our response times. Our containment protocols."

"That's reactive," Elena said. "We're always chasing. Always responding. We need to go on offense. Find Volkov. Find the laboratory. Stop the source before the next plague is deployed."

"Interpol is working on it," Antoine said. "All three suspects. Volkov, Gomez, Ashford. Cross-referencing travel patterns, financial transactions, and equipment purchases. We'll find them."

"Before the next deployment?" Elena asked.

Silence. Because they didn't know.

New York. Tokyo. Singapore. Mexico City. Moscow. Shanghai. Six more targets. Six more plagues are waiting. And somewhere, in a laboratory they couldn't find, someone was preparing the next one.

Elena's phone buzzed on the table in. front of her.

Text message.

Eighteen dead in London. Not bad, Dr. Voss. Better than Cologne. You're learning. But so am I. Next city, next plague. You can't stop them all. And when you fail—when thousands die instead of eighteen—you'll realize you never had a chance. The plagues will fall. One by one. Until Shanghai. Until Babel. Until extinction—G.

Elena looked at the map on the screen. The nine points. Three crossed out now. Central Africa. Cologne. London. Six remained. New York. Tokyo. Singapore. Mexico City. Moscow. Shanghai. Six chances to fail. And somewhere, Guiomar was already preparing the next deployment.

Friday, 2:00 PM
London City Morgue

Reza Ahmadi's body lay on the autopsy table in a special room, one designed for biohazards. Dr. Chen, in a biohazard suit, had completed the full examination. Tissue samples collected. Pathogen isolated. Cause of death: respiratory failure, secondary to Plague 3 infection.

He'd been thirty-four years old. Born in Tehran. Studied chemistry at the University of Tehran. Disappeared in 2020. Recruited by the Guild. Trained. Infected. Deployed. Dead.

Interpol had contacted his family. Parents in Iran. They were devastated. Hadn't heard from him in three years. Thought he was working in Europe. Didn't know he'd become a terrorist. Didn't know he'd died deploying a bioweapon in London.

Elena thought of Reza's family in Iran—how Islamic tradition called for burial within a day, the washing and shrouding, the quiet prayers. They would never have that closure. They would never even see his body.

Dr. Chen stood over the body. Looking at a young man who'd been willing to die for Guiomar's cause. Who'd let himself become infected. Who'd smiled as he spat on Liam, trying to take him along to his death.

"Why?" Chen said quietly. "What makes someone do this?"

Elena stood beside her in a biohazard suit, the soft hiss of filtered air filling the space between them.

"I don't know," she said. "Maybe ideology. Maybe money. Maybe coercion. Maybe he believed the world deserved to end."

Chen's voice was quiet. "Do you think he knew about the others? Central Africa? The four hundred who died there? Cologne? The six remaining plagues?"

"Probably. Guild operatives are compartmentalized, but they know the broad strokes. They know they're part of something bigger. Something apocalyptic."

"And they still do it."

"Yes," Elena said. "Because some people want the world to burn. And the Guild gives them matches."

Chen pulled the sheet over Reza's face, "Eighteen people will die because he succeeded, partially. But thousands lived because Liam stopped him. I hope Reza knew that in his last moments. I hope he died knowing he failed."

They left the morgue. London is continuing outside. Traffic. Rain clearing. Normal life resuming. Leicester Square station will reopen tomorrow. Decontamination complete. Business as usual.

Plague 3 had been stopped. But the cost had been paid. In blood.

Friday, 6:00 PM
Interpol Headquarters, Lyon

Antoine sat in the secure conference room. Video call with CIA, MI6, FSB, BND. Intelligence agencies are coordinating. Sharing information about the three bioweapons suspects.

"We've narrowed the field," said the CIA representative. A man, late forties. Senior analyst. "Dr. Pascual Gomez. Last confirmed sighting: 2022, Prague. Financial transaction traced to a shell company in Cyprus. We're investigating."

"Dr. Nigel Ashford," added the MI6 officer. "Spotted in Belgrade, 2023. Purchasing laboratory equipment through intermediaries. The trail went cold in Eastern Europe."

"Dr. Konstantin Volkov," said the FSB representative. Reluctant to cooperate with Western agencies. "Moscow informants report he relocated in 2022. Exact location unknown. But communications intercepts suggest he's operating somewhere in former Soviet territory. Possibly Moldova. Possibly Armenia. We're investigating."

"We need more than investigations," Antoine said. "We need locations. Coordinates. We need to find these laboratories and destroy them before the next plague deploys."

"We're working on it," the CIA analyst said. "But these men are professionals. They know how to disappear. How to operate in shadows. Finding them will take time."

"We don't have time. The next deployment could be tomorrow. Or next week. We don't know."

"Then we work faster," said the MI6 officer. "All agencies. Full cooperation. We find these scientists and shut down their operations. We end this."

The call ended. Antoine sat back. Stared at the three photographs on his screen.

Gomez. Ashford. Volkov. One of them was creating the plagues. Synthesizing bioweapons from medieval medical texts. And somewhere, in a laboratory hidden from the world, they were working on the next one. Plague 4. Plague 5. Plague 6. All the way to Plague 9. The Plague of Babel. The end of everything.

Antoine closed the files. Stood. Looked out the window at Lyon. The Rhône River. The city lights. Normal life. People going about their evenings, unaware that somewhere, extinction was being synthesized in a lab, paused for release.

"We'll find you," Antoine said quietly to the empty room. "Volkov. Gomez. Ashford. Whoever you are. Wherever you are. We'll find you. And we'll stop you."

But even as he said it, he wondered if it was true.

30 - Heroes and Ghosts

Saturday, 10:00 AM
One week after Leicester Square

Antoine stood outside the quarantine facility, watching the taxi carry Liam away into London traffic. He had saved thousands. Now he was done. Antoine didn't blame him.

Six plagues remained.

They had to find the laboratory—and the man creating them—before the next canister left the building.

He drove to Vauxhall Cross. Work waited.

We'll find you, he told the unseen scientist. We'll find your laboratory. We'll destroy every plague you've created. And we'll make sure Liam's sacrifice—everyone's sacrifice—means something.

Commander Mills met Antoine in her office, closed the door, and set a thin folder on the desk between them.

"Your credentials checked out," she said. "I had to verify before granting full access. MI5 doesn't open its systems to private security consultants on a handshake."

"Understood."

"Your file is… impressive. And heavily redacted." Mills leaned back. "DGSE. External intelligence. Eight years. Counterterrorism. Bioweapons division. Syria.

Libya. Macau. You weren't consulting, Mr. Rousseau. You were an agent. The kind of field work that doesn't end up in briefing rooms."

Antoine didn't confirm. Didn't deny.

"You left DGSE in 2019. 'Retired.'" She tapped the redactions. "But whatever you did afterward didn't look like retirement. Contract work. Quiet assignments. Still connected."

She studied him. "Tell me—why are you here? Why this operation?"

"Because four hundred people died in Central Africa," Antoine said. "Because my colleague almost died in London. Because six plagues remain and someone is manufacturing them. I have the training, the background, and the access to help stop this before thousands more die. So yes—I need full access."

Mills held his gaze for a long moment. Measuring. Testing. "Fair enough," she said at last. "You'll have full MI5 access, Interpol networks, and joint operations authority.

But you're here as a liaison from the WHO—*not* DGSE. Not France. You operate clean. Understood?"

"Yes ma'am."

"Good. Because if this goes sideways, someone will answer for it. And it won't be me."

Antoine nodded once.

Mills stood, opened the door, and motioned him out. "Welcome to the team, Mr. Rousseau. Let's go find this laboratory."

MI5 Operations Room

The screens were everywhere. Every news channel. A wall of headlines.

BREAKING NEWS: BIOLOGICAL TERROR ATTACK THWARTED IN LONDON UNDERGROUND. HERO PHOTOGRAPHER STOPS PLAGUE

DEPLOYMENT. 18 DEAD, THOUSANDS SAVED IN LEICESTER SQUARE INCIDENT.

The footage looped, distorted, but unmistakable.

Reza pulling the canister from his bag.

Liam sprinting.

The collision.

Both men slamming into concrete.

The canister spinning through the air, striking the platform edge, cracking—just enough to release two seconds of aerosol spray.

The crowd pressing in, phones raised, live streaming the beginning of a nightmare.

Then the arrival of WHO hazmat teams.

The sirens. The lockdown.

The media owned the story now.

Elena stood beside Commander Mills in the MI5 Operations Room, watching Liam's face frozen mid-tackle on the screen—heroic, frantic, seconds from disaster.

"The media wants him," Mills said. "Every outlet in the UK. BBC, ITV, Sky. They're calling him the Leicester Square Hero. They want interviews, exclusives, morning shows. They want to know who he is and why he ran toward a canister of death."

"He won't talk to them," Elena said. "He doesn't think he saved anyone. He blames himself for not being fast enough."

"Classic hero complex," Mills muttered. "Save thousands, fixate on the ones you lost." She flicked through a tidal wave of interview requests on her tablet—journalists, documentary crews, podcasts, late-night hosts. "We can shield him from some of it. National security gives us leverage. But his name is out. Liam Hayes. Photographer. The man who stopped a plague."

"He doesn't want attention."

"He's getting it anyway." Mills exhaled. "The Prime Minister wants to award him the George Cross. Highest civilian honor for bravery. A public ceremony. Cameras. Nationwide coverage."

"He'll refuse."

"He can't refuse. Not officially. The PM recommends it; the Crown approves it. It's already in motion."

"Then make it private," Elena said. "No stage. No reporters. Just give him the medal and let him go home."

Mills hesitated. Considered it. "I'll push for that. But the government wants this win. They need the public to believe terrorism can be stopped. That heroes still exist. That we're turning the tide."

Elena stared at the screens—at the headlines, the looping footage, the rising death toll.

"Are we?" she asked quietly. "People are dying. Six plagues remain. Guiomar is still out there. Somebody is still building these weapons. That's not winning. That's surviving."

Mills didn't argue. She looked at the screens, her voice low.

"Let the public have this moment. Let them have Liam. Hope is as much a defense as any vaccine. Without it... the panic will kill more people than the plague ever could."

Liam's Flat, Camden

The phone wouldn't stop ringing. Journalists. Producers. Reporters. All wanting the same thing. An interview and an exclusive. Liam ignored it. Let it ring. He sat in his flat with curtains drawn. Lights off. Sitting in the dark.

On the coffee table, his camera. The one he'd dropped on the Leicester Square platform. MI5 returned it yesterday undamaged. It still had the last photos he'd taken before everything went to hell.

His phone chirped. A text message from Elena.

The PM wants to give you the George Cross. National honor. You don't have to do a public ceremony. Private if you want. But they're doing it, regardless. You saved lives, Liam. Let them acknowledge that.

He deleted the message.

A medal. For what? For tackling a terrorist? For watching eighteen people die because he was two seconds too slow. For spending forty-eight hours thinking he was dying, only to survive and feel guilty about it?

Heroes were supposed to be brave. Fearless. Sure of themselves. Liam was none of those things. He was a photographer who'd been in the wrong place at the wrong time and made a split-second decision that saved some people and killed others. That wasn't heroism.

That was chance. Luck. Chaos.

His phone rang again. Unknown number. He answered without thinking.

"Mr. Hayes, this is Sarah Walker from BBC News. We'd love to speak with you about Leicester Square. Get your perspective. Share your story with—"

Liam hung up. Turned off the phone and dropped it on the table.

He didn't have a story. He had guilt. Trauma. Nightmares. Phantom coughs he heard even when the room was silent.

That's not what the media wanted. They want a brave man who stops terrorists and saves thousands. Everyone claps at the end of *that* story.

His wasn't a story people wanted to hear. So, he wouldn't tell it.

London, Various Locations

The funerals began. Eighteen services. Some private, some public—every one of them devastating. Dr. Sarah Chen attended three, representing the WHO. She stood quietly in the back, offering what little comfort she could as families mourned lives stolen in seconds.

Alina Wellington, forty-two. Marketing director. Mother of two. She'd been waiting for the Northern Line after a late meeting. Heard the commotion. Lifted her phone to record. Stepped one meter too close. Dead four days later.

Henry Carr, twenty-eight. King's College graduate student. He'd already bought the engagement ring he never got to use. Dead five days after exposure.

Debra Wells, seventeen. On her way home from football practice. Wrong place. Wrong moment. She never reached her eighteenth birthday.

Suzy Hartung, seven years old, and her grandmother, Gladys, were returning from a friend's birthday party—a joyful evening that became their last.

Eighteen stories. Eighteen futures.

All cut short because they paused—just for a moment—to look, to help, to understand what was happening.

Curiosity had drawn them closer.

The pathogen had done the rest.

Saint Paul's Church
North London

Chen stood at the back of the funeral. Small church. Family and friends packed the pews. Crying. Mourning. The priest spoke about tragedy and about senseless loss. But he didn't mention that without Liam's tackle, this church would have been filled with coffins. Hundreds of funerals instead of eighteen.

That wasn't how grief worked. You didn't mourn the lives saved. You mourned the lives lost. The ones you knew. The ones you loved.

Chen left quietly and drove to the next funeral. Then the next. Bore witness. Carried the weight. This was the cost. The real cost. Not statistics. Not numbers on a screen. Not "acceptable casualties" in a report.

They had to find the laboratory and put an end to all this suffering and loss of life. Because every number was a person. Every casualty was someone's mother, brother, daughter, or friend. Every statistic represented a life that mattered.

Saturday, Morning
London Quarantine Facility

Elena watched them leave the quarantine facility. Twenty-four people. One by one. Families waiting outside. Embraces. Relief. Joy. Gratitude for being alive.

"They're alive because of you," Dr. Chen said quietly, beside Elena. "Your team coordinated with MI5 and the WHO. Fast quarantine. No secondary spread. Without that, some of those twenty-four would have gone home and infected entire families."

"And the eighteen?" Elena asked, voice barely above a whisper.

Chen had no answer.

Elena watched the last survivor walk out: a young woman in her early twenties, clinging to her mother. Both crying, holding each other like the world had almost ended.

Because, for a moment, it almost had.

Saturday, 2:00 PM,
Interpol Headquarters, Lyon

The video call was tense—CIA, MI6, FSB, BND on screen, old rivalries simmering beneath forced cooperation. Antoine joined from a secure conference room, sharing updates on the three bioweapons suspects.

The CIA analyst—mid-forties, calm, precise—began. "Dr. Pascual Gomez. We tracked his financial footprint to a shell company in Cyprus. That company purchased bioreactors, centrifuges, gene-synthesis machines—everything needed for a bioweapons lab. The shipment's final destination is unknown, but it moved through Turkey."

"Turkey to where?" Antoine asked.

"That's what we're trying to determine. Turkish customs records are... incomplete. We're working with MIT—Turkish intelligence—to track it forward.

Could be Syria.

Could be Iraq.

Could be Georgia or Armenia.

We'll narrow it soon."

The MI6 officer picked up the thread. "Dr. Nigel Ashford. Spotted in Belgrade six months ago. He used intermediaries to acquire chemical precursors. We traced the materials to a warehouse in Moldova. Raided it last week. Empty—he'd moved on—but the site showed fresh activity. Lab equipment. Residue consistent with pathogen synthesis."

"Moldova," Antoine said. "He's in Eastern Europe?"

"Possibly. Or he moved farther east. We're coordinating with Romanian intelligence to locate secondary sites. He's close—we just need to tighten the net."

Antoine turned to the FSB representative. "And Dr. Konstantin Volkov?"

The Russian officer's expression didn't change. "Moscow sources say he relocated in 2022. Signal intelligence points to a former Soviet territory—rural Armenia. About two hundred kilometers from Yerevan, near the Turkish border. New construction. Electrical usage consistent with high-energy laboratory work. We're investigating."

His tone cooled a degree. "We can only say so much on a multilateral call. Some confirmations rely on sources and methods we cannot expose. We will deploy ground assets—but specific coordinates will not be shared on this channel. We won't burn people embedded in Russia's networks."

The room went quiet.

Everyone understood the translation:

We'll help—but only on our terms.

"Armenia," Antoine said. "How certain are you?"

"Sixty percent for Volkov. Could be Ashford or Gomez though. Maybe just an unrelated industrial site, but the timing, the location, the energy signature—it all fits. We're preparing a reconnaissance mission. Ground assets. Visual confirmation. If it's a laboratory, we'll know within the week."

"A week is too long," Elena said. She'd joined the video call from London. "Guiomar is accelerating. Cologne to London was ten days. London to the next deployment could be less. If there's a laboratory in Armenia—we need to move, now. Before they ship the next plague."

"Moving now means moving blind," the FSB officer said. "If it's not a laboratory—if it's just a factory or a mining operation—we've wasted resources and money.

Exposed our intelligence capabilities. Alerted whoever we're hunting that we're close."

"We take the risk. If it's wrong, we regroup. If it's right, we destroy plagues four through nine and end this."

"Dr. Voss is right," Mills said, joining the call from MI5. "The longer we wait, the more plagues deploy. We've stopped two out of three so far. But each one gets harder. Each one costs more lives. If there's even a chance this Armenian site is the laboratory we're looking for, we need to act."

Antoine looked at the faces on screen. All carrying the weight of Leicester Square.

"Recommendation," Antoine said. "Coordinate a multinational operation. The WHO, Interpol, MI6, FSB. CIA satellite intel. Scout the Armenian site. We get visual confirmation. If it's a laboratory, we go in. Fast. Overwhelming force."

"When?" the CIA analyst asked.

"Seventy-two hours, max. Gives us time to position assets. Coordinate logistics. Plan the operation. But not so long that they move again or ship another plague."

Silence. Then nods in agreement.

"Seventy-two hours," the FSB officer confirmed. "Ground assets in Armenia by Monday afternoon. Reconnaissance Tuesday. If confirmed—raid on Wednesday."

The call ended. Antoine stayed still, listening to the click of the encrypted channel closing. Then he shut the laptop, reached for his phone, and thumbed a number buried behind multiple authentication layers—a DGSE back-channel no one at MI5 knew existed. Thirty seconds later, the encryption light blinked green. A familiar voice answered—dry, unhurried, undeniably French.

"You want eyes fast?"

Antoine didn't waste breath. "Armenia. I need a close-up before anyone wipes it clean."

"Understood."

The light flashed red.

Connection severed.

No names. No details. No traces.

A satellite tasking would be pushed. And a trusted contact in the region—former BRDM reconnaissance—would attempt discreet boots-on-ground intel within twenty-four hours.

It wasn't authorization. It was leverage.

And he'd just spent one of the last favors he had left. Antoine exhaled and stared at the map glowing on his tablet—Armenia.

Two hundred kilometers west of Yerevan. Near the Turkish border. Remote. Rugged. Almost perfect for a hidden laboratory.

Was this where the Guild was synthesizing the next weapon? Where the answers waited? Or another dead end—another diversion—while someone, somewhere, prepared the next deployment?

Sunday, 6:00 PM London

Elena walked through the station during evening rush hour. Thousands of people. None of them knew what had happened here a week ago. Or if they knew, they'd forgotten. That's what people did. That's how they survived and coped. They didn't dwell. Didn't carry the weight.

She stood on the platform.

The exact spot where Liam had tackled Reza.

Nothing marked the spot. No plaque. No memorial. People waiting for trains, as if nothing had happened. But something had happened. A hero had emerged and then walked away. The fight wasn't over. And Elena had seventy-two hours until they'd know if the Armenian site was real.

Monday, 4:00 AM
MI5 Command Center

Forty-eight hours until the raid

A satellite image snapped into view, filling the portable white screen. "This is the site," Mills said. "Two hundred fifteen kilometers northwest of Yerevan. Near the village of Gyumri. Population: around three hundred. Closest city two hours away. Remote. Perfect for a covert laboratory."

"What's the building history?" Elena asked.

"Construction began eighteen months ago," Mills replied. "Officially registered as a pharmaceutical research facility. Private company. Ownership runs through shell corporations in Cyprus and Malta—same financial networks tied to previous Guild fronts."

"That's circumstantial," Antoine said. "Not confirmation."

"No," Mills agreed. "But the image shows thermal signatures—here, and here—consistent with high-energy lab equipment. Power consumption is nearly triple what a legitimate pharmaceutical site would require. And comms intercepts picked up encrypted transmissions from the compound to Moscow, Tehran, and Shanghai."

"Shanghai," Elena repeated quietly. "That's where Plague 9 deploys. The final plague. If they're communicating with Shanghai..."

"It indicates coordination," Mills said. "This site isn't isolated. It's part of the larger operation."

She brought up additional imagery. "FSB ground teams are moving into position. We'll have visual confirmation later today—security layout, personnel, vehicle traffic. Everything we need for the raid."

"And if it's not a bioweapons lab?" Chen asked. "What if it really is just pharmaceuticals?"

"Then we apologize, compensate, and stand down," Mills said. "But if Elena's right—even partially—we can't afford to wait. We engage."

"When?" Elena asked.

"Wednesday. Joint operation," Mills said. "WHO, Interpol, MI6, FSB, and Armenian military forces. CIA for satellite intel. We coordinate with the local government. Hit the facility fast and hard. Secure the samples. Capture anyone inside. Destroy whatever's left."

Her expression tightened. "And we do it with Yerevan's full approval. No unilateral action. Armenia wants evidence before allowing foreign boots on their soil—and they'll scrutinize every move."

"They should," the CIA analyst added. "This is a diplomatic minefield. If we step wrong, we spark an international incident."

Elena looked at the satellite image—the stark buildings, the rugged terrain, the isolation.

Was this where the scientist was hiding?

Where the plagues were being synthesized?

Or another misdirection, while the Guild prepared its next strike?

Wednesday would answer one of two things:

Whether they were about to stop a catastrophe...

...or walk straight into one.

Forty-eight hours.

And the window was closing fast.

31 - The Raid

The ceremony was small. Private. Just as Liam had requested. Intimate space. Wood-paneled walls. Portraits of past prime ministers looking down. Twenty people maximum.

The Prime Minister. Commander Mills. A handful of government officials. Five journalists. Two photographers. Elena wasn't there—she was in Lyon helping to coordinate the Armenia operation. But she was watching the live stream from Interpol headquarters.

Liam stood at the front. Uncomfortable, in an old suit. Tie feeling like a noose. Hands in his pockets because he didn't know what else to do with them.

The prime minister spoke. Words about bravery. Sacrifice. Heroism in the face of terror. How Liam Hayes represented the best of humanity. How his actions saved thousands. Britain was grateful.

Liam barely heard it and just wanted this over. He wanted to go home, to forget Leicester Square. Forget Reza. Forget the spit. Forget the forty-eight hours thinking that he was dying. But he couldn't forget. Would never forget. That's what made this so hard.

The George Cross was presented. Small. Bronze. Cross-shaped. Simple, but it meant something. Highest civilian honor. Given for acts of greatest heroism or courage in circumstances of extreme danger.

Liam accepted it.

Shook the Prime Minister's hand.

Nodded. Said thank you.

Then the journalists were allowed to ask questions, just a couple. That was the agreement.

A woman raised her hand. BBC. Mid-thirties. Professional. "Mr. Hayes. When you saw that man take the canister out of his bag and try to deploy it, what went through your mind in that moment? Do you consider yourself a hero?"

Liam looked at the medal in his hand. Turned it over. Thought about the question.

"In that split second, I thought of my friends," he said quietly. "Antoine and Dr. Voss. All that we went through together. I thought of the people on the platform. But I didn't think of myself."

He looked up and met the journalist's eyes. "Is that what makes a hero? If so, then I suppose I am one—but I don't feel like one."

Silence. The room absorbed his words.

"Thank you, Mr. Hayes," the Prime Minister said. "Britain is grateful for your service."

Liam nodded and turned to leave. He walked toward the exit.

And then—

A single clap. From the back of the room, one of the journalists. Then another joined. Then another. Applause building, filling the small hall. Not loud. Not overwhelming. Just genuine. Respectful. Grateful.

Liam stopped and turned. Looked at the faces. People are clapping for him. Acknowledging what he'd done.

He smiled. Small. Brief. But real. Then walked out. Down the corridor. Through security. Outside into the London afternoon. Gray sky. Cold. November was settling in.

A taxi waited at the curb. He got in and gave the driver his address. Camden, home. The driver recognized him. "You're the Leicester Square Hero. I saw the news. What you did—that was incredible, mate."

"Thanks," Liam said. Didn't elaborate. Just looked out the window. He watched as London passed by.

Tuesday, 12:30 PM
Liam's Flat, Camden

The flat was quiet. Empty. He set the George Cross on his nightstand, next to his camera. Two objects. One representing what he was. One representing what he'd become. Photographer. Hero. Both. Neither. He didn't know anymore.

His phone chirped. A text message from Elena.

Thank you. For everything.

Liam stared at the message. Thought about Elena and Antoine. They were his family now. Not by blood. By choice. By shared trauma. By bonds forged in crisis.

He typed a response.

You guys are my family. I had to do something.

Sent it, then set the phone down on the nightstand. For the first time since Leicester Square, Liam felt something other than guilt. His actions had mattered. He'd saved people. He'd saved his friends. Elena. Antoine. Dr. Chen. They were still alive because he'd stopped Reza. He'd been in the right place at the right time and made the right choice.

He wasn't just a photographer who got lucky. He was someone who'd faced death and won. Someone who'd protected the people he cared about. Someone who'd made a difference. Maybe that did make him a hero. Even if he didn't feel like one.

Elena had watched the ceremony again on her laptop. She saw Liam accept the medal and heard his answer to the journalist's question. She watched him smile as people clapped. Watched him leave. She wiped her eyes. Didn't realize she'd been crying.

Antoine appeared in the doorway. "You watched?"

"Yeah."

"He did well. Said the right things. Accepted the honor gracefully."

"He meant it. What he said about us being his family." Elena closed the laptop. "He almost died for us. He saved us, Antoine."

"He's a good man. Better than most." Antoine sat beside her. "You sent him a message thanking him?"

"Yes. I thanked him for everything." Elena looked at her phone and saw Liam's response. Read it again. "He said we're his family. That he had to do something."

"We *are* his family. And he's ours. That's what this is now. Not just a team. Not just colleagues. Family." Antoine stood. "And families protect each other. That's what Liam did. That's what we'll do tomorrow in Armenia. Protect each other."

Elena nodded. Tomorrow. Wednesday. The raid.

Forty-eight hours of preparation is coming to a head. They'd know soon if the Armenian site was real. And Liam would be in London. Safe. Healing. Carrying the weight of Leicester Square but also the knowledge that he'd made a difference. That he'd saved his family.

Commander Mills reviewed the final operation plan. The large screen showed the Armenian site in layers: satellite imagery, infrared, thermal, radio intercepts—everything gathered over the past three days.

"FSB ground assets confirmed visual surveillance," Mills reported to the assembled team. Elena. Antoine. Dr. Chen. CIA liaison. MI6 officers. Interpol coordinators. All present and accounted for.

"The facility is active. Personnel movement is consistent with laboratory operations. Security is present but minimal. Four guards. Perimeter fence. They're not expecting us."

"Or they're confident they don't need heavy security," the CIA liaison said. A man in his fifties, career analyst. "Remote location. Middle of nowhere. Local authorities were paid off or intimidated. Why would they expect a raid?"

"Because we've stopped two deployments," Antoine said. "Cologne and London. Guiomar knows we're adapting. Learning. She must assume we're hunting the source."

"Then why isn't the security heavier?" Elena asked.

"Maybe it is. Maybe what we see is just the visible layer." Mills pulled up thermal imagery. "But infrared shows only four heat signatures outside. Inside, twelve. A total of sixteen people are at the facility. Some could be scientists. Some support staff. But sixteen is manageable."

"What's the raid plan?" Dr. Chen asked.

"Fast, professional breach," Mills replied. "Wednesday, zero four hundred local time. Armenian Spetsnaz lead, FSB backup, MI6 technical team. The WHO biohazard element on immediate standby for pathogen containment. Simultaneous entry at three points: north, east, south. West side is a solid wall—no doors or windows. Secure all personnel, locate any plague samples, contain for transport and analysis, capture whoever's in charge."

"Rules of engagement?" Antoine asked.

"Non-lethal, if possible. But personnel safety is a top priority. If anyone resists, if there's any threat of plague deployment, we respond with necessary force."

Mills looked around the table. "This is it folks. If the Armenian site is real, if we find the laboratory, tomorrow we pull the plug.

Then the real hunt begins: Guiomar. We'll squeeze the lab personnel until they cough up her hiding place Then, cleanup and prosecute."

Mills pulled up the communications intercepts. "This site is connected. It has to be. Even if it's not the primary laboratory, it's part of the network."

Elena studied the data. The connections. The patterns. Mills was right. This was Guild. Had to be. Tomorrow they'd know for sure.

Tuesday, 6:00 PM
Armenia FSB Surveillance Position

Two kilometers from the target site, hidden in the mountains. The FSB ground team, including six operatives. Waiting. Watching. Documenting. Feeding intelligence back to command.

The facility sat in the valley below. Concrete buildings. Three structures. The main building is two stories. Lab equipment was visible through the windows when the lights were on.

Secondary building, single story. Storage. Maybe living quarters.

Third building, small. Generator. Power systems. Perimeter fence. Chain-link. Three meters high. Four guards are patrolling. Rotating shifts every four hours, rifles are visible. AK-pattern. Standard security. Nothing sophisticated.

The FSB team leader—codename Orel—radioed to command. "Target site confirmed active. Security, minimal. Recommend green light the operation."

"Confirmed. Operation proceeds at zero four hundred local time. Coordinate with Armenian forces.

Full tactical package authorized."

Tomorrow, they'd know if they'd found the source.

Or if they'd found something else entirely.

Tuesday, 10:00 PM
Interpol Headquarters, Lyon

Elena sat in the operations room, watching live feeds from Armenia. FSB surveillance. Thermal imaging. The facility sat silently in the valley. Lights off. Night shift minimal.

Tomorrow couldn't come fast enough. If they were wrong, Plague 4 would deploy while they chased ghosts in Armenia.

Elena's phone buzzed. A text from Liam.

Can't sleep either, huh?

She exhaled, smiling despite everything, and typed back:

How did you know?

Because I know you. Big operation tomorrow. You're worried. Running every scenario in your head. Every possible failure.

Am I that predictable?

You're that committed. That's different. You care. That's why we trust you. Why I trust you.

Elena paused. Trust. That's what tomorrow hinged on—trust that the lives already lost would mean something. She typed:

Thank you. For Leicester Square. For everything. I know you don't want to hear it, but you saved us.

You would've done the same.

Maybe. But you did it. That's what matters.

A long pause. Then:

Good luck tomorrow. Stop them. Before its too—he didn't finish. He couldn't.

We will. I promise.

Elena set her phone down and looked at the monitor—the grainy satellite image of an isolated compound in rural Armenia.

Quiet. Dark. Waiting.

Tomorrow.

Zero four hundred.

The raid.

And finally, the truth.

Wednesday, 3:00 AM., Armenia
One hour until the raid

The assault teams assembled. The WHO biohazard unit stood ready, Dr. Chen at the front—full suits, sealed respirators. Containment gear.

Antoine moved among them in tactical gear, officially a WHO liaison, unofficially the sharpest strategist on the ground. His DGSE past didn't need explaining; everyone felt it in the way he assessed every angle, every blind spot, every risk.

Thirty-seven personnel in total.

Against an estimated sixteen inside the facility.

Overwhelming force.

Fast entry.

Full containment.

No mistakes.

Commander Mills coordinated from London via secure video link. Elena watched from Lyon. CIA monitored from Langley. Multiple agencies. Multiple countries. All focused on one target.

The FSB representative finally leaned in toward the speaker, "We will share precise coordinates with a stripped-down assault plan," he said. "But Russian assets will lead the initial approach and handle any nationals. We will not allow an uncontrolled leak that exposes our HUMINT in Russia."

Antoine answered without sarcasm. "You want control, you contribute the pieces that prove it—names, a vehicle manifest, a time stamp. We'll provide airlift and a unified command channel. If we run into resistance, we move together; if we find nothing, we close ranks and issue a joint statement."

The room negotiated in three-minute increments—jurisdiction for arrests, custody of captured scientists, who would gather samples, and how to brief the Armenian authorities. It was efficient, but not easy. In the end, the compromise was simple: share enough to act; save the sources.

The teams moved into position. North entry point. East. South. All synchronized. Waiting for the signal.

3:45 AM.
Fifteen minutes to raid.

Dr. Chen checked her biohazard gear one final time. Positive-pressure suit. Breathing apparatus. Sample kits. If there were plagues inside, her team would secure them and contain them.

Antoine inspected his weapon. Officially, the WHO liaisons didn't carry arms—but Mills had authorized it.

3:55 AM. Five minutes.

Teams confirmed readiness. All positions. All equipment. All comms. The facility's occupants were working. Unaware that in five minutes, the doors would breach. Armed operators would flood in. The laboratory would be captured.

4:00 AM. The signal came.

"All teams: Execute. Execute. Execute!"

32 - The Satellite

Wednesday, 4:00 AM,
Armenia Rural Laboratory Site

The doors breached simultaneously. North. East. South. All at the same instant. Explosive charges. Flash-bangs. Smoke. Then, armed operators flooded in. Armenian special forces. FSB backup. Shouting in Russian. Armenian. English.

"Hands up! On the ground! NOW!"

The facility erupted in chaos. People scrambling. Scientists in lab coats. Security personnel were stunned. Alarms blaring.

Antoine entered through the East breach with the FSB team. Tactical vest. Sidearm drawn. Moving fast. Clearing rooms. His DGSE training taking over. Expertise from operations in Syria. Mali. Libya. This was what he knew best, what he'd been trained for.

First floor: offices. Storage. Living quarters. Personnel surrendering immediately. Hands up. No resistance. Scientists. Support staff. Not fighters.

But upstairs—

Gunfire. A single shot. Then return fire. Shouts. Confusion.

Antoine took the stairs two at a time. FSB operators behind of him. Moving toward the sound. Toward the laboratory level. He emerged into a corridor.

Glass walls on the right. Looking into a large space. And there, is the biohazard room. Four people inside. Lab coats. Masks. Gloves. Working at the benches. Cleaning equipment. Sterilizing. Unpacking empty vials from shipping containers. Preparing for the next batch of plague raw materials to arrive.

Outside the biohazard room, three men stood. Not in lab coats. Casual clothes. Jeans. Jackets. Weapons nearby—AK-47 rifles leaning against the West wall. Twenty feet away. Guild operatives. Guards. Watching the scientists. Making sure the work continued and that no one ran.

The raid had been so fast, they hadn't reached their weapons. But now—

One of them moved. Lunging toward the rifles. Fast. Trained.

"STOP!" Antoine shouted.

First in French. "Mains en l'air! Maintenant!"

Then in Russian. "НЕ ДВИГАЙСЯ!"

The man didn't stop.

He grabbed a rifle. Spun. Raised it.

Antoine saw it happening.

Saw the barrel coming up.

Saw the finger tightening on the trigger.

Saw the angle—toward the east wall. Toward him. Toward the FSB operators behind him.

Antoine fired first. Two rounds. Center mass.

The operative dropped, the rifle clattering across concrete. But even dying, he got one shot off—wild, reflexive, uncontrolled.

The round slammed into Antoine's left thigh.

A clean pass-through. Pain detonated. His leg folded. He hit the ground hard, hand clamping instinctively over the wound—hot, wet, blood pulsing through his fingers.

"CONTACT DOWN!" an FSB operator yelled.

Another operator swept in, kicking the fallen rifles out of reach. The two remaining operatives raised their hands immediately—shaking, surrendering, no fight left in them.

One of the FSB agents dropped to Antoine's side, already pulling a tourniquet from his vest. "Hold still." He cinched it tight around Antoine's upper thigh. White-hot agony flared, ripping a gasp from Antoine's throat—but the bleeding slowed. Stabilized.

Not arterial. Just muscle. A through-and-through.

Lucky. It could have been so much worse.

"Secure the lab!" The FSB team leader—Orel—directed his men. "Get the WHO in here ASAP! We need biohazard protocols. NOW!"

An MI6 operative approached the observation window. The four scientists inside kept working—unaware of the raid.

Tap. Tap. Tap. Suppressed Glock on glass.

A silent order.

The scientists put their hands up immediately, moving to the air lock. Terrified. No resistance. No training for this. They weren't fighters—just technicians following orders. Now being captured.

Dr. Chen arrived with the WHO biohazard team. Three people in full positive-pressure suits. Breathing apparatus. Sample collection equipment. "Clear the area!" Chen ordered. "Everyone out except biohazard-certified personnel! If there's contamination, if there's any breach, this entire floor could be exposed!"

The tactical teams backed out. Fast. No argument. Bioweapons were beyond their training.

This was now the WHO's domain.

Chen entered the biohazard room through the airlock, two team members following. They moved carefully, examining the workspace, the benches, and the equipment. Cleaning supplies. Sterilization chemicals. Autoclaves running. The scientists had been cleaning up. Sanitizing. The work area was mostly empty except for empty matte black containers and biohazard stickers.

"They were preparing for the next batch," Chen said over the radio. "The equipment's clean. No active synthesis. This is a bottling facility. They receive the plagues already made and bottle them here. Prepare them for deployment."

""Where are the plagues?" Mills asked from London, watching the raid through the secure link.

"Searching now," Chen replied.

She moved toward the temperature-controlled storage room—sealed cabinets, refrigeration units humming quietly.

She opened the first cabinet.

Inside were two hard-shell, biohazard-rated transport cases—the kind used in BSL-3 and BSL-4 facilities for moving dangerous agents. Reinforced locks. Shock-resistant. Vacuum-sealed. Foam-lined interiors designed to hold small cylindrical containers.

Chen lifted the first case and unlatched it.

Case 3 — Plague 3

Twelve molded slots.

Eleven filled with matte-black aerosol containers.

One empty.

"Plague 3," Chen reported. "Eleven containers. One slot empty—the one from London. Reza carried it. These are the remaining containers from the production run."

She opened the second case.

Case 4 — Plague 4

12 slots.

11 containers present.

1 empty.

Chen stared at the gap. Cold dread settling.

"Plague 4," she said. "Eleven here. One missing. It's already out—presumably with an operative."

Silence filled the secure channel.

Then Elena's voice crackled through from Lyon—tight, controlled. "How long ago?"

"Unclear," Chen said. "But the equipment's been cleaned. Sterilized. They finished bottling Plague 4 and were setting up for Plague 5. Could've been days ago."

"And we have no idea where it is," Mills said, her voice flattening. "Or who has it?"

"No," Chen replied. "But we stopped the rest. Twenty-two canisters total. Eleven of Plague 3 and eleven of Plague 4. Twenty-two deployments that will never happen."

"One is already out there." Elena exhaled.

Wednesday, 6:00 AM
Two hours after the raid

The facility was fully secured. Fifteen personnel were in custody. Four scientists from the biohazard room. Two surviving Guild operatives. Nine support staff. One operative was dead. Shot during the breach. His body had already been moved to the containment area for forensic handling. The rest sat on the main floor, zip-tied, guarded, silent.

Armenian police arrived. Ambulances came. Media held back at a perimeter, two kilometers away. This was an international operation. No information would pass to the press until the governments were ready.

Antoine was loaded into an ambulance. His leg stabilized. He'd be transported to Yerevan. Surgery to clean the wound. Remove any fragments. Repair muscle damage. Then recovery. Weeks of physical therapy. But he'd walk again. He'd be fine.

Elena had watched the entire raid via secure video feed. She'd seen Antoine get shot and thought he was dying from an arterial bleed. Femoral artery. Fatal if not controlled immediately. But the tourniquet had worked. The bleeding had stopped. Antoine was still alive.

Another friend who'd almost died. Another person she cared about who'd been hurt because of the fragments she had decoded. The guilt never stopped—just accumulated—layer upon layer.

"He's going to be fine," Mills said over the video link. "Clean through. No arterial damage. He'll recover fully."

"He got shot because we sent him into that facility," Elena said. "Because I decoded the fragments. I started all of this."

"No. He got shot because the Guild is deploying bioweapons and someone needed to stop them. That's not your fault. That's Guiomar's fault. The Guild's fault. Don't carry guilt that belongs to someone else."

But Elena carried it anyway. Because that's what she did. That was her M.O. That's what they all did.

Carried the weight. The guilt. The cost.

Wednesday, 10:00 AM
MI5 Command Center, London

Mills reviewed the preliminary interrogation reports. The fifteen arrested personnel. Most were talking.

Cooperative. Scared. Facing terrorism charges. Bioweapons violations. Life in prison. They wanted deals. Reduced sentences. Witness protection.

The scientists were the most valuable. They knew details, processes, and timelines.

One of them—Dr. Arman Petrosyan, an Armenian national, age 39, a biochemist, provided critical information.

"This facility is distribution only," Petrosyan said through a translator. "We don't synthesize the plagues here. They arrive already created from the primary laboratory. We bottle them into aerosol dispensers. Twelve canisters per plague kit. We handle quality control, testing, and storage. Then Guild operatives collect them for deployment."

"Where do the plagues come from?" the interrogator asked.

"Dr. Konstantin Volkov. Russian bioweapons expert. Former Soviet program. He operates the primary laboratory. Synthesizes the plagues, then ships them here."

Elena sat forward in Lyon. Finally, a name. Confirmation. Not three suspects. Just one. The video feed from Yerevan flickered. Antoine sat propped up in a hospital bed, the white sheets stark against the dark blood beneath the bandage on his thigh. His eyes were sharp, but his movements were sluggish.

Morphine drip. He hated it.

"Sorry if I sound drunk," he muttered, voice rough. "They've got me on enough meds to kill an elephant." Mills glanced toward the screen. "You shouldn't even be on this call."

"I'm not sitting this out," he said. "I got lucky, that's all. Two inches higher and I'd be a headline." Elena could see the strain behind his defiance—the twitch in his jaw when he shifted, the way his fingers clenched the bed rail every time pain stabbed through.

"You did your part," she said gently. "Let the doctors do—"

"My part isn't done until Volkov's found," Antoine interrupted, his voice cutting through the static. "That's the job. It doesn't matter if I'm sitting in a hospital. I'm not done yet."

"Just... try not to pull your stitches out while you're saving the world, okay?"

A faint, humorless grin crossed his face. "No promises."

"Where is his laboratory?" the interrogator asked.

"I don't know. I've never been told. The Guild compartmentalizes everything. I know my job, bottle the plagues. That's it. I don't know where they come from and don't want to know.

"How are they delivered to you?"

"Armed couriers. Guild operatives. They arrive in refrigerated containers. Sealed. Biohazard labels. They hand them to us. We sign a log—just a number, no names, no paperwork—and they leave. No return addresses. No shipping manifests. No trail."

"Have you ever met this scientist? This Volkov?"

"No. Never. Only heard the operatives mention him. Slip-ups. 'Volkov's latest batch,' or 'Volkov says this one is more stable.' That's how I know he's the one creating them. But I've never seen him."

"How many plague kits have you prepared?"

"Four."

"Plague 1 — twelve canisters. Shipped nine months ago. Destination unknown.

Plague 2 — twelve canisters. One taken five months ago—later heard it went to Cologne. Eleven stayed behind.

Plague 3 — twelve canisters. One was used in London. Eleven remain in refrigeration.

Plague 4 — twelve canisters. Finished five days ago. One collected three days ago. Eleven are still here."

"Do you know where Plague 4 is going?"

"New York City," he said immediately. "The operative mentioned it. Deployment soon."

"How soon?"

He swallowed. "I don't know. Days. Maybe a week. They don't tell me schedules—only when a batch must be ready. But it's imminent."

Mills pulled up the intelligence summary. "We know Volkov is synthesizing the plagues and shipping them to Armenia for bottling. One canister of Plague 4 is with an operative. Target: New York City. Deployment: imminent. But we don't know where the primary lab is or who the operative is. We are also unsure about when or exactly where in the city."

"We're blind," Antoine said from his hospital room in Yerevan, still groggy from the morphine drip, but cognizant. "New York City is eight million people. We don't have a photo or a timeline. We don't know the exact location. How do we stop a deployment when we don't know anything except 'New York City' and 'soon'?"

"We coordinate with NYPD," Mills said. "FBI. CDC. Homeland Security. Put the city on high alert. Increase surveillance at high-traffic areas. Times Square. Grand Central. Penn Station. Airports. Train stations. Subways. We watch. We wait. And we hope we get lucky."

"Lucky," Elena repeated. The word tasted bitter. "We got lucky in Cologne because we had a photograph. Lucky in London because Liam was in the right place, at the right time. How many times can we rely on luck before it runs out?"

No one answered. Because there was no good answer.

They'd raided the satellite facility. Seized twenty-two canisters. Stopped dozens of potential deployments. Identified the scientist—Volkov—as the primary threat. But Plague 4's deployment was already in motion. Already with an operative and heading toward eight million people. All they could do was watch and wait. And hope.

Wednesday, 2:00 PM Continued Interrogation

Petrosyan provided more details. Operational security. Guild protocols. How the facility operated. Shift information. He willingly answered questions, telling them everything he knew. Cooperating. Hoping for a reduced sentence.

"The operatives who collected the canisters—they were careful. Professional. Military training. They'd arrive at night. No phones. No digital trail. They'd inspect the canisters, then take them and disappear."

"Describe the operative who took Plague 4," the interrogator said.

"Middle Eastern. Late twenties. Dark hair. Beard. Spoke Arabic. Maybe Syrian. Maybe Iraqi. He was calm. Professional. Not nervous. He knew what he was carrying. Knew what it would do but didn't seem to care."

"Did he say anything about New York? Specifics?"

"Just that it was the target. He mentioned Times Square once. Said something about big crowds and maximum exposure. Then he left. That was three days ago."

Times Square. Maximum exposure. Elena felt her blood run cold. On a normal day, Times Square saw 300,000 people. During an event—New Year's Eve, a concert, or a celebration—that number could triple. A million people packed closely together. Perfect for aerosol deployment.

"When is the next major event in Times Square?" Elena asked.

Mills pulled up a calendar. "Nothing until New Year's Eve. That's a couple of weeks away. But there are smaller events. Concerts. Performances. Any night of the week could have fifty thousand people in the area."

"We can't predict when," Antoine said. "Could be tonight. Could be tomorrow. Could be next week. We just know it's coming."

"We need to alert the appropriate New York agencies," Mills said. "Maximum security. Biohazard protocols. We prepare for the worst and hope for the best."

But Elena knew. Hope wasn't enough. Preparation wasn't enough. Somewhere in New York, an operative was carrying a canister, waiting for the right moment to release its payload. They couldn't stop it. Not without knowing who, when, or exactly where.

Wednesday, 6:00 PM Armenia Site Secured

The facility was being dismantled. The WHO teams are cataloging every piece of equipment. Every document. Every sample. All twenty-two canisters—eleven of Plague 3, eleven of Plague 4—all being transported to Switzerland. Maximum security convoy. Armed escort. Dedicated air transport. No risks.

The bottling equipment went first—autoclaves, centrifuges, refrigeration units—torn apart and destroyed on-site. Dismantled. Incinerated. Erased. Nothing left that could ever bottle another plague.

The satellite facility was done. Shut down. Neutralized. But the primary laboratory was still out there—still functioning, still producing.

Plague 5.

Plague 6.

All the way to Plague 9—the *Babel strain*, worse than everything before it. An extinction-level weapon waiting its turn.

"We need to find him," Elena said to Mills via secure video link. "Volkov. The primary lab. We only shut down distribution. He'll just build another bottling facility and ship plagues somewhere else. We need to cut off the head of the snake."

"Agreed," Mills said. "The CIA is analyzing financial data. Signal intelligence. Satellite imagery. Looking for patterns. Connections. We'll find him. But it takes time."

"How much time?"

"Weeks. Volkov's been operating in shadows for years. He knows how to stay hidden."

"We don't have weeks. Plague 4 deploys soon. Maybe in days.

"We have analysts working around the clock. We won't stop until we find him." Mills looked tired. Exhausted. They all were. "But Elena... we won the battle today. Twenty-two canisters seized. One satellite facility destroyed. Fifteen arrests. Antoine's alive. We saved thousands—maybe millions—of lives by shutting this place down.

Take the victory. Mourn the cost.

It didn't feel like victory. It felt like a delay. A temporary reprieve before the next crisis. It was a roller coaster ride.

Plague 4 was already in the hands of an operative.

And no one knew who had it.

Wednesday, 7:00 PM
Joint Operations Center: London / New York Link

Elena leaned over the digital map of Manhattan. Red zones blinked across the screen—Times Square, Grand Central, Madison Square Garden.

"We've got every camera in Midtown feeding through facial-recognition software," Mills said. "NYPD counter-terror and the FBI are running it in shifts. Still nothing."

Any hits on the Guild courier description?" Antoine asked over the secure line from his hospital bed in Yerevan. His mind was clearer now, though the pain still throbbed.

"Too many," Mills replied. "Feels like half of Manhattan has a beard and a dark jacket tonight."

Elena scanned the live feeds—crowds packed shoulder-to-shoulder around holiday displays; thousands bundled in heavy coats. "He's out there," she murmured. "Waiting for the right opening."

"We'll never spot him in this crowd; it would be a miracle." Liam's voice crackled over the link.

MI5 had cleared him to monitor the briefing remotely—still sidelined, but trusted, and they needed every set of eyes they could get.

Elena allowed herself a small smile. "Welcome back to the chase, Liam."

"You've seen me play football with the children at Father Miguel's church. I'm not the sit-on-the-bench type."

"We don't need a miracle," Elena continued. "We just need him to make one mistake."

But he didn't. Not yet.

Ten hours later, still no trace of the operative. The crowd count in Times Square climbed past a million. The countdown clock to midnight glowed above them all. And somewhere in that sea of faces, death waited.

Wednesday, 11:00 PM Elena's Apartment, Lyon

Elena couldn't sleep. The raid played out in her mind. Antoine getting shot, blood all over. A dead operative. Eleven canisters of Plague 4 in the storage cabinet, and the empty slot where the twelfth canister should have been. One missing. Already with a Guild operative. New York. Times Square. Soon.

She lay in bed. Staring at the ceiling. Exhausted but unable to rest. Mind racing. Thinking through scenarios. Possibilities. Failures. What if hundreds of thousands were exposed? What if— Her eyes grew heavy.

Finally. Exhaustion winning. Sleep coming.

She closed her eyes.

The world kept turning.

Three Weeks Later.
New Year's Eve — 11:55 PM
Times Square, New York City

Elena's phone rang. Loud. Jarring. The kind of call that meant disaster. She grabbed it. Fumbled in the dark. Unknown number. Her heart was already racing. Sleepiness replaced by adrenaline.

"Dr. Voss." A voice. American. Panicked. Peter Dotzler, Director of the CDC.

"New York. Times Square. A Plague deployment. We need you here. Now."

"What?" Elena sat up. Fully awake. Adrenaline flooding. "When?"

"Midnight. New Year's Eve. Mass exposure event. Hundreds of thousands. Maybe more. It's—it's catastrophic."

Elena grabbed her laptop. Opened it. Typed frantically. News sites are loading.

BREAKING NEWS: BIOLOGICAL TERROR ATTACK IN NYC. TIMES SQUARE NEW YEAR'S EVE CELEBRATION EVACUATED. MASS CASUALTIES REPORTED. HUNDREDS OF THOUSANDS POTENTIALLY EXPOSED.
"

Oh my God. NO!"

Live footage was shaky. Cell phone videos. News helicopters. Times Square. The ball had just dropped at Midnight. Hundreds of thousands of people. Packed. Celebrating. Confetti falling. Cheering. Counting down. Three. Two. One. Happy New Year!

And then, chaos.

The operative. Moving through the crowd. The black canister barely visible. Raising it. Spraying. Aerosol mist disappearing into the confetti. Into the celebration. People are breathing it in. Not noticing. Not realizing. Just celebrating. Now breathing in death.

Security footage showed multiple angles. The operative moved methodically. Spraying in bursts. Covering ground. Maximizing dispersal. Then, disappearing into the crowd. Gone. Lost among a million people.

Within ten minutes: Coughing. People collapsing. Panic spreading. The crowd turning. A stampede. Thousands trying to flee. Crushing. Trampling.

People were dying before the plague even manifested. Emergency services responded. NYPD. FDNY.

Ambulances. But the scale is too massive. Too sudden. Too overwhelming.

Elena watched. Frozen. Hand over her mouth. A cold sweat. Fighting back tears.

Dotzler was still on the line. "We're implementing quarantine protocols. But the exposure zone—Dr. Voss, we estimate that 400,000 people were in Times Square at that time. Perfect conditions for aerosol transmission."

"Symptoms?" Elena asked. Voice hollow.

"Started to appear immediately. Sneezing. Watery eyes. Coughing. Hour three post-exposure: fever, respiratory distress, and coughing up blood. It's fast. Faster than Cologne. Faster than London. Hospitals are overwhelmed. Every ER in Manhattan. Queens. Brooklyn. We don't have enough beds. Don't have enough ventilators. Don't have enough—"

The connection cut out. Signal overwhelmed. Too many people are trying to call at once. Trying to reach loved ones. Trying to understand what had happened. Elena switched to news feeds.

Live coverage. Every channel. Every network. The same Breaking News story. Hospitals. Hallways packed with people. Coughing. Blood on their lips and teeth. Eyes wide with fear. Medical staff in hazmat suits. Moving quickly. Triage.

Quarantine tents are being erected in parking lots.

Central Park. Yankee Stadium. Anywhere with space.

NYPD barricades are going up. Blocking bridges. Tunnels. The Lincoln Tunnel. Holland Tunnel. George Washington Bridge. No one is getting in or out of Manhattan. Quarantine. Containment.

But it was too late. Always too late.

The numbers flickered onto the screen—CDC mortality projections updating in real time:

Hour 3: Symptomatic: 50,000

Hour 6: Symptomatic: 150,000

Hour 12: Critical: 90,000

Hour 18: Dead: 25,000

Twenty-five thousand dead in eighteen hours.

And the curve wasn't slowing. It was accelerating—too fast, too steep, too catastrophic to comprehend.

New footage streamed in: rows of body bags; refrigeration trucks lining hospital docks; morgues overflowing. Ice rinks converted into temporary storage. Warehouses chilled to preserve the dead. Anywhere cold enough. Anywhere available.

The National Guard was fully deployed now. Armored vehicles blocking intersections. Military checkpoints sealing off escape routes. Manhattan under martial law. Soldiers standing shoulder-to-shoulder, weapons ready—trying to hold back panic as a city of millions unraveled.

Elena's phone rang again. Mills.

"Elena. We're coordinating the response. The WHO. CDC. NYPD. FBI. Everyone. But the containment—it's failing. People fled Times Square before we locked it down. They're spreading secondary infections unknowingly. We might be looking at half a million exposed before this is contained."

""Half a million," Elena whispered. It didn't sound real. "In one city."

"We're doing everything we can," Mills said. "Quarantine. Treatment. Contact tracing. But Elena..."

A long, steady breath on the line.

"This is what happens when we're too late. This is the cost."

Elena stared at the feeds—Times Square abandoned, barricaded, silent under floodlights. Biohazard teams moved through the empty streets in bright suits, spraying, swabbing, sealing. But it didn't matter. The damage was already done. The operative had released Plague 4 into the air. Hundreds of thousands had inhaled it. Now they were dying—and soon the ones they'd brushed past... hugged... spoken to... sat beside on the last trains out of Manhattan would die too.

A new update flashed across the screen.

Hour 24: Dead: 50,000
Hour 36: Dead: 100,000
Hour 48: Dead: 150,000

One hundred fifty thousand dead in forty-eight hours. And the curve kept rising—unstoppable, merciless.

Plague 4 was loose in the most crowded city in America. Every hour, more bodies. Every hour, more families shattered. Every hour, the world slipping closer to collapse.

Elena saw the faces in her mind. Mothers holding children. Both coughing up blood. Doctors collapsing from exhaustion. Working twenty-two hour shifts. Trying to save people who couldn't be saved. Security footage of people looting pharmacies. Fighting over supplies. Civilization breaking down street by street, hour by hour.

Her phone rang again. Antoine. Still in the hospital in Yerevan. Watching the same footage.

"Elena. I'm watching the news right now. Times Square. It's—" His voice broke. "We were too late."

"We tried. We raided the facility. We stopped twenty-two canisters. But one got through. Just one. And look what it did."

"Five more plagues remain," Antoine said. "Tokyo. Singapore. Mexico City. Moscow. Shanghai. If we don't find Volkov—if we don't stop the source—this happens five more times. Five more cities. Every plague gets worse. Potentially millions dead."

""We must find him," Elena said. "Fast. We don't stop until he's caught—and every remaining plague is destroyed."

"And if we're too late again?" Antoine asked. "What if Plague 5 is already with an operative somewhere?"

Elena didn't answer. Because she couldn't. She just stared at the screens—the footage, the graphs, the body counts climbing with every refresh.

Hour 60: Dead: 200,000
Hour 72: Dead: 250,000

Two hundred fifty thousand dead. One week after deployment. From a single canister. From one operative. From being three days too late.

The news cut back to Times Square. The giant screens—normally glowing with Broadway ads and holiday banners—now flickered with something else.

A message:
THE BLACK CHALICE EMPTIES OUT,
DROP BY DROP. PLAGUE BY PLAGUE.
A chill ran up Elena's spine.
Guiomar.
The Guild.
They'd hacked the public screens. Broadcast their signature in the middle of the lockdown. And beneath it, in smaller text—quiet, chilling:
FIVE REMAIN.
Elena stood and crossed to the window. Manhattan was a dim, wounded silhouette—floodlights, roadblocks, military convoys. Two hundred fifty thousand dead, and the number kept climbing. Society was holding together by threads—martial law, checkpoints, curfews, fear.

Somewhere out there, Volkov was already working on Plague 5. Preparing the next deployment. The next city. The next catastrophe. And unless they stopped him now, New York would only be the beginning.

She slammed her laptop shut, the hinge snapping under the force. Then she grabbed it and hurled it across the room. Plastic and glass burst against the wall.

She screamed—hands in her hair, pulling.

The images wouldn't leave her.

Times Square. Bodies. Blood. Death everywhere.

Two hundred fifty thousand people. Gone.

Because they'd been too slow. Too late.

Because *she* decoded the fragments.

Horror filled her.

They couldn't save everyone. They couldn't save *anyone*. She could only watch as people died and the world ended person by person, minute by minute.

"NO, NO, NO!!"

Her chest tightened. Breath fractured.

"This is my fault..." Her voice was barely a whisper.

"I should've stopped all of it.

I should've stopped after Plague One..."

She sobbed—uncontrollably. Collapsed to the floor on her knees. The weight too much to bear.

Guilt too heavy.

Cost too high.

Two hundred fifty thousand dead.

And five plagues remained.

✠✠✠

Elena jolted awake.

A siren wailed outside—sharp, rising, cutting through the quiet street below. Not unusual for Lyon, but loud enough to break the nightmare's grip. She pushed herself upright, breath uneven, eyes adjusting to the dark of her flat.

Her laptop sat on the desk. Intact. Closed. Exactly where she'd left it.

No shattered screen.

No broken hinge.

No images of Times Square bleeding across the display.

She exhaled slowly, trying to steady the tremor in her hands. The nightmare still clung to her—the bodies, the chaos, the certainty that millions had died because she was too slow. Too late.

It hadn't happened.

Not yet.

Elena slipped out of bed and crossed to the window. Lyon slept under the soft wash of streetlights, cars drifting by, unaware of the nightmare she'd just lived through.

"We can't be late again," she whispered.

The siren faded.

The city settled.

But Elena stood there in the dim room, fully awake now, carrying the weight of a disaster that hadn't happened—and the knowledge that if they failed, it easily could.

Epilogue - Gone Viral

News footage flickered across screens around the world. Not a disaster—yet—just warnings. Analysts on every network debating the raid in Armenia, showing aerial shots of the facility, animated reconstructions of how a single canister could bring down a city in hours.

A medical correspondent held up a model of a human lung, explaining how Plague 4 would have spread if deployed in a crowd.

A security expert compared Times Square's New Year's Eve density to a "powder keg waiting for a spark."

Politicians promised tighter borders. Agencies issued new alerts. Airports raised screenings to maximum.

Nothing had happened.

Not here. Not yet.

But the world had seen just enough to understand the scale of what almost occurred—and how narrow the margin truly was. While the world exhaled, the people responsible were already moving on.

✠✠✠

The laboratory existed in a place that no satellite could see.

Buried beneath two hundred meters of granite. Carved into a mountain that had no name on any map. Accessible only by a single road that wound through forests so dense that they swallowed light. The facility had been built during the Cold War. Soviet program. Bioweapons research. Officially decommissioned in 1991. Officially abandoned.

But the equipment inside was new. State-of-the-art. Bioreactors humming. Centrifuges spinning. Gene sequencers run 24 hours a day. The air was sterile. Filtered. Temperature-controlled, perfect conditions for creating a death-in-a-bottle.

Dr. Konstantin Volkov stood at the main workstation. Sixty-three years old. Tall. Gaunt. Wireframe glasses. White lab coat pristine despite hours of continuous work. His hands were steady. Precise. Forty years in bioweapons research. Post-Soviet freelance. Now this. The culmination of everything he'd learned. Everything he'd perfected.

Before him, the screen displayed the molecular structure. Pathogen design. Plague 5. Optimized. Enhanced. More contagious than Plague 4. Faster incubation. Higher mortality. Tokyo would be the next target. Eight million people. Dense population. Perfect conditions.

A soft tone. Incoming message. Encrypted channel. Text only—no voice, no video. Security protocol.

Run the Plague 4 New York simulation again, Doctor. Projected fatalities must stay near four hundred thousand. Confirm and proceed with final preparations. —G.

Volkov read the message twice. Then deleted it. No trace. No evidence.

The simulation numbers appeared on screen: four hundred thousand dead. A projection. A model. Numbers calculated from his designs—unproven, but realistic. Expected.

He felt nothing.

No satisfaction.

No remorse.

Just data. Probabilities. Confirmation that the next phase was ready to begin.

Volkov returned to the screen. Plague 5 required final adjustments.

The Tokyo deployment would need different parameters. Humidity. Temperature. Population density. All variables affecting transmission efficiency.
He'd been working on the calculations for three days. Refining. Perfecting.

Behind him, twelve refrigerated containers. Stainless steel. Biohazard seals. Each contains enough raw pathogen to fill twelve aerosol canisters. Twelve deployments per plague. Simple. Efficient. Scalable.

Plague 5 was ready. Plague 6 was in early synthesis. Plagues 7 through 9 existed as genetic sequences. Mapped. Designed. Waiting to be created.

The door to the laboratory opened. Heavy. Reinforced. A man entered. Guild operative. Late forties. Russian. Former Spetsnaz. Now head of facility security.

"Dr. Volkov. The Plague 5 shipment to the bottling facility. Is it ready?"

"Yes. Container seven. Refrigerated. Handle with extreme care."

"Understood. Destination?"

"The Armenian facility is compromised. Use the secondary location. Moldova."

The operative nodded. "And after Tokyo? What's the timeline for Plague 6?"

Volkov didn't look up from his work.

Three weeks. Mexico City deployment.

Then Moscow.

Then Shanghai.

He paused. Adjusted a variable on screen.

The operative shrugged, then left—the door sealing behind him.

Volkov was alone again. The way he preferred. He pulled up a file. Hidden. Encrypted. The master plan with his notes included:

- *Plague 1 — Central Africa. Proof of concept. 400 dead.*
- *Plague 2 — Cologne. Intercepted. Acceptable loss.*
- *Plague 3 — London. Partial deployment. 18 dead. Acceptable loss.*
- *Plague 4 — New York. Scheduled. Projection: 400,000 dead.*
- *Plague 5 — Tokyo. Sent to bottling in Moldova. Use multiple operatives for deployment?*
- *Plague 6 — Mexico City. Time/Date: TBD. Larger canisters? Improve aerosolization.*
- *Plague 7 — Singapore. Time/Date: TBD. Remote-triggered dispersal viable?*
- *Plague 8 — Moscow. Time/Date: TBD. Water-system deployment? Confirm plague properties.*
- *Plague 9 — Shanghai. Final deployment. The Plague of Babel. Dispersal method: TBD.*

He studied the list. The sequence. The design.

The chalice would empty, drop by drop.

And the world would drown in every one.

Shanghai. Twenty-four million people will die. The largest city deployment to date. The culmination. After Shanghai, the world would understand and would finally see what Volkov had seen for forty years. Humanity is a plague. Consuming. Destroying. Breeding without restraint. Seven billion people on a planet that could sustain only two billion. Resources depleting. Climate collapsing. Extinction inevitable. Unless someone acted. Unless someone had the courage to do what needed to be done.

Guiomar's plan will be executed in full. A new Order will rise from the ashes. Death brings new life.

Volkov had no illusions. He wasn't a savior, or a hero. He was a scientist. A realist.

Someone willing to make the calculation.

To accept the cost.

To do what others couldn't.

The plagues would fall. One by one. Nine cities. Millions dead. And from the ashes, humanity would emerge smaller. Sustainable. Balanced. That was the plan. That was the purpose.

Creating. Perfecting. Preparing.

His phone vibrated. Guiomar again.

The WHO raided Armenia and seized twenty-two canisters. Petrosyan arrested. He's talking like a parrot. They know your name. They're hunting you. Be cautious—G.

Volkov read the message. Deleted it. Felt nothing.

They knew his name. So what? They didn't know his location. Didn't know about Moldova. Didn't know about the twelve containers already prepared. Didn't know that even if they found him tomorrow, Plague 5 through 9 were already designed. The genetic sequences already exist. He had been copious in his notetaking. They could be recreated anywhere. By anyone with his notes, a basic knowledge of bioweapons, and a BSL-3 lab.

The plagues were inevitable. Stopping him would only delay them. Not prevent them. He returned to his work. Final calibrations.

Tokyo in twelve days.

Then Mexico City.

Then Singapore.

Then Moscow.

Then Shanghai.

Nine plagues. Nine cities.

The Black Chalice was emptying. Drop by drop.

And Dr. Konstantin Volkov had never been more certain the world deserved every single drop.

A shadow of unease crossed him, faint and fleeting. Not doubt—calculation. He wasn't blind to the horror he was crafting. He simply believed it necessary. Mercy was the sickness. He was the cure.

He saved his work. Locked the screen, then walked to the window. Reinforced glass. Two meters thick. He looked out at the mountains. Forest. Wilderness. No civilization for a hundred kilometers. Beautiful. Pure. Untouched. Everything humanity wasn't.

Volkov pressed his hand against the glass. Cold. Solid. Real.

"Five more plagues," he said to the empty room. "Five more cities. And then silence."

He turned back to his workstation. Plague 5 awaited. And somewhere, far away, Elena Voss was hunting him. Trying to stop him. Trying to save a world that didn't deserve saving.

She would fail.

They all would.

Volkov had spent forty years preparing for this. And nothing—no raid, no arrest, no heroic effort—would stop what was coming.

The plagues would fall. One by one. Until the Plague of Babel. Until the end of humanity.

He extinguished the lights. Darkness swallowed the lab except for the monitors' pale glow. On the main screen, the Cipher's pattern quivered—shapes aligning, breaking apart, reforming. For an instant, it almost pulsed like a living thing.

Volkov walked out, certain of his next steps.
The door sealed.

✠✠✠

High above, in the ceiling return, a camera clicked alive—
one he didn't install, didn't monitor, didn't even know ex-
isted.
It turned.
Focused.
Captured every line of the Cipher still glowing on the
monitor screen.
Not his system.
Not his feed.
Not his secret anymore.
The Cipher was no longer his alone.
And somewhere beyond the mountain, the Black
Chalice was already tilting—its next drop gathering,
trembling, ready to fall.

About the Author

Rich Petrelli writes stories that blend suspense, mystery, and high-stakes discovery. His imagination has fueled a diverse range of works—from children's adventures to RV travel guides and thoughtful nonfiction—but his passion lies in crafting page-turning thrillers that keep readers up late, eager for just one more chapter.

When he steps away from the page, Rich is on the road with his wife, Zona—exploring the U.S. in their motorhome, finding new sparks of inspiration, and meeting readers who love a gripping adventure.

Enjoyed the story?

If The Hidden Cipher kept you turning pages, please consider leaving a quick review on Amazon. It takes only a moment, and your feedback helps other readers discover the book.
Thank you for being part of this adventure!

Sign Up For My Author Newsletter

Be the first to learn about Rich Petrelli's new releases and receive exclusive content.

www.TheHiddenChalice.com

Stay Connected

Thank you for reading *The Hidden Cipher*.

If you'd like early access to upcoming books in the **Templars Legacy Trilogy**, join my ARC team below:

https://thehiddenchalice.com/join-the-arc-reader-group

Stay up to date on new releases, behind-the-scenes updates, and upcoming thriller projects:

Facebook
https://facebook.com/ColorAndQuillPublishing

Official Website
https://thehiddenchalice.com

Your support makes all the difference, and I'm grateful to have you on this journey.

— **Rich Petrelli**

Turn the Page
For More!

- Character photos
- An exclusive bonus scene from the next book in the trilogy, The Black Chalice.
- A sneak peek at the Black Chalice book cover.

The Black Chalice

A brilliant cryptologist and expert in ancient languages.

The operative governments
refuse to admit exists.

A lens, a laugh, and a knack for surviving impossible moments.

— **COMING SOON**—

THE BLACK CHALICE

Book Two of the Templars Legacy Trilogy

They stopped a bottling facility. They seized twenty-two canisters. They uncovered the Babel Codex and the true purpose of the Cipher.

But the war is only beginning.

Plague 4 is already in motion—redirected, hidden, and aimed at New York City. The world believes the crisis was narrowly avoided, but Elena Voss now understands the fragments for what they truly are: a timetable. Each plague is a step. Each deployment a drop from the Black Chalice.

And far from the public spotlight, deep inside a mountain laboratory, Dr. Konstantin Volkov continues his work—perfecting Plague 5, accelerating Plague 6, refining Plagues 7 and 8.

His designs are ready.

His cities are chosen.

Yet Volkov is no longer unseen.

A hidden camera inside his facility—one he never installed—has captured everything. The plagues. The timelines. The next targets. Someone else has the Cipher now. Someone watching from the dark. Someone who has just shifted the entire battlefield.

As global agencies scramble, as the Guild prepares its next strike, and as countdowns tighten city by city, Elena and her team are thrust into a race that spans continents.

To stop Plague 4 before it ignites.

To intercept Plague 5 before it launches.

To break a conspiracy that is already years in motion. Because if they fail—even once—the world moves one step closer to the Plague of Babel.

And the Black Chalice continues to empty.

Drop by drop.